# MAGICAL MIDLIFE CHALLENGE

# MAGICAL MIDLIFE CHALLENGE

## By K.F. Breene

# CHAPTER 1

I TRAILED MY fingertips along the muscular arm draped across my middle, which was illuminated by the butter-yellow sunlight pouring through the window.

Crap. It was morning. The challenge was in a scant few hours.

A flare of nervousness jiggled my stomach. Closing my eyes, I pulled in a deep breath, expanding my chest, and then let it out nice and slow as I opened them again. I looked at Austin, soaking him in, and flattened my palm on his big shoulder. He lay on his stomach with his left cheek buried in the pillow, his face pointed at me. The sheets bunched across his hips, revealing his broad, muscular back.

A sense of profound serenity welled up inside me, calming the swirl of turbulent emotion from the moment before.

Ever since we'd claimed each other as mates three weeks ago, I'd felt utterly at peace within his presence. There was a new warmth inside of me that grew with every glance he gave me, sang with every touch. I felt weightless and as though I were always glowing.

Most people would attribute this to love.

It wasn't love.

Well…it wasn't *just* love. Because yes, I loved this man with everything in me. He'd earned my trust through friendship before he captured my heart. But there was more to my feelings than adoration and romance.

My gargoyle was expressing a primal satisfaction in the strength and prowess of her mate. Which, great, I could handle that. I liked it, in fact. What I couldn't handle was the insane jealousy that came with it, or the crazy protectiveness. If anyone so much as looked at Austin the wrong way, I had to fight the incredible urge to throw that person across the room.

I didn't always win that fight.

A rhythmic buzz pulsed from the alarm clock, startling me. I reached over and turned it off.

I'd learned in the past that Austin would ignore the alarm's loud blast for ten minutes or more before finally rolling over to slap it. Given it was ten minutes of agony for me, a mother who'd acquired the curse of light sleeping after my son was born nineteen years ago, I'd decided that I'd be the guardian of the alarm and make sure he got up. It really wasn't so hard.

I turned on my side, facing him, and trailed my fingertips across his cheek. I felt along his soft, plush lips and over his square chin. Moving on down, I brushed my fingers across his throat.

He shivered, and his exposed eyelid fluttered open. A beautiful cobalt-blue eye regarded me for a moment before it drifted shut again. His mouth curled at the corner, a sleepy smile, before his arm constricted.

I squealed as he dragged me closer, turning me onto my back. In a powerful, fluid movement, he settled his large, hard body over mine, pushing me into the mattress. Sleeping naked, the way we almost always did, had its perks.

"Morning, baby," he murmured, capturing my lips with his. His kiss was deep and passionate, and the slow thrust of his body pushed out all the breath in my lungs.

I meant to say good morning back, but instead I hugged him closer and moaned into his continued kiss.

"We don't have as much time as I'd like, so we're going to have to knock this out quickly," he murmured.

A wave of nervousness stole through me again.

"*Shh, shh,*" he said, feeling my reaction through the Ivy House bond or our mating bond—probably both. "It's going to be fine. Just focus on me right now. Focus on this."

He reached between our bodies to massage me right

where I needed it. His movements increased in speed, his body working between my thighs, and I did what he said. I let the pleasure of his body sliding against mine— the delicious ache of him inside me—crush the fear and anxiety. I lost myself in his touch.

Almost too soon I was writhing under him, hitting my high and crying out his name. He wasn't far behind, shuddering against me.

His kiss turned languid before he backed off, both of us breathing heavily.

"Good morning," I finally managed. "Sleep well?"

His smile tightened me up all over again. It was a great time for this midlife lady to be hitting her sexual peak. Although...I guess I was no longer middle-aged. Thanks to Ivy House magic, I didn't have an expiration date anymore. The only way I'd exit this life was by murder. And if I shared the fate of the past Ivy House heirs, my murder would be gruesome and at the hands of my mate.

Luckily, I hadn't chosen a young, power-hungry jerk who would try to steal my magic and take my life in the process. Austin didn't even want what was offered, which was the protector's magic. That magic was supposed to boost his power and likely his speed and strength. He'd be like a super shifter, or so everyone guessed. But he didn't want the baggage that came with it. He said he had enough darkness swirling within him—he didn't need to add my gargoyle's brand of dark violence.

I definitely saw his point. When my primal urges rose to the surface, I wasn't exactly stable...

"How about some breakfast?" he asked.

I smiled. "Yes, please."

He kissed me one last time before getting out of bed.

"Do you want a day off from cooking?" I asked, swinging my feet over the edge of the mattress before standing. "Mr. Tom would be all too happy to come in and take care of it."

He paused with his boxers in his hand. The flat look he gave me spoke volumes.

I laughed and threaded my arms around his middle. "I feel bad that you've been cooking so much for me. You never let me help."

"You hate helping, and I love cooking for you. It's not a chore, baby. You know that."

"I know, but..." I paused as he kissed my forehead before moving away to finish getting dressed. "Usually I don't spend so much time over here."

"I like that you're spending so much time over here." He stepped into a pair of sweats. "And I *really* like the way you look at me when I'm cooking."

Heat rushed to my cheeks. I turned away and grabbed some underwear and sweats from the drawer he'd given me for my things.

It was true. I'd always dreamed of having a man cook for me, and Austin had the added benefit of being incredibly hot. Cooking shows had always bored me, but to this one, I was riveted.

That wasn't why I was spending so much time over here, away from Ivy House.

Another flurry of emotions rocked me.

He paused, his gaze turning intense.

He knew this surge of anxiety wasn't about the challenge later today. He could feel through the bonds that this unease was rooted more deeply, the implications more extreme. He also knew from experience that I didn't want to talk about it. That I used the dreaded "I'm fine" when he asked.

But honestly, what was there to talk about? I didn't know what was causing this rush of anxiety. This was different than the crazy, violent side of my gargoyle, but it still seemed primal somehow. I just had this horrible feeling that danger loomed heavy around me. It crouched in the shadows, waiting to strike.

I had no proof. In the three weeks since Elliot Graves's meetup, all had been quiet on the mage front. Rumors about my magic and power level abounded on magical social media, but there was no speculation about what might happen next. I'd received no threats nor any invitations from mages. It seemed as though life was continuing as normal.

Until I set foot on Ivy House soil. And then, suddenly, it felt like storm clouds were drifting in, carrying disaster within them. It felt like a drum beat through me, warning of danger, urging me to take arms, preparing me to fight.

But was that actual danger or just this blasted gargoyle freaking me the hell out? Like when that random guy at the bar patted Austin on the back in thanks for a free beer—throwing said guy across the room and against the wall hadn't been rational. Not even remotely. And neither was this situation. There had been no warning signs. No one had snuck in to attack. There hadn't been any word from the Mages Guild, either requesting information concerning Graves or just wanting to make contact. There was absolutely no reason to feel worried, especially since it had only been *three weeks*. Three weeks of rumors did not a panic situation make.

So yeah, to avoid the feeling of impending doom, not to mention Ivy House harping on about accepting the gargoyle's inherent craziness, I avoided the place. I stayed at Austin's, where my gargoyle was (mostly) soothed, the environment was tastefully decorated and incredibly comfortable, and my hot boyfriend turned mate cooked for me and pampered me and made love to me.

Though yes, I also knew this couldn't last forever. I'd have to return eventually. Mr. Tom had made that abundantly clear, often from just off Austin's kitchen balcony, where he waited for me every morning.

Austin, half-dressed because he knew I liked to watch his bare upper body when he cooked, turned me toward him and braced his hands lightly on my cheeks. I looked up into his eyes.

The turbulence raging through me eased...and then dimmed...and then fell away altogether.

"I love you," he said, his gaze rooted to something deep inside of me. "I will protect you. I will make sure nothing happens to you."

I melted against his touch. "I know," I whispered.

He held our gaze—our connection—for another moment before kissing my forehead and stepping away. "I'll get breakfast started. No need for that bra."

"There is definitely a need for this bra. It's morning. Mr. Tom is already waiting for me, I can feel it. Along with Edgar and, for some reason, Ulric."

I could feel them through the magical bond created by Ivy House. They were all gathered outside Austin's house in Mr. Tom's usual spot.

Usually, it was just Mr. Tom waiting below the balcony off the kitchen every morning. I wondered what was up with the others.

Austin headed down before me, leaving me to finish getting dressed, and I followed him a few minutes later with a shirt on but no socks or slippers.

He'd already set to work in the kitchen, pulling out eggs and sausages from the fridge. There was a cluster of fruit on the counter, waiting to be cut up. I grabbed a couple of mugs from the cabinet, laughing when I noticed his apron—a large arrow pointed up to his face, followed by *This guy rubs his own meat.*

Austin noticed and grinned. "Kingsley sent me a care package. He said Earnessa has some things for you, but you'll have to retrieve them in person. It's his way of inviting us to his territory."

I set the mugs onto the counter before lifting the pot filled with freshly percolated coffee. Austin was excellent at timing his morning routine.

"Did you tell him that Sebastian thinks Momar plans to wipe him out? Soon, I mean."

Momar was a big-shot mage in the magical world who was currently trying to take out shifter packs. We'd heard Kingsley was next on the list, but we didn't know exactly when he planned to attack.

Austin didn't respond for a long moment. I felt his unease through our bonds.

"Not in so many words," he finally said. "He's seen the signs, though. Mages have been skirting the periphery of his territory. He thinks they're assessing his sentries. Based on what he's heard from the shifter community, next they'll assess his defenses. After that…"

"They'll attack."

A huge swell of power filled me, darkness swirling within the magic. My anger heated to rage, my frustration only making the mixture more combustible. My vision blurred, and my head went light. A loud crash had me stepping back. Scalding liquid splashed across my front, but I barely felt it. My gargoyle pounded inside of me, feeling the call of war—wanting to rush to the aid of an ally in danger.

"Whoa, whoa. We have a bit of time." I felt Austin's hand smooth down my back and then over the area where wings would sprout in my gargoyle form. "Sebastian confirmed it, remember? Not much, but we do have some time. It's okay."

"I know." I squeezed my eyes shut, tempering the surge of power. "I'm good."

A bit of an overstatement. My gargoyle was soothed in Austin's presence…until incited. That was where the *mostly* part came in. Unfortunately, inciting it was pretty easy, I was discovering.

"I'm good." I breathed deeply, focusing on his touch. "I'm good."

I took another couple deep breaths until the power and strong emotion started to ebb, and then I let my eyes drift open.

The mug lay in pieces on the floor, resting in a puddle of steaming coffee. The liquid surrounded my toes and most of my right foot, but it still didn't hurt. More coffee had splattered the counter. The mug must've hit the edge and shattered before continuing to the floor.

"Careful, there." Austin hooked his hands under my arms and lifted me like a child, swiveling and depositing me out of harm's way. "You don't want to step on one of those shards. It'll take me forever to get the glass out of your foot."

"Sorry," I said. "Here, I'll get—"

"No." Austin stopped me with a hand on my shoulder. His eyes were so warm, so kind. "Why don't you head outside and talk to your people? I'll bring out a fresh cup, okay? Take a breather."

I couldn't stop the thankful tears welling in my eyes. I rested my palms on his hard chest. "Why are you so amazing?"

His thumb traveled lightly across my chin. "Only

you think I'm amazing. Everyone else thinks I'm a stone-hearted SOB."

I smiled as he leaned down to kiss me.

"Probably for the best," I murmured against his lips. "That way, they leave you alone, and I don't get the urge to throttle them or toss them through doors."

He laughed, turned me around, and gave me a small shove toward the sliding glass door that led to the balcony. "Go talk to that weird collection of people you have working for you. Tell Mr. Tom not to crush all of my flowers."

# CHAPTER 2

T HE FRESH MOUNTAIN air greeted me as I stepped onto the balcony. I took two deep breaths, further clearing my mind, and then walked around the grill and approached the railing.

Standing just before the slope covered in azure-blue wildflowers and buttercups were Edgar, Mr. Tom, and Ulric, a little removed from the others.

"Hey, guys." I bent to lean my elbows on the railing. Austin met me a moment later with a fresh mug of coffee. He set it on the railing beside me, glanced down at the others, and left without saying a word.

"Ah, yes, your morning cup of brew," Mr. Tom said, entwining his fingers at his waistline. His wings, draped down his back like a cape, fluttered in irritation. "Pity you have to traipse all the way down to the kitchen to get it. If you'd just let me see to you in the morning instead of making me wait in this makeshift garden like a common criminal, you wouldn't have to do things the *shifter* way."

Mr. Tom wasn't completely on board with my mating a shifter. He'd really hoped I'd find a gargoyle for that "honor."

When I didn't respond, Mr. Tom continued. "How about breakfast, miss? I trust Mr. Steele is seeing to that for you? He must know how you hate to cook. It isn't something the mistress of Ivy House should lower herself to do, anyway."

"He cooks for her regularly," Edgar said as he scooted forward a little. "She is always so delighted with his creations. What's for breakfast this morning, Jessie?"

I ran my fingers through my unruly hair. They got caught halfway through. "Eggs and sausage, maybe? Fresh fruit."

"Hmm, sounds delicious." Edgar rubbed his belly, the action for show. He was a vampire, and all he'd eaten in the last…way too many years to count was blood. I doubted he even remembered how food tasted. Still, he knew how much I liked to gush about Austin's cooking and gave me ample opportunity to do so.

"Edgar, did you have something to tell the miss?" Mr. Tom asked. His tone dripped with disapproval.

Edgar wilted where he stood. He clasped his long, spindly fingers with the yellowed, pointed nails. "Jessie," he began, "I regret to inform you that I have made a grave oversight. I must ask you, therefore, to retire me. I am not fit for my post."

I wilted just like Edgar. For the undead, "retiring" didn't mean sitting around in a houseboat or tapping a cane grumpily whenever anyone came near them. Retiring Edgar would force him from existence— something he asked me to do every time he felt he'd messed up.

"Mr. Tom, really?" I asked in annoyance. "I thought we talked about this. No one will be retiring Edgar. Stop goading him into asking for it."

"First, I had hoped he'd lead with the grievance and not go straight to retiring. I apologize for that. I should've known better—"

"Oh, no, Jessie, in this case, he is dead right," Edgar said, then leaned forward a little and winked at me. "See what I did there? *Dead* right?" He chuckled to himself before sobering. "No, there really is nothing else to be done. Aside from trying to rid Ivy House of the infestation, of course. I'll do that posthaste, don't you worry. I know my job, even if I did lapse on it a little."

"A *little*?" Mr. Tom asked.

"Infestation?" I asked, my brow furrowing. "What has infest—"

"Tell her what you've done, Edgar," Mr. Tom pushed.

Edgar regarded me solemnly again. "Miss Jessie, I

regret to inform you that I have allowed a gnome infestation on Ivy House lands. I knew one of the creatures had made its home there but forgot how quickly they colonize. I should have seen to that instead of spending so much time here amongst the lovely wildflowers and few weaponized flowers while chasing the perfect doily—"

"Weaponized flowers?" I said, looking around the forest floor. "Like the ones the basajaun had to wrestle after they got out of hand and tried to kill everyone? Where are they—"

"The good news is I have gotten very close to perfection, I think. Very, very close. I've left a few of my very best doilies on the welcome mat for Mr. Alpha to peruse at his leisure. I think he will be very happy with—"

"For the last time, Edgar, he doesn't want your doilies," Mr. Tom cut in irritably. "There is a specific style of décor that can be outfitted with your doilies, and that style belongs to insufferable Irishwomen with no taste. It is rude to force doilies on the unsuspecting. A better use for them would be to give them to Hollace and Cyra. Hollace likes to throw them up like the clay targets in skeet shooting so Cyra can try to burn them out of the sky. Now *that* is a great use of your talents in the doily arena."

"Here." Austin set a second cup of coffee on the railing, glancing down at the Ivy House crew. Ulric had scooted farther away from Mr. Tom and Edgar. "Drink up. It sounds like you'll need it."

I couldn't help chuckling. Grabbing his apron to keep him put, I leaned into him for a moment, and we shared in the joke that was Mr. Tom and Edgar. You just had to be incredibly patient to get to the punch line.

"Breakfast in fifteen," he said gruffly when I let him go. "Don't invite the others."

I laughed harder.

Mr. Tom and Edgar ignored Austin, immersed in an argument about doilies and how appropriate it was to use them as the equivalent of clay pigeons.

"Did you need something?" I asked Ulric.

His eyes were tight. He hooked a thumb at Edgar. "Just so we're clear, I have nothing to do with...whatever is going on here. I'm not with them. I didn't notice the gnomes when I was walking out this morning."

"They are quite wily, I assure you," Edgar said, quickly changing gears. It left Mr. Tom arguing with himself. "They are good at hiding in the garden. But when you least expect it—*bam*! Gnome attack."

"No," I said in a long release of breath. "Tell me they aren't like the dolls."

"Yes, miss." Mr. Tom slid Edgar a narrow-eyed look. "I am afraid they are. Ivy House likes to pit them against the dolls when she's feeling particularly...cantankerous. I do not mean to call into question your decision-making, but hiding away here, leaving behind your duties as the Ivy House heir, has created some...turbulence in the house."

"I know about the house's mood, Mr. Tom," I said dryly before finishing the first cup of coffee and starting on the second.

"Um...if I may." Ulric took another step away from Mr. Tom and Edgar. "Miss, you know how you said I had a green light to tell my mother she could gossip about my place with you? That she could feed the chatter about a female gargoyle so word would get out more quickly to prominent cairns, since she's a world-class networker?"

"Yes?"

"Well, most of the gargoyle community, with my mom's help, is in a fervor. You're getting connection requests from all over the world. My mom has never seen gossip spread this quickly."

"I assume—"

"Hmm, now that smells good, Miss Jessie," Edgar interrupted me. "You are really going to enjoy today's breakfast."

Everyone paused to look at him. He was clearly no longer following the conversation.

Mr. Tom pursed his lips, taking up the conversational baton. "Usually, the larger, more prestigious cairns would send an invitation, wanting any new cairn to attend to them as a way of showing their status. The lower-status cairns would send a connection request. That is their way of saying they realize your status is above theirs and, if you should want to meet them, they would come to you."

"And so far I've only received connection requests from the smaller cairns?" I surmised. "How long do the larger cairns usually take to send an invite?"

Ulric grinned and shook his head, his pink-and-blue-dyed hair ruffling in the breeze. "The larger cairns haven't been sending invites. Most of them, anyway. They've been sending connection requests. They're already declaring you of high status in the gargoyle community."

"Well, of course they are." Mr. Tom puffed up his chest. "She is the Ivy House heir. She is of the *highest* status."

"It's sounding like they will bend over backward to gain the favor of the only living female gargoyle in the world," Ulric said. "Those who believe, anyway, and most of them seem to. I don't think we've heard from the cairns with the highest status, but my mom thinks that's because they want to make a show of their connection requests. They want to stand out."

"Well…that's good news, right?" I asked, my mood lifting.

Austin was working on getting his shifter pack organized so we'd be ready to help Kingsley stand against Momar. The basajaun was off visiting his family, trying to arrange a meeting between them and my crew. If they chose to support us in the coming battle, I would have to do them a favor in return.

My piece was getting the gargoyles united and into a sort of army of my own, something Ulric and Sebastian had said was the duty of a female gargoyle. To be the commander. The *leader*. Ulric had thought his mother would be our best bet for alerting the masses. So far, so good.

"Very good news," Ulric said, although I could feel through the bond that his pride was tempered by discomfort. "There's only one thing."

I lifted my eyebrows for him to go on.

He grimaced. "She's convinced you are going to need someone knowledgeable in gargoyle politics to help navigate the…fragile egos, she called them. Cairn leaders can be prickly, but more than that, they act a lot like shifters in that they force you to show dominance.

If you don't, they won't respect you."

"They are much harder-headed than shifters," Edgar said. "Much more stubborn. And also…quite a bit stinkier. They don't seem to know what a shower or deodorant is for—"

"Yes, thank you, Edgar." Mr. Tom glowered at him. "The gargoyles in town are just young, that's all. They're bachelors. Not all gargoyles exhibit a lack of hygiene."

"Of course, yes. But certainly much less hygiene than shifters, that's all I'm saying. Much less washing, I think. Less soap—"

"Breakfast," Austin said, leaning against the frame of the sliding glass door.

"Gargoyles have different rules than shifters," Ulric continued, frowning at Edgar. He probably wondered if Edgar was talking about him. "Their politics are different. My mom is convinced that you need someone to help you navigate these meetings."

"Dominance is no problem," Austin growled. "As her mate and the alpha of this territory, I can take that role if she can't." He looked at me. "But he does have a point about politics. I can probably navigate it, but you should be in the lead when it comes to the gargoyles."

"And that is what she has me and the miserable old woman for," Mr. Tom said indignantly, standing up a little taller. "I can help her navigate the demands of gargoyle cairn leaders—I've known many in my day— and the old crone can work with the miss on politics. I hate to admit it, but Niamh has quickly gotten up to speed on the goings-on in the magical world. She used to be a political animal. Excessive drinking and an overall disregard for social conformity aside, she does know her stuff. No, we'll be okay. Go in and eat, miss. I'll watch over things from my dirty dwelling down here, sequestered to the plant life like some sort of wild creature."

"Yes, you'd do the job very well…if you weren't so far out of the loop," Ulric said to Mr. Tom delicately.

"He probably doesn't even know there *is* a loop," Edgar added, not so delicately. "Even in his prime, he probably wasn't aware of the loop."

"Right." Ulric's lips twitched, probably with the effort not to laugh. "I, myself, don't know the politics of cairn leaders. Nathanial was being groomed to take over a cairn, but he wasn't there yet. He only has the broad strokes. Even just to go through the connection requests, you'll need someone who can read nuances. I wouldn't know what to look for."

"So what do I need to do, then?" I asked. "I'd rather not try a summons. I'm not…in the right frame of mind just now. I worry about what I'd call."

Ulric tensed. "Um…well…my mom decided that

since you don't have anyone trustworthy to help you…" He cleared his throat. "She volunteered. Then just…accepted her own invitation and made plans to come here and help."

Mr. Tom turned just his upper body in Ulric's direction. His wings fluttered in agitation. "I beg your pardon?"

"Sorry, Jessie," Ulric said, wariness and anxiety rolling through the bond now. He was usually the happy-go-lucky member of our team. I wasn't used to this change in demeanor. "I told her that you'd need to be consulted before she just turned up and took over. But…you see…my mom is a really hard woman to say no to. You can try, but she just doesn't listen. So…she's on her way." He put out his hands in a stop motion. "But don't worry! I got her a room at the hotel. I'm sure the alpha can scare some sense into her. I mean, no cairn leader has been able to yet, but…well…" He shrugged helplessly. "Or Ivy House can keep her from bombarding you. You won't have to be the bad guy, Jessie, I promise. *I* have a hard time saying no to her, but I'm sure someone else can figure out how so that you don't have to." He wilted like Edgar had earlier. "I'll probably need to join Edgar in asking to be retired after this."

"Yes, that sounds like something worthy of retirement." Edgar nodded solemnly. "At least in our final hours we'll have each other."

Ulric looked over at the vampire. "Awesome," he said flatly.

I couldn't help but burst out laughing. No matter what happened, or how much power I had, or how many problems I had with that power, I could always count on my team to be the most absurd bunch of weirdos in the history of the world. How could anyone take us seriously? The mages certainly hadn't...until we scared the crap out of them. I doubted the gargoyles would be so easy to intimidate. Regardless, this was now my lot in life.

"Sure, fine." I took up both mugs and turned for the kitchen. "If she can help us unite the gargoyles, she'll be welcomed."

"I just hope she won't be bringing her own cooler full of food?" Mr. Tom asked as I crossed the threshold.

I laughed again. My parents' visit had clearly scarred him.

Taking a deep breath, I set the mugs on the counter and saw that the table had been set. Given we almost always sat at the island, this was unusual.

I quirked an eyebrow at Austin.

He refilled one of the mugs. "I thought the table might ground you more," he said by way of explanation.

He motioned me toward it.

I didn't budge, waiting for the real reason.

If controlling his expressions weren't part of his role as alpha, he'd absolutely be giving me a sheepish grin right now. "I can't hear Mr. Tom and Edgar bickering as well from the table."

"Hmm," I said noncommittally, a smile threatening, then took a seat. "Was my discussion with my crew just now how your meetings with your advisors go?"

He snorted. "My territory would be in a world of hurt if that's how my meetings went."

He lowered a plate in front of me. Eggs Benedict took up the center focus, the sauce whipped up to perfection. Chives provided a pop of green against the glistening, lemon-colored sauce. Fresh fruit was clustered to the side, far enough away that none of the pooling liquid touched it. I was weird about food touching on my plate unless it was supposed to, like a child. Another plate held two sausage links bathed in maple syrup and crispy hash browns beside a glop of ketchup.

"Wow," I said, picking up my knife and fork and just looking over everything.

He took his seat next to me at the round table, a set-up that allowed him to watch my reaction to each bite. He loved seeing me enjoy his handiwork.

"A Sunday morning breakfast on a Tuesday? What's the occasion?" I cut into the egg and was rewarded with the delicate ooze of yolk over the Canadian bacon and down to the fluffy English muffin below it. "My God, you are good at cooking. The egg is perfect."

His smile was soft as he watched me pop the bite into my mouth. After that, I lost track of him as my eyes drifted shut of their own accord and the flavors exploded across my tongue.

"You need fuel for your challenge later this morning," he said, and nervousness fluttered in my belly at the reminder. Austin had been challenged plenty of times, but this would be my first. "Magical creatures who shift require more sustenance than those who don't."

"If it were anyone else's cooking, I'd be too nervous to eat." I cut another bite. "But it would be a pity to let this go to waste."

He chuckled softly before attacking his own meal. "Can I speak to you about Kingsley or should we…wait?" he asked.

Nervousness was replaced by another swirl of anger and motivation—the urge to inhale this meal and take to the sky. To go to war.

My spinning emotions, like a disco ball of violence, were exhausting. They were so much worse since the mating. Or since Elliot Graves's meeting, at least. It was like the gargoyle within me had fully woken and now wanted a reign of terror.

"It's fine," I replied.

Austin nodded as he speared a piece of sausage. He didn't share my love of coating them in maple syrup. "Kingsley forwarded an email detailing a mage attack on a smaller pack. The pack wasn't completely wiped out, but they were essentially chased off their land."

"Another one?" I asked, because that had been increasingly happening. We had a lot of people in our territory who had lost their homes to something like that. They'd come here looking for a safe haven.

"Yes. It doesn't sound like Momar, though. Too small-scale. I think instead that mages are taking the cue from Momar and seizing desirable land. Or maybe they're just flexing their power. I haven't had a chance to look over the report in detail yet."

"If it doesn't sound like Momar or relate to Kingsley's situation, then why did he send it?"

Austin looked at me silently for a moment. "It's his subtle way of saying we have to work together and push back against the mages."

"He already tried to unite everyone, though. It didn't work."

"He was initially met with resistance, correct. Alphas are used to making the rules. If someone wants leadership over them, they expect to be challenged. Kingsley wasn't trying to structure the league in that way, though. He wanted to organize it more like a company, with a board of directors and someone like a CEO."

"Right, right," I said, remembering talking about this here and there. With mages, gargoyles, and shifters, there were a lot of balls in the air. "They all wanted the big role."

"Yep. And while most of them didn't dare challenge Kingsley, knowing he'd dominate, a few are on his power scale. They were ready to challenge for placement. He was trying to decide how to best navigate it when the mage attacks on shifters started ramping up. At that point, the shifters realized Kingsley's logic made an awful lot of sense. It was too late, though. Packs started falling—especially the ones willing to work with Kingsley."

"You're already planning to step up into that CEO role," I told him. "I thought Kingsley knew that."

"He does."

"So is he trying to get you to hurry up about it, then?"

Austin took a bite, quiet for a moment. "I think so. That's what I wanted to get your opinion on. I don't see how I'll have the time before we need to help Kingsley—assuming things keep progressing like they have been. We need to get your gargoyle team up and running. That's a priority, especially because we can do it while I make this territory more cohesive. Another priority. A good portion of our new shifters are coming from these fallen packs, and they're shellshocked. Like Brochan."

Brochan, whom a lot of people called Broken Sue because of a naming issue at Elliot Graves's meetup, was new to the pack. He was a powerful alpha in his own right, nearly at or equal to Kingsley's level. His ferocity, though, was in a league of its own. You couldn't blame him for that. Mages had come through and wiped out his pack, including his pregnant mate and child. Loss like that left a scar.

He was finding purpose again in Austin's pack, with Austin's confident and patient guidance. He'd challenged for beta—and won—soon after arriving home from Graves's meetup. Mostly, he was thriving. The one exception was the night he'd attempted to drink as much as Niamh at the bar. They'd verbally sparred, and he ended up staggering out in a black mood, leaving her not even a little perturbed. He should've known better than to tangle with a Master Grump.

"And you said that Kingsley is seeing the signs of Momar's people testing the sentries?" I asked.

"Yes. They're gearing up. We need to be there before they attack." He speared a piece of fruit. "I want his defenses to appear weak when Momar's people test them. Then, when they attack, I want to hit back with an offense that will back Momar and his Mages Guild way up. And then I want to unify the shifters so absolutely that the Mages Guild will need to reassess who is really at the top of the magical food chain."

"And if the other pack leaders challenge you for the title of CEO?"

He smirked, all confidence. "Then they'll learn what it's like to be dominated by the meanest alpha in the world."

My skin pebbled, and my small hairs rose all over my body. The darkness within me rolled and twisted. I met Austin's burning cobalt eyes and felt the world tilt. Felt myself falling into his gaze, my blood rushing in my ears.

I recognized the ruthlessness in his eyes. I felt in tune with the ferocity behind his words.

I meant to tell him that we'd obviously need to play things by ear. I had to deal with the gargoyles, and he'd have to strengthen his pack, as he'd said. If we had time to make some visits to other packs, great, but we definitely needed to knock out our priorities first.

I meant to tell him that, but instead, all I could focus

on was the delicious heat unfurling within me and his strength and power. I was up and ripping off his clothes before I could stop myself. My gargoyle was fueling this frenzy, and I was inclined to let her.

# CHAPTER 3

L ATER THAT MORNING, I stood on the outskirts of a large field. Shifters crowded along the edges, two and three people deep. It almost looked like all the magical people in town had come to watch the challenge.

"Now, miss, let's go over things again, shall we?" Mr. Tom stood at my side with his hands wrapped up like he was a boxer. He wore a dull green sweatsuit with blue stripes down the sides that looked like it was left over from the seventies, and a white sweatband around his head. To complete the look, he had slung a white towel over his shoulder. I was thankful he hadn't brought a boombox and put "Eye of the Tiger" on repeat.

"Sure she knows all she needs'ta," Niamh said from a few paces behind us, standing with the rest of the Ivy House crew, her arms crossed over her chest. "Look at all the space they're givin' ya, Jessie. Most'v'um know what they're about, so they do. They've seen ye lose control a time or two."

Across the field stood the female shifter who'd challenged me. The woman, half my age, waited with her arms at her sides and not a stitch of clothing on her. She was ready to shift and attack. It would have been less intimidating if I knew what animal would be coming at me, but no one would tell me. I had no idea why.

I took a deep breath.

"Honestly, lads," Niamh went on, "what sorta gobshite challenges the alpha's mate? What is she hoping to achieve?"

"If you would listen rather than bluster and blow," Mr. Tom replied, "you'd know she is challenging the miss for placement in the pack. If she beats the miss, then she will rise to the upper echelons in the pack hierarchy."

"Fer feck's sake, I know all that." She scoffed at him. "But that *eejit* shifter can rise just as high by challenging any of the other highly placed shifters, female or male. She's choosing the alpha's mate for a reason, like. Is she tryin'ta get in his pants—"

"Don't." I put up a finger as my darkness boiled just below the surface. "Do not follow that train of thought. I'm barely keeping things together, and I don't need to add a shot of possessive rage to the boiling inferno that is my gargoyle. I'm trying to stay a little chill so that I don't fly off the handle and accidentally kill this person. Control is my friend right now."

"You shouldn't be trying to keep control of your animal, Miss Jessie," Nathanial said from my other side. He was dressed appropriately for the occasion in house sweats. Hell, nude would have been more appropriate than what Mr. Tom had decided to wear. Nathanial was a gargoyle alpha who acted as my general. Soon, I hoped I'd have more people for him to command. "You should shift and let your gargoyle lead the charge—or at least use her strength and power. Our gargoyles are part of us. We lose strength if we try to separate their primal drive from our consciousness."

"She's still thinkin' like a Jane, that's all." Niamh unfurled her hands and reached into her pocket. "Here, Cyra. See if ye can get this one." She pulled out one of Edgar's lopsided doilies, bent her knees, and hurled it into the sky like a Frisbee.

"Give her space!" Hollace shouted, jogging a few steps away from Cyra.

Everyone quickly followed Hollace's lead as a big smile spread across Cyra's face. She stepped forward before clapping her wrists together.

"Oh, now, Niamh, that was a gift," Edgar said from behind them as he watched the white doily hit its zenith before starting to arc back toward the dry grass. "It was the other stack that was meant for Cora's training."

"Her name is still Cyra, big guy." Ulric clapped Edgar on the back and then grimaced and slowly removed his hand from the spindly vampire.

"There was a difference in the stacks?" Niamh asked, not taking her eyes off Cyra.

Cyra's black brows pinched, and her face screwed up with determination. A bright stream of fire burst from between her palms, less than an inch wide, and seared through the sky after the falling doily.

A loud *ooh* issued from the crowd around the field, all looking at the doily, the nearly blinding stream of fire, or Cyra herself. The blast seared the very edge of the doily. The rest of it caught fire, and a ball of flame tumbled down toward the brown grass below.

"That's a miss," Niamh said. "Catching fire after the fact doesn't count."

"That's going to set this whole place on fire, you guys," I admonished them.

"Jessie, if I may," Edgar said as flames immediately caught and started spreading. "This might be a great time for you to practice your elemental magic. You should be able to suck in the heat from the fire, and in so doing, smother the flame."

"Yes, Edgar..." I was already building up my magic to do exactly that when Sebastian and his pal, assistant, and co-criminal mastermind, Nessa, jogged up from where they'd been waiting within my crew. "It's just that elemental magic is at the very top of my power scale and takes a lot of finesse. I can't seem to manage it."

"But that was in practice," Edgar replied patiently. "Now we are all at risk of being burned alive. Sometimes all we need is pressure, right?"

Nessa—Natasha only during formal occasions— stared at Edgar in utter bewilderment for a very long moment. Thankfully, Sebastian was accustomed to Edgar's oddness and could mostly ignore it.

"Focus, Jessie," Sebastian said, crowding in close. "Focus on the intent of the spell. Don't worry about it working or not working. Then, when you feel it—really *feel* it—work on your technique as you cast."

I did as he said, mimicking what we did in practice sessions, and from the way the power thrummed through my body, I knew it would work. A burst of it hurtled toward the growing flames. Thankfully, the grass was well tended and cropped close to the ground, otherwise we'd all need to be running. Instead of dousing the heat, though, my spell fanned the flames higher.

"Crap, that's wind," I said, rooting through the easy spells at my disposal for a Plan B.

"Oh, fantastic! Wind!" Edgar clapped. "That is at

least an element, Miss Jessie. Well done! I knew you could do it."

"She's made it worse, ya gobshite," Niamh replied.

"I've got it. Nessa?" Sebastian didn't even bother looking at her to confirm she was on board. They worked their magic side by side, sectioning off a portion of the field in a pink-tinged magical box. The sides stopped the flames from spreading, and the top clamped down to cut off oxygen. Without fuel, the fire dwindled to nothing but smoke rising from the blackened ground.

"Thanks," I murmured.

"That was my fault, Miss Jessie." Cyra raised her hand. "I forgot about the likely repercussions of my actions. I'm used to Ivy House handling things." Hand still up, she turned to the spectators. "Sorry, everyone. So sorry. My fault."

"Do you normally think about repercussions when there's a game afoot?" Hollace murmured, stepping in beside her again.

"No," she said out of the corner of her mouth, "but it's polite to take the blame, I think."

"Or maybe not start fires in the first place," Ulric said, laughing.

Sebastian slipped his hands into his jeans pockets as Nessa nodded and jogged away. I had no idea where she was headed, but she always seemed to be on the go.

"Like most sane people—" Sebastian said before his words cut off.

The crowd parted to my distant left, and Austin stepped through the mass in a tight white T-shirt and well-worn jeans. Broken Sue followed on the side closest to me. Kace, Austin's longtime friend and the former beta, strode on the other side.

Sebastian shivered, and his magically altered face wobbled a little.

He'd decided that he would make O'Briens his residence for the foreseeable future so he could train me, but he didn't want anyone knowing he was the infamous Elliot Graves. He preferred to keep the world's mages guessing about his whereabouts—being elusive boosted his reputation, not to mention it made him more difficult to hunt and kill.

To keep his anonymity within the town, he'd assumed the disguise he'd worn before. The shifters would have recognized his scent, anyway. Our story was that he'd never actually died, and Niamh yelled at anyone who asked questions.

"As I was saying," he continued, "like most sane people, I regret to mention this, but I agree with Edgar. Crap!" He flinched dramatically, looking over his shoulder. Edgar stood almost directly behind him, smiling with his large canines.

"Hello," Edgar said. "I'm so glad you agree."

Sebastian stepped away, dragging me with him. "I hate when he sneaks up on me," he murmured. "He must know that because he does it all the time. I think he's trying to psych me out."

I couldn't help my smile. "Actually, I think he's just happy you notice him."

Sebastian glanced back at Edgar again. "I'd like to learn the trick to ignoring him." He shook himself out of it. "Anyway, Jessie, you may not have worked the fire element, but you did work air. The differences in the spells are very small. One detail out of place, and you get a different result. Elemental magic, as I've told you before, is the work of a master. You're the only mage on the planet who has the power to do it solo. The rest of us have to work together, and we hate that." I could hear the smile in his tone, but it didn't show on his face. His magical disguise masked almost all of his expressions. "So even though your spell didn't provide the desired result, you should take it as a win. That's the first bit of elemental magic you've successfully done. It's a huge achievement."

"You have to be uplifting. You're my teacher."

"I certainly do not, no. I've heard and read that most magical teachers are very hard on their apprentices. I have no idea why."

"To make them tough," Nessa said, lifting up her hand as she passed us. "The side effect is a fragile ego." She curled her hand into a fist. "We like fragile egos. They're easy to break. Mind-fuckery, the best kind of offense."

"She's really good at her job," Sebastian murmured, watching her go. "We have some things we need to discuss when you get back to Ivy House, hopefully sooner rather than later. Now, however…"

He didn't finish his sentence, instead watching as Broken Sue approached us, and then swallowed dramatically before melting away behind me. Apparently, Edgar's creepiness was preferable to Broken Sue's menacing stare.

"Well hel-*lo*, mister." Nessa stopped to gawk and then wink at Broken Sue.

He ignored her, his focus entirely on me. "Ironheart," he said, using the name this territory had given me. His dark-eyed gaze beat into mine, something within his eyes slightly off-kilter. His haunting pain lurked just below the surface.

Recognizing it, and thinking of those who'd wronged him, I felt the darkness within me boil again. This time, though, the emotional disco ball was accompanied by a strange wooziness that made my thoughts hazy. The air between us seemed to pressurize, and little sparks of energy danced in the open space. And then a solid force slammed between his chest and mine, pulling taut and locking home.

I sucked in a startled breath.

"*What just happened?*" I asked Ivy House desperately.

"*What you were meant for. If you'd worked through it at home instead of hiding from all this at the bear's house, it wouldn't have come as such a shock.*"

I waited patiently, hoping for more. When she was in a bad mood, she really made me pay for it.

His emotions curled around him—I could feel them!—shock and delight and sudden determination. It was like he'd taken the first deep breath after almost suffocating.

"*He has sworn to protect you and your mate,*" Ivy House finally said. "*He has spilled blood for you. He is a brother in arms. A battle partner. Your gargoyle has found him acceptable and therefore secured your bond. He is one with you now. He's part of your cairn.*"

"*Is that why I can feel his emotions? Because of this bond that...my gargoyle...initiated? Also, I don't like that the gargoyle, on my behalf, is randomly forcing bonds between unsuspecting people.*"

She made a sound that said her patience was wearing thin. *"As I said, if you'd dealt with all of this instead of hiding, you'd have more control over your primal abilities. And if your mate would accept the protector's magic as he ought to, you two could work through it together. Your whole situation is tits-up. I've never known an heir to be so reluctant to assume her full abilities."*

*"If we could just skip ahead?"*

Her pregnant pause felt like some kind of threat. *"No bond can be placed unless both parties are willing. He felt your influence and welcomed the deeper connection, securing him at your side and into your cairn."*

*"Do male gargoyles have the ability to create bonds like this?"*

*"Male cairn leaders have but a fraction of the strength you do. They can create bonds, but not so fluidly. Reading emotions is part of your primal magic. You need to assess those around you in order to properly lead and protect them, and to do that, you need to intuit more than what they are saying."*

*"Why is this just happening now? Broken Sue is the only one I can read outside of those I have an actual bond with."*

*"Because you are slow? Because you are fighting the gargoyle's influence at every turn? Because you are more*

*stubborn than any male gargoyle I have ever known or ever hope to know? And that is saying something. Ask around."*

*"Right. Okay. Good talk."*

I passed the back of my hand over my forehead like a woman in an old movie.

"I gotcha." Ulric grabbed my hand and linked our arms together. "What's going on?"

"Here we go," said Mr. Tom, moving behind me. "Let's loosen you up." The sides of his hands started chopping my back in a very bad rendition of a massage.

"I feel like I'm in a circus," I grumbled.

"Ironheart," Broken Sue said again. He had a new light in his eyes. He felt our connection, I could tell, born in blood at Graves's meetup. "You're being challenged as the alpha of this territory, co-ruler with Austin Steele. It's a sanctioned challenge for pack placement. That means the pack's rules of engagement will be followed, or the offending party will be ostracized or punished. Do you understand?"

I widened my eyes a little, snapped back into the moment. "Understanding the rules has nothing to do with obeying those rules. Maybe you can talk some sense into Austin? I lose control very easily. This is a very bad idea."

"We're on hand to keep you from killing her," Sebastian called out.

"No." Broken Sue shook his head and lowered his voice. "Only the alpha can interfere, and he won't unless one of the parties is under duress and taps out."

"Austin won't get the chance to interfere."

Broken Sue nodded slowly. "I don't make a habit of speaking for the alpha, but he knows that."

He stepped a little closer. He towered over me, a foot or so taller and with shoulders so wide it almost made him look shorter. Sebastian would've been evacuating his bowels at this proximity.

"Listen, Jessie, the pack isn't going into this situation blind. We made sure your challenger, Zoe, knows what she's getting into. We've made her listen to stories of your magic, both when it works the way you want it to and when it doesn't. She knows you took down a phoenix and a thunderbird. She's challenging you anyway because she doesn't think a non-shifter should be ruling this pack. She doesn't think you're a fit mate for an alpha—especially *this* alpha, whom some are now referring to as the king of the shifters. She wants the pack to ridicule you. If she succeeds, it will unsettle the whole pack structure. Do you hear what I'm telling you?"

I flared my hand out helplessly. "You want me to make an example of her, yes, I get that. Do you hear what *I* am telling *you*? That example might be death. Then…what? Austin has to punish me or ostracize me? In what world is that going to happen? He won't harm me, and I'm the heir of Ivy House. I'm not going anywhere."

"Of course you're not, miss." Mr. Tom made fists with his hands and kept firmly beating at the muscles in my back. I could've told him to stop, but it was just as easy to ignore him. He was my personal white noise. "No one will run you anywhere. I'd like to see them try."

Broken Sue kept his gaze steady on me, apparently unfazed by Mr. Tom's whole situation. He nodded, not much more than a jerk of his head. "You'll do what needs to be done. In an official capacity, to prevent favoritism, that's all I can say."

"All right, monkey, off ye git now," Niamh said from right behind me. "We'll handle it. Bugger off. Ye did yer part."

Broken Sue's eyes flicked over my shoulder. "Remember in which territory you reside, puca," he growled. I might have taken a step back if his magic hadn't cocooned me in a protective embrace that shielded me from the aggression emanating from him. He was magically communicating that I was safe within his proximity.

"I know which territory, ye great lummox," Niamh replied. "*Hers.*"

The tension coiled. Power pulsed from Broken Sue, from Niamh, from the others around me sensing a possible confrontation.

I knew this wasn't a big deal—their squabble would amount to absolutely nothing. At the bar, Niamh antagonized Broken Sue mercilessly, always stopping her taunting just shy of an altercation. She knew exactly which buttons to push, how hard, and for how long. She used it to distract him, to break him out of his cycle of self-loathing and get him to direct his pain-turned-anger at her instead. I knew all of this.

But he was silently threatening a member of my crew. A crew it was my duty to protect. In a bar, I could ignore it. On a battlefield, when my gargoyle was already feeling the call of blood and the darkness within me was at a rolling boil...

"Please stop," I whispered, pushing Ulric away. If my magic kicked off, I didn't want to accidentally fling him. "Stop going at each other. Now isn't the time."

"It's never the time," Broken Sue said in a rough voice, like rocks dragging over concrete.

"That's only because you're on borrowed time," Niamh returned.

"Ha! What amazing wordplay. Two masters," Edgar

said from somewhere behind me.

"Enough!" The darkness surged up and stole over me. Magic ballooned out, sending a pulse into the sky.

I knew that pulse meant, *Come to me,* calling all the gargoyles around us. I didn't have any more control over that than I did my new talent of creating blood bonds.

Mr. Tom's pounding on my back ceased. My beast itched to get out.

Another pulse blasted out into the sky, across the field, across the town.

*Prepare for war.*

"Damn it, damn it, damn it," I said, balling my fists, trying to clamp the magic back down. "Think happy thoughts. Happy thoughts."

"Fall into it, Jessie." Niamh was right at my side. "Fall into it. Let yer primal side out for a walk. Shift. Take to the sky. Or waddle around—whatever ye gargoyles do. *Do it.*"

*"Listen to her,"* Ivy House said. *"She created this opportunity for you. Shift and let your beast handle this challenge. Do not let your mate down."*

"You baited him on purpose," I gritted out.

"Well, o'course I did," Niamh replied, keeping pace with me as I stepped away. "I've got him down to a short fuse, and he's got a lotta power. He's helping me push ye. Let the beast out."

"You can't let that challenging shifter ridicule you," Ulric said, popping up at my other side again. The others pushed away, probably worried I'd explode. "Show this pack your power. Show them they're in good hands with you as their alpha."

My power pumped higher, the pulses coming faster. Stronger. Calling my brothers and sisters in arms.

Broken Sue lost all his tension and sucked in a startled breath.

"Feels good, doesn't it?" Niamh told him, breathing faster. "The female gargoyle is a born commander. A magical commander. Not even Austin Steele can unite an army the way she can. Jessie-the-Jane just has to get out of the way."

"What if I lose control?" I said. "What if I kill her? What if I accidentally overreach and hurt innocent bystanders?"

"I got that," Sebastian said. "I can handle protecting the onlookers so you can focus on the challenge. Nessa, I could use some help."

"Coming! How do *you* do, sir?" Nessa said as she jogged by, laughter in her tone. She was talking to Broken Sue again.

"There, now. Ye won't hurt any bystanders, sure ye won't," Niamh told me.

I could feel my power thrumming, pulsing into the sky where several gargoyles now soared, waiting for my next command.

Ulric swore under his breath. "I can't resist this," he said, strained. "She's calling us, Jessie. Your gargoyle is calling us, and it feels incredible. It feels like what we were made for."

Wings snapped out ten feet away, like a sail swiftly catching a hard wind—Nathanial, his clothes shed, and now in his other form. Jasper was next, his wings not as large but the snap of their opening just as eager.

"Yeah, I gotta join." Ulric jogged away with a huge grin, tossing aside his clothes.

"Let yer primal side rule," Niamh pushed. "Ye aren't just a mage, you are also a gargoyle. Remember? If ye want to meet the cairn leaders who are sure to come, ye need to act like one of their kind. One of *yer* kind—Jaysus, Earl, shift quick, would ye? If your bollocks were any lower, they'd trail along the ground behind you."

Sweat ran down my face. My shirt was plastered to my back.

I shook my head. I hated this. I'd made peace with the necessity of killing enemies in order to protect myself and my people, but Zoe was part of the pack. She was an ally. I didn't want to kill her, but if I completely gave in to my gargoyle, I wasn't sure I could stop myself.

*"Nature is savage, and so is magic,"* Ivy House said. *"The shifter was warned."*

Before I could shake my head again, I felt another wave of Broken Sue's power. This time, though, it wasn't directed at Niamh, and it wasn't hostile. It was directed at me—a message of support from my brother in arms—and it pushed me over the edge.

# CHAPTER 4

Austin stood stoically, as befitted his position, trying to temper his boiling rage at Brochan's proximity to Jess. He knew his beta had pure intentions, but Austin's animal didn't care. What in God's name were they doing?

"Should I head over there, Alpha?" Kace asked so quietly that Austin barely heard.

"No," he answered in an equally hushed voice. "That'll make the delay look worse. Brochan can handle it."

He sure as hell hoped so, anyway.

A thrum of wings vibrated the air, and gargoyles started flying in from all directions. Those in the audience shed their clothes immediately and rose into the sky.

Nathanial rose to join them with a snap of wings that reverberated across the large field, drawing everyone's attention upward. Jasper followed suit. In a moment, Ulric joined them. Then Mr. Tom.

Nathanial sailed to the middle of the field and then stopped, working his wings in fast, shallow movements. A loud, rhythmic throbbing, almost like the wing beats of an enormous hummingbird, permeated the space. In a moment, more gargoyles joined from God knew where, easily finding their place in the formation of those already present. Within five minutes, the entire host was soaring around the field in a tightly kept formation, waiting for their leader.

Waiting for Jess.

Pride filled Austin's heart.

It was time for his mate to shine.

Brochan turned around with the fluidity born of a predator, but his shoulders were tight and his hands fisted. He walked across the field, not looking up as everyone else had done. Instead, he stared straight ahead before rolling his head. His shoulders were next before his hands flexed and fisted again. He was fighting his animal. Austin was all too familiar with the signs.

Kace adjusted his stance, his disapproval plain. The beta was showing lack of control. But Austin knew Niamh wouldn't have caused such an extreme reaction in a man who was usually so collected. No, Brochan must be reacting to Jess.

Moments later, a huge wave of power washed over the field, blistering in its intensity. Brochan stopped in his tracks, his whole body going taut.

"Holy—" Kace tensed as well.

A heady pulse thumped in Austin's chest, wild and raw and free, vicious and primal. Fuck, but it felt good. The power pulsed all around him, constant and insistent. It was like a drumbeat. A command to march.

Jess's gargoyle had emerged.

Brochan started walking again, his pace faster. His eyes burned with purpose and drive by the time he reached Austin, the usual pain and misery buried.

A spark of fire drew Austin's notice. Flame raced across the grass as the phoenix lifted off the ground. Sebastian's and Nessa's hands started moving, containing the spread of fire as a peal of thunder jiggled Austin's stomach. Hollace followed Cyra upward, his great wings like those of the gargoyles. His lightning streaked the air around him, following Cyra's trail of fire.

Jess walked forward, and in the time it took for the others to get airborne, she'd shed her clothes without any of her usual modesty or hesitation. She walked toward her challenger, strong and sure. Her hair blew in the soft wind, flaring out and catching the sunlight.

She let out another pulse of power, and Austin tore his gaze from her to marvel at the crowd. All around the field, people stepped forward almost eagerly. Unwittingly. Pack members.

A second group had all shuffled back, clutching at each other or themselves, stunned mute. Non-pack.

She was separating her army from the onlookers.

Sebastian and Nessa followed her for a short distance before stopping, leaving Jess to span the final distance separating her from her challenger.

Zoe's confidence had leached out of her, and now her doubt was plain. She'd been warned, though, and there was nothing Austin could do to stop this. She would have to face Jess and bear the consequences.

The two mages worked together, their hands moving in unison. A dome grew from the ground up. Translucent but tinted mustard yellow, it enclosed the challengers. Spectators, mages, and flying creatures...all were locked out of the battle.

"I apologize," Brochan said as he turned and assumed his position just a little to the side and behind Austin. "I couldn't keep control. I barely kept myself from trying to join her crew. I've never felt anything like it."

"Good or bad?" Austin asked as Jess stopped within the dome.

"Incredible, alpha. Her gargoyle reached my animal and connected us...somehow. Honestly, sir, I can't properly describe it."

In a flash of light, Zoe shifted into her animal, a large golden eagle. She was agile in the air and great with her talons. She'd clearly thought those traits would render her the dominant animal, since it was well known that flying wasn't a female gargoyle's strong suit.

Jess shifted next, a seamless transition of a beautiful woman into a jaw-dropping creature. Her purple skin was rough, a natural defense against claws, but it shed a gorgeous pinky-purple glow, a light show when she moved.

Zoe screeched as she took to the sky. Jess watched for a moment before flaring her wings. She didn't roar or rush, nor did she hesitate past showing her challenger that she moved to her own rhythm. She bent her knees before jumping, beating her wings once she was in the air.

Jess couldn't fly as well as the male gargoyles did— her wings were smaller and slimmer, hindering both her speed and ability to maneuver. Nor did she have their strength and power. But she was still a gargoyle. Her wingspan easily topped that of her challenger. More importantly, she was made for *battle*, not swooping down and catching her dinner. It was like comparing apples and pizza. Their only commonality as creatures was that they both shifted.

Zoe hadn't done her homework.

"The puca played me for a fool," Brochan said in a low tone as the entire field watched Jess gain altitude. Her pace was leisurely. It was like she wasn't even interested in the fight. "She used me to pull out the gargoyle. I fell easily into her plans." He paused for a moment as Jess stopped a little below Zoe. "Ivy House chose well in Niamh. All this time, I thought she was just a miserable old woman, but she'd been working on me so she knew exactly how to manipulate me when the moment came."

"Is that why you lost your composure on the way back here?" Kace asked.

"No—"

Brochan cut off as Zoe pulled in her wings slightly and dove.

Jess didn't so much as tilt to get out of the way.

Zoe stretched out her feet, readying her talons, before leveling out at the last moment. She raked her claws along the side of Jess's face and across her shoulder.

Jess didn't flinch, nor did she show the bite of pain Austin could feel through the bonds. She just stayed still in the air and took it quietly.

The gargoyles above her weren't so composed.

Angry roars rained down from the sky. Gargoyles swooped, ramming into the dome to try to break through. The contact set off a buzzing sound, accompanied by shooting sparks. Still more tried, crashing into it and bouncing off, slashing with their claws, twisting and screeching in pain but still attacking the magical deterrent in their eagerness to intervene.

Zoe dove again, scraping the other side of Jess's face. When Jess didn't react, Zoe got a little bolder, aiming for the center of her back and raking across the fragile interior of one of Jess's wings.

Pain vibrated through her now. Austin's animal gnashed against his hold, wanting to break free and go to his mate. The beast didn't give a damn that he'd need a very tall ladder to reach her.

"Why isn't she fighting back?" Brochan whispered.

Austin shook his head. He didn't know. All he could feel from her was a pleasant sort of calm, like the battle was enjoyable and she didn't want to rush it.

Zoe came in again, aiming for the other wing. Jess didn't let that attack land, though, tilting at the last second. Zoe flew right past. Still, Jess didn't fight back. She stayed stagnant in the air, waiting.

"I lost my composure because my animal didn't want to walk away from Ironheart right before battle," Brochan explained in a rush. "Her gargoyle was calling me. I had to fight to maintain control and keep walking."

Zoe dove again, scratching down Jess's back. She

flapped her wings and circled, readying for another dive.

As challenges went, this one was almost boring. Without Jess moving, Zoe couldn't show off her superior maneuverability. She also clearly wasn't doing much damage. Given Jess was likely healing the wounds almost as quickly as she got them, they could be at it all day until one of them tired.

Zoe circled yet again, screeching out her challenge. Her patience was clearly starting to fray. She knew this wasn't going anywhere.

This time, she dove toward Jess's front. Talons out, coming in hard, Zoe aimed for the face. The eyes.

Austin could feel himself tense and sent a warning through the bonds. Her eyes would probably heal like anything else, but he didn't want her to take the chance.

He needn't have worried.

A surge of heat and adrenaline roared through the bonds. Zoe stretched, almost there, ready to make contact—and it was at that exact moment that Jess finally slashed, the movement looking lazy but still incredibly fast. Her claws dug into the bird's body at the underside of the wing and ripped down to the beginning of her leg. Jess's left hand came down a moment later, raking across Zoe's other side and tearing through part of her wing. Zoe screeched in pain and surprise and fright. She flapped and fluttered and would've lost altitude, but Jess grabbed her by the neck to keep her from getting away. She then brought up her feet and clawed Zoe's stomach.

Even from there, Austin could see the damage Jess was doing. Large tears in Zoe's body gushed blood that fell in crimson drops like a rainstorm. Feathers fluttered down as Zoe thrashed in the larger predator's hold.

Still holding the bird by the neck with one hand, Jess took the other and grabbed Zoe by first one wing, and then the other. Each contact elicited a loud *crack*. The sound must've been amplified by magic, because it blasted down through the crowd. She was breaking Zoe's wings so that the golden eagle would be completely at her mercy.

Zoe still thrashed and squawked, trying to escape, but Jess changed her hold, grabbing Zoe's legs and hanging her upside down. The broken wings hung limp, probably too painful to move.

Now Jess did fly. She dove down and then pulled out of it, did a sort of loop-de-loop, and dove again, all the while holding Zoe like a chicken waiting to be plucked. Like a prize to be shown off. Blood was flung every which way, dotting the field below. The flow tapered off, though. Jess was clearly healing her enough to keep her from bleeding out. The display was no less vicious for it. Zoe had come to make a mockery of Jess, and Jess had turned the tables.

The crowd fell into an uncomfortable hush, watching as Jess did one more tour of the dome before flying low and unceremoniously dropping Zoe to the ground. Zoe thumped down and stayed there for a long moment. The spot flared, and the bird shifted into her human form. She kicked out her legs, flipping onto her back, and then lay limply.

"We don't need to worry about Ironheart making a statement," Kace said softly. "I doubt anyone will be in a hurry to challenge her after this."

Austin had to agree.

"She hasn't used any magic, though," Brochan murmured. "She's still trapped in the dome."

An issue that became obvious when Jess scraped her claws against it. Sparks flew all around her. Still it held. Sebastian hadn't released the spell. He was showing that he held the power here, and with it, control over her. Over them all.

# CHAPTER 5

"**S**HE'S NOT LETTING me take down the spell," Sebastian said in barely contained panic.

He watched Jess climb to the top of the dome before scraping her claws against the magic. Sparks rained down, and zags of electricity rent the air.

He tried to pull the spell down again, to disintegrate it, to seep power from it. Nothing worked! She'd laid her own spell over his to lock it into place without changing any of the properties. It looked like he was intentionally keeping her magically confined.

"Crap, Nessa. Crap, crap. What do I do? I can't run. Animals love to chase."

"I thought ye said they shouldn't be called animals." Niamh sauntered up with a beer in her hand. How that woman always seemed to find alcoholic beverages, Sebastian did not know.

"They turn into animals, and animals love chasing gangly mages running for their lives," Sebastian said, trying to break through Jessie's spell lock. "Help me,

Nessa. Maybe if you help, we can manage it together. Hurry, before the alpha decides to free his mate by breaking my neck."

"I don't have the power to even try," Nessa replied, fear evident in her voice. "Why would she turn on us? I thought you said these people were loyal and trustworthy."

"Calm yerselves, would ye? Listen to the lotta'ya. Here, Nessa, have one of these. It'll help calm the nerves." Niamh motioned behind her.

Edgar jogged up, doing that strange, lurching, high-kneed lope of his, and held out a beer wrapped in a doily. It was only then that Sebastian noticed the cooler behind them.

"Earl gives Jessie a lotta grief over her oul pair bringing a cooler everywhere," Niamh said, watching Jessie plow into the dome a little more violently, like she was starting to get seriously pissed. Seriously, horribly, terribly pissed. At Sebastian. Which was crazy, because she had done this to herself.

Did she really want to sic the alpha on him? Because that would certainly make a statement—at his expense.

"But if ye ask me," Niamh went on calmly, "her oul pair know what they're about. Drink that down, Nessa. Yer nothin' but a spectator."

"Wha—what?" Nessa asked, ignoring Edgar's outstretched hand and attempting to work her magic with Sebastian. They worked very well together because they'd been doing it forever, but Nessa didn't have a third of his power. She wouldn't be of much help if an enormous, angry shifter charged him without warning.

"No one is goin'ta kill ye, ya donkey," Niamh told Sebastian. "They like ye for some reason. Jessie needs ya, in any case. No, no, yer safe. But ye heard Ulric. The town needs to know *they* are safe, and to do that, they need to know Jessie can combat mages. Mouse, meet hawk. Go on, now. She's waiting for ye to go in and meet her. She wants a magical duel. Here, Nessa, take that beer. Don't you worry, I got plenty. I brought two twelve-packs in case this dragged on. Go on, ye might as well. Go on, take it. *Go on.*"

Her confusion evident, Nessa hesitantly took the doily-wrapped beer.

"Now." Niamh nodded and looked back toward Jessie.

"How do you know all of that?" Sebastian asked, his body starting to shake. "Are you sure the alpha isn't going to come for me?"

"I know all of that because it is my job to know all of that. Also because her call to arms, as it were, has reversed. See how the gargoyles have backed off, letting her be? She's sending out a sorta all-clear. And I can feel her impatience through the bond. In just a minute, that gobshite Earl will be down, wondering what is keeping Jessie waiting."

"But why wasn't I told?" Sebastian whined, lowering his hands.

Trying to get around that spell was no good. When Jessie did a spell like that, correctly and putting all her power behind it, he was sunk.

A gargoyle broke from the others, flying in their direction.

"See? What did I tell ye?" Niamh chuckled and shook her head. "He's like a mother hen. It's a good thing Jessie doesn't mind being fawned over."

Mr. Tom landed somewhat gracefully before shifting.

"Ye weren't told because Jessie didn't know herself," Niamh told Sebastian. "Ye were here—I had to basically yank that gargoyle to the surface. It's taking point now, and a good thing, too. She made a show of that bird a moment ago, and now she will prove she can handle a mage. That's what's needed to cement her position as alpha. Sure you must see that."

"But why would she pretend to be stuck?" Sebastian asked. "Isn't that undermining her?"

"She's showing how strong ye are, giving the people what they most fear, and then she will show that she can best ya. She will show them that she can overcome it."

"What is happening over here?" Mr. Tom said once he'd regained his human form. "What is the holdup? The miss is impatient—No, Edgar, I do not want a— Why is there a doily around that beer? Your obsession with doilies has gone too far. Go back to the flowers. At least that was useful. Old woman, are you distracting Sebastian from doing whatever it is the miss needs him to do?"

"Me, old? I'm not the one with his bollocks dangling down around his ankles," Niamh replied.

"I'd really rather not die today," Sebastian said softly.

He knew he sounded like a coward, but he couldn't help it. Usually, Jessie was his security blanket around all of these very dangerous and somewhat unpredictable magical types. Unpredictable to him, at any rate. The idea of her turning on him, even for show, crushed any sort of courage he'd thought he possessed.

"Come, now. We all must do our part." Mr. Tom patted Sebastian on the back, getting much too close for his level of undress, and began forcibly shepherding him toward the dome. "She won't kill you. She likes you for some reason."

"I think they're right, Sabby," Nessa called, cracking open her beer. "She didn't kill you when she thought she hated you, so it stands to reason that she won't now. Like they said, she likes you for some reason."

"Why does everyone keep saying *for some reason*?" he murmured in a wispy voice.

"There, see?" Mr. Tom pushed him at the dome. "Nothing to worry about."

Deciding to trust the Ivy House crew, because he really had no choice, Sebastian walked into the dome. The spell was a magical trap of sorts—one people could enter but not escape—and he regretted showing Jessie how it worked.

"Why didn't you shift and take to the sky?" Mr. Tom demanded of Niamh.

The dome wasn't soundproof, an intentional decision on Sebastian's part, because he'd wanted everyone to hear the squawks of Jessie beating her challenger. Which had happened. Had he known the next set of squawks would be his own, he might've rethought the matter.

"I couldn't be arsed," Niamh replied. "What good would it've done? All yer doin' is flyin' around in circles. And anyway, someone had to watch Edgar. All we needed was for him to gallop into the dome like some crusty vaudeville act hollering *whoopee* at the top of his lungs. Now that would be embarrassin' to us all."

"I'll try not to be offended," Edgar said.

"Show a little support for the heir and your employer, would you? Team spirit," Mr. Tom said.

"Sure I *am* showing team spirit," Niamh said. "I've got an Ivy House doily, a beer, and a front-row seat. I'm all set. Now feck off. Yer ruinin' the taste of me beer."

Sebastian lost the thread of the conversation as Jessie caught sight of his loitering at the edge of the dome. Swirls of pinkish-purple light drifted behind her as she altered her course. One minute, she was beside the dome walls, and the next, she was cutting a path through the center of the space, flying directly toward him.

"Fight with everything ye got," Niamh hollered at him. "*She* might take it easy on ye, but her gargoyle sure won't."

"Fantastic," he murmured, inching out a little farther.

"And for the love of God, lad, look like the powerful mage ye are. Yer embarrassin' yourself."

He took a deep breath and tried to straighten up. It was easy to strut and swagger and look like he owned the world when he was playing the Elliot Graves role. His alter ego was ruthless and vicious and morally gray at best.

But he wasn't Elliot Graves in this shifter town, and it was impossible to maintain any kind of swagger at Ivy

House. For one thing, Niamh loved to poke holes in people's confidence. For another, everyone was just too weird. Sebastian was sort of weird, too, and he'd enjoyed being himself here in a way he couldn't in the magical world. He hadn't needed his usual armor.

He had to remember, though, that Jessie was also playing a part. She had helped him feel safe, and now she was trying to help the rest of her territory feel the same way. This was her job. As part of her team, he needed to help her with it.

Besides, didn't they do this exact thing in practice? Granted, they weren't usually trapped in a magical dome, surrounded by lethal creatures who hated his kind and would give anything to rip him apart, but even so…

He blew out yet another breath, closed his eyes for a moment, and rolled his shoulders.

Time to hide the nerd who wanted nothing more than to work magic. Time to resume his cloak as the most notorious magical villain this world had ever known.

✧   ✧   ✧

"NOW, HERE WE go." Niamh drained the last of her beer and handed it back to Edgar as excitement unfurled through her.

Sebastian straightened out of his usual hunch. His shoulders rolled back, and his head came up. He went from a mousy-looking guy to a magical badass owning his space. He strutted forward, his arms loose at his sides, his steps purposeful and aimed directly at Jessie. Even from behind him, Niamh could tell his gaze was hard and direct. A challenge.

A surge of rage tumbled through the bond. Not from Jessie, though—from Austin Steele. The big alpha didn't like someone challenging his mate.

"Well, now, this isn't something I'm used to seeing with Sebastian," Mr. Tom said, forgetting the other gargoyles were still in the sky and crowding close to the dome.

"Git yer nekked arse away, would ye?" Niamh shoved him. "Jaysus, Mary, 'n' Joseph. Yer all sweaty, like."

"Sebastian's ready to play hardball," Nessa said before draining her beer.

Jessie paused in the air for a moment. Sebastian paused as well, his stance cocky. He leaned in such a way that said he was bored with his opposition.

A thrill curled through Niamh's bond with Jessie. Excitement. The gargoyle had found its match. It was time to play.

She snapped out her wings before tilting her head

up and roaring into the sky. The gargoyles above followed suit. The great thunderbird and mighty phoenix added their voices before the shifters on the ground joined the call. All around the dome, the challenge was voiced on Jessie's behalf.

"Whoopee!" Edgar pumped his fist and accidentally crushed the full beer he'd been about to give Niamh. She sighed.

Within the dome, Sebastian shivered.

Nessa did as well before shaking herself out. "It's never going to be a bunch to one, though," she said. "It'll never be this lopsided of a battle. A mage by himself would never go head to head with her in this sort of way."

"Well, o'course they wouldn't." Niamh waved that thought away. "They're in a magical dome, for feck's sake. This is a spectator sport. It's marketing. We need this territory to know that we have powerful magical people on our side. If those fool mages come calling, we have more than just a bunch of paws to answer the challenge."

Sebastian lifted his hand before doing a little circle in the air with his finger.

"Oh, crap," Nessa whispered, leaning forward.

Jessie's wings crunched in to her sides. Her feet kicked for a moment.

Then she dropped like a stone.

"Oh, sh—" Niamh leaned forward as well.

Emotions rolled through the bond from the Ivy House crew. Cyra dove through the soaring gargoyles toward the magical dome, her fire zigging and zagging in the air around her. Her beak hit first, and an explosion of fire followed. It raced across the surface of the dome and nearly down to the ground. Pressure cracks spiderwebbed the spell, rough and angry. Niamh could feel the heat before it dwindled.

"Crap cones." Nessa looked more closely at the spell before glancing up. "A few more of those dive bombs, and she'll crack it wide open."

"I think that is the point," Mr. Tom said. "She seems to think Sebastian has turned on us."

Jessie plummeted toward the ground, nearly there, still frozen. Sebastian didn't move, watching her fall. Niamh wished the mage were connected to the house so she could get a read on him. From what she could see through the clearing webs of fire, his posture conveyed the confidence of a victor.

"C'mon, girl," Niamh said. "Don't wait until after ye've bounced."

A burst of bright purple light exploded around Jessie, and then her wings snapped free again. She pulled out of her dive and headed straight for him, flapping her wings to get more speed.

Sebastian raised his hands, working magic, but she barreled into him before he could get a shot off, ripping him from the ground.

"Holy—" Nessa reached her can back. "I need another, Edgar. Please."

"Your command is my...order." Edgar hurried to comply.

"Didn't quite get that one, Edgar," Niamh muttered.

"She does know not to kill him, right?" Nessa said with a slightly shaking voice. "She knows that? I believed you earlier. Was that a terrible judgment call on my part?"

"You have to be careful when inciting a gargoyle," Mr. Tom said before stepping back and readying to shift again. "We are very unpredictable."

"The good ones are, at any rate." Edgar handed Nessa another doily-wrapped beer. "Like you used to be, right, Mr. Tom?"

Holding Sebastian suspended by an ankle, Jessie carried him to the top of the dome. He hung upside down without thrashing or even wriggling in her hold. Unlike Zoe, he was perfectly composed in her grasp.

Jessie roared near the top, spun, and let go.

Nessa shook her head as Sebastian flew. "He could've gotten a shot off before she threw him."

"She could've pulled his legs off during the journey to the top of the dome," Edgar countered, pushing in a little too close to Nessa. He unconsciously made it his duty to creep people out. He was very good at it.

She didn't seem to notice, though, watching Sebastian's trajectory.

Sebastian hit an invisible impediment in the sky that slowed him to almost stopping. He dropped straight down again until he hit another. And then another, like a series of nets catching him and then releasing, dropping him to safety.

Jessie was after him. She streaked through the dome in swirls of colorful light. Nearly on him, she blasted magic in his direction. It spread out under him in a sea of bright blue and then almost seemed to peel away. He crashed through the failed spell and thunked onto the ground.

The landing wouldn't have kept a shifter down for more than a moment, but Sebastian rolled onto his side and curled up in pain. The fall must've knocked the wind out of him.

"Good show," Niamh muttered.

"What?" Nessa asked, her whole body tense.

"Mages aren't as durable as shifters. They hide behind their magic. Jessie just showed everyone here what waited behind the smoke and mirrors. He might as well be non-magical with that sort of fragility. Take away the magic, and you will have no problem killing the enemy."

Jessie landed a ways away from Sebastian and fired off a spell. He rolled onto his back and erected a shield, catching her spell and tossing it back at her. She waved it away and fired another, and another.

Sebastian got to his feet in between deflecting her spells, playing defense now. Once he was up, though, he was ten times more active. Approaching her at an angle, he fired off a spell. Before it hit, he quick-stepped in the opposite direction and hit her with another.

Her shields caught and threw the spells, but they were designed to counter an attacker who was staying in one location. Sebastian was rendering them useless.

She countered, hitting him with harder spells. He braced as they came in, then shrugged them off. He fired two to her one, much more experienced and savvier in a magical duel.

"Get mad, girl," Niamh said. "Get mad and hit him with yer power."

Jessie took to the air again, making Sebastian bend back to fire spells off. It hampered his effectiveness, slowing him. And then she went for it, slamming down spells of pure power.

"Yes!" Niamh shook her fist, the call of battle singing within her. She knew from watching Jessie and Sebastian practice that these spells lacked any sort of complexity. Most mages wouldn't dare use them in a life-or-death situation because of how easily they could be torn apart. Except, as Sebastian had explained to them, most mages didn't have as much pure power as Jessie did.

When in doubt, beat them with brawn.

His shields were durable, but he didn't have anything to brace against. Her first spell shoved him back three paces. Her second one, fired off right after the first, made him stagger. The third made him roll across the ground.

She dove, hit the ground, fired off another spell, and shifted to her human form. Here, she used her more agile hands and added complexity to the spell, pounding it into his shield.

His protective spell started to tear away, and he rolled, trying to get more distance. She walked faster, catching up.

A loud *bang* hit the dome again as Cyra dive-bombed it. Fire ignited within the spell's cracks. It burned anew, momentarily cutting out their view into the dome. The spell pulsed before dimming, losing power.

Cyra pulled away, and then thunder rolled. Lightning sparked around the thunderbird as Hollace followed Cyra's previous path. He slammed into the dome with his much larger size. Lightning followed the route Cyra's fire had burned. It fizzed and crackled, and the spell groaned like an old man getting out of bed before it shattered. The orange glow diminished until the spell was no more.

"Well, that's not good," Edgar said with his crochet hooks in hand. "That dome was keeping Augustus Steele from going to his mate's aid. Jessie isn't the only one whose animal dunks them into violent darkness. She's just the only one who shies away from it."

# CHAPTER 6

M Y BREATH CAME in fast puffs, and fatigue dragged at my limbs. We were almost to the end of this battle. I just had to make Sebastian submit, and my job here would be done.

His head thunked against the ground as his shield shoved back against him. He tried to roll away from my advance, but I put up a block to pin him in. I slashed at his shield, then slammed him with another powerful spell. Slashed then hammered, slashed then hammered. In a moment, I'd push my claws against his neck and scare the life out of him. He didn't have any fear of magic, but he had a distinct fear of monsters.

Right now, most of me was lost to the monster, anyway.

He crumpled under the onslaught, giving me déjà vu for the first time we'd battled. He could've hit me with over a dozen kill spells that would've burrowed through my defenses and taken me out, or come up with more creative ways to combat my power. But he wasn't trying to kill me, then or now, and had tempered his spells so I didn't get hurt.

Not many mages would willingly allow themselves to look *lesser*. And yet here he was, allowing me to look mighty, trusting I wouldn't hurt him, so that the people of this territory felt safer.

My heart swelled, and then a crashing noise from above stole my focus.

I looked up in confusion. Fire rolled over the outside of the dome right before Hollace slammed into it.

A spell hit me center mass. I flew backward, caught off guard.

*Stupid!* I'd been almost done with this fight!

The dome winked out. Sebastian scrambled to his feet and hit me with another brutal spell, singeing away my shield.

That wasn't what freaked me out, though.

Rage pulsed through my bonds, drowning out all other emotions.

Austin.

I glanced over as another spell came at me, ripping through the skin on my arm. Sebastian's expression turned into one of confusion. I should've easily blocked that spell.

The great polar bear raced toward us.

He'd been on edge since the shifter fight. His animal

had been riding him hard; I'd felt it. I hadn't thought Cyra could get through the dome—I'd been counting on it—but Hollace must have pushed her magic over the edge.

I'd be proud of my team later.

Sebastian followed my gaze. His eyes widened, but he'd noticed too late to react. Austin's powerful strides had him only a few paces away now.

"Jessie. Oh, God, Jessie!" Sebastian turned and threw up one hell of a shield, larger than he'd ever used with me. He curved it around him but left the back open, probably inviting me in to help.

Austin hit it full on, and the spell seared through his white fur. A shock of intense pain filled the bonds, but I already knew it wouldn't faze him.

He rose on two legs and roared before slashing at the spell. One giant paw raked across it, and then the other. Sparks flew, and smoke curled up, but still he worked at it, shoving and scratching and cutting through it with his power and perseverance.

"Holy—Oh—oh cr—" Sebastian fed more power into it, hunching down. The bravado of Elliot Graves clearly wasn't sustainable under this style of attack. "Help!" he screeched, shooting a spell in sheer panic. It wasn't well aimed, thankfully, and it just slashed across Austin's side. A line of red appeared, and then blood pooled.

My monster threatened to overwhelm me, sensing trouble to her mate. Red lined my vision before darkness crowded in.

I gritted my teeth, holding on to my logic with everything I had.

"No!" I shoved my magic between Austin and Sebastian, creating a wedge. With all the strength I could muster—not worrying about spell complexity or anything beyond getting them apart—I closed my eyes and forced the wedge wider, pushing Austin back. He railed against me, thinking it was Sebastian fighting him. I let him, thickening the blockade when he clawed it too thin. It wasn't hurting him, though.

Sebastian knew the magic was mine. I snapped my eyes open in time to see him stagger back and fall onto his butt. He gripped his heart as he watched Austin struggle to get at him.

"Should I run?" Sebastian asked with a quivering voice.

"Austin, it's fine." I stepped in front of Sebastian, continuing my magical *push*. Cyra circled just above us, ready to help.

Head bowed, sweat dripping freely, I forced Austin back a little farther. By God, he was hard to move.

"It was a challenge, Austin," I said. "Just like with

shifters. It was a challenge! I was about to win, damn it. You aren't supposed to interrupt unless someone calls for your aid. I didn't call you!"

Austin's exertions slowed. I felt sudden understanding leak through our bonds. I didn't know if that was him realizing the magic he railed against was mine or that I hadn't been in any danger from Sebastian.

He lumbered back a few paces, still on hind legs, before roaring so loudly it felt like the ground was shaking. A moment later, he reduced down to a man. A cut, sweaty man with fire in his eyes. I let my magic drop.

"Today's challenges are over," he announced loudly before stepping toward me in a rush and swinging me into his arms.

"Sabby, look, I'm riding a scary unicorn!" Nessa called from above.

Glancing up, I saw Niamh flying past, Nessa on her back.

"Why…" I squinted up at them headed in the direction of Ivy House.

Austin didn't comment. Instead, he turned and spared a few words for Kace: "Make sure the mage isn't harmed. Get him back to Ivy House. He's going to be a little shaken by all of this. Make sure the people here see that but don't exacerbate matters. He is still incredibly dangerous. You don't want him going into survival mode and accidentally killing someone."

"Yes, alpha," Kace said dutifully, and hurried toward Sebastian.

The way before us opened up quickly, everyone who'd run forward to see the show now giving us a wide berth.

I waited until we were at his Jeep, out of earshot of anyone else, before I spoke. "Did you honestly think he was going to kill me? Is your animal in control or something? Because he was surrounded by your entire territory. All my gargoyles and crew were above us. He would've had nowhere to run."

Austin tucked me into the Jeep, got in the driver's seat, and started it up without replying.

Gargoyles still flew overhead, but my crew was starting to land, probably ready to get their gear and head home.

"And why the hell was Nessa flying on Niamh?" I asked in utter confusion. "Niamh hates when people ride on her back."

It wasn't until he was turning onto the highway that Austin finally spoke. "I didn't know you intended to challenge him. At first, I thought he'd trapped you in that dome."

"He didn't know I intended to challenge him, either.

Neither did I. It just didn't seem right to use magic against that shifter. She was no match for me. But I had to use magic in some way. Sebastian is the only person who can handle it, so I had to force him to challenge me. Or someone did, at any rate. I think it was Mr. Tom who finally pushed him into the dome."

"Yet he kept that dome up after you won your first challenge."

I checked the back seat for a blanket or something. He had doors on the Jeep but no top, and I didn't have any clothing. I wasn't in the habit of giving people such an eyeful on the highway.

"*I* kept that dome up. He was trying to rip it down, but I wouldn't let him."

Austin looked over at me, realized what I was doing, and shook his head. "Sorry, I wasn't thinking. I just wanted to get you away from that field as quickly as possible. I don't have any cover."

"So you did actually think he was stupid enough to try to kill me?"

"No. When he was pushed into the dome, I could tell he didn't want to be there. It just…" He shivered, and a surge of rage flooded the bonds. "He's learned a thing or two from shifters."

"What do you mean?"

"His challenge. His posture, his confidence, his

bearing... He could've been an alpha at the top of his game." His voice was low and rough. "I am not used to ignoring challenges to me *or* you."

His body flexed, and I could feel him wrestling for control.

I put my hand on his shoulder. "He has learned a thing or two, yes. He was playing Elliot Graves because he knew that's what I needed. He was doing it for me."

"And yet he nearly dropped you straight to the ground."

I rubbed my hand over his shoulder and around to the back of his neck. "Yes. And that was the fifth time he's done it to me. The other four were in practice last week. Poor Ulric had to endure it, too, so I could practice relieving someone else of the spell. We want to make sure a mage can't drop the fliers from the sky."

Austin exhaled slowly as his rage cooled. "I didn't know that."

"You can't train with me all the time. No one can. Everyone has things to do."

"As the battle wore on, I was pretty sure things were going in the right direction. I was starting to calm down. And if you'd officially beaten him, I would've led the pack in a victory roar."

"So what happened?"

"Cyra and Hollace tore down the dome. I needed to

act."

"By killing the only teacher I have?"

"By *attacking* the only teacher you have. I could've gotten through his magic to kill him."

"You could've?"

"Yes. But I couldn't have gotten through yours. Not unless you tired out faster than I did." I felt his pride glowing through the bonds.

"I would've tired out faster, no question. I was already exhausted. But I still don't understand why you needed to act."

"I needed to get control of the situation. I didn't know what Cyra or Hollace would do. I didn't know how the people watching you would react. There were just too many unknowns. In order to assume control, I asserted my dominance."

"By attacking."

"Yes."

"And how does this work out for me? You undermined my challenge. People will think I couldn't finish off a mage."

He chuckled softly as he turned onto Ivy House's street. Thankfully, I'd been so wrapped up in our conversation that I hadn't noticed anyone staring at the naked couple in the Jeep. Then again, most of the people in our town and the surrounding area were now magical. The houses and establishments of the non-magical were selling for way more than they were worth. Those few who had decided to stay were used to turning a very large blind eye to all the strangeness in town. It was the only way they could preserve their sanity.

"Babe, after what went on today, the last thing people will be thinking is that you couldn't finish off a mage." He started laughing as he parked in front of Ivy House. "Everyone knew what the outcome would have been, and you only gained status because your team broke into that dome. Then there's the way you made a mockery of your first challenger." He laughed harder, bent over the wheel. "I've never seen a challenge go so pear-shaped for a challenger. Usually, they're just made to submit, and that's that."

"What did I do that was so...extra?"

He turned off the engine and gave me an incredulous look. "She has so much pride in her eagle form, in being the only predator flier in the pack, and you flew—" He shook with laughter. "You flew her around like a dead chicken."

I scowled at him before getting out of the Jeep. "I wasn't in control for that bit. Not that I'll admit, anyway. But seriously, she ripped me all up. I think the victory lap was warranted."

"You *let* her rip you all up." He wiped his eyes as he climbed from the Jeep. "You just sat there and let her do her worst. Which wasn't much against a gargoyle's skin."

"No, it wasn't. I've never appreciated the rough skin of my other form as much as I did today."

He met me on the grass before swinging me up into his arms. "I want to do my own victory lap with you. After a shower, maybe. You have chicken smell all over you."

"Not funny. Her broken arms are going to hurt for a while. I healed her a good bit but left a bunch for her to heal herself."

The door opened as we got there.

*"It's about time you came back,"* Ivy House said.

*"Don't sass me, or I'll leave again."*

"To answer your question about Niamh, she probably had Nessa on her back to either protect her or annoy Brochan," Austin said as he carried me up to my room. "I sent him to grab Nessa when the dome was falling. I worried someone would think it was a free-for-all against the mages."

"Ah. Then she's probably upset Broken Sue didn't get a chance to grab her. She doesn't mind being squished against his muscles."

"That's why I sent him instead of Kace."

I arched an eyebrow at him.

He gave me a lopsided grin and shrugged before setting me down in the bathroom. "The guy could use a little…fun. She doesn't seem scared by his intensity or concerned about his past."

"I think she deals with some pretty shady characters. Broken Sue is intense, but he's safe. *Beyond* safe. He's protection incarnate, like you. I get the feeling she's used to dealing with the kind of people who'd slip a knife in her back as soon as it's turned." I wiped my hand down my face. "We need to discuss plans with Sebastian and Nessa. I've seen them in training, obviously, but we only talk about magic. I've been too busy running away from what's waking up inside of me to get a handle on the outside world."

"We will." He turned on the shower and stepped in, reaching for my hand. I joined him. "For now, let's celebrate your victories. News of today is going to spread quickly. Any doubts about you will be thoroughly put to rest."

"Let's hope so, because soon, I'll need to use all my focus for the gargoyle cairn leaders." I let the warm spray beat down on my back as he grabbed the fluffy purple loofa. "I still have two empty places in the circle, too. And shouldn't I try to connect with some mages? I need to talk to Sebastian about that." I leaned my forehead against his shoulder. "Running away from my problems was so much easier."

He laughed softly. "It's easier in the beginning, definitely. But your problems will always catch up to you. The longer you avoid them, the worse your reunion with them will be."

He couldn't have been more correct.

# CHAPTER 7

"GOOD MORNING, MISS." A dull thunk announced my coffee mug being set on the bedside table. The bed was empty beside me, Austin having left earlier to deal with pack matters.

Mr. Tom stood over me with a pleased smile and a sparkle in his eyes. "I trust you slept well? When you did sleep, of course. Late one, hmm?" He gave me a wink.

I felt my eyebrows pinch together but didn't respond. It was best if you ignored him and hoped he went away.

"How's Sebastian?" I asked, feeling him down in the bowels of Ivy House. "How long has he been in the crystal room?"

"Lost track of things last night?"

His grin was a little embarrassing and very annoying. I was a grown woman. I shouldn't have to blush about adult activities.

Then again, Mr. Tom wasn't the kind of person you'd want to confide in about your sex life.

He must have sensed my discomfort through our Ivy House bond, because he switched gears and answered my question. "Sebastian's been in there since Kace and Broken Sue brought him here after the challenge. They practically carried him. Austin seems to have given him quite a fright. From his constant mumbles when I was bringing him food, I assume he has lost his mind. Fear can do that to a person. Ivy House will keep him from spinning out of control and killing us all, though, don't you worry. She isn't helping with the gnomes, but she will help with a homicidal mage, I am certain."

*"He needs a moment to collect his thoughts,"* Ivy House said. *"Or maybe he needs to be forced to sleep at this point. He is harmless to you, but...he sounds a little wound up. His mumbling has only increased in fervor and volume."*

I rubbed my eyes. "I'll check on him in a bit."

"Of course, miss. What are we thinking for this morning?" Mr. Tom looked at the little table near the window. "Shall we have our breakfast at the table today? It's a lovely day to look over the grounds. Or how about you drink your coffee, get showered, and I'll set up a late breakfast for you out on the grass? I can have Edgar put up the canopy."

I pulled the sheets to cover my chest as I sat up.

"Oops." Mr. Tom held out a finger. "Just a moment." He bustled toward my closet as I reached for my coffee.

A knock sounded at the door.

"Yep?" I called.

Ulric poked his head in. "Morning, Miss Jessie. How goes it? Late night, huh? You must be sore."

I paused with the coffee mug nearly at my lips. "Did I forget to cut off the links last night or something?" Our links could be silenced prior to private moments, and I was usually good about remembering.

"No, you did not. You definitely cut it off...for all six or seven hours." Ulric laughed as he stepped farther into the room. "Gargoyles have good stamina, but I gotta say, the alpha should get a medal. He was clearly delighted with the show you put on."

Before I could stammer out a response, Mr. Tom bustled back in.

"Here we go, miss." He held out one of Austin's T-shirts. "Only lightly used. I assume you want to wrap up in his smell after last night?"

I blinked at it for a moment. "Why do you have one of Austin's lightly used T-shirts? *How* do you have one of his shirts? He takes all of his laundry home to wash."

"He hasn't even missed them. As soon as you're done with this one, I'll swap it out for another. I have a few stored up should you want or need them."

"You've been stealing his clothes?" Ulric asked.

"What do you take me for?" Mr. Tom sniffed. "I do not steal. I am simply borrowing a few items for the miss. I'm sure he doesn't mind. Or wouldn't, if he knew. He's not as observant about his T-shirts as he is about other matters. He gets a clean T-shirt from the drawer before he leaves, and while he is otherwise occupied around the house, I do a smell test on the things he's gathered to take home and grab what we need. Simple. I don't see why this is an issue."

Ulric held up his hand. "Just so that I am under-standing this...you wait until he's not looking and smell your way through his dirty laundry? And then...borrow his dirty clothes for Jessie? Without asking?"

Mr. Tom blinked at him. "How else would I get his lightly used T-shirts? I dare not break into his home. There are some lines we shouldn't cross."

Ulric and I both stared at Mr. Tom for a long moment.

Then I relented and reached for it. I *did* want to be wrapped in Austin's smell. I slipped the shirt on and went back to sipping my coffee.

"So. Now that the overindulgent question-asking

has finished, let's get back to breakfast." Mr. Tom gave Ulric some side-eye before returning his focus to me. "Brunch in the grass? How about it? Most of your people are wandering around aimlessly after missing you for weeks on end. They might like a catch-up."

I sighed. "Sure. Fine. I should probably check in with Sebastian first, though."

Mr. Tom's expression flattened. "If he hasn't completely lost his mind, you'll need to sort him out, miss. He can't just go to pieces every time a shifter attacks him. He was positively embarrassing to Ivy House yesterday. We can't have a show like that again. It'll make us seem less than professional to the magical world at large."

Once again, Ulric and I stared at Mr. Tom for a long beat. This was coming from a guy who wore ridiculous disguises to mask himself in broad daylight and sniffed his way through other people's dirty laundry.

"Right," I said slowly. A grin wrestled with Ulric's lips. "Well, I hardly think facing Austin in a temper is the same as going head to head with another shifter. I doubt many people would've responded any better."

"You did, miss. *You* responded better," Mr. Tom replied, taking my now-empty coffee cup. I was tired—I'd need a heavy dose of caffeine this morning.

"I knew Austin wouldn't hurt me. It's different."

"All due respect, Jessie, you would've stood up to him anyway." Ulric beamed at me. "You did us proud. Everything went brilliantly well."

"I wasn't really in control," I muttered, pulling back the sheets and swinging my legs over the edge of the bed. I pulled at the shirt to keep everything covered. "My gargoyle basically took the lead."

"Learning how to harness your primal side will come in time." Mr. Tom shooed Ulric away. "Go, go, she needs to wake up and to get ready for the day. I'll bring up another cup, miss. You're probably still tired from your late-night activities."

"Oh my God, please drop it," I said, groaning.

"Of course, miss. But given your drowsy mood, maybe we'll settle for a lovely breakfast in your room today, and we'll plan to set up the canopy later this week. I'll just go refill your coffee for you, or you'll be dead on your feet." Mr. Tom bustled out of the room with Ulric in front of him, and I could feel his absolute delight through the bond. He'd missed taking care of me in the mornings, that was clear. My returning had given him a sense of purpose. It had restored his duty.

I shouldn't have stayed away for so long, even though the general feeling of impending doom was starting to hang heavy over me again.

My vacation was over. It was time to get to work.

✧ ✧ ✧

WITH A CUP of coffee in each hand, I made my way through the secret tunnels and into the very heart of the house, where Ivy House's crystals throbbed with magic. When Sebastian first came to this territory, he'd been tickled with the fear he felt around the shifters. That tune had clearly changed. I wondered if the novelty had worn off and now it was just that primal terror a large and powerful predator could bring out in people.

Sebastian had two camping stoves set up, each of them with a pot on top, currently bubbling away. He leaned over a book stand with a large volume splayed open on top of it. A portable table behind him held a plethora of ingredients for potion making.

"Except there won't be time to actually apply it," Sebastian was murmuring. "By the time the attack comes, it's too late for most things. Even if I *do* manage to ingest the potion, it'd take a bit to work. I'd be dead by then."

"Hey," I said.

He jumped and turned, eyes wide. Upon seeing me, he released a ragged sigh and sagged.

Dark circles shadowed his eyes, and his hair stood on end in places where he must've dragged his fingers through it. His pale blue eyes looked a little haunted and a lot exhausted. It made me feel much better about what I was preparing to do.

"Hi, Jessie." He noticed the extra mug in my hand and reached for it with a thankful smile.

"Have you slept at all?"

He gulped a few mouthfuls, then hissed. "Hot," he wheezed. He shook his head and looked back at the book. "Not since I nearly pissed myself yesterday when your boyfriend attacked me."

"But you didn't piss yourself, so I call it a win." I gave him a soft smile before walking by him and peeking into the open book. "Wow. Advanced."

"Yes. You aren't there yet. Maybe *I'm* not there yet. I can't seem to figure out a solution for surviving an attack by an alpha shifter."

"But you did survive."

"Yes. Because he chose not to kill me. My shield wouldn't have stopped him."

So he knew.

He looked at me for a beat, realizing *I* knew. He nodded.

"That was the strongest shield I had," he continued, standing at my side, looking over the book. "Granted, yes, I was already tired. But I'll be tired in battle. I need to come up with something that will protect me. I just can't think of anything that will work quickly enough, or for long enough. You never know when an attack might come. If it's at the end of the battle, like yesterday, any potion would've waned and not been useful."

"You didn't fire a kill shot at him. You fired more of a warning shot. If you *had* fired a kill shot, he might not have gotten through your defenses. Maybe instead of finding a potion, or whatever it is you're thinking, you need to work on your reaction times. You need to practice fighting in close combat, like I do."

"That notion scares me. It's not really the mage way."

"It is definitely not the Jane way, and yet…"

He nodded slowly. "The other thing is…" He scrubbed his free hand through his hair. "What if there's more than one shifter? What if I'm surrounded? A kill shot wouldn't get me out of it. Not against the number of shifters out in that field yesterday."

"Except you—*we*—won't be against shifters. We'll be on the side of the shifters."

He gave me a long, dry look. "Jessie, all due respect, but you're much too honest and kindhearted for the life you now lead. Austin—" His expression slipped into anxiety. "Can I call him Austin with just you, or would you prefer I call him alpha? I know better than to use anything but alpha in town, but—"

"Austin is fine. Wow. He really shook you up, huh?"

This time, he rubbed his hand down his face and gulped the rest of his coffee. "More than shook me, yeah. Your mate is terrifying. The amount of power in that shifter... I mean, other than you, I'm the most powerful mage in the world. He would've, like..."

He made claws with his hands and moved them through the air like a rabid animal.

"He would've scratched through my shield. Kill shot? Sure. I could've tried. If I'd kept my composure and landed it, I might have even slowed him down. But a kill shot is only deadly if you have more power than the other person's defenses." He dropped his hands limply to his sides. "Jessie, I don't think I do. I don't think I have more power than that polar bear. I didn't even know a shifter could possess so much power against actual magic."

He turned to the book and randomly traced a line down the page with his finger.

"Though I guess I should have," he mumbled, "since I can't take down a phoenix, and he managed to. I thought that was all physical ability, but no, his physical power manifests into the ability to combat spell work. Or at least resist it." He dropped his hand again. "I had no idea. I know for a fact that none of the other mages are aware of that possibility. How could they be from their positions hiding behind mercenaries? They attack from a distance. Momar has no idea what's coming for him. *No* idea. I've had to completely rework all my plans. I'm now way behind..." His voice trailed off, and he looked at nothing for a while.

"Okay, let's..." I stepped away from the book stand, giving myself a little space. "Let's just unpack this a little more slowly, okay? First, you need sleep. You look and sound like a mad scientist."

Sebastian blinked at me. "Probably, yeah. I get a little intense when I have a major problem that doesn't want to be solved."

"Right. Except it *does* want to be solved. I'll help you. Together, we can figure it out—"

"I love you." His smile was grateful. Then it slipped. "In a way your large boyfriend won't be mad at, I mean. You're so lovely and helpful—"

"But we need to back up," I interrupted, laughing. I'd never seen him like this. "You were saying I was too honest and kindhearted, and then you mentioned Austin. Let's finish that train of thought."

"Oh, right, yeah." He pointed at my mug. "Are you going to finish that? I could use it."

I frowned at him but handed it over. I needed the caffeine too, but I was half worried he'd start crying if I said no.

"Austin is the ultimate alpha. I think we can all

agree on that," Sebastian said. "And he wants to succeed where his brother failed and bring the shifters together to stand against the mages. Noble plan…" He raised a finger, then tilted his head. "You know what, I bet Edgar is so odd because he doesn't sleep much. He just randomly says creepy things and messes up names and stuff. That's not normal, even for a really old vampire." He paused to drink the coffee, downing it incredibly fast. "Is it normal? I confess, I don't know any really old vampires."

I clapped my hands. "Focus, buddy. Focus, and then bedtime."

Sebastian shrugged and set the second empty mug to the side. "I just need more caffeine. Sometimes, the best answers come when I've been up for days." He held up a finger again. "Anyway, Austin plans to unite the shifters, as you know, and many will go along with that because there is power in numbers. But some of the packs won't want to be ruled. And while that might be fine, what if the people in power are corrupt or violent or just plain bad for the people in their pack? What are the odds that Austin will let them stay in charge?"

"Zero. Because if he doesn't help the people trapped there, I will."

He pointed at me. "Exactly. Actually, that's an even better point. How are they going to react to you, a gargoyle, sticking your nose into shifter affairs?"

"I don't need to be one of their kind to help them."

"The people in danger aren't the ones in power. Anyone with something to lose will push back. And they might not do it by challenging you or Austin. What I'm trying to get at is that I don't just need to figure this out for myself, but for you. They might try to catch you in the shadows, like mages do. If it's just one or two of them, you'd win, no question. But at a certain point, numbers will win."

"I have wings. I can fly out."

Sebastian blinked rapidly. "Yes. This is true. Let's hope you can carry me. But what if you're inside or trapped somewhere or... I don't know. What if you can't? Or what if I'm the one who's surrounded? We need to prepare to protect ourselves against that sort of attack. We have shields for magical attacks, but we're less prepared for attacks that combine a physical charge with magical resistance."

I put up my hands. "We have a lot of time to think about this. We'll be confronting mages before we try to unite the shifters, I think. Kingsley's issue, remember?"

He ran his hand down his face. "True, yeah. That's true. Combating mages, I got. Combating mercenaries, I got. Lurking in shadows—I got all that. So at least we're good there. Still...this problem..."

"Will keep," I said firmly.

"Yes," he said softly, staring at nothing again. "Speaking of combating mages and mercenaries…"

He turned to me, and his gaze was direct, as though he was preparing to deliver some bad news.

My fears came spiraling out, nearly choking me. If it was bad news, I didn't think I was ready to hear what he might say. I wasn't ready for the incredible danger that would be Momar and maybe the Mages Guild. Or other mages. The unknown made me wary, but the volatility of the magical world freaked me out. Maybe it was all in my head, but maybe it was even worse than I imagined.

Before he could, though, his eyes squinted and glazed over a little. His head tilted. "You drugged me, didn't you?"

His question hadn't been accusatory. He was just information-gathering.

"Wow. You're good," I said, letting the previous matter drop. I breathed a sigh of relief I definitely shouldn't feel. "Mr. Tom said it would take about twenty minutes to kick in."

"Am I going to die?"

I spat out an unexpected laugh at his nonchalant tone. "No. You're going to sleep. Mr. Tom did it to me once, and then I woke up with the answer to a problem that had been plaguing me. I figured you needed a little help shutting off. I definitely thought you'd need help sleeping once I told you that we need to make an appearance at the bar tonight. We have to present a unified front and show that you're very much a part of this territory."

Sebastian sagged, then started shaking with silent laughter. "Ah, Jessie, you are a real treat. At once soft and hard, loving but ruthless. You might as well walk me to my room."

I stepped forward immediately and hooked an arm around his.

"Do you know," he said as we made our way through the narrow stone passageway and into the secret tunnels, "there are only two people in the *whole world* whom I'd trust enough to not react if they drugged me?"

"That right? I'm guessing one is Nessa."

"Yes. I trust her with my life. If she thought it best to end that life, I'd trust it was the right call."

"Dark."

"We live dark lives."

"The other person you trust, at a guess…is Mr. Tom?"

"No." He started laughing as we found a narrow set of stairs within the hidden passageway. "It is not Mr. Tom. It is *certainly* not Edgar, though his natural vampiric drug would act too quickly for me to do anything about it."

"It must be Mr. Tom, because he's the one who did up your coffee. I had him do it exactly like the one he prepared for me back when I needed to sleep. We were about to be attacked, and I had to work out the particulars of a spell you'd done."

"Oh yeah? You had to be forced to sleep to knock that out? Huh." He shrugged. "Well, then, I guess there are three people, but one of them is only to be trusted when you administer the agent."

"And why do I rank so highly?"

He sighed. "I don't know, honestly. But you do. You always have. Even before you took Ivy House's magic, I wanted to know you. And once I did get that privilege, I didn't want to stop knowing you. Mark my words, you'll be a powerhouse in the magical world. But I'll always feel blessed to have known you when you were just a Jane doing nothing more than chasing her stars."

My eyes stung. I could tell he really felt this way. It wasn't the sleep deprivation or the sleeping agent talking. I knew he loved the house, too, and my weird crew. He'd actually bought a place just outside of town—a large house with extensive grounds—but he chose to stay here most of the time. He wouldn't take a spot in the circle, but he was every bit a part of our team.

"One thing, though," he said as I led him into his room. His speech started to slur. "You shouldn't be surprised by how quickly I knew you'd drugged me. We're going to need to do some poison training. You'll need to know when something is amiss immediately so you have more time to combat it. The amount of times I've been poisoned…would probably shock you."

"I think your entire life outside of this town is going to shock me."

"Probably. I hope you don't think less of me."

"Just as long as you don't think less of me when the gargoyle takes over and I'm as dark as Tamara Ivy."

He sat on the edge of the bed. "Trust me, Jessie. Tamara Ivy had nothing on me. She wasn't inherently bad. Or dark. She was just young and inexperienced in love and fell for the wrong man—a small, insecure man who couldn't handle her strength and power. She had a lot of power, but she died before she could truly discover herself and her place in the world. When she died, she wasn't someone to fear. She was, instead, someone to use. Don't let yourself be used, Jessie Ironheart, and you won't falter."

# CHAPTER 8

A FTER A FIVE-HOUR nap from which Mr. Tom eventually roused him with a non-drugged cup of coffee, Sebastian waited just inside the front door of Ivy House. Mr. Tom was still upstairs, fussing with Jessie's outfit. The rest of the gang who were headed to the bar waited somewhere out of sight for the star of the show.

*The star of the show.* For once, it wasn't Sebastian. He wasn't the one assembling an outfit and donning a stage persona. He wouldn't be the one leading the crew or sitting in the limelight. The feeling was almost…surreal.

Most mages craved attention, but Sebastian loved his position in the wings. It was easier. He hated donning costumes and pretending to be someone he wasn't. Most importantly, this just felt right. It felt like he'd finally found the role he'd been meant for all along: backup.

Soon, he'd have to earn his keep. The world of mages was restless. It wouldn't be long before they came pounding on Jessie's proverbial door. The question Sebastian had, though, was whether the shifters would be targeted, or whether it would only be Jessie under the knife. His sources didn't have that answer for him, just that Jessie was on the radar and would be in grave danger soon. The kind of danger from which a mage didn't return.

"You good, bud?" asked Hollace as he walked down the steps, his long, muscular arms swinging gracefully and his powerful thighs straining his snug trousers. The guy was so effortless in his confidence.

"Yeah. Fine." Sebastian shrugged, and Hollace quirked a dark eyebrow. "Nervous," he admitted, an emotion that would cover his wariness of shifters—something they would understand, coming from him—and also his growing concern for Jessie, something he hoped they didn't notice just yet. He didn't want questions about that, not until he had more information from his informants.

"Good nervous or bad nervous?"

Sebastian hesitated. "I didn't know there were varieties of nervousness."

Hollace paused as he reached the bottom of the stairs. The front door opened, and a baby-faced girl doll tottered in with mud on its cute little black boots and glistening red on its chubby fingers.

"Ma-ma," it said in a high-pitched doll voice. It was a voice that would usually need to be released by a pull cord. Not in Ivy House, though. Magic was the pull cord.

Sebastian grinned as it tottered by, its little feet leaving small dirt clods as they thumped against the floor.

Hollace kicked out as it passed, catching it with his shoe and sending it skittering off into the next room.

Sebastian frowned. "That wasn't very nice."

"But it *was* very fun."

"I don't get why Jessie is so afraid of those things," Sebastian said. "They can hold knives and form an army, sure, and they *do* love climbing trees and dropping down onto their unsuspecting prey, but we all have party tricks."

It was Hollace's turn to frown. "Have you gone screwy, bud?"

"I really think so. Or maybe I'm just fitting in. At this point, it's hard to tell."

"Fitting in *is* going screwy."

"Well, then…here we are, I guess."

"You'll be grand." Niamh crumpled a can in her fist as she exited the sitting room to the right. She unceremoniously tossed it over her shoulder and into the room behind her. Having disposed of it, she reached into the pocket of her black trousers, pulled out a crumpled handful of yarn, and tossed that back as well. When she caught Sebastian watching, she said, "That muppet Earl gets his bollocks in a twist when he sees litter. Watch and see. He goes *ab*-solutely mental."

The yarn wad hit the floor and ballooned out, revealing itself as one of Edgar's doilies. It was like all the others, lopsided and with gaping holes in places.

Edgar's doily habit seemed to be escalating. He produced so many that he pawned them off on everyone. Sebastian had had to give a bunch to Cyra on the sly just to keep his room fire-hazard free.

"Those doilies have to be a joke he's playing on us," Sebastian mused aloud as Ulric jogged down the steps in a pink dress shirt and bright blue slacks.

"As does that getup," Niamh said to Ulric. Jasper followed him in a much more subdued outfit of navy and white.

"The ladies love when I'm overly eccentric." Ulric flashed her a smile.

"No, the ladies love your due diligence in facilitating their pleasure," Hollace said eloquently as he moved to the side, making room for them. "They suffer through your eccentricity." He turned his attention to Sebastian. "If the doilies are a joke, I don't see the punch line."

Sebastian lifted his hands while raising his eyebrows. "Don't you? He's spent half a century learning to make those doilies. *Those*. I mean…is he allergic to patterns? Even if patterns were cheating—something he doesn't seem to worry about in the flower world— surely he could've come up with one that was at least round. Almost round, even—we'd settle for *almost* round. I mean, *fifty years*.

"Instead, they seem to get worse, don't they? We keep saying, 'Good work, Edgar, almost there! Maybe next time!' But he's probably having a big chuckle as we root him on. 'Ha-ha-ha! They keep decorating with those horrible doilies. What idiots!' Seriously, you guys, it *has* to be a joke. And honestly, they just aren't right, these doilies. People are concerned about clowns, Jessie is worried about the killer dolls, but I honestly think a vampire who makes lopsided doilies is the real trouble spot in this situation. They look like something a fun-house mirror threw up."

The room fell silent, all eyes on him. Niamh leaned against the frame of the door, her expression unreadable.

"Wow," Ulric said, pausing at the foot of the stairs with his hand on the banister.

"I apologize," Sebastian said quickly. "I know that sounds harsh. I'm just wound up, I guess."

"You're definitely starting to fit in." Hollace shook his head sadly.

Niamh held up a finger. "Are ye telling me that ye've been *encouragin'* him to do better at the doilies?"

Sebastian stilled, which was saying something, because he'd already been pretty still. "Um…I thought we were supposed to be supportive of our team members?"

Ulric burst out laughing. Hollace kept shaking his head.

"First," Niamh said, "I don't know how ye got it inta'yer head that we hold hands and pat backs while singing 'Kumbaya' and braiding each other's arse hair—"

"Well, I didn't necessarily mean—"

"—but this ain't that kinda outfit. Second, ye don't want'ta be encouragin' Edgar to do anything but keep asking to be retired. Maybe then Jessie will pity the poor wee lad and finally give in. He is Froot Loops, that vampire, and he gets worse all the time. Just pretend he isn't creeping around and hope he's there when ye need him. That's all ye can do with Edgar."

"But you take his doilies," Ulric said, unfreezing from his location and moving so Jasper could finish his descent.

"Yeah. It keeps Earl outta me house. He can't stand me, and he can't stand those doilies. If he does have to come in, the sight of them helps put him right back out."

Ulric's lips turned down, and he nodded thoughtfully. "Smart. Your sandwiches are the trifecta, huh?"

Niamh's brows pinched together. "What about me sandwiches?"

Ulric's expression cleared. "I meant... I just meant..."

"They are dry," Mr. Tom said, coming down the stairs. "Beyond dry. They are like eating sand. No vegetables of any kind, no mayonnaise—butter isn't enough to support one piece of ham and a bit of cheese. You don't even cut them!"

"Do ye want me to hand-feed ye as well, ya miserable goat?" Niamh replied.

"And then there is that wretched tea to wash it down with," he continued. "Do you ration your sugar? There is never enough. I'm surprised you're not using a fork in the sugar bowl to keep people from using too much."

"Well, if ye wouldn't take—"

"Okay, okay, let's all just calm down a bit," Jessie said as she made an appearance at the top of the stairs. "Her sandwiches aren't that dry. And I had plenty of sugar the last time I was there."

"See—what do ye mean, *not that dry*?" Niamh asked, suddenly suspicious. "Do none of yis know what a good sandwich should taste like?"

"Really?" Mr. Tom thrust his hand toward the sitting room doorway. "Were you born in a barn, woman? We don't just throw things on the ground like the world is our own personal trash can."

"I'm helping you," she said. "I figured you needed something to keep you busy while she spends hour upon hour shagging Austin Steele."

"Oh my God," Jessie said on a release of breath. "Would you guys just let it go? It wasn't that big of a deal."

"Wasn't that big of a deal?" Ulric's eyes widened. Everyone's focus zoomed to Jessie. "How often does he pull all-nighters? Anyone been keeping track?"

"What am I missing?" Sebastian asked.

Niamh filled him in, much to Jessie's obvious dismay. He couldn't help laughing at her crimson cheeks and look of utter bewilderment.

"Seriously, let it go. We're newly mated," Jessie said. "These things are normal for shifters."

"They most definitely are *not* normal for shifters, no," Niamh said with a sparkle in her eyes. "Austin Steele has been making light of things. Ye ask any shifter at the bar, and he or she'll be just as impressed as Ulric and the lads are."

"I am not going to ask—"

"Don't worry." Niamh put up her hand while momentarily bowing her head. "I'll ask fer ya."

"You're not impressed?" Ulric asked Niamh as they all waited for Mr. Tom to clean up the mess she'd left on the floor.

"Not a hope." Niamh walked to the door. "I do not have the patience for that sort of thing. Maybe when I was young and bored and wanted to experiment, but now, I'd rather watch a little telly and call it a night. A couple pumps, a little holler, and that'll do me."

Ulric looked at Sebastian as he pointed to Niamh. "Now, *that* has to be a joke. That can't be legit."

"Okay, let's go. Miss, do you have everything?" Mr. Tom stopped beside Jessie. "You're without your clutch. Where is your phone?" He held up his hand. "You go on. I'll run and get it."

Niamh jerked her head for Sebastian as she opened the door. "C'mon, lad. Weird before beard. Out ya git."

"Maybe those doilies fit into this fun house," Sebastian murmured as he followed directions. But he still had a smile on his face. He wouldn't ask what beard she was referring to. He was afraid she'd answer.

He was musing on the possibilities when he tripped over something and fell down the steps.

The spell he threw out to catch himself came too late, and he bashed his cheek on rough cement. His momentum kept him going, and he rolled over his shoulder, finally flopping down and sprawling half in the grass and half on the walkway.

"Oh, my—are you okay?" Jessie was down after him in a flash. He could feel her healing magic flow into him before she could physically scan the damage.

Niamh guffawed.

"Fantastic start to the evening," Sebastian murmured.

"Oops, that's my fault."

Out of the corner of his eye, Sebastian saw Ulric scoop up a medium-sized box sitting in front of the door and turn for the house.

"I should've grabbed this earlier and forgot. They're starting to pile up. Don't worry, though, when my mom gets here, she'll go through all of them with you. It'll probably take a few days. At least."

"What is it?" Jessie called over her shoulder, still bent to Sebastian.

"A connection request from one of the cairns." Ulric jogged back out as Sebastian was sitting up. "I didn't see who it was from. The box is on the smaller side, but that doesn't mean much. You can pack a lot of jewels in a box that size."

"How many of these things have come?" Jessie asked as she helped Sebastian up.

"A…bunch," Ulric said vaguely.

Jessie studied him for a moment, then looked away.

"We'll figure it out tomorrow."

The edge in her tone drew Sebastian's attention. He looked at her closely.

Tension tightened her shoulders and etched the soft lines in her face. A strange swirl of emotion nearly colored the air around her, something he really shouldn't feel, since he wasn't a shifter, but did all the same. Wariness, anxiety, uncertainty, fear...all mixed in a strange sort of dark, murky soup of violence. Was this the gargoyle peeking through? Why?

But in a flash of understanding, he knew why. For the first time, it felt like he could really *see* her. His stomach flipped.

She wasn't as ignorant as she was trying to pretend. Her holiday with Austin hadn't been mating bliss, not entirely. She was starting to feel the pressure of the outside world bearing down on her safe haven. Meeting cairns was synonymous with protection, her greater defense against mages and what was to come. A lot rode on her ability to connect with them, just as a lot was riding on her ability to show well for Austin's pack. Yesterday had been a baby step, but soon, she'd need to sprint, and she knew it. Or maybe her gargoyle did, and she was cluing in.

All of this was suddenly clear as day. If he'd paid attention, he would've seen it before now.

His heart went out to her. He'd half forced her into all of this. He hadn't had a choice, but still, he felt responsible. And before the end, he'd be responsible for a whole lot more. For things he didn't want to do. For things she might not forgive.

"There's no hurry." Ulric shrugged. "You might as well wait for my mom."

"When is she coming?" Jessie started walking, tugging Sebastian along with her. She probably considered him a flight risk. Niamh was still laughing.

"Tomorrow or the next day. She's not a great traveler, but given her excitement level, she'll likely be here within a few days of her original plan."

"She's a gargoyle's wife, and she's afraid to fly?" Jasper asked as everyone headed down the street. "Was she a Jane and didn't get used to the life, or...?"

A dark shape with a huge wingspan drifted overhead—Nathanial taking the bird's-eye view. He'd cover them from the air.

Something rustled away in the grass, drawing Sebastian's notice. The being hid just beyond the veil of darkness, a random, small shape he couldn't quite make out. A doll, maybe. Or one of those gnomes Edgar was so worried about.

He sent out a scan even though the noise was on Ivy House property. You could never be too careful. It was possible to circumvent the magical house's detection abilities. He should know—he'd managed it himself.

"No, no. Nothing like that," Ulric replied. "She's a gargoyle's daughter. She knows the life. She just meets random people and gets to talking. She's missed more flights and trains than you would believe. Then she makes friends with whoever she was talking to and goes for dinner, or boards their train with them, or…with her, you really never know. She's the best networker in the world, but she's not very reliable with schedules. This is the biggest news in the gargoyle world, though, so she'll very likely make a special effort to get here as quickly as possible."

"So when *was* she due to arrive?" Sebastian asked as his scan came back void. Nothing human—or from the animal kingdom—waited out there. Definitely a doll or gnome, silently watching them all pass.

"Two days ago. So it's still early."

Sebastian worked magic as soon as they stepped off Ivy House land. He sent out spells in waves, throwing them way off to the sides and then closer, setting up a framework to catch anyone who might attempt to sneak in.

The first wave would hopefully be derelict mages or musclemen. They'd come solo or in pairs to make an easy grab or get information, nothing more. As long as

Jessie had powerful people around her at all times, she'd be okay. For a while, anyway.

That was, unless Momar realized the sort of power he was dealing with. Then the attack would come later but be larger. Much larger, more than this territory could likely handle. He'd come in hot and take her away, killing everyone in his path.

Sebastian had thought it would be the former. He'd heard through his network that Momar wasn't buying the stories surrounding Jessie. Sebastian had then altered his plans accordingly. But if that were the case, surely someone would've come to grab her by now.

The inactivity was making him nervous.

He brushed his fingers against his chest as he walked, his heart suddenly hammering. If he'd read the situation wrong, the whole territory would be in jeopardy.

# CHAPTER 9

WHEN WE REACHED the bar, I saw a familiar, shaggy shape lingering next to the open door. Light flared from the end of a cigarette.

I paused and narrowed my eyes at my nemesis, the man I called Sasquatch. He was the type of guy who gave all shifters a bad name.

His overgrown hair looked like it hadn't been washed in a week and likely had fleas. His long, scraggly beard reached nearly to his chest and was in no better shape, and his hairy arms sported patches of dirt. He was brusque and rude and always seemed to be in my way.

His brows pinched together when he caught me looking at him. Instead of making some offhanded quip, he grunted before turning away from me. He didn't want to tangle this evening, it seemed. For now, anyway. Maybe he wasn't feeling surly enough, the butthead.

"You better be outta her stool, ye dirty bastard,"

Niamh said as I passed him and crossed the threshold into the bar.

"I don't have to move," he replied.

"You don't have'ta, no. But yer goin'ta, or I'll make bags of yer night. Think it through."

Laughter and talking filled the bar, along with the sound of jostling bodies, the smash of pool balls on the lower level of the bar, and the clinking of ice cubes in dozens of drinks.

But all the noise and bustle seemed to fade and dim the moment I saw him. He stood behind the bar with his hands braced against the edge. He stared straight at me with his cobalt eyes, ignoring anyone trying to get a drink or engage him in any way. I knew this was an alpha's way of telling everyone that I was the most important thing in that bar. To him, at least.

I smiled like a dope and felt like I was walking on air. People in front of me cleared away to the sides. Those in the seats at the bar scattered, leaving me room to greet my mate.

"Hey," I said softly.

"Hey, baby," he replied, his gaze drinking me in. "You look beautiful."

I barely spared a glance at the casual black dress Mr. Tom had picked out for me. I hadn't bothered with makeup, and my hair wasn't anything special. I hadn't tried at all, basically, but I knew Austin would find me beautiful even at my absolute worst.

"I love you," I told him, reaching for his hand.

"I love you too—"

"Are you going to stand around all day, lady?" Sasquatch said somewhere behind me, much too loudly. "People want to get through."

"Lady?" Niamh replied indignantly. "Well, I beg yer pardon, ye dopey-faced lummox."

Uncontrollable anger surged through me at the interruption. I turned slowly, power pumping. My gargoyle moved and shifted within me. Darkness rolled.

Sebastian and Niamh stood a few paces back, waiting patiently. Sasquatch was behind them, making a show of trying to get around.

Something violent twisted my guts.

"If you annoy me right now," I told Sasquatch in what I thought was an even voice, "I'll yank off your head and toss it like a volleyball."

Sasquatch's eyes rounded. His mouth clamped shut, and he spun around with a stiff back. Without another word, he walked right out of the bar.

Thank God, because I wasn't sure I'd be able to stop myself from throwing him.

Niamh braced her hands on her hips, turning to watch him go. "Well, there he goes. Damn, I would've liked to see that."

In a moment, it was as if the sound in the bar turned back on. People started to move, and laughter and the crack of pool balls rose in a fresh chorus. I belatedly realized that all had been still and quiet a moment ago.

I turned back to Austin's glittering eyes.

I knew that look. It matched the delighted, smug pride flowering within the bonds.

"I just made everyone watch me greet you again, didn't I?" I said with a heating face.

A grin worked at his lips. He nodded slowly.

I leaned against the bar, suddenly exhausted. "Why didn't you stop me? You know I hate when I do that. My stupid gargoyle is making me into a diva."

He ran his thumb across the back of my hand. "You are my mate and the co-ruler of this territory. You *should* be a diva. Besides, I like when you flex your power. I wouldn't dream of stopping you."

I shook my head at him. "Incorrigible."

"Yes. What can I get you?"

✧   ✧   ✧

AN HOUR LATER, Austin was finally able to get away. He walked through the bar with a stoic face and powerful yet graceful movements.

The crowd peeled away, out of his path, giving him plenty of space. Their gazes lowered. Their bodies stooped just enough to ensure he couldn't take their postures as a challenge in any way. They were showing their deference to their alpha and my mate.

My gargoyle practically glowed with the display, humming inside of me as Austin stepped in behind our group. I ran my hand down my face, trying to breathe through the sudden desperation to get to him.

"Hey, babe," he said.

Sebastian hopped up like he'd been goosed and cleared out of the way. "Here. Here you go, alpha."

"We were *just* talkin' about all of that," Niamh said, exasperated, having given Sebastian a rundown on how to act near shifters. He was apparently starting to embarrass her.

"There is confidence, and then there is dealing with *him*," Sebastian murmured. "When dealing with him, asserting myself will just get me killed."

"Or at least in a world of pain." Austin gave him a nod of thanks before pulling the seat out a little, widening the triangle into a circle. I doubted Sebastian could tell that he was joking. "I'll stand. Have a seat."

Austin slid his arm around the back of my chair. I leaned into his hard body, soaking in his warmth. Lost as I was to his proximity, I didn't notice Broken Sue walking up with a glass half filled with brown liquid.

"Alpha Steele." He looked at Austin. Then me. "Alpha Ironheart."

I frowned at him. "*Alpha* Ironheart? Since when do you call me alpha?"

It was Austin that answered. "Since you annihilated your challenger yesterday, spanked a mage, and owned your place as the co-ruler of this pack. No offense, Sebastian."

"It's fine," Sebastian murmured.

Broken Sue's eyes glimmered, and it was as close as he ever came to a smile. "All due respect, alpha, but I don't know about spanked. Sebastian's power shocked the whole territory." He directed his next comments to Sebastian. "I think it was your collectedness under fire that people are talking about most, though. You showed your experience. Well done. You've inspired confidence here."

"Hear, hear," Logan, a shifter who often sat near us, said quietly from the stool beside me.

Sebastian ducked his head. "Thanks. I'm in no hurry to repeat it, but thanks."

"I get that." Broken Sue shifted his attention to Niamh.

"I don't need yer praise," she told him.

"Good. I couldn't bring myself to give it."

Austin's phone trilled. He reached behind and pulled it out of his back pocket, looking at the screen. A hard expression clicked onto his face as he answered the call.

"Yeah?" His eyes stared straight ahead. I felt his blast of emotion through our bonds. "Where?" He paused for another moment. "Get him to storage. We'll be there shortly."

He ended the call and slid his phone back into his pocket. His gaze zipped down to me. "We found a mage at the edge of the territory. He booked a room, and when asked if he was going to present himself to the territory alphas, he sneered. The hotel reception clerk called our people. When the mage went to get a bite to eat, my people joined him. He tried to attack them, but they managed to knock him out and haul him away. He's being kept now. We need to question him."

Sebastian let out a large sigh of what seemed like relief. His expression was lost behind his placid magical mask, though. I couldn't get a read on his emotions.

Regardless, it didn't really matter. An enemy was in our territory. That, or a friend who didn't know how things worked here. This situation needed to be approached with caution.

So why was my gargoyle gearing up to approach it with violence...

✧   ✧   ✧

THE PULSE OF power from Jess stole Austin's breath. Sound and movement within the bar ground to a halt. Another pulse of power raised his small hairs.

Brochan, standing beside him, shivered. His drink sloshed over the side of the glass.

Ulric and Jasper pushed through the throng of people, all of whom had suddenly gone still, and Mr. Tom stepped into the bar a moment later, followed by Hollace. Jess was calling her people and had encouraged the bystanders to freeze so her foot soldiers could get to her more easily.

The gargoyle had been roused. She was preparing for battle.

The darkness within her swirled, calling to him, whispering of the power he could wield if he accepted the protector's magic. With it, he could easily sweep all the nation's shifters under his umbrella of dominance. He'd own them all.

He shuddered and ran a hand down Jess's back, wrestling away those enticing, manipulative whispers. He shifted his attention to Sebastian.

Then he couldn't contain his shock.

A moment ago, the mage had been slouching beside Brochan, wanting to be anywhere else but here. Now his eyes gleamed, even through the magical mask, his posture straight and his shoulders squared. He regarded Austin with a direct gaze that wasn't a challenge.

"All due respect, alpha," Sebastian said, "this is a job for me. I know all the players, which will help me figure out which questions to ask. I'm sure I don't have to tell you that I can handle magic better than any of your people." He dragged his phone out of his pocket and looked at the screen. "I'll need to know a few things from you, though. A photo of the mage. Where they likely entered your territory—alone or with friends?— where they're staying, things like that. I'll need all that before I go into the interrogation area. Or the…storage place? Wherever the mage is."

Sebastian looked up from his phone and paused for a response.

The silence of the bar rang out around them. Austin could feel the nervous wariness suddenly crowding the room. Mages had ruined the lives of many in this territory. They'd torn apart or crushed packs. And now they were showing up here, in their new territory.

"This is what you're here for," Austin replied. "Brochan, get him what he needs. Gather some people together. We'll be Jess and Sebastian's backup. We'll leave as soon as we're ready."

Sebastian nodded, just about ready to tap the screen

of his phone for a call when he paused and looked at Jess. "I know you're grappling with that gargoyle, but if there was ever a time to let her out to play, this is that time. You remember what mages are like from Graves's meetup?" He paused for Jess to lick her lips and then nod. "Well, those mages were upstanding citizens in comparison to what we're very likely about to deal with. Things are about to get gruesome. Prepare for it now so that you don't shy away from it later. This is when it gets real. Okay?"

Jess smiled thinly. "Haven't you met the basajaun? He literally spikes heads like footballs. It'll be fine."

Sebastian's smile was lopsided. "That's true. Okay. I need to get Nessa. She's the captain in these matters. I'll meet up with you at Ivy House so we can all go together." He tapped his phone and put it to his ear, already turning for the door. "Nessa? Yeah, the pack found one... *One*, yeah." He paused for a moment, nodding. "I know, me too. It looks like the games have begun. Remember what we talked about. I'm going to get you a picture in a minute. I need..."

His voice drifted away as he left the quiet bar.

"An' here I was trying to give him a pep talk and support him and all that bollocks." Niamh huffed. "All he really needed was an enemy to focus on. He came to life like one of those Ivy House dolls. Let's hope he's as mean as them. Well, c'mon, Jessie, let's get ready. We need to change and grab the others. I can't wait to see how he handles that mage. This'll be good craic."

Austin wasn't so sure.

He waited until the others had left before leading Brochan and Kace from the bar. "If I'm reading this situation right, this is only the beginning," he said in a low tone so no bystanders would hear. They paused by Austin's Jeep.

"He seemed relieved to just have the one," Kace said.

Austin nodded, looking out at the night. "That means it could've been worse right out of the gate. It also means he's been keeping information from us. Keep your eye on him. I don't want any more surprises."

"Yes, alpha," Kace replied.

"We might be starting more slowly in this thing than what we could be," Austin said, hand on a roll bar, "but only a fool would think it won't speed up. Learn all you can from this encounter. I have a feeling it'll only get harder from here on out."

# CHAPTER 10

I CHECKED MY watch. The half-hour was nearly up.

My power throbbed, vibrating through the whole house. A flurry of nerves turned my stomach. Time to do my duty and deal with the intruder.

After a deep breath, I left my room and started descending the stairs. I stopped dead near the bottom.

"No." I shook my head. "Just no."

Mr. Tom paused in exiting the house. He wore something like a purple muumuu, but lopsided and with even less shape. It was like he'd gone to the fabric store, picked purple at random, and had Edgar sew it up for him. It puffed out at the middle before flowing around his ankles. He held a suitcase that I knew contained some of his various "disguises."

"First, I realize muumuus are great for fast shifting," I said, "but do you notice how I reserve them for training? I don't wear them in a professional setting where I likely won't be shifting. So…your outfit doesn't really fit in right now, right? It looks…" I didn't know how to politely say it looked ridiculous on him. "And the disguises? No. You can blend into stone. You don't need disguises."

"Miss, you need a lookout. I will provide that for you. In order to do that—"

"No." I leveled a finger at him. "Seriously, no. No disguises. We'll be a laughingstock. Go change."

"No one would dare laugh at the Ivy House heir," he said indignantly.

"Indirectly, yes, they would." I finished descending and brushed by him.

Then I stopped on the porch.

My team waited on the sidewalk in a line whose order echoed their positions within the Ivy House circle. All of them wore the same long purple muumuu things. Edgar's, at the end of the line, was much too big. The extra material pooled at his feet like he was a child playing dress-up. Austin waited at the other end, his hands clasped in front of him. I could feel his utter bewilderment. He hadn't adorned the same piece of loose cloth, thank God, and was instead still wearing jeans and a T-shirt.

"What…?" I was suddenly at a loss for words.

"Mr. Tom hid our sweats and told us this was the new uniform," Ulric said with the utmost seriousness, but I could feel his delight through the bond. "I requested pink and was denied."

Two headlights appeared at the other end of the street, then more, the shifters showing up to provide transportation.

"This cannot be happening," I said as I spied Niamh holding a beer. A cooler waited behind her. "Of all the times you don't push back, you chose this one?" I asked her.

She shrugged. "It actually isn't so bad, like. It airs everything out. Much less hassle. And if everyone looks like a muppet, it's probably easier to blend in."

The first car, a five-year-old Honda Accord, pulled around. It was Sebastian and Nessa's "blending in" vehicle.

The passenger door opened, and Sebastian got out. Even from this distance, I could see his gaze roaming those gathered in front of Ivy House. A crooked smile lit his face as he walked around Edgar and stopped.

"They'll change real quick," I told him. "I wasn't aware they'd… I wasn't aware this was happening."

Cyra put out her arms and twirled a little, hitting both Austin and Hollace with her hands. Austin stepped away, looking down at her. Hollace settled for slapping her hand out of the air.

"I don't mind it," she said, smiling at me. "It's very comfy. I didn't wear underwear. Did anyone else wear underwear?"

"You never wear underwear," Hollace told her.

"True. I don't much understand the point," she replied. "And now I definitely don't. This is so nice and airy."

"Let them keep this on," Sebastian said as large SUVs and vans stopped behind the Accord. His crooked smile was still firmly in place. "If I've learned one thing as a mage, it's that eccentricities make people nervous. The inexplicable, the joke no one is acknowledging, a team wearing purple muumuus while one of them carries luggage—it's good. This is good."

"It's not eccentric, it is practical," Mr. Tom told him, walking around me. He hadn't put his suitcase away.

When he was halfway to the sidewalk, something zoomed out from the shadows at the front of the house. Tiny but incredibly fast, it darted across the grass and straight for Mr. Tom.

"Watch out, a rat!" I yelled, waiting for Ivy House to kill it on the spot. We didn't usually have rodents here. They were afraid to stay.

But it wasn't a rat.

A little garden gnome with a pointed red hat, an angry scowl, and a pair of garden shears cackled as it charged at Mr. Tom. It lowered the shears into "cut mode" as it closed the distance.

"What on God's green earth…" I gasped.

Mr. Tom tsked, facing the thing. Then he apparently thought better of waiting for those shears to close over his ankles, because he danced backward and then ran for the sidewalk with high knees.

The horrible little creature raced after him, faster and gaining. It clipped the shears shut as Mr. Tom vaulted onto the sidewalk, nicking him.

"Ah!" Mr. Tom bowled over Jasper.

They fell off the sidewalk in a tangle of limbs before rolling onto the street. The suitcase went flying, tumbling end over end. It burst open, and various horrible disguises spewed over the concrete. The last to settle was a pair of Elvis glasses with fake sideburns glued on.

The gnome stopped at the edge of the sidewalk. It dropped the shears to one side before leaning forward and cackling again.

"Honestly, Ivy House." Mr. Tom untangled himself from Jasper, flailed a little to get up, and then showed everyone way too much real estate.

"And *that* is why you should wear underwear," Hollace told Cyra, turning away quickly.

"It's a compelling argument," she replied thoughtfully.

"Will you do nothing to control those horrible

things until at least *after* we take care of business?" Mr. Tom said, trying to smooth his hair, which was standing up all over his head in messy wisps.

*"They all look like that, and he's worried about a homicidal gnome?"* Ivy House asked.

*"We're all worried about homicidal gnomes!"* I thought-hollered at her.

As if hearing me, the gnome turned. It stood in the middle of the sidewalk now, staring directly at me. It slowly brought up its little shears, and an evil smile drifted across its face.

"It's okay, Miss Jessie, I'll get it!" Edgar lurched forward with his hands out, preparing to run to my aid. Except he hadn't lifted up his muumuu.

He stepped on the hemline, got tangled up in fabric, and flattened across the sidewalk with an *oomph.*

"Ye can change into a swarm of insects," Niamh said, watching him. "Why didn't ye just do that rather than fall on yer face?"

Edgar struggled with the fabric, trying to get up. The gnome cackled with glee, its little shears opening and closing in anticipation of a battle.

I frowned at it, then decided to fight fire with fire.

Little legs ran through the halls of Ivy House. They thundered down the stairs, then reached the opened front door and poured out. Little knives were held high in small hands. Chubby little legs tottered down the steps to the ground. And then a dozen or more dolls were charging the gnome.

The gnome's smile drooped on its bearded face, and it screamed, a high-pitched, nails-on-chalkboard sound, as it darted across the grass. The dolls gave chase.

I didn't saunter in glory. No, I *ran*.

As fast as I could, I sprinted down the walkway until I made it to the sidewalk, safely off Ivy House's soil. I doubted she'd let one of those things kill me, but it was clear she had no objection to a little chase and a nip or two. She'd always felt the same way about the dolls.

"Edgar," I said, breathing hard. "You have some serious explaining to do."

"Yes, Miss Jessie." He stepped too high on the muumuu as he straightened from his fall and ripped it. A tear turned into a hole, exposing a bit too much down his front. Everyone groaned in misery at having witnessed it. "I have egg on my face for this one," he continued.

"Egg on your face and a hole in your crotch," Hollace replied. "I'd say you're betting aces."

Sebastian's glamor mask wobbled as he struggled not to laugh. And then it melted away, showing his real face. He bent over, hands on knees, and guffawed.

"You're dead to me," I told him.

"I'm sorry." He put his hand over half his face, trying to block it from sight. The shifters were thankfully still back near the cars and likely couldn't see him. "Sorry! You always seem to take something I say, like to roll with your crew's eccentricity, and amplify it."

"Shall we?" Austin asked, his bewilderment at my crew having turned into wariness. He must've been none too pleased with the gnome issue.

"You can go with us, Jessie Ironheart, if that's okay?" Sebastian said, wiping his face. "And the alpha. We can talk on the way."

"Put your glamor back on," Niamh told him. "You're scaring the gnomes with that face."

He furrowed his brow at her, but his smile didn't dwindle.

✧   ✧   ✧

TEN MINUTES LATER, after Mr. Tom had repacked all his ridiculous disguises and wrestled me for the right to get them into one of the SUVs, and Edgar got a new muumuu, and everyone was loaded, we *finally* set off to the interrogation. Nessa was behind the wheel, Sebastian next to her, and Austin and I were in the back seat.

"Problem one, the butterflies in my stomach are turning ravenous, and I'm suddenly not sure I can do this," I said, directing my gaze out the window. Austin held my hand, rubbing his thumb back and forth across my skin. "Problem two, my crew isn't eccentric. The whole setup is plain madness."

"You're going to get a lot of challenges from visiting shifters," he said. "They'll see this and think you're as weak as your outfit looks."

"They will challenge," Nessa said, still cheerful regardless of what she must know waited for us, "and then they'll get flown around by their ankles as they drip blood on everyone below."

I could see Sebastian nodding. "Only an absolute moron would challenge her. I definitely didn't want to. Now, to business. The alpha was kind enough to send me a picture. This clown is a low-level collector for Momar's enterprise. On one hand, his sending such an idiot here is an absolute insult."

"A slap in the face," Nessa supplied.

"I went to all that trouble at the meetup, showed you off, freaked out the visiting mages—"

"The ones Jessie's crew didn't kill," Nessa said.

"—and he sends a peon to grab you." Sebastian rested his elbow on the window ledge and looked out. It was hard not to think of him as Elliot right now. He was in his element. He might not love this role, but he was very good at it. "It's perplexing. But you know what? It's also great news. For a moment there, I'd been thinking the worst, but…no, this is good because now you have a chance to send a message."

"Like a very strongly worded letter, only in blood," Nessa added.

"Right. Bottom line, Jessie, is that Momar clearly doesn't believe the stories about you. In the grand scheme of things, that'll work in our favor."

"Sorry, what's a collector?" I asked. "It sounds like it isn't for money."

"Not money, no," Nessa said. "People. Collectors are musclemen. They collect the *people* who owe the money. Or, in this case, the people Momar wants to question."

"And the Guild doesn't care about this since I'm not in the actual Guild? He can kidnap me and question me and do whatever he wants without them getting involved?"

Nessa toggled her hand. "See, it's like this. Ordinarily, a new mage, especially a powerful mage, would draw interest from the community. What form that interest takes would depend on the power scale. Someone with a lot of power, like you, would be checked out. Like when that mage Kinsella came here. The new mage—you—would also start trying to get invited to parties, dinners, that kind of thing. You'd try to get your foot in the door, basically. Maybe you'd even offer to work for someone for a while to prove your worth.

"Somewhere in that timeline, the Guild would approach you. Now, that could also go a variety of ways. They might be standoffish or friendly, depending on your perceived worth in the community at that point. That worth is obviously all about power and money. Whatever their disposition, their goal would be to make you pay a membership fee to be in the Guild, pay more to be protected, and grease their palms to get the gilded treatment."

"What's the gilded treatment?" I asked.

"It's an unofficial tier in the Guild," Sebastian said. "I call it the gilded tier. It's essentially paying them to turn a blind eye to your activities. That service is only offered to a select few, those with the most power and prestige. Those who can pay a hefty sum to buy the Guild's silence or help cover things up, in some cases."

"Is that the tier you had?" I asked.

Sebastian gave a humorless huff. Nessa glanced over with an uncharacteristic straight face.

"No, I have never been part of that tier," Sebastian said into the quiet car. "I've been on the receiving end of that tier."

I shook my head. "What does that mean?"

"Killing one of their gilded lilies, as I call them, gets you an inquisition—"

"Torture," Nessa said. "Killing one of them will get you tortured."

"An excellent way for them to extort money. Pay me, and you can walk away now. The fees for that are always extravagant."

"Sebastian killed one of their lilies," Nessa supplied unnecessarily.

"Who did?" Sebastian looked her way.

She glanced over for as long as she could before crashing. "Really? After all these years, you're suddenly going to *out* me?"

"Why not?" Sebastian shrugged. "Jessie won't ever get the chance to be a lily. What will it matter if she knows?" He went back to looking out the window. "A mage broke into my lab—"

"This was a long time ago," Nessa said.

Sebastian nodded. "Yes, I was a new, up-and-coming mage. I'd made the rounds and then some and earned a reputation for having a lot of power and being good with potions and spell work. Naïvely, I'd also been open about the setup of my lab. I didn't have any allies to give me helpful tips."

"I was his friend," Nessa said, "but had too little power to warrant status in the mage community. I'm better at making friends, but none of the people Sebastian was meeting could be bothered to speak to me. So I couldn't help him get allies."

He took a deep breath before continuing. "The mage who broke in was looking for my journals and spell books. An alarm spell tripped him up. By the time I arrived, he was breaking out of it. He pinned me with magic and was about to deliver the killing shot when Nessa stuck a knife in the back of his neck. She's never been very squeamish about that kind of thing."

"I would've made a really good gargoyle," she said, half turning back with a grin.

"He went down like a sack of flour," he said.

"I might not be powerful with spells," Nessa said, "but I'm pretty damn good with knives."

"The problem was, in the Guild's eyes, she was nothing," he said. "Killing a powerful mage would've almost certainly been a death sentence for her. But I was powerful—*am* powerful. I knew they wouldn't want to destroy me, so I said I did it."

"But you were protecting yourselves," I said, horrified.

"They didn't care," Sebastian replied. "I killed one of their elite. They're supposed to protect their elite. If they don't, why would anyone bother paying for that status? They weren't prepared to kill me, but I had to be punished. They tortured me for hours at a time each day. On the third day, they had a talk with me before they got started. 'I'll tell ya what,' the guy said. I'll always remember that. 'I'll tell ya what, you pay us what we're owed, and we'll forget about this whole thing.'"

"What they were owed?"

"The money they wanted to extort from me," he replied. "Money they claimed they would have raked in from the mage if he'd lived."

"Did you pay?"

"No. Screw them. They continued torturing me for another few days. How many exactly, I lost count. Each day, they gave me the same offer. Each day, I ignored them. I didn't utter a peep during the sessions. Not a cry or a scream, nothing. Nor did I acknowledge their attempts at extortion. I wouldn't even look at them. Finally, they got fed up and just let me go."

"With a warning," Nessa added.

"Right, with a warning. Don't mess up again, or they'd kill me next time."

"So we killed them instead," she said.

"Yes. That's when I started killing in cold blood. I already had the stage name, but I started using it as a weapon. I *became* a weapon."

"That wasn't cold blood," Austin growled.

"Maybe not. But by then, I had no emotion left about it. I'd paid the price, and I returned to get my change. In blood."

I shivered. Sebastian hadn't told me any of this before, just hinted at it.

"There are some places in the shifter world as bad as that," Austin said. "Maybe worse. This place was lawless when I arrived. Those in power hunted or stole or extorted as they desired. The weak were used as punching bags or killed for sport."

"So you know what it's like." Sebastian's tone was lifeless.

"Yes. The body count I racked up was very high."

"But you fixed things," I said.

A pause. And then Austin said, "Yes."

"Well, then." Nessa patted Sebastian's arm. "That's good news, isn't it? We can finally help build something, Sabby. Rather than always tearing it down, hmm? Won't that be nice?"

"Leave me alone. I'm moping," he replied grumpily.

She laughed at him. "But the Guild will react differently to Jessie. Her setup is nothing like what they're used to."

Sebastian coughed out a laugh and then started chuckling helplessly. "Oh my word, is it different. Let's count the ways, shall we, Captain?" Sebastian held up a fist and then peeled a finger away from it. *One.*

"Well, Vanna, the most obvious is also the gravest offense as pertains to her status," Nessa supplied. "Until very recently, she was a Jane."

"*Blech.* That makes her lower than any magical person on the planet, yes." Sebastian glanced back. "If you haven't caught on, mages are horribly snobbish."

He peeled away another finger. *Two.*

"She inherited her magic," Nessa said, and I could see her nose crinkle in the rearview window. "She has some sort of weird historical magic. Magic that comes from a *house.* There are legends about it, but since when are those actually real? I don't buy it."

"Yeah, a *house*?" Sebastian's tone was comically skeptical.

"A house, yes. And this house apparently changed her from a Jane into some sort of shifter. A gargoyle, of all things, even though everyone knows female gargoyles don't exist." She shook her head. "Honestly, it's too absurd. She must be making it up."

He turned up his nose. "There is no way anyone could take that sort of thing seriously. No wonder Momar sent a lackey to collect her."

"Agreed." She nodded, her ears lifting with a smile.

Sebastian put up another finger for Nessa. *Three.*

"Well, the obvious, of course," she supplied dutifully, glancing in the rearview at Austin. "She hangs out with filthy animals. Hell, she's almost a filthy animal herself, and then she doubles down and beds one?

Disgusting. She might as well go back to being a Jane. She'd at least have some self-respect that way. *Blacklisted.*"

Austin looked out the window, his thumb still stroking my skin.

Sebastian started to laugh. "She wouldn't be black-listed if she could do something with all that power. But…" He held up a fourth finger.

"She doesn't know a damn thing about magic," Nessa said immediately. It was clear they'd been working together for a long time. They'd long passed the completing-each-other's-sentences stage of their friendship. "She can't even hide her past Jane status with an impressive array of magic. Which is great, of course, because she can easily be killed. There's really no point in keeping her alive, honestly."

"Yeah. Let's round her up, get some information out of her, and kill her." He wiped invisible dirt off his shoulder. "It's the cleanest way to deal with the situation."

"Agreed." She nodded exaggeratedly.

"Of course…one thing doesn't really fit." Sebastian looked over at Nessa. "It's the one thing that suggests she might not be what she seems."

He held up the fifth finger.

"Well, she was claimed by the great Elliot Graves, of

course," she supplied.

Austin's thumb stopped its ministrations. His head turned slowly, and the pressure in the car changed dramatically.

"No, no—" Sebastian said, his hand up in a stop gesture.

"Wow, I physically felt that," Nessa exclaimed with a wide smile. Her eyes flicked into the rearview at Austin. "Sure, yeah, your eyes are terrifying, but wow. I actually felt the change in your demeanor. It's making me want to cower in fear."

"Take a hint, Nessa," Sebastian said as he did just that. "She didn't mean 'claim' as in…like…'*claim.*' Just that I…"

"Reserved her," Nessa supplied.

"No!" He held up his first finger again. "No, not reserved. I called dibs. But in a very unromantic way."

"A professional way," she said.

He pointed at her. "Yes! A professional way. I professionally showed interest in her."

"Not even in a permanent way," she replied.

"Not even in a permanent way," he repeated. "It's just an act of professional interest. In this case, given my…renewed reputation, it'll make most people give you a wide berth. The Guild knows I'd kill—and have— if anyone encroaches on my territory."

"Kinsella, anyone?" Nessa said, turning off the highway. "We made it very clear that Kinsella was killed because he came here and acted like an aggressor. Then we invited Jessie to the caves to show off her power."

"Which probably would've worked better if we hadn't killed everyone or forced them to go into hiding," he said drolly.

"Hindsight," she said. "Anyway, we *tried* to send a clear message. Mess with what is ours—"

"Not ours!" he yelled out.

"Mess with the lady we're professionally interested in—man, Sabby, this is exhausting."

"It's fine." Austin resumed stroking my skin. "I know what you mean."

"Except now they're sending a low-level collector," Sebastian said, rubbing his chin.

"Well, you went off into hiding, leaving everyone out to dry." Nessa slowed, turning right before making a left. We were clearly getting close.

"True," he said quietly. "So maybe number five is off the table."

"On the table or off," she said, parking. She yanked the brake and beamed back at me. "We're about to rocket into the next phase of this thing. It's about time for some new stories to be spread about you. You'll be the infamous Jessie Ironheart before you ever sit down to a mage dinner."

# CHAPTER 11

NIAMH WAITED AS everyone filed out of the shifter vehicles. As expected, Austin's pack immediately cleared away to the sides in orderly lines or rows. Also as expected, the Ivy House crew gathered in clumps or spread out, a few people here, another couple spaced there, and that *eejit* Earl unpacking his disguises because he hadn't a clue left in his balding gray head. Compared to Austin's pack, they looked absolutely ridiculous.

It was perfect.

Niamh hadn't worn this stupid getup to fit in, as she'd told Jessie. Nor had she worn it because it was handy for shifting. She'd worn it because she *wanted* them all to look like fools. There was nothing better than being underestimated.

Jessie stepped from the car with tight shoulders, clearly worried about how this would go. She didn't like causing people harm, something she'd need to get over if she was going to dance with corrupt mages. Magic pulsed from her, strong and enticing. The gargoyle was getting everyone on the same page.

As if yanked by an invisible string, Broken Sue took a halting step forward. His body tensed, muscles bulging. There he stopped, though, a pace in front of where he was supposed to be standing.

Kace, behind him, jerked too. His eyes widened minutely, and his gaze swung to Jessie.

She caught it, and an intense moment passed between them. Niamh remembered something similar happening between Jessie and Broken Sue on the field yesterday. In a moment, Jessie nodded slightly, and acceptance rumbled through the bond.

Confusion marred Kace's expression as he stepped forward to where Broken Sue struggled, and then kept going. He stopped nearer Jessie, as though his allegiance was shifting from one alpha to the other.

*Jaysus,* Niamh thought with glee. *Austin Steele won't like that one bit.*

As if on cue, Austin came around the back of the Honda, his eyes hard and his bearing hostile. He stared Kace down, and then his gaze flicked to Broken Sue before settling on Jessie.

That bear loved Jessie more than any other man had ever loved a person, at least in Niamh's perception, but he had his limits. Her gargoyle trying to rule his people would absolutely rub those limits raw. If only they didn't have an enemy mage to manipulate, she'd grab a chair right now and settle in. The fireworks promised to be spectacular.

Jessie's voice was emotionless yet firm as she said, "I'm calling my people to me. My gargoyle is, I mean. I don't have much control over this. It's some sort of primal drive that only seems to kick in when a battle is near. Like feeling people's emotions. Those who have spilled blood by my side have the option to establish a deeper connection with my gargoyle. It's like the Ivy House bond. It'll help me keep track of their well-being, and I can call them to my side when they're needed." Her troubled gaze met Austin's. "I don't know how to stop it. I know what these pulses of magic mean, and I know they'll likely come in handy, but other than that, my gargoyle is steering this ship. Brochan is resisting me. Kace doesn't seem to have the power. Or maybe he just doesn't want to."

"It feels… I can't…" Kace shook his head.

"Doesn't want to, then," she said, her eyes pleading for Austin to understand. Damn it, she was too good at navigating that big alpha. She never really leaned far enough into the extravagance of war for Niamh's taste. For her enjoyment, at any rate.

"This is her role," Sebastian said from the side, some

of his Elliot Graves act diminishing in luster within the proximity of Austin's dominating aura. "She brings them together. She *keeps* them together. The mate protector is supposed to lead them into battle. She is the queen, and her mate is her commander. The leader of her army. The might behind her power." The frustration of a researcher bookworm talking to idiots crept into his voice. "If you'd just take the mate protector's magic, as you're supposed to, you could help her harness her gifts. The previous heirs erred because they got tangled up with mages who didn't have any battle sense. But Jessie is a gargoyle, first and foremost. They're a battle species. And now she's found her commander. She just needs him to rise to the occasion."

Austin's intense focus slowly swung Sebastian's way. The only thing that moved was his head, but suddenly, the area felt stuffed with the alpha's dominating power. Niamh felt it pressing along her shoulders and crawling across her scalp like insects. Sebastian visibly quailed.

Nessa whistled long and low. "Probably shouldn't shame an alpha, Sabby. He looks pissed."

"Yes, I just remembered that," Sebastian muttered. "I'll just hunch here for a while. Let me know if I should start running."

So this power struggle was going down because Austin Steele wasn't taking the protector's magic. He didn't like to be forced into anything.

And while this was prime entertainment, they had more important things to do. Gathering her strength, Niamh stepped closer to him. "Right so. Austin Steele, you know the score here. Let's go pay a visit to our trespassing friend inside. I doubt you've upped the magical wards on this place, so he might not stay put much longer."

It was Niamh's turn for that vicious, blue-eyed stare. She was ready for it, though. When her limbs felt like freezing and her spine tried to bow, she muscled through it.

After an intense beat that made sweat pop out on her forehead, Austin Steele redirected his focus to Kace. "Back in formation," he growled.

Kace visibly shook from the command, pulled by Jessie, pushed by Austin. He took a shuddering breath...then slowly started backing up. Little by little, inch by inch, he back-pedaled until he was where he'd started.

Austin looked at Broken Sue now, the command evident within his posture. Broken Sue didn't need much help. He took a deep breath and easily stepped back into place.

Lust and gratitude swept through the bond—Jessie's emotions. Like Austin, she clearly enjoyed when her mate flexed his power. She also seemed to like that he couldn't be bullied by the magic she struggled to control.

"Shall we?" Austin turned, pausing with his arm out to shepherd Jessie in front of him, and then headed for the door.

Niamh released a sigh as the pressure suddenly eased.

The shifters fanned out, heading to their positions around the building. They were there to secure it in case some of the trespassing mage's friends showed up. Or, more likely, mercenaries he'd hired. Only a few shifters followed Jessie and Austin Steele to the door.

"That's going to be a problem," Ulric murmured as he fell in beside Niamh. "Them fighting for power like that."

"Not a'tal," Niamh replied, making sure she and Ulric ruined the orderly line heading to the storage facility doors. "It'll just give our friend the alpha a new challenge. He seems to love those."

Ulric shook his head, falling behind a little so Niamh could enter the single doorway first.

"I fortified the spells."

Niamh nearly jumped out of her skin from the surprise of Sebastian's unexpectedly close voice.

"Janey Mack, lad. Yer as bad as Edgar at sneaking

up."

"That is *quite* the compliment," came Edgar's disembodied voice from somewhere behind them.

"Last week," Sebastian went on as they made their way through the recently redone halls. The concrete floor reflected the bare bulbs dotting the way above them. Orange metal gleamed along the walls, the doors to what were very likely vacant storage cells. "Alpha Austin—I mean Austin Alph—Dang it."

"Yer also as bad as Edgar in getting names right, hmm?" Niamh said.

Nessa started laughing.

"That alpha has a way of reducing me to a blubbering mess," he replied, shooting a glare backward, probably at Nessa. "Anyway, the alpha asked that I fortify this place with magic for just such an occasion."

They turned one corner and then another. The place was seemingly set up like a maze. It wouldn't take a genius to figure it out. Edgar had made his plant maze much harder to navigate.

"Did you tell him that you were expecting to need it?" she asked.

"No. I didn't want to worry him unnecessarily. I figured the first mage in would be easy to navigate. Well…hoped that would be the case, at any rate."

"Did ye, now? And how did you think he'd react to

you withholdin' vital information that directly related to his mate's safety?"

Sebastian was quiet for a moment. "I...I mean..." He struggled for words. "I'm always around. I've been paying attention. Watching for signs that mages are near, I mean. I've had my eye on things."

She shrugged and said, "I'm sure it'll be grand," somehow managing to subdue her sarcasm. She wouldn't trade places with him for all the world.

They turned a final corner, and the building opened up around them. The storage units that should've been there weren't, creating a warehouse-like space three stories tall. Within the area sat what looked like a large white cube with a narrow door embedded in it. This would've been what Sebastian had fortified. The enemy mage's prison.

They stopped in a chaotic sort of mass, the few shifters perfectly aligned on the outskirts and the Ivy House crew randomly spaced between them.

Nessa practically danced through everyone to stop beside Jessie. "Okay, everyone, if I may. Here's how things are going to go..."

"Send Edgar in first," Niamh said, putting a little power behind that command. She hadn't ever used that particular magical ability with this crew. She'd been saving it for when she really needed it. Now was the time.

Nessa snapped to attention, and Cyra and Hollace, standing right in front of her, looked back with furrowed brows. Austin Steele's gaze beat into her for the second time this evening, but she didn't let that bother her now. She wasn't messing with his people, so he wouldn't mess with her.

One and all then shifted their gaze to Edgar, who was hanging in the back. He held one of the Ivy House spell books and stood much too close to Broken Sue. If it was any other time, Niamh would've burst out laughing at the mildly uncomfortable expression leaking onto Broken Sue's otherwise stoic face.

"Who...me?" Edgar asked with raised eyebrows, looking around. "Go first?" He straightened a little. "My, this is an unexpected honor."

"Well, but..." Nessa hesitated. "If that mage has somehow escaped his restraints, he'll be dangerous. He'll be able to fire magic..."

"Ah, sure, it'll be grand," Niamh said, still hiding her sarcasm. "Jessie practices on him all the time. He's right as rain."

"Well, I do still have nightmares from that one time, but I try not to sleep or daydream, and it seems to be okay," Edgar said with a smile.

"See? He's grand." Niamh motioned him on. "Edgar, while we get organized, go break the ice, will ya? Fill our trespasser in on the perils of flower growing. Or your quest for the perfect doily. Or all your medals from cheating in the flower shows."

Edgar skulked closer to the cube—in fairness, it was his version of *walking*—and waggled his long finger at her. "You know very well I do not cheat in that flower—"

"Yeah, yeah. Tell him all about it." Niamh walked him forward, pulled the door open, and shoved him in. "Mind ye don't get hit with magic. Ye wouldn't want to rob Jessie of retiring you. I'm sure she'll look forward to it one of these days."

She shut the door behind him with a click.

Jessie lifted her eyebrows at the scene but was content to let Niamh handle it.

Nessa stared at the door for a moment. "Okay. That was unexpected, but not a problem. Let's roll with it." She faced Jessie. "He had the spell book you'll be using. As you all know, our goal is to get some answers from our friend in there. To do that, we'll use a mixture of intimidation and pain. I wondered, Mr. Alpha Steele, if we could use"—her finger moved through the air in front of the gathered people—"your rather dashing gorilla?" She winked at Broken Sue. "We promise to return him in one piece."

Austin nodded, and Broken Sue walked forward, his

expression hard and his eyes pinning Nessa to the wall behind her. Well, he tried, anyway. Her smile grew until she was practically beaming at him.

"I haven't been in one piece for a great many years," he growled softly.

"Even better," she replied at the same volume. "I won't have to be gentle."

He stiffened just slightly, his muscles popping along his arms.

"Right, so." Niamh resumed control. "I'll be goin' in, too, obviously." She braced her hands on her hips. "Curses. I forgot to tell Edgar to grab the cooler."

Nessa grimaced. "This first part might be a bit...tough to watch."

Niamh laughed. "Dearie, ye don't know what *tough to watch* looks like. Here, Ulric, go get me beer cooler, would ya?"

Cyra raised her hand. "Can I participate? I bet I could show you what 'tough to watch' looks like."

"That sounds like a good challenge." Hollace rubbed his hands together. "If only the basajaun were here. He'd be good at this."

"He feels like he's on his way into the area, and no"—Jessie stepped forward and put out her hand—"there will be no full-on torturing. Scare him, fine. Rough him up, okay. But I draw the line at torturing.

That's not how we do things." She grimaced. "Hopefully."

She meant *hopefully, my gargoyle complies.* Niamh had a feeling it wouldn't.

"Well, okay, why not?" Nessa said, never troubled. "Let's see if we can frighten information out of him without too much pain. I'm up for trying new things."

Broken Sue glanced down at her, a question.

"Yes, you're still needed." She motioned him toward the cube.

"Wait." Niamh held up her hand. "Give Edgar a little more time. He'll have our trespasser plenty loosened up in another few minutes. That vampire can unsettle the hardest of 'em."

# CHAPTER 12

M Y MAGIC THRUMMED through me in strong waves. Austin stood beside me, waiting for Niamh's cue to enter the room. She had apparently taken over. When she gave a nod, Sebastian entered first, putting up a defensive spell just in case. He may not have accepted my gargoyle's offer of a connection, but I could feel the emotions of those around me now, so I knew he was in Elliot Graves mode. His emotions had stagnated, as though he didn't feel anything at all.

Nessa started to go next, but Broken Sue covered her shoulder with his hand. "Let me," he grunted, gently moving her to the side and entering the room ahead of her. He had to turn a bit sideways to make it through the door, and I knew Austin would have to do the same. I bet that was by design. It would make them look bigger, larger than life. Compared to almost all mages, they would surely seem that way.

"Quite the gentleman, cutting in front of a lady," Niamh said sarcastically.

"Don't you listen to her, Mr. Gorilla," Nessa chirped. "I am positively swooning." She flashed me a smile before bounding in after him.

Niamh put out her hand for me, peering into the room. "Not yet, Jessie." She then glanced around us. "Earl, we'll need you guarding the door. Right in front, like. Put on yer best disguise so he won't see ya."

Mr. Tom puffed up his chest. "I do not answer to you, woman. Miss?"

I shot Austin a bewildered look. Niamh clearly subscribed to the power of eccentricity. "Yeah, sure, whatever."

Ulric jogged back in carrying Niamh's cooler. He stopped near her, probably hoping the errand had granted him admission into the room.

She said to Austin, "Do you have a chair? A folding one. Battered up would be good."

He nodded to one of his people, who took off at a jog.

"What is it you're aiming for?" I asked her as she directed Ulric to join the others.

She glanced in after him, then waited for Mr. Tom to finish donning a brown coat with the sleeves rolled up, a pipe, and the Elvis glasses with the glued-on sideburns. He turned and took his post by the door.

"No, not here, ya donkey," Niamh said. "On the inside. In case he gets loose, like."

"That is preposterous," he replied. "That room is going to be crowded. I'll guard you from the outside."

"Then what is the point of ye lookin' like that? Go on, in ye git. Go on, ye might as well. *Go on*."

"Just go," I told Mr. Tom. "How about a doll, too?" I asked Niamh. "Or a homicidal gnome? We already look crazy, why not extend ourselves a bit?"

She nodded at me. "If them things wouldn't have killed us in the car ride over, I would've. Now, Jessie, listen here. I shouldn't have to tell ya that the mage in there is a very bad man. He brings people in to be beat up or tortured. Probably both. The people he works for are the most cutthroat magical people ye'll hopefully never meet. These people would sell Edgar to vampire hunters for sport. They'd rip off the gargoyles' wings. They'd try to burn down Ivy House and surely burn down the town without a care. People like them are the reason the name Broken Sue fits the man. Are ye with me so far?"

She waited for me to nod.

"Now, I'd wager Sebastian is goin'ta ask you to use that nightmare spell we tried on Edgar. The one that still makes him randomly hide in the bushes, remember?"

I grimaced. It was hard to forget that spell. Poor Edgar. He'd volunteered, knowing what it was supposed to do, but I didn't think any of us had been prepared for its potency.

She continued with a very direct stare. "If ye are only goin'ta scare this mage, then ye need to give him the shock of his life. Of his *entire* life. A shock that will never wear away. And ye can do it with that nightmare spell. That room now has all our weirdest people in it. They'd make a mage wary on a normal day. Add the intensity of alpha shifters and an actual shift or two, and we should have this. But make no mistake, this is the first battle in what will likely be a nasty war. Just like yesterday, ye need to show strong. The entire territory is on the line if ye fail."

My magic pounded in time with my heart. I could feel my gargoyle moving within me, demanding action.

"Let the gargoyle speak," Niamh said softly. "Let her out to play. This is her arena. Ye need to honor that." She held my gaze for another moment, nodded, took the chair from Austin's guy, who'd just run in, and went into the room, saying, "Ulric, get me a beer. I want to watch the show in comfort."

Austin moved to the door and waited for me to go through first. "I'll be here if you need me," he said softly, resting his hand on my upper back while his thumb stroked across the base of my neck.

His magic swirled with mine, comforting and invigorating and delicious. But I could sense that he agreed with Niamh—he was letting his animal take the lead, accepting all the vicious darkness the beast would bring forth. He was inviting me to play with him...and my gargoyle was stretching forward to do just that.

"I hate this," I said as my stomach churned. "I hate that I couldn't just be magical and still be chill and left alone."

"So do a lot of magical people," he replied. "And that's why we're going to work toward giving peace to others before taking it for ourselves. We'll get there, though. Eventually, we'll find our paradise. I know we will."

I breathed deeply and nodded. He was right. I had the power to protect people, mages as well as shifters. If we didn't stand against the people abusing their power, who would? Who *could*?

"Okay," I said, mostly to myself.

Low light greeted me, and bodies moved out of the way as I entered. A man sat in the center of the space on a wooden chair. His hands were secured behind his back, and his legs were tied to the chair. Even seated, he clearly had some girth to him, strong shoulders and thick thighs. He was the muscle, all right. He could easily beat someone into submission if his magic didn't do the trick.

Edgar waited just behind him, his hands held at the height of the man's shoulders and his fingers draping a bit, like he was a vampire in an old movie about to prey on his victim. "You can weaponize flowers if you are very good," he was saying. "I, myself, am not yet that good. It's a tricky business. You have to sing to them, you see, and some of my peers have hinted that I have a voice like a croaking frog. But Hollace has a lovely voice, and of course, the alpha is an exquisite singer. Sometimes, I just sit in the flowers—deep in the shadows so I'm not seen, of course—and listen to him sing and play for Miss Jessie. What a treat. It is well worth my newfound fear of flesh-eating crickets. Isn't it amazing what the mind conjures up when trapped in a magical spell?"

He laughed good-naturedly.

The man licked his lips, and his brow furrowed a bit. His gaze zipped to the side, but he didn't turn his head toward Edgar. It was like he was trying to ignore the vampire but the process was playing hell on his nerves.

Edgar paused, noticing me. "Oh, hello, Miss Jessie. I was just explaining to our guest the logistics of a good garden. There really are a lot of moving parts. It's hard to see that from the outside."

The mage's dark eyes found me. He gave me a once-over before lingering on my face. Recognition curled within his emotions. He'd pinpointed who I was.

"Everyone here is going to die for this," he said as though we were sitting down for coffee.

"Die for what, having a nice chat with our new friend?" Nessa asked, passing in front of him while tapping her chin.

"How would they even know who was in this room?" Sebastian asked, bracing his hands on his hips in apparent confusion. It was clear they'd done this a time or two. "If you miraculously broke out of this binding, and somehow broke out of this magically protected box, you've already shown you can't handle a few shifters. How would you hope to escape the territory?"

"Good question." She nodded, passing back in front of the captive. Pacing, apparently. She stopped, bent, and looked at his face. "I think he's bluffing, that's what I think."

"You think I'm just talking about the people in this room?" The mage smirked without humor. "If I don't come back with the woman, my boss will take out this whole dingy, backwater, flea-bitten town. No one'll miss these filthy animals anyway—"

Suddenly, I was standing in the place where his

chair had been, and he was crashing against the wall behind him. Ulric had barely managed to dive out of the way to avoid getting hit. The chair broke when it hit the ground, spilling the man out of it. His ankles were still bound to the chair legs, though, and his hands bound behind his back.

My heart thudded in my chest, but it was nothing compared to the surge of power that felt like it was stretching my skin to the point of pain.

"That's not how you address this town," I said in a low, rough voice.

He flopped, trying to pull his hands into a useable position.

I didn't give him a chance.

I hammered him with magic, red tinging my vision. He slammed back against the wall again, his head thunking. I sent a spell that would make him feel like he was being splintered into pieces. He gritted his teeth, and determination pulsed around him. He was clearly used to pain inflicted by spells. Maybe he'd even prepared for this sort of scenario. He wasn't going to yield easily.

Nessa hop-jogged over to him. She bent and grabbed his slicked-back ponytail, yanking his head back so she could look into his face. Blood dripped from a cut in his left eyebrow and a slice in his lip. That had been from crashing against the wall and the subsequent fall. The magic I'd unleashed didn't leave physical wounds.

"Let's try that again, shall we?" she said. "Only this time, don't insult the people she loves. It upsets her. She was a Jane not that long ago, after all. She still has some sentimentalities. We're working on it."

He swore at her before spitting. She yanked her head away just in time. She'd clearly been expecting that.

My magic crashed forward again. I was powerless to control the surge.

"Whoops, wrong answer, my love," Nessa said to him as she quickly rolled away, her anticipation abilities topnotch.

I unleashed another series of crushing magical blows, blunt but all sorts of powerful. Wave after wave hammered into him, stealing his breath and spinning him around. My gargoyle rode me hard, wanting to shift and claw. To exact a blood price. To *end* him.

I wrestled for control. This was not the way. Killing him and turning his body over to Niamh, who would probably send his head back to his bosses or something else horribly gruesome, wouldn't get us information. We were flying blind when it came to Momar, and this was one of his grunts. Granted, it was a grunt at the bottom of a long chain of command, but we still needed what was in this guy's head.

Not to mention that *I'd* been the one to say no torture. I needed to get a hold of myself!

Breathing heavily, I barely managed to shut off the torrent of magic. Anger still throbbed within me. My gargoyle ached for action.

I took a step back and rolled my shoulders, my whole body tingling. "You might watch what you say and do," I ground out. "I'm a little shaky on my self-control right now."

The room was utterly silent as the mage pushed himself up. Determination still rolled off him. He was ignoring the pain. Oh yeah, he'd been trained for this. He was tolerating this treatment like someone with experience.

He wheezed out a cough before he said, "The boss is going to be a bit surprised that the rumors are true." He spat blood to the side. "You got the power. That much power, and they'll use you up good and proper, filthy creature 'n' all—"

This time, it wasn't me who lost control.

The mage's eyes widened as Austin stormed toward him. The man's feet scrabbled for purchase, and he tried to back-pedal even though there was a wall behind him.

Austin wrapped his large hand around the man's

throat and hoisted him clean off the ground. Rage and menace and pain ate at my mate. I knew he was reacting to the images that must've rushed through his mind when the mage spoke of what they would do to me.

The man's face turned red, as his air supply was effectively cut off. He shook his bound hands behind him and kicked his legs. Austin didn't show any sign of strain.

"Niamh, I need your chair," I said through my teeth, still struggling for my own self-control.

"O'course." She dragged it over, beer in hand, and set it between me and the wall.

"Austin, don't kill him," I said. "Put him down."

My mate walked the man over before dropping him onto the seat.

The man hit the edge and nearly fell. He got his toes onto the ground and shoved himself fully on, coughing.

"I don't think he was expecting that," Nessa said, tilting her head toward Sebastian.

He wore that strange, lopsided grin. "I don't think so, no. He's been bombarded with magic before, sure. But an out-of-control alpha shifter? I don't think that's in his vocabulary. He looks a little shaken."

The man yelled curses at the two, obviously starting to fray. That was a good thing. We were making an impact.

"That wasn't out of control," I started, but Edgar had drifted over again. He stood like he had before, with his hands draped in that strange way, and bent a little to whisper in the man's ear.

"If we get time, I'll tell you all about doily making."

The man flinched away. His weight shifted on the seat, which overturned, sending him crashing to the ground.

"What kind of a circus is this?" he hollered, flailing. It wasn't clear if he was trying to right himself or if he was having a stress-induced tantrum.

Nessa crouched next to the guy, and Austin glanced at Broken Sue. Taking the unspoken command, Broken Sue stepped forward and planted his feet right next to Nessa. He didn't crouch, just loomed dangerously. It was enough.

"Get away!" The man's flailing turned into a strange sort of scooting, half-rolling attempt to escape.

Nessa pointed at Broken Sue. "Terrifying, right? You never really get used to their presence. It's unsettling in a very thrilling way. I love the danger of it. But then, I'm on their side. See what I'm saying?"

"I don't think he does, Captain." Sebastian picked up the Ivy House spell book Edgar had brought in and stashed in the corner. He handed it to me.

"Captain?" The man's gaze ripped from Broken Sue

and fastened on Nessa. He obviously knew it was the notorious nickname of Elliot Graves's companion in crime. "*Captain*?" His gaze darted around the room; he was probably looking to see if one of them was Graves.

"Oops, I outed you," Sebastian told Nessa. "Do you think he knows who *I* am? Disguises only work so well. Ask Mr. Tom there, by the door. Plain as day in his getup, delusional as all get out."

"Getup, get out…" Edgar chuckled and did a weird sort of crab walk closer to the mage. "Don't you just love word play?" His simpering smile showed his large canines. "I find it marvelous."

"What the…" the man said in a strangled voice, bending backward away from Edgar but clearly not wanting to retreat far enough to bump into Broken Sue.

"Usually, we like to dangle our captives by their feet from hooks and torture information out of them." Sebastian glanced at the ceiling. "But this room doesn't have a hook."

"Thankfully, it *does* have a gargoyle." Nessa winked at the man. "You know the drill, right? Tell us what we want to know, and it won't get ugly. Bonus—you'll get to walk away from here! Isn't that something? You'll get to keep your balls, too, probably. I'm just guessing, there. We aren't allowed to really hurt you. Boss's orders."

The man looked in confusion at Sebastian.

"Nope. Not that boss." She pointed at me. "I've got a lady boss now. Cool, right? Girl power." She made a fist. "So, here we go. A super-easy one first. Who do you work for?"

The man went to spit at her again.

Nessa didn't get a chance to move out of the way.

Broken Sue reached down almost lazily, grabbed the guy by his black T-shirt, and heaved him. The man struck the back wall hard, shaking the room. After making a sound like a cross between a whimper and a shout, he crumpled to the ground. He didn't flail this time—he just curled up into a ball, probably hoping the vampire wouldn't be back for more idle chatter about odd things.

"Huh." Nessa watched the mage. "Nice lob."

"I know how that feels," Sebastian told the guy. "Wanting to curl into the fetal position around these guys. I mean, it's intense—I get it. They're taking it easy on you, though, my friend. She won't." He jerked his head at me. "This next spell is very fun. You haven't seen it before, trust me. This is *old* magic."

"Who do you work for?" Nessa asked the man.

He uncurled just a little, clearly struggling to keep his dignity. "Anyone worth the air they breathe knows who I work for." He coughed. "It's no secret."

"That's why I said the question was super-easy. I'm establishing a rapport." Nessa cocked her head at him. "Do you not know how this works?"

"Maybe this is his first time," Sebastian said.

She nodded as though thinking. "I remember my first time. It wasn't very fun, either. I was with this clown of a guy, and he was all fumbling hands and hole confusion…" She feigned surprise. "Oh! Are we talking about torture, here? Sorry."

Sebastian huffed out a laugh as he pulled his hand up to point at a spell in the book. "Remember how this goes, Jessie? You need to lock in on your target and use the full range of your power."

He was pointing at the spell Niamh thought he'd have me use. She'd read the situation.

"Well, I think I'll just step away now." Edgar bent at the waist and waved down at the mage. "I think I know which spell she's going to use, and I don't want to accidentally get hit in the crossfire. There are a lot of odd things in this room. I think collectively, with that spell, they would traumatize me for life. Good luck!" He gave the man a supportive smile and drifted away.

"Good intro," Nessa murmured. "The vampire is really good at this. Let's keep him, Sabby."

"That's a dark path, Captain," Sebastian replied. "A strange, dark path with possibly no escape."

A can popped somewhere off to the side—Niamh on her second beer.

"This whole situation is..." I shook my head, refamiliarizing myself with the spell. I'd only done it that once.

"It's perfect," Sebastian told me quietly. "It is absolutely perfect from top to bottom. I have to hand it to Niamh—she brought in all the right players."

"You might've caught me, but you won't catch the next guy," the man said. He winced when he tried to straighten his legs. "They're gonna get her"—he jerked his head at me—"and then they're going to pry her—"

He was dangling in the air at the end of Austin's hand before anyone could flinch. Austin rammed him repeatedly against the wall this time, his rage not on any sort of leash.

"Never speak about her like that again," he growled. "If any of you so much as lay a hand on her, I'll tear your arms and legs off and throw you in a lake."

Fear drifted off almost everyone in the room, a reaction to Austin's unspeakable menace. Nessa reached back, grabbing Broken Sue's shirt.

Sebastian shivered where he stood. "Come on, Jessie, hurry now," he whispered urgently. "This guy is already in a walking nightmare, I think, but this spell will really send him over the edge. We're not killing him. But let's give him a good scare so he can tell his boss how off-kilter and terrifying this place is."

I ran my hand across my forehead, trying to focus my thoughts.

"Honestly, the mage should've expected that," Nessa murmured, possibly to Broken Sue, whom she still clung to. He wrapped his arm around her back and pulled her in tightly. "We learn from our mistakes or we end up getting choked by the shifter king again."

"Drop him, Austin," I said as I started working my magic through the movements in my hands and body. When the man hit the floor, I focused hard on my target and said the incantation.

The spell fired across the room and sank into the mage's chest. This particular spell was fast-acting. We'd had Edgar racing around the woods within thirty seconds, screaming that the grasshoppers were going to eat him alive.

For a moment, nothing happened, and then the man started thrashing.

"Broken Sue, can you shift into your other form?" Sebastian asked.

Niamh set down her beer and started to strip. "I have a form that'll work right nicely."

Broken Sue did as instructed, followed by Niamh shifting into her little nightmare gremlin form. She opened her mouth to show rows upon rows of sharp white teeth.

The man's eyes got wider and wider. Sebastian fired off a few magical spells, casting shadows and throwing sparks of light to further throw the mage off-kilter. Niamh skittered around him, ran over his lap, and then bit into his arm.

He screamed, attempting to get up but falling over again and butting up against the wall. "No, no, no, no!"

He flinched when magic flared next to him. He rolled away, only to see Broken Sue rise and roar, beating his chest.

"Holy shi—! No! Oh, God, no. Please. Please!"

"What were your orders?" Nessa was suddenly right in his face, blocking out the others. Behind her back, she motioned for Edgar to come closer. "*What were your orders?*"

Edgar loped the short distance and squatted down, his canines ghastly. The man started to scream again.

"Get it away." The man flung out his hands, frayed rope dropping away. "Get that grotesque thing away!"

"Well, that is a confidence buster," Edgar murmured.

"What were your orders?" Nessa said again, louder.

Sebastian opened the door, and in a moment, Cyra jogged in with a large smile. I barely heard Sebastian ask

Hollace, "Do you do anything in your human form other than look pretty and fight fiercely?"

"Nope," Hollace replied. "I used to be okay with that."

"Fire." Nessa half turned to glance at Cyra. "Burn half his clothes off. Obviously, don't kill him or hurt him too badly, because we're not allowed to, but really give him hell."

"Okay!" Cyra set to work as Nessa got in the guy's face again. "Tell me your orders, and all of this stops. We'll let you go. I give you my word."

Cyra shot a stream of white fire into his leg. His scream turned high-pitched. She didn't seem to have understood the assignment.

I grimaced, quickly getting to work healing him.

"Call them off. Call them off!" the man yelled. He started to crawl away from Nessa, but the chair legs were still attached to him, making it difficult. She let him go a little distance before prompting Edgar to go after him.

Cyra got there first.

She pounced onto his back while cackling, burning his clothes with her touch. He turned to the side to try to throw her off, and Niamh raced up his body and bit down on his crotch.

"I promised him his balls," Nessa yelled at her. "Cyra, that's—No. Don't do—Crap. This went tits-up really quickly."

Ulric jogged closer, grabbed the man by his hair, tilted his head back, and asked the question again. "Just tell us so we can get you out of here," Ulric said afterward. "That's a phoenix burning your clothes. Trust me when I say you don't want her to get free rein. This is nothing."

A rumbling roar echoed outside of the cube room. The ground shook a little, and I could feel the basajaun coming closer. Someone must've stayed behind at Ivy House and given him a ride. Or else Austin sent someone back for him after I'd mentioned he was coming. However it had happened, he was here now.

His roar built through the walls.

"You want to get out of here, bro, trust me," Ulric said urgently, feeding the man's fear. He shook his head a lot, inviting the mage to notice his brightly colored hair. That had seemed to freak out Edgar when he was under our spell and hiding in the shrubbery. Ulric had actually been trying to help that time. He hadn't been successful. "Tell us what we need to know."

Ulric moved to the side, showing the man Mr. Tom, waiting by the door in his disguise. Then Broken Sue in his gorilla form, on all fours with his mouth gaping. Saliva dripped from his large teeth. Then Austin, watching the scene stoically now, power rippling out all around him. Niamh skittered by again, pausing to scratch the man. His clothes burned along his back.

He started to hyperventilate and clutched at his chest.

"Crap-sticks," Nessa said. "We might accidentally give him a heart attack." She motioned Cyra off him. "Give him a little space."

The basajaun burst into the room, squeezing to get through the door. His hair bristled all over his body, and his roar drowned out all other noise.

"No, no. Oh my God." The man froze in fear...and then the words started pouring out. "I was supposed to sedate her and rendezvous with a jet at LAX. They were going to fly her to headquarters to question her about that meetup at Elliot Graves's place."

"What do they want to know, specifically?" Nessa asked, taking Ulric's spot.

His whole body shook with fear. "I don't know."

"Guess!"

His mouth opened and closed a few times before words came out. His eyes were glued to the basajaun in blind terror.

"Word is, Momar wants to kill Graves before Graves builds momentum. First, he needs information on where to find him. A few people were at that meetup. He's got the location of one of the mages and is closing in on the other. She was the third and final piece, I think."

"What do you know about her?" When he didn't immediately answer, Nessa shook him. The basajaun stepped closer, growling low.

"Please don't let that thing get me," the man said, squeezing his eyes shut. "Oh, God, please—"

"That makes me feel a little better about myself." Edgar grinned at the basajaun. "It must be the spell after all. I was nervous he was put off by me specifically—"

"*What do you know about her?*" Nessa asked again.

"Her location. That she's some sort of filthy creature. She beds animals, too. Disgusting."

His lip curled, and I barely kept myself from rushing over, ripping him up, and making a liar out of Nessa, who'd promised to preserve his balls.

"How much power did they say she has?" she went on.

"They think she's a joke. Word is that Graves is playing games. He was always playing games before he went dark. Taunting. People are saying he used that meetup and some strange magical creature he'd found to taunt Momar and the Guild. The Guild would've dealt with her, but they're letting Momar handle it. He wants that information first."

"What about the pack? What did they tell you about the pack?"

His confusion was evident. "The pack?"

She shook him just as the basajaun roared.

"Oh no! No, no!" The man started to flail again. "Please. *Please!*"

"The shifter pack," Nessa pushed. "The shifters in this town. What do you know about them?"

He waved his hands in front of his face to keep the basajaun out of sight, then just covered his eyes and started swearing softly to himself.

"Back off." Nessa waved the basajaun farther away. She repeated the question in a gentler tone.

"Nothing! I don't know anything, I swear. It's just a shifter pack. They've got a couple of strong animals, but what pack doesn't? It's nothing. It wasn't a concern."

"Is he coming for this pack?"

He started to cry. "I don't understand the question! Why would he? The pack is nothing. Some upstart situation, I don't know. This is about Graves, not some filthy shifters. *No one cares about them!*"

"What else do you know?" Nessa asked him.

But he was done. He curled up again and started screaming.

Nessa straightened with a confused expression. She glanced at Sebastian. "Is there a way to temper that spell? Because this is a little overboard."

Sebastian put out his hands. "I..." He shook his head in confusion. "I mean, we tried it on Edgar. He went a little panicky and weird but...not *too* weird. You know, for him. I didn't think it was this bad."

"That vampire is old as dirt," Niamh said after she'd changed back into her human form and grabbed her muumuu. "Magic and spells affect him differently than they would a mage. Less power is probably better."

"It doesn't work with less power," I replied, grimacing at the man.

"We've gotten all we're goin'ta get off this one. He's lost the plot altogether."

"We're definitely not following Jessie's original orders." Nessa looked down at the man. "Then again, she *is* at fault, so I guess we're absolved of blame, right?"

Ulric started laughing.

"Well...okay." Sebastian motioned for the basajaun. "Can you help me carry him out? I need to get him into the trees before we let him loose."

"I got here just in time." The basajaun bent down and hauled the man up by one ankle. "I would have been sad to miss this."

That was certainly something I'd expect him to say.

"There." Sebastian pointed at the basajaun's hold. "See, Nessa? We don't even need a hook now."

"So we don't. Whaddya know?" She looked around the room. "Even though it ended prematurely, I think we got way more out of him here than we would have with our crew, Sebastian. He's been schooled to resist painful magic. He might even have a spell against it we couldn't detect. He's low level, but they've clearly upped their game when it comes to training their people."

"Yeah, good point. Okay, let's—"

Austin grabbed Sebastian by the shirt as he was trying to get past and pulled the smaller man in close.

Sebastian screeched and blasted a spell off nearly before I could get a defensive layer up. As it was, the spell shot harmlessly off Austin's shoulder. Sebastian's aim was still not great when he was under pressure.

"That mage was here to capture my mate, take her to get questioned and then killed, and you plan to *let him loose*? Whose side are you on, mage?" Austin asked.

Niamh snickered, heading for the door. To Sebastian, she said, "Told ye so."

"She didn't tell me so!" Sebastian hollered, staying very still in Austin's grasp. "She definitely did not tell me so. She told me"—he affected a very good Irish accent—"*it'll be grand.*"

"Didn't ye hear the sarcasm, like?" she replied, and left the room.

"I didn't. I swear I didn't." He squeezed his eyes shut. "Please don't kill me."

# CHAPTER 13

"I T'S FINE." I put a calming hand on Austin's shoulder and tried like hell to cut off the thrumming magic still vibrating through my person. My gargoyle didn't seem appeased. Worse, Austin's display of protectiveness was spreading heat through my body that was hard to ignore.

I swallowed and leaned into him.

"It's okay," I said. "Let's meet at Ivy House and talk about it. I haven't been around. Neither have you. That's my fault. Let's open the lines of communication. It's time to get control of all this."

He stared at Sebastian for one more tense beat before letting go. He didn't step back, though, but rather waited for Sebastian to stagger away before he turned just slightly toward Broken Sue, who was nude and standing near the wall. For once, Nessa wasn't winking or poking fun at him. She watched the scene solemnly.

"Leave the enemy mage in this room," Austin said. "He doesn't walk free until I say so. Keep the guard around the perimeter of the building. Load up the Ivy House crew, and you and Kace meet us at Ivy House. I want you two with Nessa and Sebastian at all times until you're on Ivy House soil. If that means you need to carry them around like luggage while you see to your tasks, so be it. I want this territory locked down."

Broken Sue nodded and headed for his clothes.

Austin slung an arm around me. "Ready?" he asked, then paused. He was giving me a moment to direct my crew so it wouldn't seem like he was taking over.

"Yeah." I made a circle with my finger, about to tell the Ivy House people to head to the cars, but then the basajaun unceremoniously flung the mage across the room. My mouth hung open as Edgar sidled a little closer to the wounded enemy mage, who was still screaming and crying, and said, "We'll get to those doilies another time, okay?"

"Yeah," I told Austin again, heading for the door.

They'd figure it out. There was only so much weird a person could take, and this situation had tap-danced over that threshold in sparkly red slippers. I needed to get out of there.

"Sorry about that," Austin said as we exited the storage facility-turned-mage detention facility. I would eventually need to ask when he had done all that, because it didn't look freshly built.

"About what?" I asked as he directed me toward a nondescript black sedan.

He opened the passenger door for me, handed me in, and then crossed to the driver's side. Once on the road, he said, "That was essentially your scene, and I usurped your command."

I issued a humorless laugh. "Leave it to you to apologize for what was basically securing the territory to ensure my safety. Especially after I tried—and will probably continue to try—to hijack your pack members."

"I stepped into that interrogation when I shouldn't have—"

"When you strangled him, you mean? That greatly helped, actually."

"I interrupted your mage's plans—"

"Which was logical, since no one even knows his plans—my fault for staying away…"

"And I took possession of the enemy mage, not as an alpha pair, but as a solo alpha."

I frowned. That part had obviously escaped me. Then again, I'd never cared about being a town alpha. Austin had given me that role. I was happy to let him handle the sticky stuff.

He wouldn't see it that way, though. He lived by shifter rules, most of which I didn't know. His unwavering loyalty to me meant he wouldn't take it easy on himself. He wouldn't believe me when I said I didn't care, and he wouldn't forgive himself for not believing me.

My heart swelled. The Ivy House heir could be in no better hands.

I dropped my hand to his thigh and rubbed, making light of it. "It's your castle, baby. I like when you play king. Besides, your taking control of him is infinitely better than whatever Sebastian and the basajaun would've cooked up. *Especially* the basajaun. He might listen to me, but if Sebastian said, 'Don't pull his head off and see how far you can kick it,' he'd be aiming for a head-kicking personal best before Sebastian got out the last word."

A grin pulled at Austin's handsome face. He nodded slightly, and I knew I'd succeeded in letting him off the hook.

"But seriously, I'll definitely try to hijack more of your pack. Anyone who sheds blood on my behalf is...offered that connection. *Offered* is the only word I can think of. I can't help doing it. I can't seem to stop it. I tried to pull it back with Kace, but he'd accepted before I figured out how. And then..." I shrugged. "I just can't control it yet. But I'm working on it. Know that."

He covered my hand with his. "I know. And I will assert my dominance every time you do. Your gargoyle is wrestling with my animal." He slipped his hand off mine and reached for my thigh. "She's challenging him. She's challenging *me*."

His hand ran along my inner thigh until it brushed against my apex. A shock of fire coursed through my body. I sucked in a surprised breath…and then widened my knees.

"I like it," he whispered, rubbing in a firm, slow motion. "I like the push and pull of our power merging."

His fingers left me for a moment to yank free the button on my jeans—one-handed, because he was still driving, something that only made it hotter. He pulled down the zipper before running his fingers along my skin. They dipped into the lacy fabric of my panties.

"I like the rush of heat I feel from you in our bonds," he murmured, running his fingertips along my wet center.

I let my eyes flutter shut and leaned back, giving him more access.

"I like the feeling when your gargoyle willingly submits and demands to be compensated for it." His fingers did lazy circles, stroking me. "I like providing that compensation…"

His fingers sped up, working me higher. I clutched

the leather of the seat. My breath came faster, and my hips moved to the rhythm of my pleasure.

"With my mouth," he finished, and I let out a tortured moan as the ache for him increased beyond what I could bear.

I groaned as his finger dipped inside. He rubbed firmly, right where I needed it, but it wasn't enough. Without him working to get our bodies thoroughly intertwined, it could never be enough. Not with him.

Lost as I was to his ministrations, I didn't feel the car stopping. I did feel his hand ripping away, though, leaving me empty. My door opened, and then he was there, lifting me into his arms and covering my mouth with his.

"You aren't going to like what you see in the morning," he murmured against my lips, crossing onto Ivy House soil. "Or maybe later tonight, after the meeting."

I squeezed my arms around his neck. "What does that mean? I'll always think you're the most handsome man I've ever seen."

His lips curled under mine as Ivy House opened the door for us. He took the stairs quickly, heading to my room.

"I love you, thank you, but that's not what I meant." He kicked my bedroom door shut behind him and didn't wait to cross to the bed. He swung me around and let me slide down his body at the same time, his lips devouring mine.

At any other time, I would have paused to ask what he meant, but I was desperate for him. I fumbled with the buttons on his pants as he pushed my jeans down. He bent, trailing his lips down my neck, giving me a little bite, until my jeans and panties were at my ankles. I worked them off as he pulled my shirt from me, then he unclasped my bra in no time and fastened a hot mouth to the hard peak of my breast.

I grabbed fistfuls of his shirt and pulled, bunching the fabric at his shoulders. He leaned back to strip it off, allowing me to view his hard, gorgeous body. Only for a moment, though, because he immediately leaned in and started trailing scorching kisses down my skin. When he reached my knee, he pushed my legs open, and then his tongue was feathering my center. He licked and sucked as his fingers worked.

With a fist in his hair, I pushed my hips up into him, savoring the exquisite feeling. The pressure within me built higher, and dancing lights fluttered behind my eyes. I moved faster as he worked harder until I was right there, on the edge.

"Not yet," he commanded, his power rippling through me. "Don't finish until I say you can."

My whine was mixed with a moan as he backed off

a little, teasing me.

"Yes," I drew out, rocking into the flick of his tongue. "No," I moaned as he kept backing off.

My body was strung out. Desperate. So keyed up.

Two fingers slid in deep as he gracefully rose, keeping me right where he wanted me—on that precipice, eager to jump. To fall. To turn end over end, deep into the abyss of pleasure.

His thumb barely touched down as his fingers moved, and then his mouth was back on mine. He moved between my legs, slow but deliberate, taking control. He hoisted me up and pushed me against the wall, almost roughly. His hard length rubbed against my throbbing center.

I breathed out in delirious expectation, something primal within me relishing my mate's dominance, both now and earlier. Relishing his strength and power. This wasn't just my gargoyle talking, either. It was the joy of having someone look after me the way I'd looked after others all my life. It was his way of making me feel safe in a world that had always treated me like prey.

I clutched his shoulders, struggling to get my legs a little higher, a little tighter around him, and he grabbed my neck, locking me in place. I relaxed within his hold, trusting him implicitly. His lips moved over mine, consuming me, and then he thrust.

My world exploded in color. Sensations overwhelmed me. I rocked against him, feeling like I couldn't get close enough. The pressure he'd built earlier increased until I could barely stand it. Until I was crying out his name, begging him to end the torture, but at the same time desperate for it to go on.

"Now, baby," he said, his body crashing into mine. "Now. Come with me *now*."

I shattered like a dropped crystal vase. My body shuddered against him violently—and he shook against me in return. I clenched my teeth as waves of pleasure swept me away, and then draped over him when they turned into blissful little aftershocks. He swayed where he stood, his knees about to give out.

"Let's just...head over here for a moment," he murmured.

I laughed when he carried me to the bed, and then sighed when he gently laid me down before curling his body around mine protectively.

"I'm apprehensive," he admitted into the following stillness. "I'm worried mages will breach this territory and I won't be enough to protect you. I'm scared of what I'd become if I lost you. You are everything to me, Jacinta. It would destroy me if something happened to you. I can't be rational where your safety is concerned. I'm not like my brother, always so logical and steadfast.

I can't accept that some things are out of my control, the way Brochan's learned to. I've always been half of something twisted. I could easily turn into the nightmare we're currently fighting. I would burn down the world if something happened to you. I wouldn't apologize for the fallout."

My heart lurched, and I flattened my palm on his forearm.

"I think you and my gargoyle have something in common," I said softly.

"*And your gargoyle and you have something in common,*" Ivy House said. "*Only those worthy of the magic may wield it. That worthiness doesn't just hinge on the ability to deal with an eccentric crew. There is a distinct ferocity in you. Jane culture might've made you squash it down until it was hidden from sight, telling you women should be demure and polite and please others, but it's there. I will drag it out of you kicking and screaming if I must.*"

"*I've risen to the occasion, haven't I? I've been in enough battles by now to prove I can handle it.*"

"*No, you've been in enough battles to prove you can be goaded into action. That's not the same. You are still working through that Jane passivity. Time to stop thinking like a Jane lady and start thinking like an Ivy House lady. Time to stop doing as you're told by weak-*"

*willed morons with fragile egos and too much power. Time to take up a sword and, if someone bothers you, cut off whatever is dangling. The safety of your people and your territory depend upon it. Shrug off the cloak of other people's expectations and rise to your true potential. No one can tear you down if you refuse to let them."*

"I realize that probably isn't easy to hear," Austin said quietly. He must've mistaken my rolling emotions and silence as a reaction to his declaration. Before I could set him straight, he continued. "I'll do anything for you, but I won't hurt you. That magic you possess…there's something off-kilter about it. I know you heard or felt that, too, when it was trying to get you to take it. Unlike me, though, you're light and pure and good, counteracting its effects."

"Ivy House doesn't seem to think so," I replied in a flat voice. "She's urging me to lop off people's dangling bits."

He paused for a moment, and I explained what she'd said.

"Ah," he replied. He snuggled a little closer. "There's another reason I don't want to take that magic," he said darkly. "I need to address the alphas of the other packs as myself. As a shifter, nothing more. Once we're united, I can don the cape and use the superpower. Not before. Because if I do lose myself to the power, I need to make sure someone can take me down. A united pack with you at their helm should be able to handle that."

I blinked my suddenly wet eyes. The extent to which he didn't trust himself—and the precautions he was taking to protect me if he should break—squeezed my heart. I didn't comment, though. I didn't really know what to say.

So I lightened the mood.

"Will your cape be black and a little raggedy, like Mr. Tom's wings?"

His sudden release of breath said I'd been successful.

"Damn it, why did I use that metaphor?" he muttered.

I laughed and ran my hand along his arm where it had snaked around me.

"I just want you to understand where I'm at," he said, kissing my shoulder.

"I do, trust me. If I can find this hidden, very violent ferocity that Ivy House thinks I have, maybe I can temper the crazy of this house and my crew. But now…it's much easier to just walk away."

He laughed as Ivy House piped up again.

*"You think someone without a mean streak can call in a phoenix and a thunderbird? Especially* that *phoenix*

*and thunderbird? Get your head out of your ass."*

"Ivy House is starting to sound like Niamh," I murmured.

*"Well, we do have the same goal: to get your head out of your ass."*

"I really want to move into your place," I told Austin, turning and burying my face into his neck. "It's so serene there. So devoid of a pushy magical house."

*"Pushy? A useless Jane term. You want pushy? Here you go, here's pushy—"*

An electric pulse lit me up from the inside and ballooned out. It wasn't my magic, though. Not directly, anyway. It was coming from the heart of the house, the magic I had essentially awakened. It happened two more times, each time vibrating through me and seeming to signal outward.

I knew where this was going. I knew what Ivy House was doing.

"Oh, crap," I gritted out.

"What is it?"

She was issuing a challenge on my behalf. Her target was the enemy mage and anyone directly connected with him. Given that he was a peon, thankfully, we wouldn't be climbing the ladder too high. They were still mages, though. When—*if*—the enemy mage checked in with his boss and their crew, the challenge would be solidified. The mages would be unable to resist reacting to it.

I was essentially saying, "Come and get me. I'll be waiting."

My chest tightened.

"Where are the others?" I asked with dread. "We have some things to discuss."

# CHAPTER 14

A HALF-HOUR LATER, everyone made their way into the largest sitting room in Ivy House, an archaic sort of space at the western-facing rear of the building. The oversized, clunky furniture faced a central point— an empty one—with the seating spread between large, squatting coffee tables or circular end tables. Heavy drapes lined the windows with a horizontally lined pattern in green and rust. Little tassels dangled from the top.

"When are you going to redecorate this place?" Hollace asked as he took a seat at the end of one of the couches facing the empty focal point.

"When I have two moments to rub together," I responded briskly, worrying a button on my top.

"There is nothing wrong with what is here," Mr. Tom said, bustling in with a tray of sandwiches. He beelined for Hollace and offered him first pick, probably since he'd been the first to follow directions and make himself comfortable. "The office might need a little work to make sure you are comfortable there, miss. That'll help you spend more time in it, I'll wager." He gave me a pointed look. "But otherwise, it is in tiptop shape."

"It's definitely clean." Hollace took a sandwich and then looked around. "And polished. But…"

"It's ugly, right?" Cyra took a seat on the other side of the room, facing the empty focal point and Hollace beyond it. "That's what you were going to say? I think it's pretty ugly. Was the person who decorated this room color-blind?"

"I'll take care of that," Ulric said as he walked into the room, pointing back the way he'd come. "I'm not sure how yet, but I'll…figure something out. Edgar can help."

"I would love to help," Edgar said, walking in behind him. "I have so many ideas how we can incorporate it into the overall aesthetic."

"You have an aesthetic?" Jasper asked, following them.

"Of course. All good gardens have a plan."

"I don't know if we can keep it. That's a question for my mom." Ulric sat on the other end of the couch from Hollace. "She really should be here any day. We can—or she and you can—go through all the connection request stuff just as soon as she's here. Then we can figure out what to do about the thing on the front lawn."

"The thing on the front lawn? What are you guys talking about?" I asked as Niamh came in carrying a cooler.

"Now *that* is going too far," Mr. Tom said, stopping in his distribution of sandwiches to point at the cooler. "We are in a residence. We are not camping or interrogating someone or at some beach somewhere. We have modern appliances to keep things cool."

"Yes, but we don't have a spry butler to quickly grab those things." Niamh sat in the back with her cooler. "This is much faster."

"It's even stained!" he admonished her. "It's an eyesore, if nothing else, and I am plenty fast, thank you very much. I am always at hand before the need, whatever it may be, has even been realized."

"And now ye don't have to be." She pushed up the top slowly, allowing the loud plastic creak to take up several seconds before grabbing out a beer. "Here, Edgar, where is one of yer doilies? I forgot to bring a beer koozie."

"Oh no! No way." Mr. Tom pointed at Edgar. "Do not get any of those godforsaken doilies! I've had just about enough of those." He turned back to Niamh. "Old woman, you are trying to rile me up. I will not stand for it!"

"Okay, okay, settle down." I put out my hands to stop their bickering. "Ulric, what are you talking about? What do you need Edgar's help with?"

"She was otherwise occupied on the way in," Austin said from the seat closest to the focal point. He leaned back and draped an arm over the back of the couch. "I didn't fill her in."

"Yeah, we felt a little too much of that occupation," Niamh said, cracking a beer open. "It seems someone forgot to deaden the link."

My face burned hot. I hadn't even thought about it.

"Whatever. It doesn't matter." I waved it away as the basajaun stooped a little to get into the room and sat in the middle of a love seat. "I'll get to whatever it is in a minute. We have more pressing matters to discuss."

The rest of the crew filed in, and then came Sebastian, his magical mask gone and his expression closed down into one of unease. Kace followed so closely behind him that he'd give Edgar a run for his money in the no-personal-space Olympics. Nessa sauntered in next and smiled as she greeted me.

"Good work back there," she said, stopping. Broken Sue waited beside her. "You nailed the interrogation, and on your first time! That's incredible. I mean, I realize you don't want to make it a habit, but this kind of stuff does come up from time to time. Especially with high-caliber mages who have potentially valuable potions and notes."

Hollace put up his hand. "I would like to participate next time. If I have to come up with a weird party trick, so be it. I hate being left out of the reindeer games."

"It was a good time." Cyra smiled before pushing up her glasses. Then she laughed with delight. "A good time! I wouldn't mind rounding up a few enemies and seeing who can scare the information out of their mark the fastest. I bet I'd win. I really do. Dibs on Nessa, though. She's really good at moderating."

"I would win," the basajaun said. "My hobby is scaring hikers. I am very good at it. I know how humans tick."

"There will be no contests to almost fatally scare people, you guys—" I began.

"The trick is not speed, though," the basajaun continued. "The slow-sneak approach is much better. They sense danger but do not know why. Their head starts to spin."

"Okay, that's great." I counted everyone up. "I think we're all here—"

"Then you build and build until finally…" He burst up to standing, hands curled into claws, teeth bared, and let out a ferocious snarl. His hair puffed up all over his body.

His size and menace and the way his body hair accentuated his obvious threat sent a chill through me. Half of the room visibly shivered. The shifters tensed, their eyes hard.

"Or sometimes, you just let them see glimpses." He shrugged, and his hair flattened. "Just little glimpses here and there through the trees, and they think they are losing their minds. That is the long game. They come back to the mountain and are more watchful. On their guard. Then you stalk them." He sat down again. "There really are several plans of attack that work well. And each causes a different type of fear. For example—"

"Okay, okay." I put up a hand to stop him. "We'll discuss it later, okay? We can all compare notes."

"I call Edgar," Ulric said. "No question. He's a master at *creepy*. He set up that mage like no one could have."

"*Okay!*" I sent a blast of power into the room, stilling everyone. Those who hadn't yet sat took their seats. "Sorry—"

I clamped my teeth together. What was it Ivy House had told me? *Stop thinking like a Jane lady.* And here I was, apologizing for being assertive with my own team. Austin would never do that.

"Right, okay. There are a couple things we need to go over," I said, moving to the focal point of the room.

"First, it seems Sebastian and probably Nessa had some sort of idea in mind of what to do with the enemy mage. Even that the mage or someone like him might be coming. We need to meet and lay everything out in the open so that we're all on the same page. Before that, though, I'll tell you about the wrench Ivy House has thrown into whatever plans some of you might already have."

I told them about her spell, making Sebastian crinkle his brow.

"How was she able to do that?" he asked.

"I have no idea. I doubt she'll tell me. She likes to show me what's possible and then watch me scramble to figure it out. In this instance, though, I think she wants me to rise to the challenge."

"About that..." He squirmed in his seat. Nessa scooted away a little, and I knew I wouldn't love what I was about to hear. "It seems I shouldn't discuss plans with Nessa when in the crystal room."

"Explain," Austin said in a rough tone.

"I knew you'd react to that," Sebastian mumbled. He took a deep breath. "First of all, please know that I've been making schemes for years and years. I know the mage world very well. I know the rules, and when the rules are most likely to be broken—"

"Yes, yes, we're all in awe of your expertise. Please

move on," Mr. Tom said, setting aside the mostly empty tray of sandwiches.

Sebastian blinked for a moment, then complied. "I don't count on loyalty in the mage world, but I do know how to get people to do my bidding. I won't bore you with the details. Let's just say if you offer them something they covet, especially if they can't get it elsewhere, you've got them for as long as you keep offering them that thing."

"Money?" I asked.

He shrugged. "Sometimes. It's certainly always part of the equation. But a chance at being in the winning outfit, the opportunity to double-cross someone who's treated you badly—there are many pressure points out there. Nessa and I are good at finding out which ones make people tick."

"What's your point?" Austin asked.

"We have a network. When I went underground, I hinted that I would be back. I made it known to my people that they'd be rewarded if they remained faithful. Those who leaked the information at that time were killed outright—"

"I like how he does business," Cyra murmured.

He shrugged again. "In the underbelly of magical society, everyone knows the risks of betrayal. Three-quarters of that network is still active. Many have access to the enemy, and all are operating with networks of their own. So my foundation is solid, even after my hiatus."

The room was silent, many nodding. Sebastian went on. "So. Long-term goals." He inclined his head toward Austin. "Bring down the Mages Guild. I can't bring them down by myself. Momar? Probably." He paused for a moment. "Maybe. He's got a helluva setup now. I could probably take him out personally, but the Guild could easily step in and take over his operations. Or someone else might. That serpent has many heads. To fight the Guild, we need another organization equally strong. For that, I'm counting on the unified shifter pack you're planning on setting up, Austin." He flinched. "Steele. Alpha Steele."

"Close one, Sabby," Nessa muttered with a grin.

He didn't acknowledge her. "We need a large force to combat the corrupt Mages Guild. I think, with Alpha Steele leading and Jessie at his side, that would fit the bill."

"And what sort of control would you want after helping set that up?" Austin asked.

Sebastian's expression puckered, and he put his hands out. "I don't want to mess with shifter politics any more than I have to. I just want someone trustworthy and well-intentioned to be in charge—someone who can force the Guild to be a less corrupt organization. There are good mages out there. I'd like to be one of them some day. You're the shifter who can do it, Austin Steele. We all know it. So I'll do whatever I can to help you."

"You seem to do just fine in the shadows," Nathanial said. "Why would you want to mess with the Guild?"

He hadn't heard Sebastian's whole story, and Sebastian clearly didn't feel like going into it now. So he replied, "Revenge, at the heart of it. Or maybe the ability to step out of the shadows and not be assassinated. Take your pick."

"So you're doing this for you?" Nathanial pressed.

Sebastian shrugged. "For me, and for mages like me. Which brings me to my next long-term goal. Jessie needs her own network, one that Elliot Graves is not a part of. I'm hopeful that Ulric's mom"—he glanced at Ulric with raised eyebrows—"can help get that started. Regardless, she needs an army. Alpha Steele will have the shifters. She needs her gargoyles. But she also needs mage allies. And this is where it gets tricky."

"Despite yer efforts," Niamh said, "Jessie is not perceived in the magical world as any sort of threat. I've done the research. She is a curiosity to many and a joke to those with power. We got proof of that earlier this evening. They might've heard she's a powerful mage, but so far, they haven't found anyone to verify that."

"Right…" Sebastian indicated Niamh. "She's right. Jessie is…mostly a joke. *At present.* Mages won't be in a hurry to work with her."

"Not even if you ally with her?" Austin asked.

Nessa shook her head. "Elliot Graves makes for a certain type of ally. Most of the people who'd willingly work with him are bad people. We wouldn't want them for Jessie."

"Except you put a stamp of interest on me," I said. "You basically claimed me in that cave meetup. You heard what that mage said—Momar's going after the survivors. When he catches them, he'll know you favored me."

Sebastian put up his hand. "Yes. Exactly. Those things all lend weight to your perceived power. I made a show of being interested in your power, but then I disappeared. I didn't openly ally with you. That'll hopefully send the right message to the mages who aren't interested in my type of politics. *Those* mages are the ones you need to ally with."

"Which is all well and good, but you hinted that you were Graves in that…session with the enemy mage," I reminded him.

"*Hinted*, yes." Nessa shrugged. "I'm the only one he recognized. Maybe they'll think you stole me from

Graves. If anything, it'll make you notorious."

"And that's a good thing?" Austin asked guardedly.

"It is *a* thing, at any rate," Ulric muttered.

"Jessie is violent in a way mages don't understand," Sebastian said. "That's a very good thing. Then there's the way she has shifters as backup instead of mercenaries. Shifters terrify mages. All in all, she's a mage's worst nightmare—and we need all of them to know it. They'll fear her, but some of them will also flock to her power. That's what we want."

"After her reputation is forged," Nessa said, once again tag-teaming with Sebastian, "we'll let her out into the wild. We'll have her meet various mages and see how those meetings go. I have every expectation that they won't go as planned, but that's fine. We'll figure it out."

"From there," Sebastian said, "we'll start assessing those mages as allies. That's about when I'll finally reveal myself as her partner. Not before. As we said, we don't want to taint her reputation with mine. She's violent and unpredictable, but she has morals. Elliot Graves doesn't. The idea is for her to win people over that I could otherwise never get to. Then, with them and the shifters and hopefully gargoyles, we cut down the Guild and restructure it into a fair and just organization that helps mages instead of extorting them."

I ran my hand down my face. "Okay…let's hit the short-term plans."

"Sure." Nessa gave a thumbs-up. "Switching gears."

"First question…" Sebastian spread his hands. "Why on earth would we turn a dangerous mage loose?"

He didn't look at Austin, but it was clear he was speaking to him.

"Well, here's the situation," Sebastian continued. "No matter what we do here, Momar will see it as an act of war. He'll send more people to collect Jessie for questioning and then end or use her. Pretty much the same as before, except with a lot more hostility. Based on the mage's answers, it seems the shifters will just be collateral damage."

"For the moment," Nessa said.

"We're only talking about the moment, Captain, keep up." His lips quirked, almost a smile. "The original plan was that the mage would make it back to his bosses in a state that would make them extremely nervous. They'd wonder what kind of power this new mage has. She didn't outright kill him, but she messed him up in a way they haven't seen before."

"It won't be enough to get Momar directly in-volved," Niamh said from the corner. "They won't want to admit they failed in collecting her, and also that she had such an effect on their grunt. They'll send a team to collect her next time."

Sebastian and Nessa turned their heads in unison to look at Niamh in the back.

"Well...yes," Sebastian finally said. "Correct."

"And why do we want them to send a team?" Austin asked.

"Yeah, if he never makes it back, they won't know to send anyone else," Ulric said.

"They're not stupid," Niamh replied. "These types of things have a shelf life. It'll take time for them to be sure he isn't returning, yes, but they'll figure it out eventually. If he doesn't make it back, they'll consider him dead. Next time, they'll send in a team to try to kidnap her. If they succeed, they'll just add a few questions to those they were already planning to ask. Like *did you kill our man?* The weird mage and his gal pal are just trying to pinpoint the timing so we can be ready for them."

"Really?" Nessa put up her hands and turned to face Niamh. "His gal pal? I don't get my own nickname?"

"I wouldn't offer her that challenge, if I were you," Jasper said out of the side of his mouth.

"Right," Sebastian said. "They would come anyway. These are the low-level bosses in Momar's organization we're dealing with. They are like the supervisors in a huge corporation where Momar is the CEO. Unlike the higher-level management, who take time to prepare, these tend to react hard and fast if something spooks them. I have no idea why. Regardless, all that taken into account, we could expect them in a couple of weeks or so. Between two and four, really."

"And if we send him back, we can expect they will come almost immediately," I said. "They'll be compelled, thanks to Ivy House."

"Yes, miss," Mr. Tom said, now entering with more refreshments. I hadn't noticed him leaving. "Clearly, the house is tired of waiting for you to embrace your gargoyle. She is going to push the issue."

"Thank you, Mr. Tom, I hadn't realized that," I said sarcastically.

# CHAPTER 15

"WHY WOULD YOU think the mage would return to his bosses without his charge?" Austin asked, wariness still crowding the bonds. "Why wouldn't he try again?"

"Number one, there's no way that mage can keep his head on straight long enough to try again." Sebastian chuckled, and then he started laughing in earnest.

Nessa had to take over. "The basajaun did him in. He's going to have repeats of tonight for a while, like a bad acid trip."

"Yes, I can attest to that," Edgar said, looking out the window. "I'm still not comfortable with crickets. I don't trust them."

"I would win the battle to scare information out of an enemy," the basajaun said. Cyra just shook her head.

"And he'll go back to his bosses because we'll help him along," Sebastian finished. "I don't want to leave anything to chance. I don't want him dallying or for someone else to recognize him and take him out for a past grudge of some kind. As I said, a lot of my network is intact. I have someone waiting just beyond the territory line. They'll pretend to kidnap him, go through the motions of questioning him to make it seem legit, and then botch killing him. They'll stick him on a plane. He'll arrive at his headquarters in a coffin, but he'll arrive alive. It was meant to be a warning that would help spur them to act. Now…it's just safekeeping. A flourish, maybe, to increase her reputation."

"Ye have it all planned out," Niamh said, crumpling her can. "Except we can't have a team of mages running through this territory. If we scramble even a little, we'll lose face with Austin's pack. We can't let that happen."

The room fell into silence, and I could feel the wariness leaking through Austin. He agreed with her.

"Luckily," she said a moment later, "the basajaun can plug that hole for ye. Can't ya, basajaun?"

He stared at her silently, which was kind of a big deal with him. He did like to talk once asked questions.

"Were you able to convince your family to see Jessie?" she prompted him.

"Ah. Yes. They want to meet her, but that does not mean they will issue their support. You will have to show them you would be a worthy part of the family. And then you would need to meet the elders. But it is a good start. Very rarely will they meet outsiders."

"There. See?" Niamh put up her hand. "You've a trip coming up anyway. Draw them away from here, and then we can combat them as messily as we please."

"And why would it be better to scramble in front of the basajaunak instead of this territory?" Ulric asked, hand raised. "Don't we want to impress them?"

"Not to mention we can't inundate the basajaun's family with my troubles." I braced my hands on my hips. "But if they're targeting me, and the magic ensures they can find me, then we can lead them anywhere we want."

"Yeah," Niamh replied. "Anywhere, like the basajaunak's bunch of trees. And then we can battle the low-level mages and show the basajaunak yer power. Otherwise, the basajaunak just see a bunch of muppets milling around saying odd things. They need a demonstration."

"Right..." Ulric drew out the word. "And back to the part where we'd be scrambling in front of people we need to impress?"

"Even when the Ivy House crew scrambles, they make a spectacle out of it," Sebastian said. "We saw it at the meetup. Why wouldn't you want this territory to see that?"

Austin shook his head minutely. "The pack structure thrives off organization. I'm still filling out the ranks. We aren't solid in our hierarchy yet. We're almost there, but I'm hesitant for them to take on mages at this point. Other shifters, mercenaries—even gargoyles—we could handle it. But mages have swept through the shifter communities and wrought horror. Confidence when it comes to mages is currently precarious. I'd rather not poke holes, even small holes, in the territory's confidence. Not if there's an alternative."

"As someone with firsthand knowledge, I agree with that," Broken Sue said, one hand fisted. "I will not hesitate to fight—no one would—but the past is a hard thing to let go of. Defending my home from invading mages again...threatened with losing everything...*again*...." His jaw clenched. "If there were an alternative, it would spare those who aren't yet ready to confront their past."

"They'll have to confront their past eventually," Sebastian said softly. "This isn't a problem that will go away."

"As soon as we're solid as a pack, we'll be training," Austin replied. "As I said, we're almost there. I hadn't realized we'd be confronted with this type of situation so soon."

His stare bored into Sebastian. He clearly wasn't impressed that Sebastian had assumed mages—even just one—would come but had failed to pass on that information. Thank God nothing had gone wrong with the mage's capture.

"Except if we leave the territory, we won't have forces with which to combat the threat," Nessa said. "We can't be sure exactly what will come, but we should expect a handful of decent mages and a crowd of experienced mercenaries or trained ground troops. Sebastian and Jessie are powerful, but they are only two, and one of them isn't very experienced. The shifters count for several fighters each, but still...if we leave the area, we won't have the numbers."

Niamh looked the basajaun's way, something Nessa noticed. Almost on cue, the basajaun spoke. "My family is fierce, and we are the masters of our lands. The mages in our wood would not even see one of us before they were killed. It would be great sport."

His smile stretched, showing his large teeth.

"I also agree," he went on, "that this new family of mine needs to show its strength to the basajaunak. The basajaunak have listened to my stories with great rapture, the younger basajaunak especially. I *do* weave a good yarn. But they have no proof of my claims. Battle is the best place for a demonstration."

Almost everyone nodded.

"With the other basajaunak on our side, the battle

will be nothing," the basajaun went on. "The basajaunak would not even need your help to cut out the threat. But with shifters and mages and gargoyles adding to our numbers, it will be the best way to show our prowess without much danger. The perfect plan."

Nessa stayed unnaturally still, and Sebastian fidgeted. They didn't agree with him. Not wholly, anyway.

I voiced what they hadn't. "Mages can use spells to suss out what lurks in the woods. If a few of their people suddenly went missing, or they saw or heard something to make them nervous, they'd use magic to reveal their attackers."

"Bah." The basajaun waved that away. "They would be dead before they could." He adjusted in his seat. "The only issue is the village elders, I think. They do not tend to have a sense of humor. They do not have patience for the younger basajaunak, like me, who want to get out and see the world." He put his hand on his chest smugly. "I am somewhat rebellious. I left to follow my stars, and I have found my purpose. I felt the calling. That is the only reason they didn't try harder to keep me put. But the others do not have such a strong conviction. They are told they will starve, and they believe this. They do not have stars to follow. They have no guidance. No protection away from their lands."

"But we can offer them protection," Niamh said.

"Have ye mentioned that?"

The basajaun held up his finger. "Yes, and it is part of why they have invited our Ivy House crew for a visit. Once they meet you, they will not be so worried about the outside world. They will be more inclined to venture out, with or without the elders' blessing."

"Except that means we're a threat to the elders," I said.

"Once they meet you, they will understand," he replied, though I didn't see how. "The only issue I anticipate is that the elders might not take kindly to us bringing danger into their lands. On principle, of course. They would see that as a slight."

"And as we all know," Mr. Tom said, "a slight means certain death."

The basajaun shook his head. "I am confident I can lessen the punishment from death to mutilation or a sound beating. It will not be so bad. They can be reasonable."

I now stared with my mouth agape.

"And that is if we do not talk them around," he continued, much too chipper. "Given how easily we will defeat the mages, I see no trouble there."

"I hadn't realized he was prone to overconfidence," Ulric murmured to Jasper.

"I'm not sure if that is a good thing or a bad thing in

this situation," Jasper replied.

"I'd have to agree with them." Sebastian pointed at the gargoyles. "It might not be as easy as you're thinking. I mean, I'm all for getting their help. We probably need it. But I don't want to win a mage fight only to get killed by basajaunak."

The basajaun didn't seem to hear him. "My family has heard stories of the skirmishes we have been in, as I said. I tell them all. They know you walk within a cloud of danger, and yet they still invited you." He leaned back, getting comfortable again. "It will be okay, I think. As long as we follow the rules of the lands and village, the lead basandere should be lenient with any punishments. We cannot help if someone attacks us there, after all. Besides, if the mages do not apply for the right to pass through the lands, it is a basajaunak problem, anyway. We will be tied together in this skirmish, and through it, the basajaunak will get to remember the ways of old. Yes, this is a good plan. I feel it. The stars are guiding us. The timing is too perfect. As long as we do not mention that we knew about the trouble beforehand, I think it will all go smoothly."

Ulric and Jasper's expressions matched mine: lots of grimacing.

It was clear the basajaun had an agenda of his own. He wanted more of his kind to venture out of the lands and to join him on his journey. I couldn't fault him for that. And honestly, it would help us greatly if they did.

However, if we omitted key details from our story to the elders, we'd be lying. If we were caught doing so, it could mean death. Basajaunak were temperamental, prickly creatures. I knew that from my acquaintance with the basajaun. Now he was telling us he was on the younger side, a little wilder and not as much of a stickler for the rules as the rest? What the hell would we be walking into?

"No," I started, "this is just too dangerous—"

"What choice do we really have?" Niamh asked. "We either take a risk with the basajaunak or we stay here. We stand to gain more with the basajaunak than we would here."

"Or we head out to some nondescript place," Nessa said, "with *very* little time to prepare, and hope we're better and more experienced than we think."

"I still do not see much of a risk in my territory," the basajaun said. "A slap on the wrist, maybe, but we have seen worse."

I looked at Austin, who was looking at the basajaun. He swung his gaze slowly to Niamh in the corner before moving on to the mages. Finally, it landed on me, and his eyebrows inched up. He wanted to know what I thought.

I shook my head. I didn't like any of our options. In the past, we'd taken a stand on Ivy House soil, but that was before Austin and I were alphas and had the welfare of the pack to worry about. Taking a stand in some nondescript location wouldn't work, either. It seemed like the best option was the basajaun's lands, a decision made more promising by his obvious confidence.

I swore under my breath, then braced my hands on my hips and turned to look out the window. "We could just kill the trespassing mage. It would buy us some time."

"Not enough," Nessa said.

"I really don't want to take the basajaun up on his hospitality, though," Sebastian murmured. Then glanced at the basajaun. "No offense."

"Miss," Nathanial said, leaning forward with his elbows braced on his knees and his fingers entwined.

"Yes, Nathanial, go. What are your thoughts?" I said.

"We don't want the resident gargoyles to see us…scramble, I think the word was. We certainly don't want them to see us falter. We'll have prestigious cairns coming. Cairns that are used to being the top of the social hierarchy. They will look for ways to diminish your standing so as to keep their perch at the top. If you falter here, it'll affect your standing with them."

"Jesus, you guys aren't making this easy on me." I blew out a breath. "Fine." I turned to the basajaun. "Thank you for your offer. It seems you're giving us a way to help Austin and me both. To help this territory. I only hope it doesn't jeopardize yours."

"Well, then, I guess we'd better get flea spray," Mr. Tom grumbled.

# CHAPTER 16

"MAGICAL SECRECY, PLEASE," Nessa whispered as she and Sebastian made their way to the front door of Ivy House.

He looked behind them to make sure no one else had come out of the meeting room. The others were staying to plan for the trip, but Sebastian and Nessa had been in a hurry to leave. They'd given the excuse of needing to take stock of their supplies before the trip, but truthfully, he had wanted out from under the intense alpha's gaze.

Austin had been shaken to hear what was in store for Jessie. He'd been much more terrifying than usual, and for him, that was saying something.

Sebastian cast them into a soundproof bubble that not even Ivy House could splinter. "You're good," he said. "What's up?"

"Are we going to talk about the puca or what?"

"Talk about Niamh?" he replied. "I can't talk about her. I'm too busy wetting my pants about the prospect of trekking into the basajaunak lands. Did you hear what he said? We're practically going to our deaths. If someone lets slip that the danger we brought was intentional, the basajaunak are going to take offense, and we'll pay with our lives."

"Yeah, and all because of Niamh. She had this whole situation on lock, did you see that?" She pulled a piece of hair behind her ear. "From perfectly orchestrating the interrogation—she clearly knew what spell you were planning, and you didn't discuss that with her—to goading us all into the basajaunak lands. She was one step ahead of this whole situation, and the crazy part? No one realized it. They chose me or Edgar for their torture teams, not the mastermind behind tonight." Nessa shook her head. "She's good, Sabby. Really good. I have a lady crush, but more importantly, I'm worried what this will mean."

"You think she'll read into our plans?"

"Don't you?"

He shook his head as they neared the front door. "She knew all the pieces to this puzzle. We already know she's excellent at putting them together, and also manipulating people. But she doesn't know any of the pieces to the puzzle we're crafting. She can't know, not without the contacts we have, and she doesn't have a network."

"We better hope she doesn't develop one. I should've looked into her details before now. I don't like being surprised. It's easy to assume these people are incapable."

"Just like everyone used to always assume you were incapable."

"Touché. Let's check out that carriage before we go," Nessa said as he opened the front door.

They'd noticed the shiny red carriage sitting on the front lawn when their shifter guards delivered them. It had golden spokes and undercarriage with real gold, by the look of it. Some sort of crest adorned the door, glimmering in the low light, and intricate scrollwork— also gold—decorated the body. He'd tried to stop and take it in earlier, but their shifter guards hadn't given them the opportunity.

"I'm incredibly intrigued about these connection requests," Nessa said. "Like...why would someone send a carriage? No horses or anything, just a random, old-school carriage left on someone's lawn. What is *that* about? Such a strange gift." She paused. "Is that what they all are, gifts? They're basically buying a meeting with her?"

"Must be. Have you seen all the boxes and baskets and all the stuff showing up? There's a ton of it. Ulric just keeps putting it away. He says there's no point going through it until his mom gets here."

"It's like Christmas," she murmured in excitement. "How does he not peek? I would. I'm dying of curiosity."

"Me too. I don't know anything about gargoyles. I'm eager to see how all this plays out. From what Nathanial has said, the cairn leaders are really intense. The whole lot of them are prone to fighting, I think."

"Hello? Battle creature! I wonder if they'll be more intense than the shifters." Nessa was practically giddy.

He shook his head at her. "You have dangerous taste in men, Nessa, do you realize that?"

"Only if I'm the enemy."

"You are often the enemy, though."

"Sure, but they don't know that." She laughed, apparently unconcerned with the dangerous game she was playing.

He was about to speak on it as they stepped onto the front porch, but the sound dried up in his throat.

"What in the holy hell?" she said breathlessly.

Gnomes straddled the golden trellis on the carriage roof. They sat in a row on the driver's bench. They leaned out of the windows. A couple of them even sat on the wheels. A few held shears, others had trowels or garden forks, some had pruning items, and one had some sort of lawn dart. Worse, they all wore identical homicidal smiles below gleaming eyes.

"I can't believe I'm saying this," Nessa said, shivering, "but this is definitely grounds for retiring Edgar. It's mean, and I feel bad, but this… I mean, *this*…" She shook her head. "Should we get one of the shifters?"

"You wound me," he said, starting forward slowly. "I have magic."

Just as slowly, the gnomes moved to disembark the carriage. They were clearly going to try to murder them.

"Ivy House wouldn't let them kill us…right?" Nessa said, readying to do a spell beside him. She didn't have much power, but she more than made up for it with courage.

"I'm guessing, but I've gathered that Ivy House loves to play horrible jokes. I think she tends to take those jokes further than most people think is decent."

"It's certainly horrible. I didn't get why Jessie was so worried about those dolls—"

"Me either."

"—but I get this. I get this deep in my bones."

"We need to start hand-to-hand combat." He descended one step. One of the gnomes slid off the wheel, waiting for its friends or his next step, Sebastian couldn't tell.

"But why?" Nessa stepped down the next step in tandem with him. "Why not fire an attack at them from the porch?"

"Because we need to learn spell work on the fly. Also because there are a lot of them, I'm not sure what works best on homicidal gnomes, and if I get it wrong or miss a few, we're sunk. Consider this practice for when one of the shifters comes at us. Okay, are you ready? In two seconds, we're going to start running, and we need to erect the defensive electrical shield—the one that shocks the enemy when they run into it. We need to get it right, too. I don't want to get my legs chopped off."

"Getting legs chopped off is more than a joke."

"Get them cut up, then. Still terrible."

"Point made." She paused, getting ready. "Go!"

They ran like their lives depended on it. Gnomes jumped from the carriage, way too high to stick the landing and yet somehow managing it. They hit the ground and skittered after them.

Sebastian wasn't sure who started screaming first, him or Nessa. They both worked at the spell, hard to do when they were terrified and sprinting. The sound of metal sliding against metal drew too close, too quickly. At this rate, they'd lose a leg!

"Cast the spell," he said, already out of breath. "Cast the spell!"

She did as instructed. He did the same. But their

work wasn't perfect.

One of the little garden demons slammed into the magic. It bounced off...and then started to cackle as it pivoted and moved around the spell.

"Crap, I didn't think about them going around it," he said. "Why didn't I think about them going around?"

"Probably because you thought the blasted thing would work—Ow!"

"Help is on the way!" they heard. It sounded like Edgar.

It was *not* reassuring.

Nessa staggered and fell into Sebastian, who turned and grabbed her, hustling her along. They were only a handful of steps from the sidewalk that marked the end of Ivy House property. Her leg was bleeding, he noticed, and then a sharp pain grazed his thigh. One of the little devils had thrown a lawn dart at him.

"Hurry!" he urged, working that spell again, and this time, getting it mostly right.

A gnome hit it full on. Sparks blasted out around it, and then the horrible creature jetted backward with a cute little squeal that somehow rendered it more terrifying.

A swarm of bugs materialized into Edgar. "I'll distract them. Get to safety!"

"No, Edgar, come with us. We can make it," Nessa

said, limping toward the sidewalk and yanking Sebastian with her. "We have a spell up. It'll hold."

Another gnome hit the barrier and went flying with a little *eeeeeeee*.

"Nessa—" Sebastian tried to struggle out of her grasp. "Let go. We can't just leave Edgar to fend for himself."

"Oh, it's okay—Ow!" Edgar kicked at a gnome that had just stabbed him in the leg with a garden fork. "They never cut anything off. I just have to get them to the weaponized flowers. I have two that can scratch them up. Don't tell Jessie. I was supposed to wait for the basajaun to make more of them, but these gnomes are really creating a problem. I needed a little backup. The temptation was just too much. Here we go."

He started running, his distinct lope with high knees and hands out in front. He ran to the side, drawing half of the gnomes with him, and the others eyed the barrier warily as Sebastian and Nessa made it to the sidewalk.

Breathing heavily, they watched the leftover gnomes staring back at them. One put a stubby finger to the side of its throat and dragged it across.

"This house is so messed up," Nessa whispered. "*So* messed up."

"Do you think we should go save Edgar?"

She stared at nothing for a moment. "I have no idea how we could."

She had a point. Plus, he had a suspicion the gnomes who'd stayed behind were ready in case they tried.

"Well...he did say they never cut anything off—Oh, look." He pointed at the still-open door. Dolls tottered out with knives and swords, and one had a miniature machete. "How cute—look at its little doll-sized weapon."

"Why are the dolls so cute and those gnomes so terrible?"

"It's one of life's great mysteries."

The dolls ran down the stairs. Some split to the right, hopefully going to help Edgar, and some ran directly at the gnomes waiting just behind the spell's barrier. In a moment, the two factions were fighting, trying to stab or cut. They all took off around the house.

"Come on, the dolls will save Edgar." Nessa plucked at Sebastian's shirt to get him walking. "Just to circle back..."

She paused for a beat as they put distance between themselves and the house. She must've known he'd had to drop the privacy spell when trying to erect the other.

"We're going to have to be careful about Niamh," she whispered. "We can't have her knowing…everything."

Unease settled in his gut. He looked away to the side as he sent out magic to assess danger. "I know."

"You need to only talk to the house when it is something she—it?—can help with. Like now."

He took a deep breath, feeling something constrict within him. Regret.

"I know," he said again, and thankfully, she let the matter drop.

# CHAPTER 17

NERVOUSNESS ATE THROUGH my middle as we pulled into the motel parking lot. The tiny town we'd elected to stay in sat at the edge of a natural forest preserve near California's coast. Hiking trails criss-crossed the outskirts of it, open to people who wanted to marvel at some of the oldest and tallest trees in the world. Beyond that, deep in the thick of the preserve, lived the basajaun's family.

We'd just let the basajaun off at the trail we'd use tomorrow. He would go now to meet them and prepare them for our arrival the following day.

I blew out a breath as Austin parked. He turned off the engine and looked over at me.

"No," I said.

"No?" he asked.

"No, I'm not good. I figured you'd ask."

He nodded, studying me silently.

I looked away, out the window. "I know I've asked this a couple of times by now, but I'm going to ask it again. Was there any other way?"

"You were in that meeting, same as me. We didn't have a lot of options. The basajaun is confident his people can handle it."

"If they don't take offense at a random slight and try to kill us all," I said, feeling my nerves pulse. "This is a no-win situation, Austin. There are just so many risks. What were we thinking?"

"We were thinking that the people in our territory aren't ready for a magical battle like this." He put his hand over mine, resting in my lap. "I'll grant you, this situation isn't ideal. Not even close. But we can handle it. The basajaun will help navigate his family, and hopefully, they'll help us defeat them. Worst case, they can help us get set up to make a stand. If they don't want to get involved, they'll be able to disappear into the trees. They won't be in the crossfire."

I rested my head against the seatback and nodded. "Thanks. I needed that pep talk. Again. I'm just...nervous."

"There are going to be a lot of hard decisions in our future. It's good to keep talking about them, keep affirming that we're doing the right thing."

He squeezed my hand as Mr. Tom appeared beside my window.

"How was the spread in the jet, miss?" He opened

my car door. "I noticed that you helped yourself quite a bit. I made sure to have a little bit of everything for you in there. All the snacks you could hope for. As soon as you and Austin get your winery underway, I'll keep that stocked as well. Flying in luxury, that's the only way to do it."

I brushed off my misgivings so they didn't spread to the crew and stood from the car. "Great, Mr. Tom, thanks."

"Did ye consult Elliot Graves before you stocked the jet?" Niamh asked as she ambled by. "Because there weren't any gifts."

The first time we took a jet, Mr. Tom had thought the company we used would provide snacks and refreshments. He hadn't realized we were supposed to bring our own. I'd been so excited for a private jet and all the little perks that I hadn't been able to contain my disappointment when there were no actual perks. Besides no lines or security, obviously.

Then, when we got to the meetup, Elliot (a.k.a. Sebastian) had supplied more snacks than one person could possibly consume. He'd even included baskets of thoughtful gifts. Mr. Tom had been wounded ever since.

"The only gifts people really need is the gift of your silence," he told Niamh as I moved around to the rear of the black sedan that had transported us here from the small airport.

"Like I said," she replied, "there weren't any gifts on the jet."

"Here, let me do that, miss." Mr. Tom took my place in front of the trunk as Austin walked back toward the other black sedans parking behind us. "Actually, first let me go check in for everyone. One thing at a time."

I removed myself to the curb in front of a little grassy knoll. Car trunks were opened, but nothing was removed, since we didn't have our rooms yet.

The small group of shifters, about a dozen in all, fanned out immediately, looking around. They'd all been told about Sebastian's second identity. He wouldn't wear his magical mask here. We were trying to cut down on the lies and omitted truths we were working with.

Ulric joined me as he slipped his phone into his pocket. "My mom took a detour. Well...another one. Or a third? I can't keep up." He sighed. "Sorry about that. I really thought she'd get to Ivy House at least *near* the date she'd said."

"It's probably for the best, since we now have our own detour." I indicated the quiet street. "Though after seeing that carriage, I'm interested in what else has come in."

"Yeah, the carriage." He shrugged and shook his head at the same time. "I have a lot of questions about that carriage. How'd they get it there? It looked brand new, so they clearly didn't drive it. No horse poop, either. *Clearly* didn't drive it. Why weren't we alerted that someone was on the property to drop it off—"

"I asked Ivy House about not alerting me. She said that I was busy learning how to be a gargoyle, and that was more important—it was when we were with the enemy mage."

"Be that as it may, the main question is, why a carriage? It must signify something. Is the cairn calling you royalty and giving you a symbol of that or something? I could see royalty of old riding in a carriage like that."

"Will your mom know any of that?"

He waved his hand through the air. "Oh, yeah, definitely. And if she doesn't, she'll make a bunch of calls to figure it out. Don't worry about that. In the meantime, though, it has piqued my interest."

"Maybe that's the actual goal—to be unique. To stand out."

"Maybe so." He looked off down the street. "Quaint, huh?"

The tiny strip of town was half the length of O'Briens. A couple of store signs jutted out over the sidewalk. Buddy's Auto Repair sat beside a gas station. A burger joint and some sort of café seemed to encompass the downtown eateries, and a dive bar lurked in the middle. Other than that, there didn't seem to be much.

"Yeah," I said, breathing in the fresh scent of trees. I crinkled my nose. "Is it just me, or does this town smell like incense?"

"Not just you." Ulric inhaled as well before glancing at the sky. "We bought out all the rooms in town, right?"

"Yeah. And we'll still have to double up. There were a couple of other places we could've stayed with more accommodations, but the basajaun said this was the closest entry point to their home. It's only for one night, though."

Ulric shifted a little, back to looking down the strip of town. "I'm not so excited about the odds of this going right."

I bit back an honest response and instead said, "It'll be good. The basajaun is confident."

"Yeah," he said noncommittally. "Do you get the feeling, though, that he might be a bit younger among their kind than you initially thought? And…you know…a bit less mature in his thinking? I mean, I can't tell his age or anything, and from the things he says, it sounds like he's been alive awhile, but I'm getting the impression that his species is longer lasting than I originally thought, and he isn't so far up that ladder."

It had occurred to me, yes. I'd talked it over with Austin at length.

"I think he just has his own agenda," I said, hedging. "I think he wants to lead the younger crowd out into the world. Or who knows, maybe he *is* following his stars back here. Maybe this is all meant to be. I honestly don't know. But he *is* confident, whether that attitude is logical or intelligent or not, and it *is* our best bet, as much as it pains me to say so."

"Take it as it comes."

I chuckled. "That's about right, yeah. And if it comes out of the trees with puffed hair and snarls, I'll take it at a run and hope to get away."

He laughed. "You know, it's funny, but I'm actually more nervous about the basajaunak than I am about those mages. That mage we caught in Alpha Steele's territory wasn't much of anything."

"He was the muscle. He wasn't supposed to be much of anything. Can you imagine going up against someone like Sebastian?"

Ulric's brow pinched. He didn't comment.

"These mages won't be of his caliber," I said, "but there will be more of them. They'll be experienced, and they'll bring their ground crew. Sebastian isn't one hundred percent certain about what we should expect, but his ears on the inside apparently told him what to look out for. He's nervous about it, even with the possible basajaunak aid. Don't lose sight of the danger here. We're going to be surrounded by it constantly." I paused for a beat. "This isn't my ideal getaway."

Ulric laughed again. "You're right. Maybe I'm just focusing on one big bad at a time."

"Wise. I should be doing that."

"Alpha." Nathanial walked up and stood beside me, watching a car move slowly down the street. "They're heading in." He motioned for Ulric to move that way. "Help with the bags."

"Yup." Ulric started off, but Nathanial didn't follow.

"A word?" he said.

He believed this plan was a good idea. Most of the crew agreed. I was the one who had the most doubts. And Austin. And now Ulric. Mr. Tom was mostly just put out he'd have to sleep in the woods.

"Sure. What's up?"

"I know you aren't used to any of this. You should know, though, that if we were meeting gargoyles and not basajaunak, they'd *expect* you to bring the fight to them. They'd *expect* to see how you handled it and, in so doing, handled them." His wings fluttered a little. "If Ulric's mother ever shows up, she can hopefully fill you in on the details, but I thought I might point that out, since we'll need to be dealing with everything soon. Maybe treat this as practice for what's to come."

As Ulric said, one big bad at a time.

"Thanks. I will," I said.

"I'd also like to say that I am honored to be part of your circle. Not because of what you are, but because of who you are. I believe in your leadership. Whether or not you succeed, I will remain by your side until the bitter end. You have my oath."

My eyes got a little misty, and I put my hand on his shoulder. "Thank you for saying that, Nathanial. It means a lot."

He nodded, stayed until I took my hand back, and then turned to help the others. I watched him for a moment, saw his long wings dusting his ankles, before I took myself over the berm and to the sidewalk. When in doubt, head to the dive bar.

The bar halfway down the street still somehow smelled like incense. It wasn't until I entered that I realized I didn't have a handbag, money, or someone with me to hold either. Luckily—or unluckily, as the case might be—it wouldn't be long before someone from the crew came to find me. Hopefully, they'd have money. *I just flew on a private jet, but I can't buy a beer.*

I barely noticed the dingy interior or blinking lights

from an old-style jukebox in the corner. The high-back seats were mostly vacant, and a bored bartender flicked the channels on a box TV strapped into the upper corner over the bar.

He lowered the remote and glanced at me when I sat. My chair leaned dramatically to the left, threatening to come apart and topple me out.

"Bud, please. Light. Bud Light," I said, clutching at the bar and righting myself. "Or Coors, if you don't have Bud. They all taste the same to me."

Without a word, he went back to messing with the TV before finding a baseball game and throwing the remote aside. He leaned over the fridge as Austin's large frame filled the doorway. The patrons down the bar, a few guys sitting on their own and watching TV or messing with their phones, glanced over. Two hunched a little more and went back to what they were doing. The third stared, his elbows coming up to rest on the edge of the bar.

Austin pretended not to notice, though I could feel his swirling aggression at what was on the verge of becoming a challenge. He took the chair beside mine before his body tilted my way. His chair groaned.

He looked down as he stilled, hands braced on the bar like mine.

I laughed. "Don't bother changing seats. Mine does

it too. They probably all do. Just be careful."

The bartender dropped a coaster in front of me before setting down the beer. He paused, looking at Austin with the same bland expression he'd used on me.

"Same as her," he responded, bracing his elbows on the bar, probably also to keep from toppling.

"You have money, right?" I murmured. "Because I didn't bring any."

He carefully reached around to his back pocket and pulled out his wallet. I stifled a laugh at his delicacy.

"Cheery place," he said after he'd laid a twenty on the bar.

"Yeah. Matches my mood."

"Need a little space?"

"Are you offering to head out and give me some alone time?"

His body tensed, and a swirl of emotions filtered through the bond. "If you'd like."

"But you wouldn't go far."

His gaze was piercing, and I knew he was trying to read me. I kept my emotions as stagnant as Sebastian did when he turned into Elliot Graves.

"I'd go far enough," he replied.

I put my hand on his forearm. "I don't need space from you. I was just seeing what you'd say."

He took a sip of his beer. "I would give it to you,

though, if you needed it. And if you were inside our smoothly running territory, where I knew the borders were secured, I'd leave you to your own devices. Here, though, with the threat and that douche down the bar..."

I let a smile bloom and leaned toward him to rest my cheek on his shoulder. "I know. I also know that if you did walk away and leave me to my own devices, Mr. Tom would be skulking around somewhere, ready to sound the alarm if anything should happen. And if I were in a bar? Niamh would come in and claim a seat at the other end, telling me that was space enough."

"She was on her way here when I stopped her. She's currently waiting for the all-clear."

I laughed, my mood lightening.

"Do you mind it?" he asked after a moment. "All the people around you all the time? It seems like you're never alone. Even in your bedroom, you're not alone. Not with the house listening or Mr. Tom liable to walk in at any time. Does it bother you?"

I shrugged, back to leaning on the bar. "I never really thought about it, honestly. But...no, I guess it doesn't. You have to understand, I was alone a lot during the twenty years of my marriage. My ex worked all the time. *All* the time. I had Jimmy when he was younger, but he'd go to bed early, and I'd be alone.

When he got older, he started sticking to his room or going out with friends. Arguing with Matt—my ex—about getting him to spend more time with us got old, so I stopped trying. In the end, it was just me. It was fine—I mean, it was my life. I accepted that. But...I guess I never really felt valued or cared for. I did the house stuff, and I got to see Matt when he was available. I cramped Jimmy's style when I got too lonely. So now..."

I shrugged again.

"It's nice to be looked after, you know?" I said. "It's nice to have Mr. Tom fawning over me or Niamh saving me a seat at the bar. It's nice that Edgar goes out of his way to ask about meals, even though he can't relate. It's nice to have everyone hanging around that big house, doing their own thing but always up for a chat. And when no one is home, if that ever happens, I still have Ivy House to keep me company. I'm not alone anymore."

I paused and took a deep breath before going on.

"Then there's you. I'm guessing I must have been a saint in a past life, burned at the stake, and karma is finally kicking in. You cook for me, and you refuse to let me help because you know I don't like it. You value me and go out of your way to show it..." I tried to blink away the tears. "I've never had that. Even when he was courting me, Matt was never like that. No one else ever was. I've never had a man make it his personal duty to ensure my happiness. Like it was his job. Like it was his *favorite* job."

He wiped the tears away from my cheeks with his thumb, looking at me intently.

I finished voicing my thoughts, wanting him to hear it. Wanting him to know that his treatment wasn't taken for granted.

"If I ever pissed you off enough that you stormed out, I know you wouldn't go far. You'd sit outside somewhere, in the rain if you had to, mad as hell but still concerned about my safety. Just like you would've left here a moment ago because I asked it of you...but stayed close by in case I needed you." I wiped another tear. "I feel more than valued with you. I feel cherished. And no matter how crappy things get, I thank my lucky stars that I've ended up in this life with you. With all of you. I feel like this is where I've always been meant to be, weird crew and sulky house and all. It took me getting to midlife to finally follow my stars, and I'm so glad I did."

I wiped away more streaks of wetness on my cheeks, smiling at him. "You probably didn't expect to have to unpack quite so much baggage with that answer, huh?"

He was watching me, his elbows braced on the bar

again. "It *is* my favorite job, Jess. One I covet. As far as the other... You're worth it. All of it. You give me a reason to be my best, and it feels good to do that...for you."

"Stop being sappy." I wiped my cheek with the back of my hand and then leaned into him. "I love you."

"I love you too. I want you to know...the mating was chosen for us, essentially. We gave in to it, but not until we were half pushed in the right direction. But if I were a Dick, and you were a Jane, I would still choose you. I'd choose you as a man chooses a woman. If I weren't so daft, with so much baggage of my own, I would've known it the first time I met you. I would've asked you out on a date right then."

"It would've been too soon."

"Okay, well...then I would've gotten shot down." He leaned his cheek against my head. "But it wouldn't have changed how I felt about you. I wish it didn't take me so long to realize it so you could've known it was me wanting this, not the attraction of our beasts."

"I do know that," I whispered. "I feel it."

A pulse of magic flowed over my skin and along my scalp before seeping in. Once there, it pulsed a second time. Then a third. And settled into an unmistakable, horrible hum.

The implications were clear.

*War. War. War.*

"Crap," I said softly, my heart starting to hammer.

Ivy House's expectation rose. My gargoyle thumped solidly within me, calling the darkness. Throbbing with magic.

They were coming. I could feel it. I could feel the danger rising. My first instinct was to get to my people, to prepare. But we weren't in a defensible place yet, and there was no point in hurrying. The basajaun was expecting us tomorrow, no sooner. I didn't dare go when not protected by the invitation, especially when I couldn't explain why we were in a rush.

"What's the matter?" Austin asked, suddenly tense.

I shook my head, getting a hold of myself. "The countdown has begun." I straightened up. My hand shook as I reached for my beer. "Apparently, I'll be a living clock when it comes to this challenge. When Ivy House wants to make a point, she really makes it." After a swallow, I set the bottle down carefully and smoothed back my hair, clutching on to logic. "We have some time. This is just the beginning. The magic announcing that they've gotten our message and will rise to the challenge. They'll have to organize, travel…"

I didn't mention that their organization would be hurried because of the magic, or that they obviously had private jets and transportation at their disposal so they wouldn't dawdle. We still at least had a few days, *minimum.*

He reached out and took my hand. "At least we know. We're not left guessing."

"Silver lining."

His presence was like a blanket of assurance. "It's too late to head into the basajaun lands," he said.

"Too early, you mean."

"Too late in the afternoon, too early for our rendez-vous."

"Right, gotcha," I muttered.

He squeezed my hand. "What do you say we give Niamh the all-clear, let her and the guys come in here for a little respite before the storm, and watch her handle that douche down the bar? It could be a fun distraction."

"I'm definitely game for a distraction."

"Well, in that case, when the fun has worn off here, I'll find another means of distraction for you back at the hotel."

A shiver ran through me. "Motel. Don't expect any-thing fancy."

"Right. Motel. As long as it has a bed, I don't care if it's a shack." He reached around the other side to grab his phone.

"Don't tell Mr. Tom I said so, but the spread on the

jet was a little overboard," I said as he pulled it in front of him. "We barely had room to put down plates or glasses with how much he'd spread all over the place. Half of it fell on the floor when we hit turbulence."

"That's between you and him. I definitely don't want to say anything and have him panic. The last time he did that, he offered you chocolate-covered Ex-Lax. That's the last thing you need before going hiking."

"Ugh. I hadn't thought about the bathroom situation. Do we dare hope the basajaunak have running water?"

"They definitely have running water. It runs all the way down the mountain and through the valley. They call it a stream."

"Cute."

"Sometimes it pools into…a lake."

"Yeah. Got it. Thanks."

"And sometimes, you'd better dig a hole, because I doubt they'll let you contaminate their water source."

"On second thought, a little space might be nice. From just you, though. Go ahead and call the others in. You can go."

He laughed and called Niamh. She would have a new playground for the night.

✧　✧　✧

THE NEXT MORNING, we entered the preserve through a tiny trail with no sign. The trailhead was about a mile away from the motel.

"Have we figured out what we should call the basajaun?" Ulric asked as we traveled in single file.

Customary to shifter protocol, the shifters took the front and rear. Broken Sue, the strongest besides Austin, took the rear, and Kace led in front. Austin stayed behind me, protecting me over the pack because he worried I was in the most danger.

The Ivy House crew walked within their ranks without any real formation. There was no point in trying to force organization on them. If something happened, they'd all react unexpectedly, I was sure.

"'Basajaun' for now," I said with a shrug, watching the green and brown grasses to either side for snakes. It was probably a little early for them to be out, but you could never be too sure.

"But, like...they're all basajaunak," Jasper said. "What do we call the others?"

"The females are basandere," Hollace said. "So there's two names for us to use."

"'Basajaun' for now," I repeated. "I assume they'll introduce themselves."

The trail turned downward. Not long afterward, our surroundings started to change. Ferns and other vegetation dotted the way, and the redwoods crowded in closer, standing like mammoths, silent and serene. The temperature dropped, cool now underneath the great branches jutting out way into the sky.

"Oh, look."

I turned to see Edgar step out from the path. He bent over a patch of clover blanketing the ground.

"I am excellent at finding four-leaf clovers," he said. "Give me long enough, and I will find them all."

"What time scale are we using, here? Is it *long enough* in relation to your quest for the perfect doily," Nessa asked, "or your ability to choke a yard with flowers?"

Ulric started to laugh.

"Would you come on, Edgar?" Mr. Tom said. "You're holding us all up. There will be plenty of time to find a clover when we're…wherever we are going."

Edgar straightened and hoisted his pack a little higher on his back. We all had food and supplies and clothes, but he had merely sweats and a cooler of blood. He didn't trust the animal resources and had decided to bring his own. I didn't ask where he'd gotten it. It wasn't something I'd ever want to know.

We walked farther along the trail, deeper into the redwoods. Moths and insects danced in the stray rays of sunshine over the ferns. Birdsong floated through the chilled air.

One of the large trees hulked beside the trail, over fifteen feet in diameter.

"I think this is it," I said, looking up its reddish-brown trunk to the top—how far up it was, I couldn't be sure. It crowded the light in comfortable stillness. A hush lay heavy around us all, almost like the trees were keeping the peace within the wild. Like they were as sentient as the basajaunak themselves. "A large redwood kissing the trail—isn't that what the basajaun said? We're supposed to communicate to them through it, letting them know we're here?"

"Sure, they know we're here," Niamh said, looking up as well. "Edgar has been tramping through the grass and brushing branches the whole time—"

"Me too," Jasper said. "I swatted a few fern leaves out of the way."

"You kicked them," Ulric accused him.

"And kicked them, yeah."

"Touching the tree is just overkill, like," Niamh said.

"It's what he wanted us to do." I laid my hand on the bark and infused the trunk with a slight vibration. The basajaun had said that would signal the basajaunak that I was in their territory and wished for an audience. Though Niamh was right—they surely already knew of our presence. They could sense life through all manner of activity in the wood, not just a single tree.

Austin placed his hand next to mine because he was the leader of his pack. He didn't have any magic to add, but the basajaun hadn't seemed to think that would be a problem. Then again, he didn't think any part of this visit would be a problem, including the near certainty of an attack by enemy mages and their crew of trained soldiers. Hopefully, a random basajaun wouldn't happen by, see an alpha, and decide it was a fine time for a challenge.

"It's a little unsettling that we really have no idea how their culture works," Austin whispered, pulling his hand away. We continued along the path.

"It is, yes," I replied. "It really is. But I've thought that since first meeting the basajaun. You at least know the rules of engagement."

"I know the rules for meeting *one* of them. I don't know anyone who's been in their home, or even met more than one at a time. This will be…enlightening."

"What I don't get is that he's supposed to be some rule breaker, right?" Ulric said, looking back at us. "He left his people, but the other youths still live in the elders' shadow or whatever. But there have obviously been other basajaunak who've moved away from their homes. How else would Alpha Steele, Kingsley, and other shifters know how to deal with them?"

"Maybe the cultures are different, depending on where they're from. The others could be from places where it isn't so strange to leave," Hollace said from behind us. "I've noticed that the basajaun—the one we know—doesn't share a lot of information about himself and his kind."

"Noticed that, did you?" Ulric replied sarcastically. "We don't even know the dude's name."

"Maybe keep that chatter to a lower volume, Miss Jessie," Edgar called up. "You're making my friend Sebastian very nervous. His heartbeat is going very fast."

"If you weren't watching the vein in my neck so closely, it probably wouldn't be moving so quickly," Sebastian responded. "But I agree with him, Jessie. Again. It's becoming a habit, apparently, my agreeing with him."

"You're done for, bud," Hollace said. "Absolutely done for."

A musty earthiness drifted through the air, as though everything were permeated with the bark of the trees. Nathanial was in front of me in line, so I rested my hand on his shoulder to keep my balance and closed my eyes as I breathed in deeply. One breath, two. The quiet around me, the serenity, calmed the beast inside. Calmed the fear of the terrible hum from the challenge that now resided deep within. I asked Austin if he felt the same way.

"No," he replied, "but my animal isn't natural to this type of climate."

"The alpha is hinting at a vacation to the Arctic, Miss Jessie," Ulric said with a laugh. "I'll sit that one out, if you don't mind. It can be your Jane honeymoon, and the shifters can be your protection."

Nathanial started, "I do—"

"The wilderness is calmed here," Niamh said, interrupting him. "It is protected. By the basajaun, I imagine. At present, we must be too. Ye can feel it in the air. In the hearts of the trees."

I felt my eyebrows climb before I looked back at Austin in surprise. I'd never heard Niamh talk like that. Maybe I'd never heard her completely in tune with her animal before. It felt like good news, though.

Austin's emotions rolled through the bond.

"What's the matter?" I asked quietly.

"If she feels protected, then the two of you aren't just responding to the natural habitats of our beasts," he murmured. "Given that I don't feel protected or at peace, I can only imagine I'm being singled out."

"What do you mean? You think they'll challenge?"

"It's a distinct possibility. If they do, get clear. It isn't your fight."

"Why do you guys keep assuming I can control what I do?"

"Treat it like a challenge."

I didn't remind him that there was a reason I never went to his challenges. Seeing him attacked was a sure way to losing my senses and freaking the hell out.

✧  ✧  ✧

AFTER ANOTHER HOUR of hiking, we were immersed in the redwoods. Clover, ferns, and moss covered the ground to either side; a carpet of it wound between the enormous redwood bases. Occasionally, one of the huge trees lay on its side, its roots higher than I was tall. Within them lay tangled brush and fallen branches. If we didn't have a trail to follow, we'd be hard-pressed to get through.

Every so often, I gently slid my fingers across the bark of a tree or ran my hand through ferns or bushes to help the basajaunak keep track of us. Not that I really needed to—more of us than Jasper were getting bored at this stage and slapping the leaves of ferns or hitting a branch reaching too close. Someone in the back must've bent a reaching branch and then let go, smacking the face behind. Their feet stomped with the small tussle that followed.

"So this is all their territory?" I asked, careful not to

step on a clover patch, or Edgar would give me a stern talking-to about minimizing his chances to find that special four-leaf. I'd heard the talk three times now.

"I imagine so," Austin replied, his tone a little gruffer than usual. While I still felt nothing but serenity, he seemed to be experiencing something entirely different. His wariness and aggression pumped through the bonds.

"In other situations, how would you know if you were on their land?" Nathanial asked.

"When you smell them, you make your way out of the area as quickly as possible," Austin replied. "Or you stick to the towns."

"And you must've smelled them as soon as you got onto the hiking trail, right?" I asked. "The basajaun used it yesterday, after all."

"Exactly. Normally, I wouldn't enter the trail. I wouldn't be walking in this wood. I'd go around. The exception would be if I were trying to find them, and then I'd go in a ways before waiting for them to come to me."

"What if it was a long wait?"

"I'd either wait or I wouldn't. That's how it works."

"A lot of bloody effort," Niamh said.

Austin didn't respond, which was as good as an agreement.

Half an hour later, I felt it. Tingles erupted along my spine and crowded the base of my neck. An itch grated between my shoulder blades. We were being watched.

Immediately, the bonds were lit with emotional turbulence. My team sensed the presences. A moment later, I felt Broken Sue and Kace's emotions as well, which meant only one thing.

My gargoyle was feeling the pressure and pushing to the surface.

# CHAPTER 18

"LET'S ALL KEEP it cool," I said as a pulse of magic erupted from me.

*Prepare.*

"Damn it, gargoyle," I grumbled. "*Keep it cool.*"

Austin put a hand on my shoulder, stopping me. Nathanial had already stopped ahead.

"Anyone see moving foliage?" Cyra called. "I didn't see any."

"None."

"No."

"Not here."

"Okay, then," she said. "We can assume it's not a game. Let me know if I should burn it all down, Miss Jessie."

I closed my eyes slowly. Could we not all stay chill *one time*? "It's fine. Just wait," I told her, looking forward through the trees.

The trunks of the old redwoods were mostly bare until quite a ways up, past the canopy, where they could finally grab some sun. There weren't many other types of trees within their ranks able to survive in the muted light. Ferns and similar plants were too small and low to hide a basajaun. Either they were hidden behind trunks or they'd be out in plain view. I didn't see any of them, not one, but I distinctly felt like I was being watched.

"Excuse me," Sebastian said from behind me. "Excuse me. Sorry. Sorry, alpha, excuse me." He worked to my side, his eyes downcast. "We've got seven, all told. I'll show you the magic."

His spell was simple, elegant, and incredibly effective. I felt rather than saw the various life forms spread out around us. There were other animals within the spell, but given the size differences, it was easy to tell which were the basajaunak.

We were surrounded.

"Well, that's terrifying," I mumbled.

"I thought so," he replied.

"I, too, am more than a little uneasy," Nessa called up.

I moved around Sebastian to Austin and pointed out their locations to him. The magic had allowed me to feel them, plain as day, but I still couldn't see them with my eyes.

Austin just nodded and put his hand on my hip, pulling me in close. I could feel Kace and Broken Sue at either end of our group pushing the Ivy House crew together. The other shifters stepped out to the right or left, guarding their people as a unit, even though we didn't need to be guarded. With the power we had amassed, it really should be the other way around, but they probably worried about our ability to keep calm.

"This is a lesson in patience, then," Niamh grumbled. "Well, I fail. Come out, would ya? We obviously know yer there. She's pointed out each of ye."

Austin's hand tightened around me, but he didn't tell me to silence Niamh.

A moment later, a female—a basandere—stepped forward. Hidden one moment, she was clearly visible the next. Their magic was something else.

I gauged her height as about the same as our basajaun, but she lacked his girth. Hair covered her body like his, but with parts in intricate braided designs down her flank or across her stomach. She had a cloth draped around her hips and hairy bulges for breasts on her chest.

"Hello," she said. "You are in our territory."

That would sound pleasant enough if not for the growl riding the words. It would be a wonderful time for the basajaun—*our* basajaun—to show up to the party.

The rest of the basajaunak in this group stayed hidden, even though we clearly knew their locations.

"We're here by invitation," Austin said smoothly. "We seek passage and to reconnect with a member of our team."

She considered us for a moment, looking down our line. "You have a lot of powerful shifters in this team."

"Yes. This is my mate." He inclined his head toward me. "Our mating bond is very fresh. I need to make sure she's well protected. These are known to be dangerous lands."

The basandere studied him for a moment before shifting her focus to me. When she looked back at Austin, she said, "We have not had a shifter with so much power come through here before. And you have another alpha in your midst." Her eyes skimmed to Broken Sue.

"He was *once* an alpha. Now he is my beta."

"That does not negate his power."

Austin didn't respond. I hoped to hell that didn't mean it was my turn to do the talking. I was anything but smooth in stressful situations.

Her eyes traveled the rest of the crew, sticking often. They came back repeatedly to Cyra and Hollace before settling on Nathanial.

"Three alphas," she said. "This one of a different breed."

There was a beat of silence, and I knew that this time, it was my turn to speak.

"He's *my* beta," I told her. "And I don't have a clue what I'm doing, so you're safe there." The thumbs-up I flashed was as stupid as it was overkill.

She didn't study me. She barely looked at me. It was probably the thumbs-up.

Instead, she took in Sebastian, who was hunched at my side, staring at his feet. "Four," she said.

"She's looking at you, bud," Hollace muttered.

"I sure hope you don't mean me," Sebastian replied.

The basandere's brow furrowed, and her head tilted just slightly. She didn't know what to make of that. Clearly, she'd never come across an alpha who A, didn't know he was an alpha, and B, didn't want any notice at all.

Her gaze zipped back to Hollace, then Cyra, then Niamh, where it lingered a while longer. She didn't say five, but her pause was just as long. She was clearly sizing Niamh up and having some trouble doing so.

Finally, she speared me with her gaze. All the other basajaunak stepped into visibility, and thankfully, one of them was our basajaun.

"We have not invited anyone into our home for many generations," she said. "The last time resulted in a death of our family. We have not risked it since."

I tried to hide my sigh of relief. Our basajaun hadn't said anything about past visitors causing trouble, but he *had* prepped me with a response to the we-don't-have-a-lot-of-visitors thing.

"I understand. You're in no danger from us. While we're here, we will protect your lands as our own. We don't know much of your culture, but we hope to learn quickly and help in any way we can."

The rest of our group nodded their assent.

The basandere looked at Austin again. "You are not the alpha of these lands. You do not rule here."

"I rule my people and my people only," he replied. "That is specific to the shifters in this group. Jessie Ironheart is the alpha of her...crew. I will defer to your dominance, as will she. In return, I would ask that you allow me to govern my people. If there is any slight or fault, take it up with me. I'll handle any punishments."

"As far as you are concerned, that is agreed. However..." Her gaze shot back to me again. It was like a physical presence this time, pushing against me. "*He* is of your...crew, is this right?"

I looked at Austin in confusion and then caught movement out of the corner of my eye. The basajaun— our basajaun—was indicating himself.

"Ah." I nodded. "Yes, he is. His choice."

"And you claim alpha of him?"

Deer in the headlights.

There was a whole bunch of emotions filtering through the various bonds, and they were all different. Clearly, everyone thought I should handle this a certain way, and none of them seemed to agree. Super.

I homed in on our basajaun, but he was as serene and complacent as could be. Not helpful.

I grimaced and just spoke the truth as I knew it. I'd never been very good at lying. "I think that's my role. Alpha, I mean. But I'm more of a team player. We respect each other and work together. I can do things like tell Cyra not to burn down the forest, but if she's left to her own devices and torches our enemies...well, I should've known better than to leave her to her own devices. If I tell the basajaun—or the shifters—not to kill people who have been subdued, and he randomly drop-kicks someone off a cliff...I'm happy for the apology. We all make mistakes, after all. But they wouldn't disrespect him—or you—on purpose. He's a valued member of our team. He's one of us, and we're one of...him, I guess. We'll do right by you with his guidance."

I suddenly had a thought and held up my finger. My magic pulsed, and I hoped I had time to meditate out here so I could figure out how to control those pulses.

"If he tells us to do something that turns out to be a

K.F. BREENE

practical joke, please know that we didn't mean it. That's his bad, not ours. I know when to stop his jokes in *our* culture—the ones that would probably give someone a heart attack—"

"Only partly true," Sebastian muttered.

"—but I have no idea in yours. So...I'm going to throw him under the bus for that. I don't want to die because of a joke."

Dang it! I got the furrowed brow and head tilt. I was as bad as Sebastian.

"I am not sure about a...bus, but I get your meaning," said the basandere. "Yes, *he* can be very immature. He doesn't seem to learn."

"I mean...I wasn't trying to talk badly about the guy. Some of those jokes are hilarious..."

"Definitely not true," Sebastian grumbled, the butt of one or two of said jokes.

"Come," she said. "We will travel to our home. Let us hope that what you have said is true."

"Still no name," Ulric whispered as we waited for the basajaunak to join us on the trail. "I'm going to die of curiosity. I totally get that Dick story about Pandora. Seriously, I'd ruin the world, no problem, to answer this question."

"Men do love to create stories about women ruining everythin'," Niamh drawled, "and yet they're the ones in power. They create wars and famine and burn women at the stake. Methinks we're pointin' fingers at the wrong villains…"

"Awesome! Ruining things to get a pointless question answered is already in my wheelhouse." Ulric put a fist in the air. "Let's get it done."

"Please don't cause a ruckus," I said. "We've only been granted passage. We're not safe from anything."

To my surprise, our basajaun filed in with us, choosing a spot just in front of me. He probably worried my crew would get me in trouble. I worried he would.

We continued along. In a while, we split from the trail we'd been following, moving onto another that quickly started to climb.

"It's been a while since I hiked," I murmured, leaning forward to get a little momentum. It didn't seem to work, not to mention the basajaun's butt was right in my face, and he'd spent the last couple of days eating Edgar's flowers. I worried about his flower flatulence problem.

Up and up the trail went, climbing the side of a mountain and lifting us out of the sanctuary of redwoods. The landscape quickly changed from a thick pelt of green back to the yellow and brown grasses and scraggly bushes. The trees up here were what I was used to—oak and pine and others I didn't know by name. The small trail hadn't been a problem on mostly flat land, but now it hugged the side of the mountain, and the price for stumbling would be a helluva tumble.

I looked to my right, watching the slope fall away at an alarming rate. There would be no saving me if I rolled down the side. Without healing magic, it would be a death sentence, no question. There weren't any roots or branches or anything to grab on to, not until you were falling so fast that they wouldn't be of any help anyway. Even *with* healing magic, I probably wouldn't have the chance to fix what was broken before lights out.

"I can see how a mountain goat would find this trail easy," I said, pausing a moment to catch my breath. My leg muscles burned. The sun beat down on my sweaty face. "Creatures as big as basajaunak? Not so much. They don't seem freaked out, though. Hardly any room to maneuver, but they're good to go." I squinted up at the sky, expanding my chest. "Good grief, this is a doozy of a trail."

The basajaun slowed and turned to look back at me. "This? No. This is just the beginning. It gets steep a little farther up."

"It *gets* steep?" I heard Ulric ask.

"Natural deterrent to attack, right here." I soldiered

on, pushing on my thighs to help them along. Not surprisingly, it didn't work. "No one is bothering to hunt you guys down."

I wondered if the mages would even be able to get to us. I doubted they'd pack for a few days' hike or whatever this turned out to be.

Lord, I hoped this wouldn't be a few days' hike.

In another hour, we all experienced what the basajaun had meant. The trail felt like it shot straight up toward the peak. Hard breathing sounded from almost everyone in my crew. I felt exhaustion from Austin, though I doubted he or his shifters showed it.

"Can I fly?" Cyra asked someone. "This is crazy. My kind aren't meant to scale mountains."

"And you think mine are?" Hollace replied. "I don't have room to shift. I'd fall off the side of this trail and tumble down until I went splat. You don't have room to shift, either. You'd probably set the whole place on fire. I doubt these creatures want their redwoods burned down. That'd be a sure way to get your ass thrown out."

"You're just trying to discourage me because misery loves company," she accused him.

"That obvious, huh?"

"You must walk the path," our basajaun said. "It lets the village know where we are and how fast we are traveling. Though...I'm sure they are laughing about our speed. I don't think I've ever climbed this slowly. We can make friends with snails at this pace."

"*You* can't make friends with anyone," Mr. Tom replied.

My legs were screaming now. My heart knocked hard in my chest.

We hit a crest, and I could feel everyone's relief as we descended the ridge a little. In a moment, though, we headed right back up.

"Why?" someone groaned behind me. It could've been Nessa. "*Why?*"

A small branch cracked under my foot. I kicked a rock and made it skitter off the path and bounce down the slope. The basajaun turned back again, probably because of the noise. Austin hadn't made a sound. In fact, aside from the heavy breathing, everyone was nearly silent.

"You guys are all good at sneaking," I said through my own heavy breathing.

I stubbed my toe and shuffled to the left. A small, leafy tree bending too far into the path smacked me with its branches. I put up my hand to push it away. My thighs flared from the pivot, and I staggered a little toward the edge.

Alarm bled through the link. Austin gripped my shoulder from behind. "Careful, there," he told me.

"I'm fine." I issued a thumbs-up to the side, not daring to turn back with a smile or even a grimace. "My legs are just a little wobbly. I'm good." I eyed the edge of the trail, which was much too close to my feet. The lip was jagged, pushing out around rocks or receding because of past runoff. "How much do we have left?"

The basajaun stopped now and turned, looking down at me. I meant to stop with him, but my legs were burning so badly that they didn't respond as quickly as they should have. I smacked my face into his chest and felt his hand steadying me.

"Sorry," I said, straightening.

"Alpha, let me take her rear," the basajaun said. "I am more adept in these mountains. If she falls over the edge, I'll be able to retrieve her much faster than you could."

"Retrieve me?" I held the straps of my backpack and dared another look over the edge. The blood pumping through me and the height made my vision distort. I didn't usually have vertigo, but I also didn't usually cling to the side of a mountain with legs that were threatening to give out. "You'd be retrieving a pile of broken bones off this thing."

"Okay," Austin said, stepping closer. "How do we change our places?"

The basajaun turned to point. "The path widens a

little up ahead. We'll adjust the line formation there."

"She gets her own basajaun security detail, huh?" Ulric asked. "Can I have a piggyback, then? I'm pretty light, I think. You guys wouldn't even notice me."

"I'd sign up for that," Hollace said.

"Me too," Cyra replied.

"I really love the gorilla hugging my backside, don't get me wrong," Nessa called up, "but I probably need a basajaun, too. This is a little beyond my expertise."

"Just don't drag me down with you," Mr. Tom said.

"Now I definitely will. You just cemented your tumble, my friend," she replied.

The trail turned, veering right over the top of the ridgeline. To either side, it fell away now, but there were a few places where it did, indeed, widen out a little. At one of those places, the whole line reorganized. The basajaunak positioned themselves within my crew, taking the places of many of the shifters. The wolves shifted into their animals, a move that Cyra pointed out was cheating. I agreed. Austin and Broken Sue were the only ones left on two feet; their animals were much too large to traverse the slim trails.

Time crawled by in a haze of physical exertion I wasn't used to. I'd built up a tolerance while flying, but I hadn't been running or scaling mountains. This was not in my wheelhouse. The basajaun hovered close as I toiled, his large hand repeatedly drifting out beside me. He clearly thought I'd lose feeling in my legs, stumble, and stagger off the side. I wondered if he was right.

"No guardrails at all, huh?" I asked when we reached a particularly hairy section. "Not even a couple of stakes people might grab hold of in a pinch."

"I was just thinking the same thing," Ulric said from up the line. "Nathanial looks totally comfortable, yet I have a basandere behind me who seems a bit nervous."

"We have trails like this where I'm from," Nathanial replied. "Our mountains are treacherous. We must walk in the storms."

"What's your excuse, Niamh?" Hollace asked. "Why are you so blasé about all this? You don't even seem winded."

"Are ye that out of shape?" she replied.

"It seems so, yes. The things we learn when visiting potentially life-threatening new friends, hmm?"

After another horrible hour that seemed like far longer, the path evened out a bit. We still traveled the ridge, and each side was precarious at best, but the path had widened, allowing for trees and brush along the sides. If we did fall now, we'd at least take a small tree or two down with us. Tiny acorns littered the ground up here, seemingly untouched since they'd fallen. Until now, obviously. I shuffled through and scattered them all around, dragging my feet in fatigue.

"What's for lunch?" I asked no one in particular, stopping for a moment with my hands braced on my hips. "It has to be lunchtime by now."

"We are nearly halfway there," the basajaun said, still hovering close. "There is a nice meadow between the mountains where we can idle for a while. I know how you like meadows."

"*Nearly* halfway there, huh? Nearly." I shook my head and squinted at the sky. "Whose idea was this? Tell me again."

"Why?" Ulric asked, stopped up the way and looking back. He was using me as an excuse to catch his breath.

"I want to poison them, obviously."

I glanced back, seeing a basajaun hovering very close to an obviously agitated Sebastian. The closer the basajaun got, the more he tensed, and the more walking mistakes he made. The more walking mistakes, the more the basajaun leaned in to help. And on the cycle went.

I leaned over and laughed. "I bet you never would've answered that summons if you'd known what you were getting yourself into," I called to Sebastian, starting forward again.

"It was in my stars to answer that summons," he

replied. "But I might've taken a little more time and gotten a large prescription for Xanax."

A ways farther along, a bluish-black bird exploded off a lower branch. It landed a couple of trees back and higher up, twitching as it watched us pass. From its beak came a gruff sort of bark, almost like a crow's call but in shorter bursts. Anyone could see it was a warning, which wasn't a big deal because it was just a bird.

Which was why it surprised me when the basajaun's hand suddenly clamped down on my shoulder. I glanced back and saw his hair was puffed out as though he were preparing for an attack.

# CHAPTER 19

S UDDENLY ALARMED, I swept my gaze to the sides and
then up to the sky, looking for the disturbance. No
way could the mages have found us already. Even if they
were on our trail, they wouldn't be able to get up this
mountain any faster than we could.

Then again, the basajaunak could sense presences
through the trees. Maybe the bird was their alarm
system that something was intruding below us.

I intended to stop and ask what was wrong, but the
basajaun pushed me along.

"Keep going," he said, looking in the direction of
that bird. "If I say so, cover your eyes. They like to go
for the eyes."

"Who do? What's happening?" I asked, bringing my
hands up to the sides of my face.

One of the basajaunak toward the front of the line
grunted. "Their memories are long, these birds. A
simple mistake, and they pass the slight down for
generations."

The bird continued to squawk in the tree. The basajaun in front of us looked from side to side as though expecting an attack.

"The birds?" I asked in confusion.

"*He* disturbed a nest when he was too young to know any better, or so he claims," our basajaun said in a low voice. Apparently, we wouldn't get names for any of them. "He liked to climb trees. He saw the nest and wanted a closer look at the eggs. Instead, he lost his balance and fell out of the tree. The nest fell out with him, and the eggs cracked on the ground. It is a grave offense to those birds, disturbing their eggs. Any birds, I guess, but those particular birds attack. They pass down the treachery to the next generation in the family line, and so on. They never forget."

The bird launched from the tree, heading straight for the basajaun ahead of me. Another came from the other side, swooping in low, and several others were quick to join in. They pecked at the basajaun in question but then spread out, pecking at Cyra and Hollace. Ulric ran out of the line, ducking for cover and waving his arms to swat the persistent avian creatures.

"Hurry. Go, *go*." The basajaun pushed me harder as the first bird reached me. It squawked loudly before trying to peck at my head.

I flung magic all around, blasting it into the sky.

Another spell was loosed from behind, Sebastian helping with our defense. Both spells ballooned out, mine creating a shield that would elicit pain should the invisible plane be breached and his a nearly solid force to keep the birds at bay.

The squawking intensified. Feathers floated down around us as the birds met our magic.

"What is happening?" the lead basandere asked, her arms held up mid-wave.

"*Miss Jessie* has created a magical barrier for us," our basajaun replied. I could feel his pride through the bond.

"Sebastian helped." I pointed behind me lamely.

The basajaunak looked back at me, moving so they could all see. One by one, they nodded in thanks. The bird's nemesis raised his pinky finger to them. I had a feeling it was their version of an offensive gesture.

"*Her* gifts come in handy," the lead basandere said. "We can take her with us when we use this trail. She can keep the birds at bay."

"Sebastian really did all the work," I rushed to say. "He probably likes hiking much more than I do."

"No," Sebastian responded. Nessa started laughing.

Finally, farther on, the trail began winding down-ward for real, no more random climbs popping up in the middle of the descent. The air started to cool as we kept descending until redwoods once again made an appearance. A stream wove through the area, trickling between steep banks and around large rocks. A little wooden bridge spanned the chasm, and on the other side, the path finally widened to the point where we were nearly sauntering along.

Not far from the stream, close enough that we could still hear the running water, a lovely meadow stretched out before us. Violet wildflowers dotted the green and brown grasses, waving in the wind.

"Thank God. I have to pee so badly," Nessa said, hurrying forward. "Where do we go? Just pop a squat or what? Anyone think to bring toilet paper?"

Thankfully, Mr. Tom had thought of the essentials. So had Edgar, of all people. Or maybe Mr. Tom had just forced the extra supplies onto him, since he only had blood to carry.

We all did our business, the ladies heading one way and the guys just getting out of the way. Mr. Tom laid out a lunch consisting of meats, cheeses, and breads while the basajaunak went down to the water or into the trees to forage. They apparently hadn't brought a lunch because they'd expected to be back by now.

Content if not full, we lounged for a while longer. The basajaunak hadn't said as much, but it was clear they wanted us to relax and rest and take in the beautiful scenery. Yes, please.

A pulse vibrated through me. Urgency sped up my heartbeat. That horrible hum intensified, indicating the enemy must've made a move. Hopefully, that move was just to get organized, like booking the jet or calling the mercenary office.

I let out a slow breath, putting my hand to my chest.

"What's up?" Austin asked.

I shook my head at him, dropping my hand. I couldn't explain here, where the basajaunak might overhear.

Looking for a distraction so I didn't advertise my anxiety, I craned my head to turn toward the stream. I let the tranquility of the gently flowing water soothe my coursing adrenaline. There was nothing more we could do right now. There was no sense in becoming a ball of stress when it wouldn't, or couldn't, change anything.

"Okay, shall we go?" The basandere leader didn't stand up, watching me placidly for an answer instead.

"Sure, yeah." I hopped up. "This is halfway, right?"

Everyone paused mid-action to hear the answer.

"A little over halfway, yes," she replied. "Do you need to be carried?"

"No, I don't need that level of embarrassment, thanks," I replied, and Ulric, Cyra, and Hollace froze with their arms halfway in the air. Given that I'd healed them of their fatigue, they were just being babies.

The shifters who'd donned their human forms for lunch shifted back into their animals, and away we went. When I saw what we'd be climbing next, I suddenly wished I'd raised my hand.

This time, there wasn't a trail slowly winding around a mountain. No, this trail cut right to the chase. It climbed in one direction steeply, turned like it was a set of stairs in a skyscraper, and aggressively climbed again, cutting back and forth until it reached the top.

"Are you ready for me, mountain?" I asked it, shaking my fist. "You will not defeat me."

The lead basandere tilted her head at me again. "The mountain cannot be challenged. It will sit there placidly while creatures tread on it. That's its lot in life."

Oh, great. Out of all of us, I was the weirdo.

My legs were screaming in no time. I sucked in air and dripped sweat all down my face and onto my shirt. Our basajaun kept looking at my feet, but I didn't care if I was being incredibly loud. Once we reached the top, the wide trail flattened out before dipping into the trees and descending. That was when the trail shrank to the width it had been earlier—on the side of the mountain again with a sheer face less than a misstep away.

"Oh, perfect," I said, still breathing heavily and now wiping my face. I couldn't spare the energy to heal myself just yet. "Another one of these death trails." I puffed out more air and tried my best to step carefully with my burning leg muscles. The vertigo was back in force as I peered over the side. "If there's an earthquake, we're all going to fall right off this mountain."

"*She* is very concerned with falling and mortality," the basandere called back, probably talking to our basajaun.

"For the record, I'm also concerned with mortality, and I've never been amazing with heights," Sebastian said. "This isn't my favorite adventure so far."

This trail was similar to the first in that it wound down to the bottom of the mountain, but the switchbacks were more frequent and the descent mild in comparison. It wasn't until we reached the bottom and passed through a gap between the mountains and over a lazily moving stream that the magic of the area presented itself.

"Wow," someone said from the front of the line. Someone else whistled.

Twisted branches littered the bank by the stream, which wound alongside a wider, packed dirt trail. Thick redwood trees shot into the sky all around, nudging the trail one way and then another. The sound of flowing water mixed with the twittering of birds and snickering of crickets. Ferns and clover once again filled in the gaps between the trees. A strange sense of peace and contentment flowed over me. The vibe in this area felt good, like the trees were giving us a gentle embrace. The canopy dimmed the light and made the air pleasantly cool.

"This is beautiful," I said with a release of breath.

The mountains rose on both sides of us, but I didn't feel trapped. A mossy slope rose on my left before falling away.

Austin fell back and took my hand, entwining our fingers. I felt his serenity through the bonds. They must've released the challenge to him. The others kept looking around as they walked, taking it all in.

The paths were all wide here, and well traveled. Cut and polished logs crisscrossed the edge to keep people from falling, and I wondered why they hadn't applied the practice to the hell trails we'd been forced to take.

I didn't see any huts or dwellings as we continued on, but there were plenty of firepits, small, charred circles in cleared spaces. Rustic wooden cups sat on rocks, and baskets had been left out or staked up. Occasionally, I saw a piece of pottery—a plate or bowl.

The feeling of being watched again tingled my senses. I sent out the spell Sebastian had used earlier. There were basajaunak all around, standing beside trees or pushed back a little from the firepits I'd discovered.

Their magic was incredible, allowing them to literally hide in plain sight. All of them, too, not just those with higher power. It was similar to how gargoyles blended into buildings, I guessed. The same type of magic in a vastly different setting.

"*He* will show you to your fire," the basandere said, gesturing toward our basajaun. The basajaunak waited for the shifters to regain their human forms and then handed back their packs. "We were told that you will not require assistance with hunting. Fishing might be an issue for you, and so we will provide fish, should you require it. Tomorrow, we will honor you as guests with a feast, and in the days following, you may address the elders. If you need anything, please do not hesitate to ask." Her gaze shifted to Austin. "Mind yourself in this village, alpha."

With that, she walked away, taking the path on the right and nodding or gesturing hello to those she passed. The other basajaunak who'd come with us did the same, staying visible as they went along. In a moment, we were left solely with our basajaun and a lot of onlookers who didn't want us to see them.

"Come this way." The basajaun took us left as the sunlight started to dwindle. My feet felt like lead after all the walking we'd done, and my legs were starting to cramp up. I needed a meal before I could get to healing.

Around a knuckle of land we went, then down steps naturally made from roots. Finally, the basajaun stopped beside an unused firepit with fresh wood layered inside and a pile waiting nearby. The undergrowth was a bit different here—spongy moss or clover beds lay in between the large trunks of redwoods. All the ferns and other spindly vegetation had been cleared. This was obviously our camp.

There was no cover from the elements. We'd be sleeping outside with nothing but our packs and our clothes. We probably should've asked a few questions when the basajaun had said accommodations would be provided.

"After tonight, I will be sleeping among you. Tonight, I must meet some others and will adjourn with them." The basajaun checked over the wood as Ulric smirked at him.

"Adjourn with them?" He waggled his eyebrows. "That's what you call an orgy here, huh?"

The basajaun's hair puffed out slightly, but he didn't comment. More eyebrows rose, and a few of the crew looked at each other with an obvious question in mind. Did the basajaun have a bed buddy?

The basajaun glanced at what would be our natural beds. "It is late now. We had thought you'd have time to hunt, but we could not have foreseen the snail's pace we'd take over the mountains. I will bring you something to eat."

"You've been around us for how long?" Ulric asked. "Did you think we moved slowly in normal life for funsies or what?"

The basajaun pointed at the firepit. "Do you know how to start a fire?"

"Yes," Austin said. "We can handle it, thank you. We can fish as well, come tomorrow. We don't want to be a burden."

The basajaun nodded and walked away without a backward glance.

"Well, this isn't exactly as planned..." Mr. Tom surveyed our camp. He pursed his lips. "I suppose we'll have to pull up a clump of dirt for our bedding, will we?"

"What a shame that the clover will be crushed." Edgar walked toward the nearest bed of clover. "I'd better hurry and find all the four-leaves or they'll be smashed."

"Isabelle, Layan, get a fire going," Austin commanded a couple of his people as everyone else looked around.

I didn't bother. I just plopped down close to the soon-to-be fire and waited patiently. I was too tired to care about a lack of bed or chair.

"Kace, take a few wolves and patrol the area. The

basajaunak are all over. Give them a wide berth. We don't want any trouble."

He chose a few others for the duty, and they all put down their packs, shifted again, and took off at a trot.

Austin pulled my pack from my back, took his off, and chose a mossy location behind us, more central to the camp than most of the other available spots. He set both packs down before sitting beside me.

Isabelle, a chiseled-faced woman with white-blonde hair who often trained with me, crouched next to the fire. She held up two sticks, a smaller one with a blunt tip and one that looked like a really thin, somewhat hollow log. Tilting the tiny log toward us, she lifted her eyebrows. It had a small groove streaked with black that would fit the blunt end of the other stick.

"When the basajaun asked if you knew how to start a fire, were you expecting he meant with sticks?" she asked.

I felt Austin's humor through the bond, but he was in alpha mode. He didn't show it. "That would've taken a minute."

"Several hundred dozen minutes." She shook her head and grabbed her pack to get fire-starting supplies.

"Cyra, they need fire," Hollace called, coming into the area while zipping up his pants.

"Oh. Sure." Cyra peeled away from Edgar, whom

she'd clearly been helping look for four-leaf clovers, and walked to the firepit. "Here we go."

Isabelle stopped rummaging in her pack.

A thick spread of flame blasted from Cyra's hand and onto the firewood. Given the blistering heat, it took no time at all to catch and start them burning.

"That is incredibly handy," said Layan, a guy with light blue eyes who turned into a snow leopard.

"I didn't know what to expect," Austin murmured a moment later, looking out through the trees. The other camps were a respectable distance away, allowing for privacy. "I've never seen the basajaun's...living quarters. I honestly don't even know where he sleeps. I'd thought a cave, but now, I'm not too sure. This is...pleasant, though. Serene."

"I can't imagine it's so pleasant in the winter." Broken Sue sat on the other side of the fire with his knees bent and his arms draped around them.

"This is the California coast," Nessa replied, stopping as she walked past, coming from who knew where. Even after that crazy hike, she was always on the move. "It's temperate most of the year, and you have the trees for protection. I'm sure it gets cold, but not like you're thinking. For you, coming from the Midwest, it would be chilly at best. Besides, they have all that hair. I'm sure they're just dandy. It gives a new definition to *fur coat*."

He barely glanced at her. "I stand corrected."

"And you are most welcome for it." She smiled and continued walking.

Sebastian, who'd been hovering around the outskirts of camp, returned and sat beside me. When Nessa walked briskly back into the area, she plopped down between him and Broken Sue.

"Miss." Mr. Tom emerged from between two smaller redwoods. "I've found a hollowed-out tree just over there." He turned and pointed. "The ground is mostly flat and soft, and great news! The opening of it faces away from camp. It's a lovely, secluded spot for you and Austin to continue your nighttime gymnastics."

I stared at him with an open mouth. Austin's humor crowded the bonds.

"We can abstain for a few nights, Mr. Tom, thanks," I said dryly.

"Give the tree to the mages," Cyra said. "They're the most fragile. Besides, that way, one of us can sleep just outside of the tree hole to keep them from getting into mischief or turning traitor and trying to kill us all."

It was Sebastian's turn to stare with mouth agape.

Nessa put out her hands with a laugh. "I'll remind you that it wasn't our idea to come to the most beautiful but scariest place in existence—"

"See? I told you," Sebastian murmured.

"We couldn't escape if we turned traitor," she said. "At *best*, we'd stumble far enough away to fall off the side of a mountain. At worst, and much more likely, one of the basajaunak would catch us and make us into a skin coat. That would probably become a staple in their winter fashion line."

He shivered. "They'd definitely catch us. No question. They probably wouldn't even need to feel the wood. They'd be able to *hear* us."

"Yeah, I got the distinct impression I was very loud," she replied.

"My watcher just flat-out told me," he returned. "I might not have been so bad if he hadn't crowded in so dang close the whole time."

"I will watch them." Edgar still stood at the edge of a patch of clover, his body bent to study the ground. "I will watch you all while you sleep. It will be my pleasure."

"Yes, fantastic," Mr. Tom said, picking up my pack. "I'm sure we will all rest easier knowing a hungry vampire is crouching in the dark somewhere, watching us while we are at our most vulnerable."

"The gargoyles will shift to sleep," Nathanial said, standing a little away. "We'll be sentinel."

"And stone." Ulric nodded at us before sitting beside the fire. "Vampires can't bite stone. Sucks for all you shifters who turn into breathing types."

"Oh, I won't be hungry," Edgar replied. "I'll have a little snack before you all tuck in for the night."

"Ever better," Mr. Tom said, looking through my things. I didn't know what for—he'd packed for me.

"What did she mean when she told you to watch yourself?" I asked Austin, leaning into him as the fire flickered and glowed within its circle of rocks.

The rest of the group joined us, Hollace putting out his hands to feel the heat and Cyra sitting at the outskirts, looking out into the trees.

"She's warning me not to push for dominance here," Austin replied. "She doesn't think I can accept a submissive role, especially if it's clear they aren't actually more dominant."

"Do you think it'll be a problem?" Nathanial asked. "I could feel their magic pushing at me. It felt like they were trying to test me somehow, and I don't have the power you do."

"They were doing the same to me," Broken Sue growled, looking out into the growing darkness. "It was annoying."

"They're trying to test us, yes." Austin pulled me in against him, resting his hand on my knee. His thumb stroked across my jeans. "You can't blame them. Hosting us here is an act of trust, and that trust is not in us—it's in the basajaun. But it seems he has a reputation for being a loose cannon. Makes sense if he's the only one who's ventured away from here in who knows how long. They want to make sure their people are safe from us, so they're prodding us to judge our reaction. They'll have sentries watching us the entire time we're here in case we slip up."

"No one is near," Sebastian murmured. "I have a large magical net around us to make sure nothing tries to sneak up and rip off our arms."

"Your constant state of paralyzing fear around dangerous creatures is quite helpful," Mr. Tom said, back from the sleeping area. "Austin Steele, might I remove your pajamas and set them out for you? How about a fresh pair of underwear? You've been walking around all day in the hot sun. We can all attest to how hot it gets in and around our...begonias, I believe the miss's father would call them. As you know, the miss is not one for general stinkiness. I will just—"

"No," Austin growled.

I elbowed him.

"Thanks," he finished.

Ulric stifled a laugh.

"And if we slip up?" Hollace asked Austin.

A flurry of emotions rolled through his bond. "We can't slip up."

"It's not them we need to be worried about," Cyra said softly, still looking out into the trees. "Something is brewing. I can feel it."

"Well…we all know what's brewing," Nessa said. "Sabby, do we need a sound-resistant bubble?"

"No, not that," Cyra answered, her tone wispy. "Something more." She looked up at the sky, her expression contemplative. "Something with an undertow. It's coming. It'll suck us all in with it. We'll have to fight our way out to survive."

Hollace brought up his knees and leaned forward over them, still staring at the fire. "She doesn't mean right now. A phoenix can sense large magical shifts. The time scope for those shifts can be a few weeks to several years. What shape they take is anyone's guess. But what she means is something has been set in motion that will lead to whatever change she's sensing. I feel it, too. It's…" He looked out to the right. Blackness crawled in between the trees as the sun dipped over the distant horizon. "It's imminent. I wonder if that's why we felt the summons as hard as we did. Like we'd specifically been called. Like we have a larger purpose in all of this."

"In all of what?" Nessa asked.

He shrugged. "I don't know. We'll see when it happens, I guess."

"I don't think I brought enough whiskey for this

trip," Niamh murmured.

"There's not enough whiskey in the world for this trip," Sebastian replied.

# CHAPTER 20

T HE NEXT MORNING, Austin escorted Jess along the path of the natural village. He held her hand, knowing today would bring trials but intent on enjoying their time here anyway. She seemed so at peace within these trees. So content.

He'd sent the wolves hunting earlier. They worked together with an efficiency few teams could achieve. Not to mention they wouldn't raise as much suspicion if a hiker or camper happened to see them. A giant polar bear wouldn't be as easy to write off as a coyote, since he didn't think they had wolves around here.

Austin would go fishing in a while. He wasn't amazing at swatting fish out of a stream, but hopefully, he could catch a few. They hadn't brought any fishing gear, and the basajaunak didn't seem to use it.

For now, though, they were showing their faces in the community, Austin and Jess, with Sebastian trailing behind them. Austin had told the others to stay at camp for now. He assumed he'd get some sort of challenge before long, and he didn't want the fervor of his pack behind him when he evaluated how to handle it. Jess was with him because he wanted her there, and also because she rarely registered when she was being challenged, making it easier for her to ignore them.

As for Sebastian, he was donning his most submissive posture by request and was here in case Jess reacted violently to something. He'd need to quell her magic or at least put up some sort of barrier between it and the basajaunak.

This was such a precarious situation. It wasn't just that Austin wanted to show well. Which he did, of course. Basajaunak support, even in name, would be amazing for their overall cause. No one wanted to mess with the basajaunak or anyone connected with them.

But he was more concerned about finishing this trip without inadvertently causing offense. He didn't want these creatures as his enemy, and the ways in which that could happen were numerous. They were prickly at best, prone to violent hysterics. If his and Jess's crews could leave peacefully, without upsetting the whole group, he'd call that a huge win. Anything else was pure bonus.

He felt the stare before he registered the presence, somewhere to the right.

"Off right and walking closer," Sebastian murmured. "Medium height. For them, I mean. Medium build. Our basajaun is bigger in all ways."

A youth, then. The basandere seemed to be just as tall if not so wide in the shoulders and chest as the male of the species.

Austin barely kept himself from grimacing. Youths were a problem in any species, all hot temper and wild stupidity.

He breathed deeply to keep the tension from winding through his body and surging his adrenaline. His strides shortened, and he pulled his hand from Jess's. He needed to focus. He hadn't had to act submissive in a while, not since his time in Kingsley's territory. It would take all his effort to subdue his reflexes and natural drives.

"Still coming," Sebastian said, and then swore. "Faster now."

Austin could sense it. The threat of danger sang through his blood like a living thing. His senses warned him of an attack at hand.

"Let me handle this," he told Jess, stopping and turning.

"Sure. But let's all get on the same page." Jess worked her hands, and suddenly, the basajaun blinked into his field of vision.

"Reveal the weapon spell, huh?" Sebastian said, falling back behind Austin and dragging Jess with him. "Nice alteration."

"Yeah, I was thinking about it last night. I figured it would do the trick."

"Right on. You could add a few embellishments, but—Oh, hell, he's not stopping."

Austin bowed his back marginally and directed his eyes slightly downward, aiming for just below the chest line. This was the position he'd had to adopt with his brother to keep the older alpha from reacting. Of course, this was a kid, and he probably wouldn't be content until Austin was bowing dramatically.

"You have no place here," the kid said as he walked up and delivered a hard cuff to the side of Austin's head.

Sudden rage nearly tore away Austin's control. He fought it while putting out his hand for Jess.

"Nope, don't release that," Sebastian told her in an urgent tone. "Stop doing that. We can't start a war. Let him handle it."

Austin straightened up slowly, focusing on his breath and keeping his eyes downcast.

"This is obviously one of those tests. Right, Austin?" Sebastian said. "You've got others coming, by the way. Larger ones. Not as fast, though. They must've heard the commotion, but it looks like they're content to watch."

*Heard the commotion.* That meant this wasn't exactly planned, but the leaders or older basajaunak were seeing how it would play out. This youth was trying to assert his dominance because he could. He was testing his limits. He clearly didn't know danger when he saw it.

Austin wished he could teach the kid a lesson that would eventually save his life, because doing this to the wrong alpha would mean death, no questions asked.

"I can reveal them," Jess said with strain in her voice. She was fighting her gargoyle. Thank God.

"No. Let this play out," Austin told her. "I won't let him kill me or hurt me beyond what you can heal."

"You won't *let* me kill you?" the young basajaun said, crowding his space now. His height topped Austin's by over a foot. His girth and strength were likely on par. This kid probably thought that gave him the advantage.

Austin saw the blow coming. He closed his eyes and took a deep breath as the fist connected with his sternum. The force carried him back a step, but only a step. There were limits to what he would do to prove his submission.

He stepped back to his original position.

The kid bristled, bending down until his face was in line with Austin's. "What have you got to say for yourself?" the basajaun asked. Spittle speckled Austin's cheek.

He didn't bother responding, keeping his posture the same and his gaze set.

The next blow seemed like it was in slow motion, aiming for the side of his face.

Before it could land, the kid froze.

"Dang it, Jessie," Sebastian said with obvious strain in his voice. "You're not supposed to get involved."

"What's happening?" Austin asked, keeping his posture. The others were watching. He wanted to make sure they knew he was still minding his manners.

"Sorry," Sebastian said, "I don't have the power to block some of her more robust spells."

The basajaun stood slightly twisted, arm curved with his large hand fisted. His eyes were fully rounded, zipping around all over. He didn't know what was happening either, and he was scared.

"What's happening?" Jess asked, stepping up beside Austin. Anger burned through the bonds.

The watching basajaunak popped into his field of vision. The lead basandere from yesterday was among them, leaning against a tree.

"I'll tell you what's happening," Jess continued, shoving her hand forward.

The kid jerked back, barely getting his feet under

him. He froze again, surprise and fear etched into his expression.

"We have a rude kid with bravado he hasn't earned, that's what happening," she said in an accusatory tone. "This is how you treat visitors, basajaunak? You let some ignorant kid assault them just to see what will happen? That's absurd. One of you can test Austin, that's fine. But this kid? No. Letting him pick on an adult alpha just because he can is fueling his sense of entitlement. What happens when he explores the great outdoors and runs into someone like Austin without the protections of this sanctuary? I'll tell you what'll happen. He'll get his bell rung, that's what'll happen. He might be killed. Is that what you want? Or are you locking him up tight because you know you haven't trained him to survive in the outside world? I don't know, but I'm not having it."

She flung her hand to the side. The kid went flying, hitting the ground and then tumbling away.

"This isn't his fault," she spat. "It's yours. All of yours. I'd never set my son up for that kind of a fall. I'd also never let him do something so disrespectful to guests without checking his behavior. If this is how it is going to be, we're leaving. I don't want a family that thinks this is okay."

"We need to make sure he is safe to be around our

young ones," the basandere said, stepping forward. "An alpha of his caliber is not used to bending."

"Oh, really? And how do you think we started working with *him*? The basajaun we know, I mean. Do you think Austin ran all hotheaded onto his mountain and demanded something? No. He showed the basajaun the respect due to a territory holder. The same respect he's trying to show you now. But I'll tell you what. How about you let that kid at *me*? Why don't you let him try to knock me around? I'm a mom. I'll take an unruly child in hand, no problem, I don't care whose it is. In the sandbox, while camping, whatever. I'll handle it."

Jess stared them down. Magic throbbed in the air, and Austin had no doubt it was beating into them. All of them bristled, their hair puffing out from their bodies. The kid stood up. Dirt clung to his fur. He sagged, having lost the bravery of youth from being tossed to the side by a matriarch. He didn't intend to take her up on that challenge.

"It is agreed," the basandere said before turning and walking away.

"Wait...what is agreed?" Jess asked Austin. "What did I agree to? Leaving?"

"It's agreed that they won't allow younger basajaunak to instigate. If there are to be more challenges, they'll leave it for the older village members."

"Oh. Well, that's okay, then. To a point, obviously."

He allowed himself a smile and squeezed her close.

A few of the others lingered for a moment, watching them, before fading into the trees as well. The younger basajaun turned and started running in the opposite direction. He'd had his fill.

"Well." Jess rolled her shoulders, but her power still throbbed in the air. "That got the blood flowing." She shook Austin off before grabbing his hand and pulling him along. "I'm really riled up. Seriously, that's bull. Who lets a teen bully a grown adult? What were they thinking, letting that happen?"

"They probably thought it would be the fastest way to break me," he replied, entwining his fingers with hers. "I wouldn't have, but I'm glad you stepped in. That sort of stuff is never pleasant."

"Well...yeah." She scoffed. "I would be so pissed if I found out Jimmy did something like that."

"How is he, by the way?" he asked to try to distract her.

A little smile crossed her face. "Really good. He still talks about Easter. He's desperate to be here for the holidays. I don't know how I'm going to convince him to spend some of that time with his dad."

"How's he liking school?"

While she talked about her son, they wound

through the village and took in the lovely day. More and more basajaunak stayed visible, making things or chatting. Some, though, disappeared quickly upon seeing them, clearly not comfortable around strangers.

He thought back to how Jess had stepped up with him. She still didn't totally get shifter culture. She certainly didn't get basajaunak culture, not that *he* could claim to be an expert. But from what he could gather, the basajaunak must think pretty highly of them to have allowed the youth to make his challenge. They'd trusted that Austin wouldn't lose control and hurt one of their young.

Now they also knew, however, that Jess was protective. She could take charge when she wanted to—and would do so if she felt it necessary. Moreover, Austin would let her. He wouldn't try to dominate her any more than he had that kid. Not when she was taking command. They'd seen the give and take of their co-rulership, and also that Jess could assert her will in an effective way without resorting to violence—or, at least, what the basajaunak would think of as violence.

She'd done well. They'd all done well, even Sebastian.

Pride glowed through Austin, drawing Jess's notice.

"What?" she asked.

"Just…" He shook his head. "We have a damn good

team. Even though your crew lacks any real structure, we always work together seamlessly."

"Have you forgotten Edgar loitering around, staring at us while we're sleeping?" she asked with a laugh.

"I had to post Cyra outside the tree hole, as she called it," Sebastian said, "just to block out Edgar. At one point in the night, I woke up to him leaning into the hole with his mouth open, exposing those big canines. Just staring. Do you know what he said when he caught me awake?"

"No," she said, laughing harder.

"He said, 'Lovely evening, isn't it, friend? All is well. Sweet dreams. I'll just stay and watch you a little longer.'" He ran a hand down his face. "I had to pretend to go to the bathroom just to drag Cyra over. I wasn't even sorry about waking her up. Had to be done."

"How have you gone through life afraid of everything?" Austin asked as they rounded a turn and started back.

"I haven't! I realize that's hard to believe, but I honestly haven't. I had a really rough childhood. I kind of lost the ability to care about most things, I think, and then my sister died, and I got tortured. I didn't think I had any room left for fear. Don't you remember my saying that when I first met you?"

"And now you're afraid of literally everything," Jess

said, glancing back with a teasing smile. "All the things."

"I think it's just that I'm meeting the most extreme examples of all these new species. Well, basajaunak are always scary, but I'm far from the only one who thinks so. You even think so. *Niamh* does! But as far as shifters, even that enemy mage was terrified of all of you, and he probably went through sensitivity training."

"Sensitivity training?" she asked, her confusion evident. "I think that must mean something different in the magical world than it does in the corporate world."

"It means they hardened him up. They reduced his sensitivity to violent acts. I bet they gave him some sort of mental spell, too, to help him combat pain. I didn't check for it. I should have. If he had a spell like that, though, it was designed against magical attacks. Did you notice that he didn't react to your battering quite like he did to being held in the air by Austin? Alpha, I mean. Austin Alpha. *Steele!* Sorry, I'm getting frazzled."

"Okay, Edgar," she teased.

"Not funny. You're as bad as Nessa," he grumbled.

"We need to give you sensitivity training for dealing with shifters," Austin said, teasing the weird mage for laughs.

"Oh, you are, don't worry," Sebastian answered solemnly. "Every day. Pretty soon, I doubt very much that lesser shifters will affect me. Not that I've met any shifters outside of this territory, or that I want to put the theory to the test, but still."

"Maybe just rile up the basajaunak," Jess said. "If you survive, you won't fear hardly anything."

"No, thank you," he murmured.

✧   ✧   ✧

BROCHAN LEFT THE camp with Niamh, Mr. Tom, and Edgar. It was his turn to face the soft challenges from the basajaunak.

It was also, apparently, his turn to be the butt of a joke. He couldn't imagine any other reason why he'd be forced to go with the three original—and consequently oddest—members of the Ivy House crew. Especially since one of them, the very grumpy Irishwoman, could push his buttons like no one else in the world.

If he could've at least brought Nessa... She seemed to have no difficulty handling Niamh or even Edgar. She just let everything roll off her back. Her smile never seemed to dim. She could be in the middle of attempting to torture someone, and she would still be light and jubilant. The pressure or the trials of life never eroded her cheery disposition.

He wished he could be like that, could feel like that again. He wished he could bottle her up and put her in his pocket to use whenever the clouds in his mind grew too dark.

The other mage—Sebastian—had scars that were etched deep. Looking at him was like looking in a mirror. But Nessa was the light in Sebastian's life, his buoy in troubled waters. His tether when things got too turbulent.

Brochan wanted that for himself.

Then again, he wasn't so sure he deserved a buoy or a little bottle of sunshine to keep with him when the memories crowded in.

"Oh, look." Edgar stopped beside the path and looked over the rustic wooden railing. "This patch of clover is all shriveled up. Their leaves are droopy, see?"

Niamh and Mr. Tom kept walking, ignoring him. Brochan hesitated, then drifted toward the vampire, not wanting to leave him for the basajaunak to find. When had he become a shepherd of odd magical creatures?

"We'd best keep going," he said. He glanced down the path, seeing that Niamh and Mr. Tom had slowed, then peered over the railing. "We're supposed to stick together."

"Yes, I know. Yes. I can always come back and scour this patch when Miss Jessie inevitably wins over the basajaunak."

As the vampire straightened up, Brochan felt a thrill. "There's one." He pointed downward. "A four-leaf clover."

"What?" Edgar looked between Brochan's finger and the ground multiple times before leaning so far over the guardrail that Brochan worried he'd tumble headfirst into the patch of clovers. "So it is." Edgar straightened and beamed at him. "How marvelous. You have a very good eye. I haven't found any yet. What should we do, pick it and ruin the fun for everyone else just so you might have a little good luck, or let it continue living its natural life?"

Brochan suppressed the urge to laugh uncontrollably. Something about this vampire pulled you into his mindset until you didn't feel completely rational.

"I think," he said slowly, pretending to mull it over, "that maybe we should let it live."

"Yes." Edgar nodded. "Yes, I was thinking that myself. Okay, on to the next patch. Unless you want to look a little more here? There might be another. With your eagle eye—actually, gorilla eye, right?" He leaned in a little closer while smiling. His teeth were ghastly. "Maybe we can find another."

Brochan turned and strode away. He probably should've just kept going in the first place.

"Are ye through with yer tryst?" Niamh asked when he caught up.

Edgar loped after them as they kept moving. "Did

he tell you what he found?" he asked when he caught up. "He found a four-leaf clover. On his first try!"

"Did he, now?" She glanced back, her expression impossible to read. "Beginner's luck, maybe."

"How do you know he hasn't been looking at camp?" Mr. Tom asked. "Have you been spying on him?"

"Edgar's been spying on everyone," she replied. "That's what he does."

"I do not spy," Edgar said. "I merely watch everyone discreetly so that they don't feel anxious."

A tremor of warning stole Brochan's focus. A shiver started at the base of his back and crawled quickly up his spine. Danger. Something hostile was near.

Niamh glanced away to the right, then back at Brochan.

"Yes, that challenge will be for him," Mr. Tom said. They'd clearly felt it too. "I'd just as soon get out of the way. I can't imagine we'll be needed."

A branch swayed gently about fifteen feet away, in line with the presence Brochan felt. But there were more. Other bodies, maybe not hostile, hiding in the brush, watching.

He straightened his shoulders and held his head high as he walked to the area of the hostile presence. The branch stopped swaying. He stared straight ahead, bristling. His power pumped out a warning.

The challenge had not yet begun, so he wouldn't be faulted for the posturing. He wanted to make sure these creatures knew exactly who they were challenging in the safety of their home.

A crackling announced the presence to his other senses. The basajaun was downwind, though, so he couldn't tell whether it was someone he'd already met.

All at once, the creature's concealment magic fell away, and he was running at Brochan. A vicious snarl ripped from the great basajaun's throat as he charged, his large arms held wide on his ten-foot-tall body. Hair puffed out all around him, making the impossibly large creature seem that much bigger.

What a way to die.

Brochan lowered his gaze marginally, since there was no fear of his meeting the creature's eyes while staring straight ahead, and bent a touch at the top of his back. It was the posture he used with Austin.

The creature continued forward, closing the space at remarkable speed. The basajaun reached him as the slavering snarl came to an end. His huge arm swung across and then out, striking Brochan across the shoulder and smashing him to the side.

Brochan flew, hitting the hard-packed dirt and sliding. Skin burned away from the contact. He hit a post with his head and then stopped when the rest of his body slid to the center of the path.

Anger curled within him. The desire to shift and fight back was almost overwhelming. Alpha Steele had never hit him like that. He'd never crossed the line, inciting the type of violence that would bring Brochan's animal rushing forward.

Alpha Ironheart wouldn't dream of it. She'd hunt down and punish anyone who did.

But he wasn't dealing with his alphas now. This wasn't about dominance, either. This was merely about his control.

The situation was triggering him, though. It brought back memories. Failings.

In his wandering days, after everything had been taken from him, he'd passed through towns where alphas did stuff like this—knock around weaker pack members, pick on people who weren't able to get up and fight back. They'd been ridiculed, beaten, and punished for fun. For *sport*.

There wasn't one day that Brochan didn't regret pretending he didn't see it. There wasn't one moment that he didn't feel like a coward for leaving those towns without trying to help. For turning a blind eye to the injustice, too sick with grief and loss to make a stand. Wishing for nothing other than an alpha strong enough to tear him apart like he'd seen others torn apart.

He'd found that someone. And then the alpha's mate, who was equally strong. But instead of tearing him apart, like he'd initially wanted, they worked every day to rebuild him. To stand him up little by little and make him stop thinking—*wishing*—for the grave.

He owed them everything. If he had to keep his composure here and take a beating to show he had control, he'd do it ten times over.

Getting to his feet, he took a deep, shuddering breath. He would remember what this felt like—being made the victim—but not because he wished for vengeance on the basajaun. They were doing what they thought was necessary to protect their kind and their young. He'd do the same.

No, he'd remember it because his alphas planned to unite the shifters, which would mean taking a stand against wicked alphas like the ones he'd come across. Next time, there'd be no walking away.

Back more prominently bent, eyes further downcast, he returned to where he'd been standing. There he waited for the next blow.

Instead, he heard a grunt and felt breath dust down on him.

The basajaun turned and strode away. The presences in the trees drifted away also. They'd gotten what they wished to see. He'd passed the test.

He rolled his shoulders and turned back toward the others.

"Right so." Niamh started forward. "Another patch of clover, then?"

# CHAPTER 21

T HE AFTERNOON WANED as I sat on a rock with what I knew was a goofy smile.

"You almost had that one!" I yelled in encouragement.

The great polar bear head turned my way, and though his animal face wasn't capable of human expression, I didn't need the bonds to tell me he was not amused.

Austin stood with three paws immersed in the fast-moving stream. Water gurgled around him, washing halfway up to his knees. The last paw was poised above the sparkling surface.

He looked back down, seeking out trout or whatever other fish lived in these regions. Then he paused, utterly still. In a moment, he swung his paw down. Water splashed to the side and across his chest. His paw arced before reemerging. No fish flew from the stream.

He turned in the stream, splashing water everywhere, and pounced. His two big paws sloshed into the water, and his head dipped. He pulled it back out and shook the water off. No fish.

"You can't let the wolves show you up," I said, switching tactics. "They got that big buck in no time. If you can't get a fish, we'll have to go find some berries in disgrace."

He huffed, resuming his original position.

The sun filtered through the trees reaching high above, dappling his snowy-white coat. The light danced on top of the water and shone on the wet rocks all around him. The massive beast looked both out of place and completely at home.

I took a deep breath and closed my eyes for a moment, centering myself in this beautiful place. I loved it here. The soft chirping of birds and the gentle sway of branches overhead calmed my gargoyle in a way only Austin usually could.

Letting my eyes drift open, I caught his swinging paw just in time for it to hit the water. The water splashed as before, but this time, a fish with colorful scales—a rainbow trout—flew with it. The prize hit the bank and flopped high before turning and landing on its other side.

"Oh, quick, get it before it gets back into the water," I screeched, pointing in excitement.

He was already moving, pouncing onto the bank

and capturing the fish. He grabbed the fish's head in his great maw and crunched down, putting it out of its misery.

"Yay!" I clapped in excitement.

He pulled back his head, still looking down at it to make sure it was really dead. The assessment complete, he returned to the water and resumed his pose.

"One down. The wolves better look out," I said, and then laughed when he gave me that dead stare again.

Minutes dragged by, pulling a couple of hours behind them. I only moved from my spot to cross the stream and organize the growing pile of fish as my mate continued frolicking in the water.

"Now you've got the hang of it," I said as he pawed out another fish, the tenth in the pile.

A wave of warning pounded inside me, intensifying that horrible hum. It ripped me out of the serene moment. I took a deep breath and palmed my chest.

The mages were definitely on the move, and they were getting closer. I could feel their vicious intent through the spell now. My gargoyle pulsed magic, gripping the bonds I shared with my crew and also those I'd connected with.

Soon, it would be time to battle. To flex my magic.

"Are you okay?"

"Hah!" I struck out with my hand in a cartoon-like

karate chop that did no one any favors.

A young basandere stood fifteen feet away just off the bank in the trees. A loud warning rumbled through the polar bear's chest as he turned in the water. He lowered his head, his gaze acute on the new addition.

The basandere's eyes flickered back and forth between us. "I mean you no harm," she said quickly.

"I know." I put my hand out for Austin. "You just startled me, is all. Which startled him. I'm supposed to have my magic feeling around me for other people, but…" I shrugged, leaning my hands back onto the large rock and pointing my face toward the sun. "It's so lovely here that I forget about the danger."

The basandere reached down, pulling a large bucket around to her front. "You aren't in danger here. Animals know better than to attack our homestead. Even if they didn't, your alpha mate would keep them back. He's very protective of you."

"Of all his people, yes," I said.

"As for humans…" The basandere bent to the stream and dipped in her bucket. "We monitor the wood. The elders do, I mean. They can use it to sense trouble from a great distance. Many, many miles. They'll know if someone dangerous is coming long before they get here. You'll have plenty of warning."

A pang of guilt hit me. This youth was assuring me

of my safety. She was offering her people as a warning system. What was I doing, knowingly putting them in danger? I was bringing an unwelcome disruption to their quiet sanctuary.

"Anyway," she said after standing again. She glanced at Austin resuming his position in the water. "If you're okay…"

"I am." I offered her a smile I didn't feel. The warning from earlier continued to pound, speeding up my heart. "Just getting used to everything."

She nodded and started to leave, but then turned back. "I'll see you at the feast tonight. It's nice to have fresh faces, even if a bit unusual…"

She'd better be talking about Edgar or Mr. Tom and not me.

"There are many stories of when the basajaunak moved around a great deal more," she continued. "But my mother says that as humans took over more spaces and trees were torn down, our kind have grown stationary. Many of us have, anyway. I have never been anywhere. Everyone thinks *he* is rash or foolish for venturing out and following the stars, but he is doing as our ancestors did." Her voice softened. "I want to do that as well. I want to see more than this wood. I want to meet different creatures and sneak up on humans. Maybe *I* can get *my* picture taken and have everyone obsess over finding me." Her eyes sparkled before dimming again. "Anyway. Thank you for coming. Thank you for giving us a breath of the outside world."

I sat quietly as she disappeared into the trees. If only that breath of the outside world wasn't a crew of angry mages intent on destruction.

A loud splash brought me back to the moment. Another fish flew out, and Austin immediately pounced after it. I took a deep breath and let my smile return as I watched him assess his kill and then back off. His large form shrank into a man cut with muscle and glimmering with water.

"That should be good," he said, bending down to grab the latest fish and add it to the pile I'd made earlier. "Or should I try for a round dozen?"

He braced his hands on his hips as he glanced back at me. My alpha mate. The biggest, baddest alpha of them all, and I got to watch him mess around in the water and debate whether his offering would be enough.

I smiled and eased off the rock.

"My hero, the hunter," I said as my heart expanded and heat pooled low. "Or should I call you the fish slapper?"

His eyes heated as I slunk toward him, all hip and breast. He turned a bit more, showing the effect I was having on him.

"Hunter, obviously," he said in a deep voice, wading into the water toward me. He stopped me on the bank before backing me toward the rock I'd been sitting on. "I am man. Hear me grunt."

I laughed, and his lips touched down on mine.

"Are we alone?" he asked softly. His fingers worked at my shorts. "I've missed the feel of your body wrapped around me."

"It's only been one day," I said with a smile, sensing with magic and then cocooning us in a spell.

"One *night*. Nearly two days."

His hands dipped into my shorts.

I sucked in a breath and closed my eyes. He did tight circles with two fingers before sliding them through my wetness.

"We're alone," I said, pulling off my shirt. "No one will see us."

His kiss was deep and passionate. My clothes were removed in record time.

"I like it here," he said, slowing down for a moment so he could feel up my body. He ran his thumb across the peak of my breast, making me shiver. "I love being with you here. Or maybe I love being with you any-where, and the beauty of this place is just a bonus. Like your beauty is just a bonus to the amazing woman that you are."

I kissed him deep and long, hooking my leg onto his hip.

"I like you just for your looks," I murmured, and then laughed when he playfully bit my neck.

He whirled me around and pushed me forward. My palms slapped down on the rock. In the next moment, he sank deeply into me, eliciting my moan of pleasure. His sigh drifted toward me, sweet and satisfied, his pace unhurried.

His hands came around me to cup my breasts. The peace and serenity I felt in this spot merged with the delicious slide of his girth.

"Faster, Austin," I said, pushing back against him.

As he complied, I directed one of his hands down my stomach and to the spot of extra sensation. He massaged expertly while leaning over me. His hips hit my butt with each thrust. I breathed hard, tilting as he rushed forward now. Sinking further into the moment. Into my feelings for him.

My cry of climax came right before he shuddered behind me, groaning. His other hand came up to grab my hair and give it a small yank. I turned my face to the side so that he could run his teeth along my neck. It felt like a physical claim, and my gargoyle sent a burst of magic with the pleasure.

"That never gets old," he finally said as both of us

breathed heavily.

"Hopefully, it never will."

He turned me before pulling me into his arms. "It won't."

I fell into his kiss. When he pulled back, he gazed down into my eyes for several long moments, and somehow, that felt ten times more intimate than any physical touch.

"What do you say we get these fish to camp?" he murmured. "All of the teams should be back by now."

"We definitely need to. The only thing is…I'm really not looking forward to carrying half a dozen slimy fish."

His eyes narrowed a little in thought before he looked back at the pile. "Good point. Why don't you run back and get some help? I'm sure Mr. Tom would fall all over himself to carry them for you."

I tsked at him. "Be nice. That's his job. You should be ecstatic that someone wants to do the menial stuff so you don't have to," I joked.

That deep look was back. It felt like his eyes were peering into my soul.

"Or maybe I'm jealous that he's doing it and I am not."

I ran my hand up his chest. "You need to think that through. Doing my menial work isn't as glamorous as you're making it out to be. Running back to the house constantly because I've left something behind isn't on the 'fun task' list."

He shook his head slowly. "I wouldn't mind, Jess. I told you: ensuring your happiness is my duty as your mate, and I feel blessed to have been granted such a duty." He paused for a moment, and a smile budded. "But no, that's not why I pick on Mr. Tom."

"Why, then?" I asked, angling my face up.

He brushed his lips across mine. "Truth?"

"Truth."

"Because I can't help myself." He threw his head back and laughed. "Your crew is so…strange. Each member is more absurd than the last, including the weird mage and his gal pal. I can't…" He shook with laughter. "I just can't…" He gripped my shoulders. "If I don't poke fun, it'll start to seem normal, and then where will I be?"

"In my position, slowly slipping into insanity to eventually rival Edgar's?"

He sobered. "I vow that I will not let you *ever* get as bad as that vampire."

I belted out laughter. "All right, Casanova, let's get these home." I took a step back and closed my eyes.

"What are you doing?"

"I'm trying to connect with my gargoyle magic so I

can more effectively call my team. You know, reel them in like I sometimes do?"

But I couldn't seem to call up the ability at will. I hadn't really merged my gargoyle's magic with mine.

"You need to find your balance," Austin said, watching me. "To do that, you have to test your limits. To do *that*, you need to fully let yourself go. To allow that darkness to pull you under."

"I've done that, though."

"No. You've never willingly rushed into that darkness. Your gargoyle has been pulled out by Niamh or the call of battle. Part of learning control is choosing when to use your darkness. Believe me, Jess, I understand your fear. You know how long I've lived with it. But I found you. I know you'll pull me out if I ever go too far. Hopefully one day, you'll put the same trust in me."

"I *do* trust you. With everything I am."

"Then run into that darkness without looking back," he said, gently stroking his thumb along my jaw, "and know that I will never allow you to lose yourself to it. Your gargoyle will never keep you from me. Nothing on this earth could. Nothing but death." I stilled for a moment. "But maybe don't rush into it just yet. If you release a whole bunch of magic and my bear has to battle it, the basajaunak probably won't be overly impressed."

I grimaced. There was that.

"Why don't you just call your crew the normal way?" he continued. "Freak out a little and wish for Mr. Tom, and he'll fall all over himself to get to you."

I laughed and swatted him. "You're the worst."

I bent to get dressed, not mentioning that I intended to do exactly that.

# CHAPTER 22

"WELL, NOW, ISN'T this nice," Mr. Tom said that night as we walked into the communal area of the village—a large stretch of land cleared of growth, the dirt packed down. Three spread-out fires burned in the expanse, each crossed by a spit. A deer and what must've been a wild pig were being hand-turned over two of them, and various vegetables and roots were cooking on the third. "Given how the basajaun always gets on with flowers, I didn't expect this kind of decorum at all."

I gave him a flat look as we meandered through the various basajaunak, all of them visible to us. We'd clearly earned their trust enough that they didn't feel the need to use their hiding magic.

The knife of guilt cut through my stomach and twisted, drawing Austin's attention. He stood beside me, our fingers intertwined, and his arm kept brushing mine. I enjoyed the shivers it gave me, being so close to him. I felt like I was a teenager again, except for this very adult guilt riding me hard.

"You good?" he asked softly.

"Yeah, I'm fine," I replied in a low tone, needing to talk to him about all of this. I hadn't found a time yet. Or maybe I was just putting it off. We'd agreed on this course of action, after all. Including the basajaun, who was all for it. I just couldn't shake my unease, or the guilt dripping acid through me every time the warning pulses—happening more frequently now—tore into me.

That teen earlier hadn't known how to handle Austin. He'd been slow and ineffective. The basandere had told me this afternoon she'd never had any contact with the outside world. Everyone here was sheltered. Talk about setting the young people up for failure.

A few drumbeats sounded from across the clearing to my right, turning into a rhythm that was quickly joined by the delicate whine of string instruments. Five musicians played at the base of an enormous redwood tree. The trunk had to be twenty feet wide. Each instrument was crudely crafted from wood or animal skins. I wasn't sure how the strings had been made, but the resulting sound was beautiful and wild, fitting the scene perfectly.

"Miss Jessie, Alpha Steele." Our basajaun strode toward us. He stopped in front of us and surveyed our party. After nodding, he waved us on. "Come this way. I made sure to leave us a section on the side where everyone could see."

"And what is it we need to see?" Mr. Tom asked as we followed the basajaun.

If the basajaun heard, he made no indication. Instead, he led us to a spit and reached for it. The basajaun turning the handle stopped and waited for our basajaun to grab off a chunk and shove it into his mouth. He moved away and looked at Austin and me, clearly expecting us to follow suit.

"Allow me," Austin told me, following the basajaun's example. He didn't put the strip of meat to his mouth, though. He offered it to me before grabbing one for himself. That done, he moved us away a little so the others could partake.

"If I had known we'd be picking off carcasses like cavemen, I would've brought plates and flatware," Mr. Tom grumbled.

"Just don't suck on yer fingers and then go back for more," Niamh told him. "We don't need yer spit all over the place."

"Talk about double dipping," Jasper murmured when it was his turn. "I'm going to need a big hunk of this stuff. Ouch! That's hot. Don't they have a knife or something?"

"Don't be such a baby," Cyra told him.

"Easy for you to say," he responded, blowing on his fingers, the meat in his other hand.

"Please do me a favor," Austin said in a low tone, moving me a little farther away. "Don't let anyone but me get meat for you. Not even Mr. Tom. Definitely don't let anyone else feed you. We—shifters—have a similar sort of setup for mating dinners or large family gatherings. A male feeds his mate. If anyone else attempts to do so, it's seen as a challenge. Logically, I know that's not why Mr. Tom would get food for you, but my animal would ride me hard, and I might not be able to control it. I don't want to put you in an uncomfortable position. Can you do that for me? Wait for me to get food for you or do it yourself?"

"I mean, sure, I'll let you rip off pieces of meat from a carcass roasting over the fire. That's not exactly a hardship. And sure, I'll let only you do it. Mr. Tom will understand, especially since I don't want his fingers in everything. But actually feed me? Like a child?"

He stood close, and the heat of his body soaked into my chilled skin. The firelight flickered across his face, highlighting his intense gaze.

He reached his piece of meat forward slowly, and the heavy emotions through the bond started to make my heart thump quickly. He brushed the meat against my lips, and I opened my mouth to take it from him.

The overall piece was too large to take in one go, though.

"Use your teeth," he whispered, his eyes rooted to my lips.

Something about the command was incredibly erotic. It was like when he ran his teeth down my throat, raw and primal.

I did what he said, savagely tearing a chunk off and eating it as he leaned in a little closer. His kiss was possessive and hard, and it ignited my entire body.

"That's why I couldn't suffer another person feeding you," he said while I finished the bite and swallowed.

"And what about the other way around? Do I get to feed you?"

His intense gaze hadn't lifted from mine. "If you like," he said softly.

So that was a big yes.

I did the same as he'd done, but as I moved, something stalled my hand. My gargoyle, obviously. What else could it be? I could sense what was happening on a primal level but didn't understand it logically. Regardless, I allowed it to lead me. My hand stopped short and a bit below his lips, hovering in the air, waiting. I knew expectation lit my eyes.

Austin's eyes sparked in return. A tiny smile flirted with his lips. He understood what was happening, but he didn't fill me in. Instead, he dipped his head and captured my offering with his teeth. He pulled back, taking my hand with him, until he was standing straight again. Only then did he rip off a chunk and eat it.

Something hot and glorious flowered within me. It seeped into my blood and coursed through my veins. An overwhelming urge to drag him into the trees had me grabbing his shirt with a fist.

"You feel it," he said, not at all perturbed by my sudden dramatic shift. Liking it, even. "Imagine some other female—"

I put a finger over his mouth. "Let's just stop you right there before I do something crazy. I catch your drift."

"When yis are finished staring at each other, can we move on, like?" Niamh asked.

Austin turned and put his arm around me, eating the remainder of the bite left in his hand. I followed suit. The meat was bland, but my hunger had dissolved my ability to care.

"I think I'll let you rip off the chunks, though," I told him as our basajaun led us to the right and stopped on the outskirts of the clearing. "I'm not really a fan of ripping off pieces of meat in front of someone and then gnawing on them. I never did get behind the turkey legs at the fair."

"My pleasure," Austin replied, and stopped beside a lush bed of clover flanked by ferns.

We dropped down onto it, taking a seat, then freezing when Edgar picked his way past...and sat directly behind us.

"Why are you at my back, Edgar?" Austin asked in a gruff tone.

"I apologize, alpha. But you've chosen the only bed of clover, and I really must work on my ability to find four-leaf clovers. It seems I am a little rusty. Broken Susan seems to find them so easily. There really shouldn't statistically be as many as he is finding, yet he keeps spotting them. I think someone is trying to pull the wool over my eyes. Just in case, though, I'm honing my skills, as it were."

Austin turned to me slowly with a bewildered look. I started laughing as he turned to face front again, and I knew he was debating moving locations and letting Edgar win.

"It'll be fine," I whispered, patting his arm. "He won't bite you. Right, Edgar? You don't bite friends."

"Not if I can help it, Miss Jessie. I remember when I bit you out of necessity. My eye still hurts sometimes. That was a mean poke. I assume Alpha Steele would rip out my eye entirely. I'd rather not endure it if I don't have to."

"There. See?" I leaned against Austin and smiled up at him. "Totally safe."

He just shook his head and leaned into me.

We fell into silence for a while, listening to the music and watching the basajaunak. Our crew and pack were spread out around us, some in larger clusters than others. Sebastian sat at the edge of the wood with Niamh. To my surprise, Nessa was near Broken Sue. They were chatting—well, *she* was chatting—and occasionally, she would reach out and pat him on the shoulder or rub the top of his knee. Her touches were always in safe zones and never drawn out, almost like she was trying to cheer him up more than seduce him.

I made a mental note to check in with him when I could. My gargoyle magic had slunk away again, and I couldn't assess his mood through our connection.

After a while, Austin left to get us food. This time, he didn't feed it to me. I could tell he wanted to, but also that he worried about his control. Mine was slippery, and I didn't want to leave what felt like a celebration of some kind to disappear into the darkness and each other's bodies. We needed to practice a *little* restraint.

"Why haven't you fed me at home?" I asked him, and immediately felt myself blush. "That's a sentence I never thought I'd ask a grown man. I feel like I should call you Daddy or something."

He huffed out a laugh and finished chewing his fish, one of the ones he'd caught earlier, apparently. Then he shrugged. "It's not the same in a kitchen with plates and forks and everything. Feeding someone off a fork is a Dick and Jane thing. Like 'here, have a bite.' It's civilized."

"I remember feeding my son when he was a baby. That was anything but civilized. But I get what you mean."

"Basically, it takes the thrill out of it. But out here with the open fire, in nature, when our primal sides are singing…" He shivered. "It's different. It's how mating should be."

"Okay, but what about sitting on the deck with barbecued meat?"

He studied me for a silent beat. "I could see that. I can tell you're eager to try it."

"When we're alone, yeah. Yes, I am. Then maybe I'll show you how fun chocolate fondue can be."

It was my turn to shiver.

"I spoke to the basajaun when I was up getting food," he said after a moment, putting an arm around me and drawing me closer. "We've passed all of the trust trials. They don't fear us."

That stab of guilt cut through me again. I knew he felt it, but he didn't press this time. Instead, he went on.

"Brochan showed very well, not to mention the others. He got slapped down, and Niamh and the rest apparently stood by placidly, not a care in the world."

"Niamh seems to be pretty good at reading him. She would've stepped in if there was a problem."

"True. Nathanial excelled as well. He took the beating, got up, fluttered his wings, and waited for more. Sebastian surprised them a little, apparently."

"He did? But he was with us the whole time."

"No, they caught him a second time, when he was out with Cyra."

I hadn't heard about that. He hadn't mentioned it when I saw him at the camp before dinner.

"The lead basandere went for him..." Austin shook his head and looked away. I felt his amusement in the bonds before he shook his head again and started chuckling. "Please don't ever mention this to me in public, because I won't be able to keep my composure."

"Why? What happened?"

He kept chuckling. "I guess he just froze up and fell over." He bent over to laugh a little harder. "He didn't swear, he didn't shout, he just fell over before the basandere could even touch him. Stiff as a board he fell, then just lay there like he was playing dead. She stopped at his feet and stood there looking down at him, not sure what to do. Nessa was laughing so hard that they couldn't ask her what was going on. The basandere actually picked him up like a baby and carried him to their version of a medic to have him checked out."

"No," I said, laughing with him now. "He did that once when we were training and the basajaun snuck up on him and scared him, but he came out of it. I bet her carrying him just made it worse."

"Nessa told me the story. She said she hadn't laughed that hard in a long time. After they confirmed he was fine, just afraid, the only thing he said to her was 'I told you so,' and he walked away."

"That's terrible, poor guy. I can't imagine that could be construed as showing well, though."

"It's confused them, I think," said Austin. "The lead basandere is supposed to be able to see people's essences. She can see their potential, basically. She reads alpha in him. And honestly, as Elliot Graves, I see that side of him too. But not here, obviously."

"He wears a different persona when he's Elliot Graves, almost like he's hiding himself with someone else's skin. He hasn't accepted a connection from my gargoyle, but occasionally, I can get readings on him. Maybe it's the teacher–student bond or something. It seems there are all kinds of connections and links and bonds in the magical world."

"Or maybe your gargoyle is just latching on to anything it can, and he hasn't shut that facet of your relationship down?"

He asked it like I might know. When I shrugged, he went on.

"I'm not sure how healthy that is, hiding oneself, but he certainly hasn't pulled on that persona here. Maybe that's a good thing."

I didn't mention that I didn't think Sebastian really wanted that persona, that he seemed happier in the crystal room with his magic and his muttering. Maybe one day.

"So anyway," Austin said, "proving our control to them is a good thing. Apparently, it's another point in our favor that they can feel the power we have at our disposal. I'm told Brochan and I flared a few nostrils. That's their version of widening eyes. They haven't encountered shifters as strong as us before."

"Did our basajaun tell them about your brother and the other shifters you hope to amass?"

"Yes. It gave them something to think about."

A group of what looked like teenage basajaunak, however old they might actually be, chatted and laughed near the music, a few of them swaying or moving to the beat. An adult basajaun bit into a chunk of meat as he passed us to sit down with a few others who'd gathered within the trees.

"Then there's you," Austin went on. "They liked how you stepped up to defend me. It showed your fire. They haven't gotten a good viewing of your magic yet, though."

I grimaced. They'd only get that in a battle.

"Cyra and Hollace made more nostrils flare. We're a group of people packed with magic and alphas. They know that if they get tangled up in the outside world, or their extended family does, they'll have good support in us."

I blurted out what I knew in my heart: "Except this group of basajaunak don't get tangled up with the outside world. They stick to themselves. They stay here in safety and peace."

He didn't comment for a few moments. One of those horrible warning pulses vibrated through me. I couldn't tell how near the enemy was, but they must be closer, because the magic felt like it was seeping their emotions into me. Or maybe it was their intent? The feelings swirled within the spell that had attached itself to me. *Annoyance. Wariness. Anticipation of victory.*

They were annoyed to have to come get me. Wary because I'd used a spell they'd never heard of. Sebastian had said that would make them incredibly nervous. Any decent mage would be, knowing most heinous spells even if they couldn't do them. But as far as the end result? They worked for a man who didn't seem to lose often, or ever. They'd always worked for the winning side.

They must be coming in a hurry, too, for the spell's danger signals to be ramping up this quickly. They'd clearly wasted no time. The spell was probably to blame for that, and their resources obviously made fast travel accessible.

I spied three young basajaunak chase each other through the open space. An adult basandere yelled at them to slow down as they sprinted by.

The guilt threatened to choke me.

"Why don't you finally tell me what's going on in that heart of yours?" Austin said.

He didn't say *head*. He knew I wasn't operating on the logic by which we'd made the original plan.

"It's just..." I wrapped us in a soundproofing spell for some privacy. "Austin, what are we doing? I yelled at them about not watching out for their kid earlier today. Their *kid*. What would I do to someone who put my child in danger? Imagine for a second that we were putting your niece and nephew in danger. How would you react to our plan then?"

A shock of rage blistered through the bonds.

"Exactly," I murmured. "This is their family. Our basajaun isn't thinking clearly. With their help, it might be a clean sweep, sure. It might be easy. But what if something happened and one of their children was hurt? What if *any* of them were hurt? They didn't ask for this. They don't deserve the danger we're putting them in. We've earned their trust under false pretenses. I know we agreed on this plan, and I know you really need their help with the mages, but…" I sighed. "I don't feel good about what we're doing here. It isn't right."

Austin nodded as he surveyed the basajaunak around us. Cyra got up and drifted to the music, bobbing and swaying. She joined the teens and started laughing when they froze to gawk at her. In a moment, though, they smiled and joined her. Isabelle got up, too, dragging Kace with her.

"I agree," Austin finally said. "When we decided on this course of action, I wasn't thinking beyond the danger to us from them. But you're right. Even if we lure the mages away from them a little, the young basajaunak seem curious and filled with ignorant courage. That youth who challenged me earlier had no idea what kind of danger he'd brought on himself. If we aren't far enough away, some of them may follow us and engage when they shouldn't. We're putting the whole village at risk."

"You're right. The young basandere I met earlier seemed eager to spread her wings, so to speak. So…" I put up my hands. "What do we do?"

He looked at me. "You know what we should do," he said softly. "We both do."

"But, like…do we tell them why we're leaving? That we intended to deceive them? I can't imagine that would go over well. Leaving early with no explanation won't exactly go over well, either."

"Missus Jessie, if I may." Edgar pushed his head up even with us, much too close. I hadn't realized I'd included him in the spell. I wasn't enthused by the idea that he was becoming the same sort of white noise as Mr. Tom. Edgar wasn't someone I wanted to entirely lose track of.

I leaned away, harder into Austin.

"Honesty is rarely the best policy," Edgar said. "If you want them to trust you, you need to be forthright about what is happening."

I furrowed my brow at him. "I'm not following."

"I don't think he meant the 'rarely' part of the first sentence," Austin murmured.

"Ah, yes, I see where I went wrong there." Edgar half smiled and shook his head as though we were commiserating about something. "Words, right? *Words*."

"What—" I rubbed my eyes. "We need Niamh or Mr. Tom to translate."

"What I think you should do is tell them you sense danger coming," Edgar went on. "That you thought you'd handled a problem back at home but now you worry it might have followed you here. I'll let you and Mr. Austin work out the details. He's an alpha. He always knows the right answer. A partial truth is still true. Mostly."

I stared at him for a moment. "That's actually a good idea."

"Yes," he replied, slinking back again. "Sometimes I have them often."

*Words*, indeed.

"When do we tell them?" Austin asked, and I knew he was actually asking how much time we had left.

I shook my head. I didn't know. But given that the pulses were coming faster and faster, and I was starting to feel our adversaries' menace, I doubted we had long. The trek through the woods would likely slow them down, but even so, we were running out of time.

I explained all that to him. "Where can we go? We can't endanger the town any more than we can this village."

"We ask them where to go," he said. "We tell them about the danger coming, apologize for involving them, and ask where we can make a stand against the threat. This natural preserve is huge. There must be a great many places we can do this that will be far enough to keep their youth from following."

I groaned. "That means more hiking."

It also meant we'd almost certainly be outnumbered and battling up that theoretical hill.

# CHAPTER 23

THE HORRIBLE HUM within me sauntered on with the night. Music flowed, food was eaten, and I tried to find a time when we were all together so I could quietly broach the subject of leaving without blowing our cover. I needed to ask the basajaun how best to approach the basandere. And also…I was freaked out about admitting our fault in all of this. I knew I had to, and I knew it was the right thing to do, but man, inciting a very violent type of creature wasn't on my list of most anticipated things to do tonight.

My only consolation was that I knew that even if the mages got near the preserve, they'd be hard-pressed to navigate it in the dark. We had a little time. How little, I couldn't be sure.

One thing I did do, though, was cut out the Ivy House links. At the crew's confused or inquiring looks, I snuggled up close to Austin and gave the impression I wanted a little privacy. They were all having such a good time, dancing and eating and even branching out and chatting to the locals, that I didn't want to spoil their fun before I absolutely had to.

I couldn't hide my feelings from Austin, though, and he hugged me tightly, knowing what I was waiting for. And why. I also couldn't seem to cut the gargoyle connection links to Kace and Broken Sue, who glanced over often, wondering what was up.

The water provided for drinking was cool and refreshing, and the homemade alcoholic fruit drink tasted like gasoline. I coughed and sputtered and beat at my chest every time I took a sip. That and needing to stay coherent ensured I didn't take many.

At close to midnight, the music stopped. I assumed the party was winding down and my death march just beginning. Now or never. I needed to grab the basajaun, round everyone up, have a quick chat, and go admit guilt to a ferocious creature and her people. Hopefully, I would live long enough to meet the mages.

Surprisingly, though, the lead basandere stepped up behind the most central firepit. She wore a sort of headdress with draping moss, adorned with bones and animal teeth. The cover over her bottom half had been changed to a deep red number adorned with beads and shiny decorations.

Firelight flicked across her stern expression. Her hand drifted out and then moved fast, dropping something into the flames. Light flared, and the flames licked the sky before dying down again. All eyes turned her way. She was focused on me.

"*Her.* Please step forward," the basandere said.

Shivers coated my body. Crap, had my soundproofing spell not worked earlier? Or had our basajaun come clean? I wasn't ready to face her yet! I hadn't properly chased away my cowardice!

Austin must've had the same thought, because wariness pumped through the bonds. He stood with me, his hand on the small of my back.

"It is okay," our basajaun said, walking closer. "They mean you no danger."

I nodded at him stiffly and walked forward. She waited behind the crackling fire for me to approach her, and then directed me around it and to her right.

"Turn to face your people," she told me softly.

Austin had followed me, and he stood by my side, sending the message that we were a team. A unit. I lifted the muffle on the Ivy House bonds, finding readiness waiting for me. Many watched me placidly enough, sitting back with bland expressions, but if the situation escalated, so would they. Sebastian had moved to the side of the clearing, by a tree, his hands out and ready. Next to him, Nessa had her hands on her hips. Broken Sue had gone the other direction, connecting with the shifters and standing just in front of them, braced and ready.

They might not know what was going on, or even that I'd been anxious all night, but they were clearly a team that could pivot on a dime. The seemingly benign evening before this didn't blind them from the prospect of these creatures turning on us and the situation turning ugly at a moment's notice.

"*Him.* Come forward," the basandere said in a loud, clear voice. As our basajaun walked to her other side, she turned her head to me and said quietly, "They guard you well. It is clear they have great respect for you. Such respect comes from trust. Trust comes from doing right by them."

"I hope so. We all do right by each other. It's how we work."

"Yes. You care about one another. Like family."

Our basajaun stopped at her other side. Expectation filled the space.

"*Him* left our community to follow the stars," the basandere said after a silent beat.

My body pulsed with the spell's warning, and this time, I felt a curl of malice from the enemy through the spell. Sweat beaded on my forehead.

"He found a lonely mountain to the southeast to call home," she said. "There he stayed, despite our protests.

Despite our attempts to bring him back. And it was there he found what he'd been searching for. He met *her* under the mountain. He followed her to distant caves. He protects her, guards her, and fights for her…as she does for him. She has provided him with food, welcomed him into her stick-builder's ways, and introduced him to her young one. She asks nothing. He asks nothing. They ask everything. They are family. Come."

She held out her hands to each of us. I followed the basajaun's lead and took her hand.

"It is time." She lifted our hands into the air and then back down. After releasing them, she dug into a little pouch I hadn't noticed on her left side. "It is time to reveal the name of his essence to his family. Given we know this name and the stick-builders do not guard the naming of their essences, you may all be present to witness the exchange."

A swirl of excitement and expectation filled the bond. Ulric was clearly beside himself to learn the basajaun's actual name.

"Alpha Jessie Ironheart." The basandere threw powder into the fire. It surged again, and the flames turned green. "Buln'dan of the Ai'Foran brood." She threw in more powder, yellow this time. "You will guard each other's essence above all else. You are family."

It sounded like essence was their way of saying soul, or maybe life force? Regardless, it was clearly an honor.

She combined the powder and threw it into the fire; the green mixed with the yellow and reached toward the heavens.

"It is done," she finished.

The village repeated the words, and I couldn't help connecting that saying to the basajaun's words whenever he finished enacting a punishment.

I murmured the phrase with them, though, not wanting to cause offense and get my head drop-kicked. Ulric lifted his hands in the air in triumph, presumably because he'd finally learned the basajaun's name.

Before whatever was going to happen next could, Edgar said, "He's going to need a nickname for public places. We can't reveal his name to non-family. I wonder if he wants to be Mrs. Smith, maybe. Or Lieutenant Dan."

I was pretty sure Edgar didn't realize he was using a name from *Forrest Gump*, and that fact made it even funnier.

Struggling not to laugh, I bowed for no real reason and then followed the basajaun's—Buln'dan's—lead around the fire to stand in front of it.

"I thank you for accepting me," Buln'dan said. "And

I will accept the nickname Missus Smith."

"Oh, no, you don't need to go by that," I rushed to say. "No, we can call you—"

"I have always wanted a nickname," he went on. "Ever since I was a kid, I have wanted my friends to come up with one. A name built on friendship and joy and humor. Even the shifter has a nickname."

"Well, Broken Sue came from—"

"Edgar has dubbed me Missus Smith," he said. "It is a good name. A generic stick-builder name, is it not?"

"I think Dan is probably a better stick-builder name, actually," I said, not to be deterred this time. "Mrs. Smith will probably make us seem even odder—"

"It's perfect," Sebastian said from beside his tree. "Calling him Mrs. Smith when mages are present is perfect."

"And at home," Nessa said, bouncing a few steps away from Sebastian now, "we can use the very familiar and a lot more fitting nickname Dave. How's that? Two nicknames. One for family, and one for…non-family."

"Dave?" I said in bewilderment. "That's not even part of his real name. Lieutenant Dan would be more fitting than randomly calling him *Dave*."

Buln'dan's smile made his beard move and shift. "Yes. Two nicknames. It is done."

"No, but…" I let out a sigh. What was the point in

steering this ship toward logical waters? I'd always lose that battle. "Right, fine, okay. Fantastic," I said as the fire surged behind us. "Great names."

"Now go. Enjoy the festivities," the basandere said.

Everyone cheered, raising their wooden cups. The musicians started playing a faster song, and Buln'dan—Dave, I guessed—grabbed my hand and lifted it into the air. The cheer went up again as Dave laughed.

"It was a long time coming, wasn't it, Jessie Ironheart?" he said as we continued to face the crowd. "The stars are shining brightly on us. Our paths were meant to cross. Teaming up with Ivy House is a great honor. I am sure of it. My family will realize it soon."

"About that." I chewed my lip for a moment. "We need to talk."

I finally gathered our crew closer together, knowing time had run out, and wrapped us all in a privacy bubble. There I laid out what Austin and I had discussed. I explained my concerns and made it abundantly clear that I would not be talked out of my decision.

When I was finished, everyone stood in quiet contemplation. I didn't peek at their feelings through the bond, worried it might shake my resolve.

It was Niamh who spoke first—not to me, though. "Sebastian, based on your best guess, can we handle what comes without the basajaunak?"

He stood at the edge of our circle, picking at his nail, *thinking*. Then he confirmed what I'd feared. "They'll almost certainly outnumber us," he said. "They were never going to show up to an undisclosed location, to meet a mage who could do strong and surprising spells—a mage who'd rattled their guy so much—with conservative numbers."

"Okay, so. Let's dissect this." Niamh got a little more comfortable. "Let's start with the mages," she said with a somewhat stronger brogue. Her fingers wrapped around one of the wooden cups, and I assumed it wasn't water inside. Clearly, she'd found a drink that could give her a run for her money. "The mages. What are we lookin' at?"

"I'm guessing they'll bring a team," Sebastian replied. "Nessa?"

Nessa stepped closer and tucked a flyaway hair behind her ear. "I'm thinking four or five adequate mages. They'll have a thorough knowledge of spells, but they won't have the power to do half of them. They *will* have potions and other aids to help them bridge the gap against a more powerful mage."

"Jessie and I can render them mostly ineffective with defensive spells," Sebastian said. "I create a larger gap than most, and Jessie widens it beyond what they could be prepared for. She's not very experienced, though. She'll really only have brute strength to work with. Anything else will take her too long to complete within the enemy's onslaught."

"Get her on defense," she told him. "She was damn good at defense in the gladiator-type battle at your meetup."

He nodded slowly. "True. Yeah. If she can run a very strong defense, I can fortify it. That'll lock up our efforts, though. We won't be able to help with any offensive magic against their ground crew."

"Do we know what to expect with their ground crew?" Austin asked. "These are the highly trained troops?"

"Yes. Think mercenaries, but much more effective. These troops are on Momar's payroll, used as needed for a variety of situations. Destroy shifter packs, for example. They've been trained to deaden their emotional response to massacres. Mercy is not in their vocabulary. They can all fight hand to hand or with specialized weapons, and they fight brutally. Viciously."

"Sir, may I?" Broken Sue asked, his arms clasped behind his back in a way that showcased his bulging muscle. I could tell he was staring down the barrel of his past. I understood his struggle with emotion. Even so, he clearly wasn't backing down.

"Go," Austin said.

"Freezing out those mages is the only thing that matters. Taking away their magic is seventy-five percent of the battle, no matter who's in their ground crew. My pack could've handled the grunts, even five to one. It was the magic that did us in."

Ulric raised his hand. "Is everyone forgetting that we have fliers? Freeze up the mages, and we can fly right over the ground crew and take the mages out. That then frees up our mages for attacking the ground crew, which we can then help with as well."

"Their ground crew aren't just grunts," Sebastian said. "It would be a mistake to underestimate them. And they have weapons that can take down fliers."

"All due respect, weird mage," Nathanial said, "but we aren't just average fliers. We're gargoyles. Their weapons are nothing."

Nessa smiled at him. "And now we're seeing how the stubborn streak in gargoyles can really benefit a team."

"It's settled, then," Austin said. "Our mages will counter theirs until the gargoyles can dismantle the mages entirely. While that's progressing, my pack and the rest of the Ivy House crew will take on their ground team until the mages can back us up."

Sebastian shook his head. "Either you guys aren't

really hearing me or your courage is completely off the charts."

"Or they're as dumb as rocks," Niamh said before taking a gulp of her drink. "Either way, we've got no other options. Unless we want to hike back to Ivy House, hope we make it ahead of the enemy, and take them on while we're attacked by flesh-eating gnomes." Another gulp. "What's the timeline on retiring Edgar fer that gnome fiasco?"

"Yes," Edgar said solemnly. "I really have stuck my foot in it with those gnomes. The dolls aren't as effective as I'd hoped. We're running out of spare parts to repair our fallen soldiers. There really is no excuse, Miss Jessie. It's a dereliction of duty, and I should finally be put out of your misery."

"Seriously, Niamh, don't get him started." I rubbed my face. "I don't think we have the time to go back to Ivy House even if we ignore the reasons we didn't want this battle in town in the first place. They were on the move incredibly quickly. No offense to our team, but they seem a lot more organized than we are."

"I must express my sadness at this new plan," Dave said. My brain really was having a hard time calling him that. "I wanted my family to witness the greatness of Ivy House. They are so intrigued about you. I have talked to many who are eager to learn more. If they saw you in battle, it would really flare their nostrils, I know it. The elders might remember the thrill of the fight. I think it would be the final straw to entice at least some of them out of the safety of the wood, I really do."

"I understand that. But the decision to fight is one they have to make on their own. We can't force it on them. We can't endanger your family, bas—Dave."

"Does anyone else think calling him Dave is absurd?" Ulric whispered. "I like Buln'dan. That's badass."

"But someone might overhear us calling him that. Like at the bar or something," Jasper replied just as quietly. "Then we might piss him off and get our arms pulled off for our trouble."

"True. But what about on Ivy House—"

"Focus," Nathanial barked, and it was the first time I saw him go hardcore alpha on them. It couldn't have been the first time he had, though, because both guys immediately closed down all chatter and looked almost remorseful as they did so.

"You are correct, Miss Jessie," Dave said. "I was not thinking. Hoping, but not thinking."

"Okay." I put my hand on Austin's shoulder for no real reason. "So then, on to the scary part. Any tips and tricks to explaining this to the lead basandere?"

"No." Dave stood and rolled his shoulders. "Honor dictates that I must fess up to this. I will take this up with *her.*"

"We should start running then, so," Niamh said, before finishing her drink and moving to stand.

# CHAPTER 24

"YOU DO NOT need to run," Dave said. "I will claim responsibility and accept the punishment. You might be exiled in shame, but you will not be killed."

I held up my finger. "Except...Edgar brought up a good point earlier." That earned me some looks. "I know. No one was as shocked as I was. Maybe we can just tell them most of the truth? That way, we'll still have an opportunity to work them around—"

He walked through the spell in determination.

"Crap," I said, scrambling after him.

"What are you going to do?" Austin asked, catching up.

"Well, go," I heard Mr. Tom say behind us. "This was originally your plan. You had all that talk about falling on swords and building empires and maneuvering people—where are you now?"

I wasn't sure what he was talking about, but Niamh seemed to know.

"Enjoying me drink, that's where I am now," Niamh responded. "This stuff has a punch—Oh, all right, keep yer wig on."

Dave found the lead basandere sitting beside one of the smaller fires, chatting with two others. They fell silent at our approach, looking between us. Without a word, the two basandere I didn't know stood and walked away without a backward glance. They must've sensed we had something important to talk to their leader about. Or maybe they were reading it in Dave's body language.

"Yes? What is it?" the basandere asked, looking at Dave.

Niamh joined us, standing a little removed. I doubted she'd be much help here.

"*Her*," Dave began. "There is something I need to tell you. May I sit down?"

"Yes." Her gaze flicked to me.

"I…uh…" I felt like a child going to a parent to confess I'd graffitied the lockers at school. "I'm here to possibly explain or at least support or"—*to hear the final verdict and blast you with magic in case you decide to kill us all*—"other stuff," I finished lamely.

"Sit," she told me. Austin and Niamh remained standing, leaving Dave and me as the focal points in this conversation. They had both just written themselves onto my shit list.

"I have made an error in judgment," Dave started, and then spun an amazing tale that was all true but with a couple of large omitted details. It was exactly the approach Edgar had been advocating.

He hung the tale on a key point: we were supposed to visit anyway and hadn't wanted to break our promise despite the danger on our heels.

We hadn't wanted to break our promise. Genius. Even Niamh was impressed with that one. I could feel it through the bond.

When he was finally done, his eyes downcast, his shoulders hunched, the basandere said, "I see." She shifted her attention to me and studied me for a long time. The firelight glinted off her dark brown eyes. "Tell me," she said, "what did you think of Buln'dan when you first met him?"

The sharp left turn had me blinking stupidly. "Um…" Thoughts jumbled in my brain. "I hardly remember. I had been kidnapped and was trapped in a cage suspended over spikes. He just added to the overall impending doom of the moment. But I appreciated his being kind when he spoke to me."

At least, I *thought* he'd been kind. That moment had been so packed full of adrenaline that I didn't remember. I just remembered he'd agreed to go for an impromptu break so that I might try to escape in exchange for magical flowers. I didn't think he'd want her to know that, though.

"And when you were not suspended above spikes, awaiting your demise?" she asked.

I lifted my eyebrows, thinking. A lot had happened since then. "Nervous, I guess. Or, at least, everyone else was nervous. Or scared. But I didn't think he'd hurt me. So I was a little taken aback when I witnessed his extreme brutality in battle. I was definitely nervous then, wondering if I'd break some random rule and get Hulk-smashed because of it."

She blinked a few times. "Hulk-smashed?" She shook her head. "It does not matter. I get the point. And coming here? Were you not worried we would uncover this ruse and seek retribution?"

"We're still worried about that, yeah."

"It's hard to believe," Niamh said, "that any member of yer family could be vulnerable. Jessie wasn't worried when confronting a basajaun the first time because she didn't know what the hell she was doing, like. She didn't know what he was actually capable of, and once she figured it out, she trusted their rapport."

"But *you* knew what he was capable of," the basandere said to Niamh. Her gaze switched to Austin. "You did. And yet you still went into his territory, uninvited.

He has told me the story."

"We went into his territory the right way," Austin replied. "We asked for his approval. And we did it because Jess needed his help. I was there in case anything happened. He had the option to say no. He chose to barter."

She studied him for a long time. "And now, you need our help."

"We don't need ye to sort this out, sure we don't," Niamh said. "We'll stumble through the wood, find a place to make a stand, and wait for the mages to come find us. We've got a plan and plenty of power. We just needed to get out of our town so as not to endanger its people."

"You preferred to endanger us?" the basandere shot back, and suddenly, I wasn't happy Mr. Tom had shoved Niamh into tagging along.

I didn't get a chance to do damage control.

"This group of enemy *eejits* aren't goin'ta trouble ye at all." She waved the possibility away. "They are the lackeys. Jessie and that other weird mage are about as strong as they come—much stronger than what is coming. That weird mage is as good as a magical encyclopedia. Don't let all the stoopin' and knee scrapin' fool ya. Once he's in his element, he's worth his weight in gold. They will block the enemy mages, and then what do ye have? Beefed-up mercenaries. Remember what those are? Or have ye been playin' hide 'n' seek with hikers for too long?"

"Maybe don't lean on the 'I offend people as my duty' angle of your personality this once," I murmured to Niamh.

She clearly didn't hear me because she didn't change her tone. "If ye have any sort of savageness left to ye, which ye must, since Missus Smith enjoys ripping off limbs and throwing them around the place, ye'd blow right through them. They can't sense ye like the shifters can, and our mages could keep 'em from using magic to locate ye. Ye'd be phantoms until ye ripped out their middles and flung their bodies over yer shoulders. It'd be nothing more than a bit of sport for ya."

Well, that explanation was a bit much.

The basandere caught my grimace. "And you tried to convince *her* of this?"

She was asking the others but clearly talking about me, so I answered. "They did. And I believed it."

"What changed your mind?" she pushed.

I swallowed and took a moment because I knew this was essentially a trial, and I didn't want to mess up more than the others already had. Thank God I could just use the truth on this one. I told her about the peace and contentment I'd experienced here, how my gargoyle felt at home. I told her that I had a son, too, and I'd realized how angry I'd be if the tables were turned. How violent it would make me—

And then I froze in panic because I hadn't meant to say that last bit.

"I mean…it's just…" I held my breath for a long moment, hoping one of the others would come to my aid. When they didn't, I made a mental note to plan horrible jokes on them and tried again. "Anyway, it would be wrong to put you and your family in danger. Even if nothing's likely to happen, something could, and I couldn't live with that possibility. It's better if we go."

Again she studied me. Everyone held silent. This was clearly the deliberation before the verdict.

"Buln'dan left to follow the stars," she finally said, pushing back onto her hands and gazing upward through the space between the tall trees. Pricks of light glimmered within the sheet of black. "It is hard to set off on one's own. You always wonder if you did the right thing. In unsure moments, insecure moments, you seek validation. You try to push other people onto your path to prove it was the right one. This is what he is doing. He is trying to force us to join his journey."

I pressed my lips tightly together to keep from saying anything but couldn't help myself. "Except he didn't try to force you to join his journey when he left." I cocked my head. "Or did he? Was he trying to get you to his mountain all this time?"

Dave's face snapped up. The basandere narrowed her eyes.

I felt my eyebrows lift of their own accord. "I honestly don't know anything. I'm just asking. It hadn't occurred to me before now."

"No," Dave said with a budding smile. "I didn't. Through loneliness, times when I wondered if I should just return and seek a mate...I never felt the pull enough to change my mind. In fact, I felt a stronger urge to stay."

"Right. So it's not—"

"This village—*you*—were trying to push *me* onto a certain path," Dave continued. "You tried to talk me into coming back every time I visited. Even now, you would prefer that I return. I do not feel that urge, though. I feel the rightness in what I am doing."

"But you are forcing us into your ways," the basandere countered.

He hung his head a little again.

"Have ye been motherin' long or what?" Niamh asked sarcastically, and my mouth dropped open. I furrowed my brow and looked between the two basajaunak. I hadn't realized they were related. Dave never used *Mom* or a similar name. "He isn't tryin'ta force ye onto his path or journey or whatever it is yer talkin' about. He's tryin' ta include ya, fer fuck's sake. He's tryin' to show off how powerful his new family is, and the only way he can do that is if ye see us in action. Ye haven't lived unless ye've seen a female gargoyle at work. Or a phoenix or thunderbird. Or even what Austin Steele can get up to when he's roused. Ye have no idea the sort of magic that weird mage can spin. The strange vampire? He'll give ye a shock with how well he fills in the natural gaps in battle. Sassy Smith or whatever we're callin' him is proud." She looked around and then glanced into her cup. "And I'm empty. Let's hurry this along. I think I might actually feel a little buzz from this stuff. It's been a while. I'm enjoyin' meself. Anyway, the other reason has got to occur to ye as well. I swear, yer bein' awfully daft. After all this time, he has finally found his purpose. Now he wants to merge both parts of his life. Cop on to yerself. He doesn't need you on his journey. He just needs everyone to get along." She pointed with her free hand. "Right. I need to go fill 'er up. I'll let yis sort out this mess."

She walked off without looking back.

"She came with the house," I said quickly. "I didn't choose her for the team, she just sorta…came with it all. Also, I'm not very astute, and I honestly didn't know he was your son. He never mentioned it." I furrowed my brow. "I actually have no idea how Niamh knew that. Was she eavesdropping or something—"

"I need to think about all this," the basandere said. "*Her*, you are absolved of blame. I will consider it an incorrect judgment call that you rectified before it affected us. Next time, however, I will not be so lenient."

"Understood. Thank you for being—"

"Tomorrow," she went on, "or when you deem it fit, I will direct you to a different place where there will be more space for your battle. We will send a small group with you to ensure you do not starve or die while waiting for this threat to find you." She hesitated. "Though I must admit your hunting and fishing prowess should serve you adequately. As a favor to Buln'dan, we will also teach you the best ways to hide and then ambush your prey. When the enemy draws near, we will depart. This is not our battle. And while you are welcomed guests, now and in the future, you are not family. We have no obligation to you, nor you to us."

"Agreed," I said, letting out a breath. It wasn't exactly what we'd hoped for, but it was better than we'd feared. I'd take it.

She nodded, spearing Dave with a look. "You and I will speak more about this later."

"Yes," he said, and I could feel the emotions swirling through him. Before, that might've made me nervous, but the knowledge of their relationship eased my worry for him. She wouldn't kill her son. Whatever she did do wouldn't be forever. Not if she'd already bent this far for him.

"Go. Enjoy the rest of the celebration," the basandere said. "I think a wager has been placed on how much your puca can consume."

"The money—or whatever it is you wagered," I said, "is going to go to the most extreme bet. She's going to drink you dry, you watch."

The basandere looked that way, but Niamh was already gone. We found her back at our area, sitting and watching the growing number of dancers by the music.

"Did it work?" she asked as we sat down. "Did she feel motherly guilt and go easy on you and him?"

I frowned at her. "That was your plan?"

"Of course that was me plan. She's a shrewd one. Hard. Good leader. But mothers are easy. They have a lot of pressure points."

"How do you figure?" I asked as Ulric handed me a mug of that awful, gasoline-tasting fruit alcohol.

"Isn't it obvious?" She waited for Austin to squeeze my shoulder before moving off toward Broken Sue. He would fill him in on what had just happened and the change in plans. "Now, I don't know this personally, but I've seen it often enough. Mothers never seem to feel like they are doing enough, do they? They tell me these stories, and I always think, the poor *cratur*! They juggle a million things at once, seems like. They're always overwhelmed. Ready to crack. They're expected to not just keep the wheels on the bus but construct the bloody thing, too. Then drive it. And wash it. And change the oil. I don't know how they don't just randomly start punching people. I would. What do they get fer their trouble? Ignored. What bollocks. I hear it all the time. Do it all, do it perfectly, and your reward is to be ignored. Is it any wonder they all feel, deep down, like they are failing? It makes me bloody furious. I tell these women all the time, I say, 'Love, you just need to burn it all to the ground.' They always laugh. They don't take me seriously."

"What's happening?" Ulric asked someone. "Is Niamh going soft on us?"

"Bugger off, ya muppet." Niamh grabbed a rock that had been resting beside her and threw it in his direction.

"Ow," Jasper said. "Where the hell did she get a throwing rock? These patches are all cleared and soft!"

"Always be ready to duck, bro," Ulric responded. "She has ammo everywhere."

"Anyway," Niamh went on after taking another slug of her drink, "oul Missus Smith's mother—I wasn't sure all that was in her baggage trolly. But lo and behold, she mentioned all that crap about him tryin' to force them on *his* journey. She's the only one around here with a son who took off and refuses to live life like everyone else. Hello, pressure point. She's probably judged for it. Or maybe she just judges herself. Or hell, maybe she's pissed she didn't get her way. I don't care. Easy pressure point to exploit, that is. She showed her hand with that one."

My head whirled.

I didn't feel that way now, with Jimmy grown and on his own, but I'd definitely experienced all of that when he was younger: frazzled and on edge, always behind, always forgetting something, always asked to do more when I was at my max. Judged for forgetting something, judged for my parenting style, my hard work always ignored by Matt. He'd expected me to do all of it while still looking perfect.

Oh yeah, I remembered those years. I remembered constantly feeling like I was failing. At the time, I'd had no idea other people felt the same way. That other people were struggling to keep up. But if what Niamh said was true, I hadn't been alone. I only wished I'd had a woman like her around when I was drowning and people kept dumping more water on me.

"Holy crapbirds," Nessa said, breaking my reverie. "You're my hero. That was incredibly vicious but super effective. I realized they were mother and son, but you're right, she's a hard one to read. I expected war because we endangered her people. I mean, she gave us that bogus warning about the last people who came through here and supposedly killed their people, but I couldn't see a way to exploit it. Well done."

"That was a bogus story?" I said wistfully. "Am I really this gullible that I just believe everyone?"

"Yes," Niamh replied.

"That's why you have us." Nessa beamed at me. "I tend to think everyone is a bald-faced liar."

"But…" Jasper shook his head at Niamh. "You just became the type of person you want to burn down. You made her feel bad about her decisions."

"First of all, boyo, if there is a hell, I've already got my seat reserved." Niamh raised her glass. "Might as well go down in flames. But no, I freed her. Shur, it'll be balls at first, the guilt and all that, but just you wait. It'll all work out. This way, she won't think her dear, sweet boy—who rips off heads and throws bodies off cliffs—is sufferin' out in the big, bad world all by his lonesome. Maybe more people will join him on his grand adventure, and she won't be the only mother with a kid who couldn't wait to leave. Whatever the reason, I'm helpin' her think of the whole thing differently. Worst case, she hates me. There is comfort in knowing it was a miserable old bag that issued the unwelcome opinion."

"Do you just sit on that stool in the alpha's bar," Ulric said slowly, leaning forward to squint at her through the darkness, "and churn stuff like this over in your mind? All the different ways your manipulation tactics could go?"

"Before Jessie, I just did it for fun, like. Now, though...yes. I have'ta hone my skills again. A long time has passed since I dabbled in ruining kingdoms and wrestled with the worst creatures to walk the earth. I need to refresh meself."

He shook his head and leaned away. "Don't mention what you've deduced about me. I don't want to know."

"No, ye don't."

Nessa started laughing.

Niamh finished her mug, then mused, "Good drinkin' buddies, those mothers on the edge. If ye can get them to talk about something other than their kids, I mean. I hate hearin' about kids. Why do I care that your little monster got a gold star for playin' nice with others? I do not relate."

"No, you do not," Jasper mumbled, and then I

heard a quick shuffle. He must've ducked just in case.

"But I'll tell ya, get a mother to let her hair down, and by the end of the night, she is dancing or crying or falling 'round the place, or all of the above. It's a helluva show. One group the other night got all riled up about some wanker sayin' something. One of 'em tried to stab him with her high heel." She tipped her head back and started laughing. "That was a grand night, that was. I picked up their tab. Great craic."

"On that note." I handed Niamh my mug and stood. "They have a bet regarding how much you'll drink. Just don't go crazy. There are no hospitals to pump stomachs way out here."

"Do ye *hear* her?" It was unclear whom Niamh was talking to.

Edgar clearly thought it was him. "I can."

"Hospital, me bollacks. I'll drink every drop and have a nice snore when I'm done."

"Dang." Ulric stood. "I guess I'd better drink a little more so I can pass out and not hear that."

"Do what ye like." She swayed just a bit, and I decided that was definitely my cue. Otherwise, she might talk me into drinking with her, or worse, tell me what she'd deduced about my personality. Like Ulric, I didn't want to know.

Mr. Tom joined me after I'd taken a few steps away

from the other group. "Since you are done listening to that godawful woman, shall I prepare your pajamas for you? Or get you a cup of water? I assume that is still within my ability, or do shifters have overly possessive tendencies around water as well?"

He hadn't been at all amused to learn he wasn't allowed to get me food or even a few nuts from what he thought of as an outdoor kitchen. He didn't like Austin taking away his duties. We needed to get back to Ivy House so he could at least still rob Austin's clothes and clean up Niamh's trash. A mother hen liked to feel useful, after all.

"Water would be great, thanks, Mr. Tom." I smiled at him as Austin joined me.

"You're not going to stay and see if Niamh will drink herself into a coma?" he asked as he ran his palm across my back and hooked it around my hip.

I mimicked the movement, and butterflies tickled my stomach as I felt across his hard back and around his waist. Goosebumps coated my skin, and I leaned against him, feeling warm and tingly all over.

"With anyone else, I would be nervous about how much she was consuming," I murmured as we took the path, and the sounds of the feast diminished.

"Don't be. She knows her limits if she has any, and I'm honestly not sure she does. I've never known another puca, so maybe it's a trait of the creature, but I've never seen anyone who can hold their liquor so well as that woman. It's unreal. Absolutely unreal."

"They're going to be annoyed when they run out of alcohol," I said as we gently bumped against each other.

He was quiet for a moment before he said, "I was glad to hear her say we'd be welcomed back. I would've missed this place."

"Me too," I whispered, finding the fire in our camp crackling merrily. Someone had tended it while we were gone. One of the basajaunak, probably, but they'd cleared out when they heard or felt us coming. No one was around. "Take it all in now, though. We don't have much longer." I looked at him, not trying to hold back my fear. "I can feel their expectation. They must be eager to find me. They're out for blood."

# CHAPTER 25

I GASPED TO consciousness and clutched the downy inner fur of Austin's polar bear form. He'd shifted to keep me warm.

Shock waves of malice coursed through me. A drumbeat of aggression rattled my bones until all I could do was sit up in a panic and grab my chest. This spell was the absolute worst. Remind me never to call Ivy House pushy again.

The pale light of dawn cast the camp in an eerie glow. The chilled morning air spread goosebumps along my skin in the absence of Austin's warmth.

He eased himself away from me carefully so he could shift. The flash of light and heat gave me a momentary reprieve before his nude form was squatting beside me.

"What is it?" he asked.

A wave of magic pulsed through me. My gargoyle was waking up.

"I'd thought we had a little time, and it is indeed a

*little* time. They've moved incredibly fast. We need to get out of here." I pushed myself to standing and turned toward my bag to put everything away. To my surprise, it was already done. The zippers had all been drawn, and when I peeked inside, the clothes were all tightly rolled for more space. Mr. Tom must've sneaked in here after Austin and I fell asleep. Apparently, I would be hiking in my sweats. Or maybe just flying, because at this point, I didn't really care if they had something to say about that.

Austin froze while looking down at his own pack, also neatly arranged and ready to go. A house muumuu, shoes, and socks had been left out for him.

"Go with it," I told him, unable to smile through the throbbing effects of the spell. "Just this once, please go with it."

"It's annoying how much I love you," he grumbled, snatching up the fabric. "Whoever thought this would become my life? Being pushed into a purple muumuu by a crazy gargoyle butler."

Now a smile did work through my low-key panic.

Niamh met me in her muumuu, her eyes bright and her face its normal sort of dewy perfection.

"Glad to see you aren't in a drunken coma," I told her. "We've got to leave. Let's get some breakfast to go, if we can, or eat quickly right here. Where's Cyra; we need—"

Cyra walked up in her muumuu. It seemed Mr. Tom had visited everyone last night.

"Can you get a fire going, Cyra?" I asked as Ulric and Jasper groggily stumbled toward us. Ulric had his muumuu draped over his shoulder, and his hand covered his forehead. Jasper's eyes were puffy and squinted, and his muumuu was on backward.

"They didn't fare so well," Niamh informed us. "I told them to stop, but they wouldn't listen."

"The basajaunak joined us after most of you had gone to bed," Ulric said, bending over and groaning. "They're actually a lot of fun. They were telling jokes and singing songs and telling stories... I had no idea we'd be up this early."

Jasper took a halting step forward and gave Niamh an incredulous look. "How do you look like you didn't drink last night?"

"Never mind that, how is she not dead?" Ulric asked. "She drank the feast vats dry, something that's never happened, apparently. Then she moved on to their storage vats and, on a dare from a basajaun, drank those, too. She just guzzled the stuff to prove a point. Then she started a fight with a basajaun, wrestled him for a while; he somehow caught on fire—"

"They rolled through the firepit," Jasper said.

"Oh, yeah, right. Well, he caught on fire, that ended the wrestling, and then she passed out on a bed of clover, cursing Edgar and his lazy eye. We had to carry her here."

"I was ab-solutely langers, lads." Niamh started to chuckle. "I haven't had that much fun in…two hundred or more years. It reminded me of the old days when I'd meet my cousins."

"Right, but how are you not dying right now?" Jasper asked.

"How did you have time to do all of this?" I asked, healing them as I took stock of everyone's position. "And why is Hollace on the other side of the camp with Edgar?"

"The mages snuck out," Cyra said as she added logs to a roaring fire. "The Irish lady was snoring so loudly, we didn't hear them—"

"Oh, shoot," Ulric said, crouching down and holding his head. "Sorry about that. We put her over there so it wouldn't bother the majority of the camp."

"When you sent that blast of emotion through the bond, it woke us up," she continued. "That's when we saw they were gone. Edgar was moving around, so Hollace went to see if he'd followed them."

I gritted my teeth as the pounding within me persisted. My gargoyle pulsed out magic. *Get ready.*

"They left?" I asked in a surprisingly level tone. Something uncomfortable tightened my stomach, though. I couldn't feel Sebastian and Nessa because they weren't in my Ivy House circle and hadn't accepted battle bonds like Broken Sue and Kace had.

Cyra shrugged as Nathanial walked up, looking fresh. "That, or they quietly went for a secluded morning walk," she said.

"Here we are, miss." Mr. Tom walked into the clearing in his muumuu, his wings fluttering behind him. He held out two steaming wooden mugs as the shifters gathered closer. Like usual these days, I hadn't even realized he'd been gone. He was one I never checked on, likely because he was always the one checking on me. "This is as close as I could get to coffee. It's tea, but it's heavily caffeinated tea, I think. I had a cup to try it. I expect it will clean out my bowels quite soon. You might heal yourself from that if you can. I'm not sure the situation will be pleasant while squatting in the insufferable wildness with a fern tickling your backside. I'm about to find out, sadly. I think I'm too far gone to be helped. It's all gurgling quite madly in there. Austin, I brought one for you as well."

Edgar and Hollace were standing close now, stationary. Hollace seemed curious, and Edgar was delighted.

"I'm fine, Mr. Tom." I held up my hand. "I'll stick with water."

"Wise choice, miss," he replied. "Would anyone else like the equivalent of explosive Ex-Lax? The basajaunak must be very regular."

I rested my hand on Austin's forearm to break him out of his befuddled stupor as he stared at Mr. Tom. My crew could rattle even the most solid of people.

"I'm going to go see what Edgar and Hollace have found. The basajaun—Buln'dan. Dang it. *Dave* is on the other side of the village—"

"Dave's at his mother's camp," Nathanial said. "She called him there to speak with him last night. From what I gather, she insisted he stay there for the night and not head back to the party."

"See? It'll be grand," Niamh said, taking one of the mugs from Mr. Tom. I was starting to think she was bionic.

I shook Austin's arm a little, bringing his cobalt gaze to me. I didn't have time for the resulting stomach flutter, especially not with all the nervous churning and pulsing panic I already had going on.

"Can you send someone to ask for that escort she promised us? Tell her it's urgent. We need to get out of here and get set up elsewhere. Then I need you to get everyone ready. Try not to be distracted by all the weird things everyone says. I need to go find Sebastian."

His eyebrow quirked, but he nodded. "I'll send Bro-chan with you."

"There's no need. If Sebastian tried to run and got caught, which is doubtful, the basajaun would handle it. I'm sure there's a good explanation for his leaving early."

Austin shook his head before lifting his hand, pre-sumably for Broken Sue. "Just in case."

Broken Sue caught up immediately. He stayed slightly behind me, giving me the prominence of an alpha, a status I didn't at all care about. Our connection was open because of my gargoyle's rising magic.

"Are you afraid of what will come?" I asked him quietly. I wasn't sure why I asked—I could feel his confidence. But his answer surprised me.

"It's not my job to be afraid. That job belongs to you and Alpha Steele. My job is to follow orders, trust in my alphas, and believe they will ensure my safety. With that trust, there's no point in fear."

I glanced back with a grimace. "Yuck. Thanks for the added pressure. I appreciate it," I said sarcastically.

I felt his humor, even though I didn't see it in his eyes or expression.

"And what happens if power corrupts?" I asked, nodding to a basajaun who'd emerged from the trees to my left. He put up a hand in salute. "What happens if blindly following orders leads you into murky territory? You might resist your fear right until the moment we get you killed."

This time, he huffed out a laugh, and I was surprised he'd allowed himself that much leeway outside of the bar and a few whiskeys. "I'm not scared to die. My family is waiting for me when I do."

Not to be a jerk, but I really didn't need the heart squish with all the other stuff going on inside me.

He continued, "Besides, I might have my reservations about a good many people—most people, actually—but I'll follow you and Alpha Steele into hell if I have to, just to pull you back out when we're all on fire."

"We'll probably have gone there to visit Niamh."

More basajaunak were on the path now, many headed in the same direction as us. Around a bend and beyond some trees, I saw why.

A large fire licked the bottom of a black cauldron, which was braced on thin iron legs over the pit. A camping stove had been set up beside it with pots and pans steaming away on the burners. A heavy volume sat on a tall book holder, opened to one of the last pages of a large tome. Off to the side, various ingredients had been spread around a rough-hewn stump the size of a coffee table. In the middle of the melee stood Sebastian with his hair sticking out at all angles.

Basajaunak of all ages formed a very large circle around the setup, watching him mutter to himself, scratch his head, and then shuffle over to the camping stove and stir in some sort of leafy plant. Nessa, Edgar, and Hollace sat at the edge of the circle, munching on something while they watched the show.

"Oh, Brochan!" Nessa raised her hand to us, drawing Sebastian's attention. "I've learned that feeding chunks of meat to someone is very erotic for shifter types. It sounds caveman-esque to me, but that could be *hawt*. Want to give it a try? I'll let you club me and then drag me back to your cave by my hair. I do like a good hair tug."

Her eyes danced above her wide smile. The basajaunak laughed around her.

"That woman," Broken Sue muttered.

"Ah. Jessie. Good, you're up." Sebastian motioned me closer. "I could use your help. I'm tired, and my magic is flagging a little. Can you help me with this potion? It's almost done."

"Nessa said we couldn't disturb him yet," Hollace told me as I crossed to him in a daze of competing emotions.

"Don't worry, Jessie," Edgar said. "I've had my eye

on him since he dosed the mythical creatures with magic and sneaked out of that tree trunk like a thief in the night."

Sebastian sighed. "Would a thief in the night have all this gear set up in an open location?"

"You tell me," Edgar replied.

I heaved a sigh of relief. Yes, it *was* easy to underestimate Sebastian. And yes, he clearly was a handful when cornered. I got what Austin was picking up. But clearly, that was a good thing for us. A great thing, maybe. Who would've thought he'd out-prepare us all and bring in a whole lab at a moment's notice to combat an enemy that wasn't even specifically his?

Offering a little smile, I walked closer. "Speaking of, how did you get all this gear here?" I looked at the rig for the cauldron. It seemed to automatically adjust to the heat of the fire. I'd never seen anything so high-tech look so archaic.

He paused in stirring the pot on the camping stove. "The basajaunak. I'd told…Dave, I guess we're calling him now, that if something went sideways, I'd need more supplies. So he told me to bring my supplies to the motel, and if we needed it, he'd ask some friends to help him get it here."

"Right, I knew you brought a bunch of stuff to the motel, but…how did he get it *here*?" I looked down on the open spell book. The complexity of the instructions was way beyond my level of expertise. This was master-level stuff. Sebastian-type stuff. I surmised that there were only a few mages on the planet who could handle spells and potions to this level of intricacy, and likely none but him could tweak and alter them to get even better results. "That cauldron would be impossible to safely carry up that narrow mountain trail."

He threw a dash of something into the cauldron and then took a step back and bent. "Get low."

I turned and did as instructed. A flash of pink light preceded a plume of purple smoke curling from the cauldron. He didn't straighten, though, so neither did I. A moment later, a loud bang sprayed liquid up and out, curling over us in an arc.

Basajaunak screeched or scrambled to get out of the way.

"Oops." Sebastian looked around as he finally straightened. "I forgot about warning them." He raised his voice. "Don't worry, it's not acidic yet. It's still harmless. You'll be okay. Maybe spotted purple for a while, but that's fun too, right? Free dye job."

He lowered a long wooden spoon into the cauldron and stirred counterclockwise three times before going clockwise once. Then he let go of the spoon. It kept stirring on its own.

"Oh, whoa," I said, venturing closer to watch.

"It's very thick and has its own mind," he told me, stepping around me to get back to the book. "You get the best results when you let it stir itself."

"Right, so how did you get all this here?"

"Oh. Yes. Well, it turns out that there's a much easier and faster way to get into this village than that horrible route we took." He ran his finger along a line in the book and paused to mutter to himself. "Right, right, yes. I remember now."

He turned and grabbed something from the stump before approaching the simmering pan on the camping stove.

"When…Dave was done speaking to his mother, I told him that I needed my stuff." He dropped in the ingredients and watched them slowly sink into the frothing liquid. Once they were submerged, he stirred it all around in a frantic zigzag. "This portion of the spell thrives on anxiety. I have plenty, so I give it good doses when I stir." He checked the pot on the camping stove before turning back to the stump. "I went straight to bed, got a few hours' sleep, placed magic on Cyra and Hollace so Nessa and I could get out, and pretended not to fear for my life when Edgar tracked me here. That vampire seems impervious to privacy spells. He sees right through them somehow. Anyway, Dave and his buddies helped me set up before Dave went back to his mother's—he was in trouble, I gather—and his buddies returned to watch Niamh beat the living hell out of a drunk basajaun. Or I assume that's what she was doing with all the screeching and clattering that was going on."

Nessa put out her hand and toggled it. "It was a pretty even match until she rolled him through the fire. Good thinking, that. She basically did a coal roll while he had all that hair to entice the flames. She won fair and square, I don't care what they're saying."

"She won the drinking portion, anyway," one of the basandere said.

"And we are all the poorer for it," another said. "Without the"—I couldn't understand the word she said—"to drown our sorrows."

"Why the hell did we have to walk over all those mountains to get here if there was a faster way?" I asked softly, grabbing an ingredient he'd pointed at on the stump.

"No idea. I didn't bother asking. They have a very strange sense of humor, these basajaunak—"

"I think *you* do," one shouted, and the rest laughed.

"Don't mind them, they're still drunk," he muttered. "Here. Drop that into the fire. No, not that one, the other one. In your left hand."

"Use your words," I mumbled, reaching over the cauldron. "Is this going to scorch me?"

"No. It's slow acting. But back away after."

I did as he said. As I backed up, the pounding within me slowed to a halt. I stopped with it and cocked my head.

"I don't know what's happening," Sebastian said urgently, "but get your little ass over to this pan and prepare to drop that what's-it-called into the stuff."

He was clearly frantic. He only got this way when a potion was about to turn. As intricate as this potion seemed to be, it was probably constantly in a state of *about to turn.*

The silence within me was deafening. No emotions. No intentions. No expectations. No danger. Nothing. It was like the magic spell had switched off.

"Are they dead, maybe?" I whispered as sweat broke out on my forehead.

*"No,"* Ivy House said. *"The spell is giving you time to focus before battle."*

And now my heart started hammering. Given Ivy House's way of doing things, that would mean *right* before battle.

"We have to get out of here," I said urgently, standing over the pan and holding the bag of powder he'd indicated upside down, securing the top with one of my hands. "Do we expressly need this potion, and if so, how long until it's done?"

"When you drop that powder, I need you to put in a burst of magic with it. You know how. Three—two—one—*drop*."

I maintained hold of the bottom of the bag and released the top, dumping the contents.

"Of course we need this potion! This will theoretically slap a cap down over the mages. A dome, I mean. Like the dome at that challenge however long ago? That's what gave me the idea. Here." He handed me a spoon. "Stir that pan stuff. Pour all the terror I see on your face into stirring. Go, go."

I did as he said. He moved faster now, visiting the book again, going to the cauldron.

"That dome will last for a bit, and then it will shrink to encompass their weakest member."

"Their *weakest* member?" I asked.

"Yes. The one we'll leave alive to tell the tale. Stop stirring. That's good. Grab the red…flower…leafy thing from the…thing there. Gotta hurry. Gotta hurry. Here we go."

I grabbed the bright red flower with green sprigs from the stump as he added more ingredients to the cauldron and started moving the spoon in the opposite direction.

"Can't let it make all the decisions, can we?" he muttered. Then he talked louder for me. "With the amount of power in the dome, we'll have probably ten to twenty minutes, give or take, before they pick it apart with whatever potions they brought. They'll have multiple things to get them out of a trap, they'll just have to find the right one. Maybe use two, we'll see. Your added power will throw them for a loop, as will the complexity of this potion. Drop that flower into the—*No!* Not the pan, the pot. Into the pot there."

"With magic?"

He paused and raced back to the book, finding the spot with his finger. "Magic, yes. A crapload, if you can manage it. The more magic you drop in, the more time you're buying us."

I did as instructed while he continued to explain, working as he talked. That combination helped him focus.

"While they're trapped in the dome, we'll unleash hell on the ground crew. Austin—Steele—Alpha—"

"You're starting to sound like your best friend Edgar," Nessa said.

"What a thing to say," Sebastian muttered as Edgar said, "Oh my! I didn't know we'd progressed that far past the 'getting to know you' stage." He beamed.

"You're making a very dangerous enemy," Sebastian told Nessa.

"I hope so. Otherwise, I'll get bored with all these new friends."

He shook his head and kept muttering to me. "Alpha has underestimated what he's walking into. The ground crew will be powerful and large. They aren't taking any chances with you this time. You've rattled them."

"How do you know that?"

He jerked his head my way before going back to the cauldron. "Stir that pot. I had the basajaun—Dave—take my phone to get a signal. Saw a message from someone in my network. It seems the fear you instilled worked too well. We don't have the people. We need a crutch. This is that crutch. We batter the crap out of the ground crew, kill as many as we can, and then we go back to the mages. When they emerge from the dome, we'll pound them with attack spells. After they get their defenses erected, we'll play defense until the shifters can *hopefully* kill the rest of the ground crew and move on to the mages. It's the best option we have—"

He put up his hands and stepped back, his signal to cease all activity. I stepped back with him.

He was breathing heavily when he was finished. "It needs to sit for twenty minutes."

I hissed. "We don't have twenty minutes, Sebastian. We have to leave *now.*"

# CHAPTER 26

S EBASTIAN WAS POSITIVE there were other, better ways to travel than clinging to the back of a very grumpy nightmare alicorn that didn't want him there. He just didn't have any choice in the matter.

"This is awesome," Nessa yelled with a giant smile. Jasper's thick arms were wrapped around her middle. Her feet dangled below her as they passed over the tops of short trees and veered this way and that to avoid the tall redwoods, which were sparser as they climbed in elevation. All he'd have to do was let her go, and she'd be done for. At least Sebastian could clutch a mane or grab a tail if Niamh tried to throw him off.

Okay, so yes, he *had* had a choice, and he'd selected the least awful option presented to him. He hadn't wanted to be hugged by Mr. Tom.

The giant polar bear raced through the trees below, graceful and sleek despite his size. Behind him ran the wolves, followed by the not-as-graceful lope of the enormous silverback gorilla. The basajaunak ran all around them, Dave among them.

"Do you also hate your life right now, bestie?" Edgar called from Ulric's grip. Ulric had drawn the short straw. Literally.

Sebastian didn't answer. He was finally taking Niamh's advice and ignoring the crazy vampire in the hope he'd go away. Sebastian didn't have high hopes, though. He'd probably walked too far down that plank.

Niamh's flanks shivered under Sebastian's legs. Edgar put out a fist like he was Superman.

"We're coming, Jessie. We're coming!" he shouted into the wind. "I'm so scared, I'm shaking. I still don't like heights. This will give me more nightmares. Better not sleep."

They must've been reacting to another pulse of Jessie's magic, which seemed to be coming faster now, urging everyone on. She flew at the front, grasped in Nathanial's arms. Her wings couldn't keep up with the others over the long stretch.

The shifters down below put on a burst of speed. Niamh's oily black wings beat at the air.

They'd waited for Sebastian's spell. He'd forced them to—or so he'd like to think. What had really happened was he begged and pleaded with Austin and tried not to piss his pants within the alpha's hard stare.

The rest of their team had hurried to get ready while

he prepared the bottle for his potion. The basandere had chosen which basajaunak would go with them and packed food for the Ivy House team, just in case. Nessa had stayed right next to him, watching the time on her wristwatch.

Still, they'd all ended up waiting, and he'd felt many sets of eyes on him while he poured the potion with a shaky hand.

He had it, though. He had it in his underwear, nestled next to the one part a man protected the hardest. Even if he fell off this alicorn, he would not drop that bottle. Since he was the one who'd be using it, he wouldn't have to gross anyone out with where it was currently stored.

Niamh's flanks shivered again. Edgar's fist shook in the air.

Sebastian squinted through the rushing wind. Sunlight had bleached the horizon and the blanket of trees beneath him.

He swore to himself. He wasn't ready for another battle, especially not one like this. He'd handled the situation with Kinsella because he knew the odds were stacked heavily in their favor. This one wouldn't be so easy. He didn't have an escape route planned, either. Not for himself, at least. He could only get one of his people out—and only then if the potion worked.

Niamh neighed, the sign for *hang on!*

She angled downward so fast that he slipped back onto her rump. She flattened out a little with an equine growl, letting him scramble up her back and clutch her mane. She'd probably hate that, but he didn't have a choice. He wasn't experienced in riding horses, especially not in the air.

The gargoyles followed their downward swoop, cutting through the jutting trees and reaching branches. He was thwapped in the face, but he held on tightly, not daring to look over her side and see what he was sure was the ground rushing up to meet them.

A streak of fire zipped under them. Cyra's flying form was more agile than Niamh's.

Niamh's golden hooves touched down a moment later, the landing soft but the galloping afterward jostling him all over the place. Maybe flying was better. She slowed to a canter and then stopped when they reached the shifters gathered within a grouping of trees, masked from sight...which would only be helpful if no one had been watching the sky with binoculars. The great thunderbird circling overhead wouldn't be easy to hide.

"No, no, don't land," Nessa shouted to the ones above. She pointed ahead of them. "Go to that meadow over there. Hollace needs space to land. We don't want to break him. Let's lead him there, and we can run back."

She looked down, caught Sebastian looking up at her, and put out a thumbs-up. Her smile was radiant. Nessa found delight and joy in everything, which was probably good, considering the horrible life she'd found herself in. They shouldn't call her his gal pal—they should call her his silver lining. Or his crutch.

Niamh shook herself as Dave and his mom emerged from the trees, breathing heavily. The shifters were winded, too, their furry sides expanding and contracting. Niamh shook again, and Sebastian took the cue to get off as the other fliers landed.

Jessie was last, watching to make sure Hollace made it okay. A beautiful swirl of color trailed her flapping wings. She shifted immediately, and Austin followed suit. No one else did. The goal for everyone else was to conserve energy.

"Basajaun—Dave, sorry." Jessie closed the distance to Austin, but her attention was in the trees. "What's the status? Can you feel them through the wood?"

"Yes." Dave vibrated with aggression. "There is a large host to the south, three miles or so. They must've seen you in the air because they sped up when you flew in this direction."

"That's what I figured." She shook her head and

braced her hands on her hips. Sebastian could tell she was swearing under her breath. "Ivy House never does things by halves. Fine. If it's going to happen, it's going to happen." She looked at the basandere. "You need to get out of here. There's no time for anything else. Thanks for the offer to help, and thanks for all you've done for us. Hopefully, we'll meet again."

The basandere studied her silently. "Your creature is the most beautiful one I have ever seen. But you are not allowing it to be the deadliest. I can feel it lurking within you, even now, kept on a tight leash. You need to free that part of yourself."

Sebastian couldn't help thinking that the basandere should follow her own advice and join the battle. But then, it was often easier to give advice than to take it, even if it was one's own.

Jessie flinched as though struck, however. Her brow furrowed. "So I've heard. But it's new to me. I'm just trying to…get used to it."

The basandere shook her head slowly. Sebastian could tell Jessie felt tense about the time all this was taking, made worse when Dave said, "They are coming at some speed. Dirt bikes."

"It isn't new to you," the basandere said, and then touched her hairy chest. "It has always been there. Basajaunak can be fierce, but we must embrace that part of ourselves. Shifters, too. Humans. We must embrace it. Your magic just adds to you—it didn't *create* you. Everything it needs to thrive was already there. Don't think of it as a separate entity; think of it as a dormant part of you, rarely used. Now, when you are protecting your family, is your time to *use* it. Use all you have. Their lives depend on it."

An emotion Sebastian couldn't identify moved in Jessie's eyes. He half wished he could've forged that connection that her gargoyle kept extending. But he couldn't allow her to keep tabs on him. Not if he wanted to stay the course he and Nessa had agreed on. Still, Jessie seemed able to read him after a fashion, even though he couldn't reciprocate, and that would have to be enough.

She nodded once. That was it. And then she turned away.

"Let's get ready. They're coming," Jessie barked, the commander side of her taking over. Her magic throbbed through the natural place. "Hide within the trees around that clearing. Let them get into their formations. Then we attack as planned."

He watched the basandere place a hand on Dave's shoulder and then move off into the trees. Dave watched for a moment, but he quickly snapped out of it. The hair on his body bristled and puffed out, making the big creature look that much bigger. There was no way to make him look more terrifying—it simply wasn't possible.

"It is time to shine, weird mage," Dave said as he passed Sebastian. "We're in our element now."

Sebastian took a deep breath. Jessie had to embrace the part of her that was distinctly violent. So did he. They all had to pull their weight.

He felt his emotions drain away. He let the worry and apprehension for what was to come seep down into the center of his being, and then he imagined covering it with a lead blanket. This wasn't a time for reflection and contemplation—it was a time for action.

It was a time for Elliot Graves.

Magical spells tumbled through his mind. Attacking spells. Killing spells. He'd need speed and power today. Accuracy. He'd need to take them down as speedily as possible.

He started walking quickly into the meadow, wanting to check in with Nessa before all of this kicked off.

"Sebastian, wait." Jessie caught up with him. Her eyes glittered with ferocity. "Stay here for a moment. There's a perch for you. It won't give you a lot of maneuverability, but it'll give you eyes."

She leaned a little more toward him. He could see her gargoyle's intense hostility peeking through her gaze. The lead blanket fluttered, wanting to reveal a reaction. Somewhere in his mind's eye, he thought about shrinking away. But that wasn't how Elliot Graves did things.

"We're their backbone, weird mage," she said with a little smile, using the nickname many of the others had adopted. The one he felt strangely proud of, especially because of how well it fit. Her magic pounded through him, shoving aside the lead blanket and reaching a place deep within him, a dark place, full of insecurity and feelings of inadequacy. It was a sensitive place, one that he tried to hide. One that he fully ignored when he was Elliot Graves.

As if she could read his mind, that spark in her eyes glowed brighter.

"Elliot Graves is a hollow mask granting you an excuse for courage. If this gargoyle is a part of me, then that courage is a part of you. Time to embrace it. The worst that can happen for you is to slip on that persona again. You need to find your courage another way. Me? I'm trusting Austin to make sure I don't fall in too deep." A wry smile twisted her lips. "I feel very vulnerable right now. You do too. Let's do this together. We can trust in Austin. He'll pull us all back from the brink."

She held out her hand, palm and elbow even. Her

power kept pounding into him, hitting that place inside of him.

Jessie knew his struggles. She probably knew he hated all of this despite the life he'd led—the darkness, the battles, the violence. She wasn't judging him, though. She was trying to build him up, like a leader should. Like a *good* leader did.

In that moment, he didn't love anyone else in the world the way he loved her. Thank God it wasn't sexual, or it would've been the scariest moment of his life due to the horror of what that big polar bear could do to him.

His hand shaking, he fit his palm against hers. She drew him a little closer, making him latch on to the ferocity in her eyes and soak in those pulses of deep, penetrating magic like a security blanket.

"We can do this," she said, finishing with a soft hiss. *Pulse. Pulse.* "We're more powerful than those mages. We're more insightful. More cunning. You're *way* more of a nerd. Your knowledge cannot be surpassed. We'll do everything—*anything*—to protect our family. You heard the basajaun's name. You're part of our family regardless of whether you sit in our circle. You expect nothing. I expect nothing. We expect everything. Help me. Don't let me brave the darkness on my own."

*Pulse.*

*Pulse.*

She stared into his eyes. Yelling and shouts erupted from behind them. The enemy had come, but she ignored it completely as she said, "You don't need a crutch. You are enough on your own."

Sebastian would never know how she understood his crippling insecurity, his fear that after his sister died, he was only whole with Nessa. But she did, and when she touched the middle of him and said those words, it was like she'd blown on a tiny spark in the middle of tall, brittle grass. It only took a moment for that spark to catch.

She nodded, squeezed his hand, and then led him into the trees.

*I don't need Elliot Graves.* The thought was foreign, but in that moment, it seemed true. *I'm enough on my own.*

"You'll have to do a little climbing," she said, weaving between the redwoods. She stopped short as they ran into the basandere. "Why are you still here?"

"I was invited to see Buln'dan's new family," the basandere replied. "I intend to."

"What you're really saying is that you'll make sure no harm comes to him, and until you have to act, you'll enjoy the show."

The basandere didn't flinch. "Yes."

"Great," Jessie said. "Well, make yourself useful. Show him to that perch. We're out of time."

She turned and started jogging away.

The basandere looked down at Sebastian before turning and continuing to wind through the trees.

"I have heard you have great power, mage," she said before stopping at a small, rocky hill. "I can feel it within you. You have found a place of belonging with this family. They will help you to flourish." She jerked her head up the incline before moving off through the trees.

"O-kay," he said softly.

He climbed up the steep slope amid the thin tree branches that scratched at him. He paused at the lip, and a huge swell of magic rolled over him. *Get ready.*

More shouts and yelling caught his ears. He took a deep breath. And then another. Showtime.

*You expect nothing. I expect nothing. We expect everything.*

For some reason, those words kept repeating themselves in his mind as he climbed onto a sort of outcropping that peeked through a couple of trees and overlooked the meadow beyond. He was plenty far away to be useful without being in the action. Jessie had posted him where he'd feel comfortable. Where all mages tended to feel comfortable—in the cowardly cheap seats.

One day, he'd get closer. He'd move into the action. His spells would be more powerful up close. He'd be able to improvise more readily.

He needed to learn to improvise.

For now, though, he'd do what he was best at.

He saw the enemy immediately—large men all, strutting through the gaps in the trees and directly into his line of sight. There must be well over fifty of them, a huge force to accompany mages of that caliber. They carried weapons and wore nondescript magical armor. They walked like machines, all in sync, large shoulders swaying and with obvious confidence.

Behind them, slinking through the trees like phantoms, the mages wore black robes and little black hats. That denoted them as Momar's. Not his employees, not his highbred staff, but *his*.

They clutched something in their hands, but he couldn't see what from the distance. Vials, probably. Or bottles. Potions. They'd come ready too.

The ground crew stopped in neat rows, waiting for their enemy to step up.

"We've come for the woman," one at the front shouted. "Bring her out, and we'll kill you quickly. Make us come and get her, and we'll draw out the pain."

One of them spotted Sebastian, standing a little

hunched on the hill. More caught sight of him until the leader was peering in his direction. He puffed his chest up, probably filling it with air to make his demand again, but suddenly, all eyes snapped to a focal point in front of them. A shiver worked through the crowd— Sebastian could visibly see their bodies roll with it. Backs snapped a little straighter. Shoulders tensed.

Austin Steele had stepped into the meadow. His movements were sleeker, more graceful than theirs had been. His shoulders were broader, his body not trained for violence but biologically built for it. They had learned to be predators. He'd been born one.

The leader spoke again. "Bring the woman forward."

Even from that distance, Sebastian could feel the rage pouring off Austin. Or maybe Sebastian just knew it was happening.

"Say please," Austin growled.

The leader stared Austin down, and then the magical light show that was Jessie rose from the trees to the right. Her wings flapped, and she flew over the center of the meadow. Magic pumped into the air around her, visible in its effulgence. It swept along the ground and ran through the trees. It rose like a tidal wave, and then it was encompassing Sebastian, fanning that fire she'd ignited within him—the one that had made him realize he didn't need Graves at all. He was ready to fight for her. Fight by her side. He was ready to give everything to this family, just as she would.

"Showtime," he said out loud.

He dug in his drawers for that bottle of potion. Working the spell with one hand, he yanked out the cork with his teeth, pushing aside the thought of how utterly gross that was. He flung the bottle into the air and then caught it with the spell before hurtling it higher.

Magic continued to swell from Jessie as she looked down on the enemy. Her wings pumped at the sky.

Once again, the gargoyle's connection was offered to Sebastian. It throbbed in his middle, asking him to join her. To become one with her. Only this time, it didn't feel like it was only her gargoyle that did the asking. This time, there were traces of Jessie woven through the magic. Soft and delicate and fiercely loyal, trustworthy—all of it mixed with the gargoyle's hard, fierce magic. She was doing as the basandere had said. She was choosing to let her gargoyle side truly meld with her.

Sebastian felt his courage rise. If she could face her fears, then he would do everything in his power to support her—and to accomplish the same.

He blasted the potion with the unlocking spell. This

was the risky part. If the mages fired before the dome was established, it might not fit into place.

He needn't have worried, though. Jessie spread out her hands, and her wings pumped faster. Those below her stared up with wide, unblinking eyes—unmoving, in awe. Then she roared. It was deep and brutal and unmistakably a challenge.

Austin shifted, the muscular man turning into an enormous snow-white polar bear, larger than its natural counterpart.

The mages in the trees started to back-pedal, but that wouldn't matter. The spell would find them. Their hands clutched at their robes.

The rest of the shifters jogged into the meadow behind Austin, and the fliers rose into the sky. Hollace had to venture further into the meadow before he shifted into a great bird that swept over the crowd and into the air. The ground crew couldn't help but duck. None of the training they'd had could've prepared them for this.

Sebastian's spell bloomed and then fell. One of the mages, clearly the quickest thinker in the bunch, lifted his hands, but it was at that moment that Jessie engaged.

Then all hell broke loose.

# CHAPTER 27

S WIRLING DARKNESS SWELLED through me as I shifted and rose above the meadow. Red tinged the sides of my vision and then spread, pulsating like my magic. Anger and aggression took over me until I felt like I was sinking into the abyss of it, down and down, drowning.

Fear crowded my senses. The desire to push back, to shift into my human self and shrug off these feelings, was almost overwhelming. I wasn't sure I could give myself over to the inky well waiting to consume me.

I clung to my humanity, to the safety net of what I'd always known, of what was acceptable in the polite society in which I'd resided for most of my adult life.

Warmth surged through the bond. Support. Austin was urging me to let go. He was reminding me that he was there for me. He wouldn't let me lose myself to the darkness.

I trusted that. I trusted *him*.

But we had a long battle in front of us. A battle where I'd be in the air, and he'd be on the ground, worlds apart, it seemed. It would be impossible to connect with him if something went wrong. If the darkness locked me in its grip, we wouldn't have time to coax me out until maybe it was too late.

*"Let go,"* Ivy House said. *"Become one with it."*

An enemy mage lifted his hands to do a spell.

Without waiting, unable to completely succumb, I slammed a spell down on the mages. They dropped their hands, and two of them sank to the dirt, not ready for that level of power.

Sebastian's potion-spell fitted itself over them, just barely large enough, locking on to the ground and solidifying with a mustard-yellow sheen. They looked up in surprise. Their hands immediately started working, some with spells, some reaching into the pockets of their robes. The countdown had begun. Time to hit the huge crowd of ground troops, six dozen or more.

I roared again, flying above the battlefield. What looked like lasers zipped around me. One sliced across my shin, but my tough skin barely tore. Nathanial had been right: gargoyles were built to withstand certain types of magic.

Those trained footmen below weren't.

I slammed down spells, crushing the enemy beneath my magic. Cyra flew overhead before diving, opening her beak and blasting them with fire. It rolled over three men standing in a crisp line—these troops were highly trained and organized, as Sebastian had said. They screamed and slapped at their faces for a moment before regaining their composure and lifting their guns to fire at her. They ignored their bodies, and I instantly saw why: their bulky gray uniforms were flame-resistant. While Cyra could increase the heat to blistering levels, the stream would be small, only able to scour one at a time and maybe taking a while to burn through. It would take too much of her focus—less than ideal, as we'd lose the brunt of one of our strongest allies.

Hollace flew overhead, and his lightning crackled down. Prongs of it hit three bodies, making them shake with the rush of electricity before collapsing. A fourth missed, though, and fire sprang up in the dry grass.

I reached for the spell to quell it but hesitated. My magic surged and boiled, rushing within me one moment and strangely subdued the next. My gargoyle was struggling with my logical side, with my Jane side, I knew, off-kilter and less effective. My fear of the dark violence was hindering me—I knew I had to let go, but I was unable to fully do it. The effect was worse than if I hadn't tried at all. If I attempted elemental magic right now, there was no telling what might happen. I would almost certainly make it worse.

Thankfully, the enemy troops shuffled through

quickly, dousing the flames as they surged forward to get at our people. Blasts flew through the air from dozens of magical guns, forcing Hollace higher. His aim up there would be precarious, and the threat of fire, burning our people as well as theirs—burning the basajaunak's forest—would increase dramatically. We were losing another of our powerful players.

*Damn it,* I thought, knowing I wasn't holding up my end of the bargain in this battle. I needed to achieve balance so I could be more effective. My people were counting on me to lead, to protect them and the forest, to make up the difference in our forces with my inherited well of robust magic.

I swelled my power for another spell as I tried again. Darkness crowded through my mind. My gargoyle pulled at me, dragging me down. Fear swirled, breaking my concentration. I couldn't quite get the balance. I needed time to work myself down into this fervor.

It was time my team didn't have.

✧   ✧   ✧

THE BLUE-GRAY BLAST of a magical gun zipped through the air right beside Niamh. She hadn't seen those types of weapons before. She wondered what they did, though she didn't plan to get hit to find out.

Austin roared as he charged onto the battlefield. His

shifters followed. Niamh, in her alicorn form, ran around to the right, wanting to pick off the enemy lingering on the edges and shooting into the melee.

Jessie slammed magic down onto the ground crew even as she dove, claws out. She sliced at them, flying by. On her way up, she jammed her hands downward with another spell.

A portion of the ground crew quailed, sinking, but only a couple stayed there.

Her spell didn't have the potency Niamh had seen at Elliot Graves's meetup. Not even the potency of handling the enemy mage in the interrogation room. It certainly didn't have the strength she'd used when she was challenging Sebastian. It was as though she hadn't completely loosed her gargoyle.

Her roar was pure frustration. That couldn't be good.

Austin Steele was obviously thinking the same thing. He put on a burst of speed, with his shifters behind him in a tight formation. Dave ran along the side, snarling like the wild thing he was.

Niamh pumped her wings to get some altitude and then clattered ahead with her hooves. The muppet fell, and she touched down in time to ram another through the back with her horn. She yanked the body over her head and nearly cracked her neck doing it. These fighters were big and wearing some sort of magical armor. Their clothes looked like normal uniforms but were harder and much heavier. Too heavy for this. She needed to switch gears. How tedious.

She landed a distance away as Austin Steele and his shifters barreled into the ground crew. He swiped with his big paw and clamped down with his mouth. Broken Sue picked someone up by the neck and laboriously swung him at someone else.

Yeah, throwing these fools around would take too much energy. Pity.

Niamh shifted into her other form and scurried forward as the gargoyles made a dash for the mages. Ulric dove, but the dome bounced him off, something she hadn't remembered Sebastian mentioning. Ulric clearly hadn't, either. He shook his head before pausing, looking down at the cowering mages beneath him.

Light from a magical gun blasted his way. Almost there, and Jessie swung out her hand. A sheen covered Ulric just in time, and the ray hit and deflected. Nathanial grunted something Niamh couldn't hear over the noise, and then the gargoyles were switching gears as well, diving at the ground crew and ripping through them with claws and teeth. Some of the enemy were flown up a ways, killed, and then tossed.

Cyra followed them, spraying down fire before

dodging, letting Hollace blast them with lightning. They could only hit in small doses of power, though, or this whole place would go up like a tinderbox. Setting these woods on fire wouldn't do anyone any good.

Niamh's heart sped up, which was unusual in battle. They'd given themselves a handicap in these woods that she, stupidly, hadn't contemplated. Another handicap was the absence of the basajaunak. She'd known there'd be a possibility that the greater force wouldn't join in, but Dave had been so confident. She'd hoped at least a few would lend a hand.

They were now operating within the worst-case scenario, and these mages had come prepared with a large force.

She scurried up an enemy's leg and bit him in the face. It wouldn't kill him, but he'd lose his sight. Good enough. There could be no frills here; they had a lot of people to get through, and there weren't nearly enough of them to do so easily.

Jumping to the next, she saw an easy opening for the jugular and took it. Fast and efficient. His scream turned into a gurgle, and down he went, crumpling to the ground.

She dodged from under his falling body before seeing a boot stomping down at the last moment. The tread hit her back and pushed her to the ground. The enemy trooper had been ready for her. Damn.

The pop in her back was unwelcome, the pain even more so. She shifted into her alicorn form, using way too much energy but keeping herself from a broken back.

Pain crushed her senses for a moment—her energy was not on par for this—before she flung the enemy off. She turned and speared him through the back, and her spine screamed in agony. Straightening again, she kicked, and her hooves made contact with the chest of an enemy behind her.

Fatigue already dragged at her, much too early. The pain hindered her movements.

A gun blasted Niamh's side, tearing into her flesh. She neighed, painfully pissed off. This battle was going all kinds of pear-shaped.

Ignoring the wound, she charged. Another enemy to her side lowered his gun and aimed for her. There were just too damn many of them. They were every-where.

She stabbed one enemy with her horn and turned to the guy with the gun at her side, flinging a dying enemy at a live one. The guy with the magical gun kept his composure even as the body was whipping through the air at him. He took aim in close quarters, and his finger turned white as he depressed the trigger.

Niamh braced for impact. She'd withstood one of those blasts, and she could damn well take another.

A spell slammed into him just as he fired. Sebastian had shown up to the party. Thank all that was holy.

The blue-gray blast went high and wide, just missing Niamh's flank. The body she'd thrown slammed into the enemy next, taking his suddenly lifeless form to the ground.

Sebastian stood on his bluff, straight and tall. Spell after intense spell hit those around her before he moved on to other areas of the battle. The spells scored across bodies and turned one poor sod almost inside out. They came at a blistering pace, as fast as Hollace's lightning.

Bloody hell, that weird mage could sure sling magic. Niamh had never seen him go all out like this. He didn't have to hold back for Jessie's safety now. He could let his violent streak out to play, and he had violence in spades. Niamh was glad he was on their side.

She crashed into the back of an enemy as he lifted his magical blaster-thing at Broken Sue, then yanked her head to get him off her horn and speared another. Kicking, she got two more.

A hole opened up to her left, just in time for her to see Edgar at the edge of the battle. He bit an enemy and ripped with his hands at the same time, severing the carotid artery and disemboweling the man in one go.

She'd forgotten about Edgar. Vampires did viciousness in their sleep, even the old, senile ones.

He ran on, and Niamh was surprised to see Nessa follow him with knives in hand, throwing weak spells before stabbing and slashing to take people down. She was using the vampire's uncanny ability to move through dangerous spaces without being noticed. Smart.

Jessie roared as she descended, ripping at someone and bombarding another with spells. An enemy got a shot off, and the blast punched a large hole through her wing. She squealed with surprised pain. Her body dipped right as the wing let out air before she started to sink toward the ground, flapping frantically to stay in the sky. She'd be healing herself, no doubt, but that took time she clearly didn't have.

Niamh neighed, shaking her head as she tried to head that way. A wall of enemy blocked her, though. They crowded in, much too close for her to snap out her wings. She'd have to clear space.

Nathanial roared, diving toward Jessie. Gun blasts zipped through the sky all around him. He was forced to weave through to protect his wings, and his speed was greatly slowed.

Over their enemies' heads, Niamh could see Austin Steele rise onto his hind legs. His mighty roar shook the earth. He crashed through the crowd like a bowling ball through pins, aiming for the spot where Jessie would fall. The hardened ground troops quailed at the sight of his rage. They cowered before him and then met their untimely fate. He bashed in chests and turned heads completely around before bodies fell at his paws.

The other shifters closed ranks, using his forward rush like the point of a wedge. They worked their way to the struggling Jessie, but they were still half a packed battlefield away.

Jessie continued to fall, almost on top of the enemy now, raining down magic to try to keep them at bay. She wasn't enough. She wouldn't be able to save herself from this. If she went any lower, the enemy would have what they came for.

❖   ❖   ❖

"OH GOD, JESSIE, no," Sebastian said through his teeth as moisture clouded his vision. He watched the beautiful spectacle that was her animal sink lower and lower, flapping her wings for all she was worth and it not doing any good. The one wing was broken or torn or something. She was tilting madly on that side.

Nathanial raced toward her, cutting through the sky, but it was as if the enemy knew he was her crutch for flight. They blasted their guns at him, forcing him to swerve madly. Body shots landed, however, and Sebastian was absolutely amazed to see how little damage they did. They'd sap his power, though. That was what those magical guns were designed for. They might not have a large physical effect on that creature, but they'd still sap his power.

"C'mon, Jessie, where are the spells we practiced?" he murmured to himself, firing off spells as fast as he could. They weren't pretty, but they were powerful and deadly. More importantly, he could rapidly fire them.

It wasn't enough, though. She was on the other side of the battlefield, sinking. He was too far away for the kind of accuracy he needed. Someone else needed to save her.

"You expect nothing," he whispered, feeling the fire she'd planted within him fan higher.

He scanned the field quickly, looking for options.

"I expect nothing."

He couldn't let the enemy have her. He couldn't let them take her. Even just a few hours in their care would be enough to crush her spirit. It would be enough to scrape out all that gooey goodness within her, to hollow her out and turn her into a shell of a person. A shell like Sebastian had been when he first found her. He couldn't let that happen. Not to her.

"We expect everything."

Austin and his shifters fought through the melee to get to her. Nothing was standing in the way of that big alpha. He took magical gunshots like he didn't even feel them. But he was still a world away. He needed more time. Someone had to give him more time. Someone closer.

"Think it through, Sebastian. Think it through."

A flare of light on metal caught his eye. And then, just beyond, he couldn't believe what he was seeing.

Edgar!

The vampire slunk through little pockets and last-second openings in the rolling crowd of enemy fighters, ripping out necks or stomachs as he passed. He was somehow ignored by almost everyone until their neck was in his mouth. He was ten feet away from Jessie and closing the distance rapidly; he'd clearly seen her in peril and was aiming to get to her.

And then Sebastian thought he must be dreaming.

The moisture in his eyes overflowed, and fresh tears followed.

Nessa followed right behind Edgar! Bent low as though hiding or using him as a shield, she remained right on his heels. If he missed an enemy, she fired off a spell to keep them put or give them a little shock before she finished the job with her knives. The captain was staying in the shadows even in broad daylight and in the middle of a battle. The perfect savior.

"Yes, Nessa," Sebastian said with renewed hope, more tears streaming down his cheeks. "We expect everything. We are family. I know how to work with family."

He sent a different sort of spell her way, withering the people around Edgar and Nessa but not killing them. Nessa noticed immediately; it was a signal they had. A call for help.

She tilted her face up, finding him immediately, then held up a knife, her version of a nod. And then he was slinging spells her way. Hard spells. Powerful, blistering spells.

She continued to follow Edgar toward Jessie. As she did so, she darted left and right, catching his spells and expertly deflecting them. It was a special spell he'd devised for her. He used their friendship and mage connection to prop her up as a mirror of sorts. Through her efforts, he could obtain the accuracy of aim that was lost to him at this distance. Through her, he could actually help Jessie.

And then Jessie dropped just far enough for one of the enemy to jump up and grab her.

# CHAPTER 28

A HAND CLOSED over my ankle. A strong arm dragged me down until I was flung onto the ground. The breath left me for a moment, and then a heavy body smothered me to keep me put.

"Now I've gotcha," a harsh voice said in my ear. It increased in volume. "Block 'em off so a team can get her out of here. Let the mages know we'll need to mask our trail from the animals."

"They seem to be trapped," came the reply.

"They're never trapped for long. Give us cover!"

I struggled in his hold, fear and panic gripping me. Rage and terror bled through the bonds from Austin, and his roar seemed like it was everywhere at once, shaking the ground, rattling my heart, infusing me. *I'm coming,* it said. *Hold on, I'm coming!*

The voice was back in my ear. "Thought you could use your filthy animals to keep you safe, huh?" He spat on my face. "You're nothing but a filthy animal yourself. A pretty little beastie, but a beastie all the same."

The roar came again, all around me now, all through me, calling me. Begging me to seek that darkness within and become one with my gargoyle. To finally find that balance and fight my way out.

"Where we at, Hank?" the voice near my ear called. "Hank!"

"Hank is currently indisposed," Edgar said from somewhere close.

My jailor was suddenly ripped away, and his fingernails scraped across my rough gargoyle skin.

"He tasted delicious, though," Edgar said, and I could just see him grab someone by the throat with his hand and rip it clean out. "He probably ate a lot of candy. I love a good candy-soaked blood source."

"Hey, Jessie," Nessa said from just behind him, strain in her voice. She smiled down at me before stepping over and straddling my prone body. "Ouch. That wing looks like it—Crap, Edgar!"

A puff of insects zoomed in on Nessa's left before materializing into Edgar. He launched himself face-first at the neck of someone reaching for Nessa.

"What the—" was all the man got out before his eyes rolled back in his head, and the vampire let him slide to the ground.

"Close one," Nessa said, her face closed down in concentration. She held knives up but didn't seem to be using them. A glowing red orb grew between her fists and then shot out, slamming into two people pushing in. They screamed and fell away. A new orb, yellow this time, immediately took the place of the first.

I hadn't thought she'd had much power, but she certainly seemed to have plenty now.

"Don't worry, Jessie," Edgar said, stabbing his finger through someone's eye. "Did you see that move? I think of you every time I do it. Anyway, Sir Steele is coming. He's almost here."

"Yeah, we're just playing for time"—Nessa's face closed down in concentration again as another glowing orb materialized between her hands—"in the number-one most dangerous place in this whole field."

"Oh, well, I don't know about—" The last of Edgar's words were muffled as he clamped down on someone's neck.

An enemy trooper shoved Nessa from behind. The orb she had zipped out to the right, splashing across a couple people. Their screaming was cut off quickly.

She turned and stabbed the man who'd pushed her, but by the time he was out of the way, three more had shoved in to remove her.

"What's all this?" a man with thin black hair said, incredibly cool under pressure.

"Edgar," Nessa said, her voice wavering. She shot a

spell forward as I struggled to get up and my wing twisted painfully beneath me.

Bald Guy took the blast with gritted teeth. His eyes flared hot, and a disgusting smile curved his lips. "Pretty little thing." He snatched forward, grabbing her throat. "I think I'll keep you."

She slashed with a knife, aiming for center mass. She should've known she would never reach, not with the difference in their arm spans. If she'd had training, she would've aimed for the arm or wrist holding her.

I curled in my wing, struggling to roll over. Gargoyles weren't great on the ground like this. Wings got in the way.

Austin was closer now, so close, but moving slowly. They'd obviously doubled their efforts to block him off. They were trying to stand between him and me so as to get me out of there. I doubted these guys cared about fallen soldiers.

Nessa was ripped away with a choking yell, and someone else dove on top of me. He rolled over to offer me up, and another grabbed me. I was hauled closer to a blond-haired man with a large overbite, my wings and arms pinned. A crowd moved around me, securing me in.

"Let's go, let's go, hurry!" an enemy shouted. "We've got cover."

I had to shift and fight. I could do more spells without my hands in my human form because I could speak the words. Hell, I could *move* in my human form, unhindered by these dang wings.

Before I could commit, I was ripped to the right. A fist smashed down on my head. Another dug into my ribs. The pain was minimal but wouldn't be in my human form. This might be a wait-and-see situation— let them carry me out, act docile, and then light them up. I was running out of options.

I closed my eyes to still the panic and focused on the moment. On my magic. On Austin working closer. He wouldn't give up on me. Even if I were taken, he wouldn't give up. He'd come for me. I wouldn't be able to stop him.

Another person pushed in close.

"I got her upper half, you take the lower," my captor said. "These things are strong—the males are, at least. Two should be enough for a female. Keep a close eye, though."

"Got her. Here we go, run her out," the guy that grabbed my feet said.

They started to move, jostled around as their cover closed in tightly.

"What are you doing with her?" the guy at my head said.

I opened my eyes to find Nessa draped over a wide shoulder. Bald Man glanced at the man who spoke. "Taking her. Spoils of war. She'll be mighty fun to play with."

My stomach twisted for what he'd do to her. For what they'd do to me. I struggled within my captors' grasp, desperate to break free, to use my hands.

"Whoops, here she goes. Hold her!" the guy at my feet said.

Nessa's hands hung limply down Bald Man's back as they jogged, knives gone. Her head, upside down, shook slowly.

"This isn't going to end well for you, my friend," she said, making no move to struggle. "Maybe it'll be fun for a while, but in the end, you'll think back to this exact moment and wish you'd made an entirely different decision."

There was such confidence in her words, such promise, such laughter, that I couldn't help stilling for a moment. If she held even an ounce of fear, she didn't show it.

"That right, lovely?" He laughed at her. "I think it'll be *very* fun for a while. Until I tire of you. Then I'll give you to the others to use."

A roar of rage from Austin followed our plight.

Another sounded, surprisingly close, an anguished

cry of vehemence.

Nessa was exactly right—I just had no clue how she'd known. I should've, but I hadn't been paying attention to anyone else's location but hers and Austin's.

Now I did…and smiled.

A shiver of fear went through my captors right before a huge silverback gorilla burst through their ranks ahead of us. Two guys went flying. Guns were lifted to fire, but Broken Sue rushed forward, his big arms swinging. He grabbed two more guys and bashed them together before throwing them away. He rose onto his hind legs and beat his chest with his fists, roaring his challenge.

The enemy froze for a moment in fear. Wolves used the opportunity to dart in on all sides, sending the clustered group of mercenaries into chaos. And then *he* came. The biggest of them all. The alpha leading this organized strike.

I could barely see the huge maw coming down, aiming for the man at my head. Austin's teeth fitted over the man's cranium, crunching and ripping away. My body fell, caught by one of Austin's huge paws and lowered quickly to the ground. He reached over me, snatching up the frozen man at my feet and ending him in a blink.

Broken Sue pushed forward again, smashing people out of his way, his focus solely on Nessa. A gun blast struck his chest, but he didn't so much as flinch. He swung his mighty arm. It crunched the upper body of the gun bearer.

Austin pushed forward until he was standing over me, protecting me with his body. The wolves darted in, taking fire now. But so were the enemy. The guns weren't meant for these close quarters, and their frail bodies couldn't handle the blasts like the powerful shifters could.

Broken Sue reached Nessa with a snarl. Bald Man held on to her as he lifted his gun, probably not even thinking about the hand clutching her.

He should've.

The sight clearly enraged the gorilla. Broken Sue took another blast as he moved, spittle flying from his open mouth, showing his large canines. He slapped the gun away like it was nothing and grabbed Bald Man by the face. With a wrench, he ended the scuffle.

Bald Man tumbled to the ground, but not before Broken Sue quickly leaned in to grab the falling Nessa. He cradled her to his chest with one great arm as he used the other to quickly move him toward Austin. It was impossible not to think of King Kong. Once to Austin, he gently deposited Nessa on the ground next to me.

"Too bad he didn't have the opportunity to prolong the grisly death, huh?" Nessa said to me, breathing heavy. She pushed herself up onto her hands and looked up at him. "Thank you, hero," she said, and even through the laughter in her voice, I could tell she meant it with everything in her person.

He held her shimmering gaze for a moment before huffing and turning away. His job wasn't done.

Neither was mine.

Austin and his shifters had cut a line to us, but there was no way they could've killed a whole battlefield of enemy to do it. If we weren't surrounded now, we would be soon. And with me beneath him, he couldn't fight as he needed to.

"I have to find the darkness," I meant to say, but the words came out of my gargoyle maw a garbled mess. "I have to allow my gargoyle to rule."

Nessa crawled closer to me, under the shadow and protection of Austin.

"How's that wing? Gonna heal?" Her fingers danced over my wing's edge. The hole was nearly mended now. All the time in the enemy's hands was time my body had had to repair itself.

It was also time the enemy mages had to get out of their magical prison. Time was ticking.

"Looks good, pretty beastie." She smiled at me, and her eyes flashed. "Let your mate unlock the power of the gargoyle, okay? Like Brochan did at that challenge, remember? We need it. Let Austin be your guide. Don't be afraid. Sebastian said you've been afraid to really let go in training, but don't be. You have friends and family waiting in the darkness for you." She touched her chest lightly, then pointed up at Austin. "And Brochan and Sebastian and Niamh and probably Edgar. We're all there. We all come and go as we please. Join us. We won't let you wander too far, don't worry. Come on in, the water's fine."

Austin grunted, and a shock of pain coursed through him. He turned, obviously careful to keep us under him, to combat a surge of people at his back.

Nessa scooted closer to me at first so as not to get stepped on, then looked that way. She looked behind her, then back at me. "I've got to go. I need to help, or we're all gonna die. Well...the guys are. We might have a much worse fate. Find that gargoyle. Let's make you the queen of this bitch, and then let's go home and ride around in that carriage!" She nodded at me in encouragement before rolling out from under Austin. "Anyone seen a couple of very expensive, custom-made, and quite necessary knives?" she called before the crowd swallowed her up.

*We expect everything.*

I had to do this. I *had* to. I had to connect these two pieces of myself, past and present. I had to cement them with the ferocity Ivy House needed me to find.

I had to protect my people. It was my duty. A duty I coveted.

I reached out through the bonds to Austin, doing as Nessa had said. My magic roiled and surged within me, feeling the dangerous darkness of my mate. She was right—he'd found that darkness within him and was currently exploiting it. Our connection suddenly felt decadent and raw, utterly primal. It felt like exactly what awaited me if I sank into the dark depths of my magic. It felt like battle and wildness and bloodshed. I would follow him down and trust him to pull me back to safety again, no matter how long I was locked below.

*"That is a mistake,"* a familiar voice whispered. *"If you trust him, he will betray you. He will be your demise."*

It took me a moment to locate the voice in my memory, but once I did, a wave of cold shivers washed over me. It was the voice I'd heard within Ivy House, the one that had been pushing me to take the magic. Tamara Ivy, I'd thought.

It had said, *"Rely on no man, for it is he who will betray you. Set yourself free."*

If it were any other man, I'd hesitate for a moment. I'd contemplate her words. Trust was a risk, and I'd been burned a great many times in my life.

But this was Austin Steele. He'd earned my trust before he earned my love. He'd proven himself. If I couldn't trust him, I couldn't trust anyone, and that wasn't freedom. That was a prison of fear, and it wasn't how I would go through life.

If this was taking a chance, it was a chance I was willing to take. A demise I was willing to face.

I took a deep breath and let go. Let myself keep sliding deeper. Terror gripped me, but I continued, intent to do as Ivy House kept pushing me to do. As Austin had eventually had to do with his animal. I submitted to it, seeking the balance, following my mate into the twisted depths of our beasts.

The darkness overwhelmed me quickly, sucking me in. Magic pumped. Power slid around me. Still I sank, feeling Austin with me, all around me. Holding me and dragging me, deeper and deeper until I was no longer sure where my sense of self ended and the gargoyle began.

I mentally closed my eyes and released my holds on humanity. I released my past and my logic. I released my control.

His approval sang through the bonds. His pride. His sweet darkness.

And that was when I felt it—a sensation unlike any I'd ever experienced, like strolling through the decadent midnight wilderness. It was raw and twisted and volatile, yet somehow heavenly and serene. It was the darkness I'd feared, but there was light buried within it. Nature was comprised of both, after all—the deep night was always followed by a new dawn. A vicious killing fed a predator's young, ensuring new life. Raging fires allowed for regrowth.

Death and rebirth.

Tamed savagery.

I'd felt a portion of this in the wood. The peace. The serenity.

And now, I would flip the coin and display the brutal savagery needed to protect my family.

As I embraced the feeling, power pumped through me, a glorious feeling.

My roar reverberated across the battlefield. Austin stood up on his back legs, matching it, letting me fly free.

I snapped out my wings, shedding swirls of pinkish-purple light. A glittery dust emanated from me, my magic taking a physical form and falling onto the ground before winking out.

My creature was beautiful. Time to show the enemy, and myself, that it was also vicious and fierce.

I was an Ivy House lady, damn it.

# CHAPTER 29

I FLEW INTO the air in a rush of power. My wing was almost completely mended, only tilting me a little. I worked a spell on impulse, one at the very top of my power scale, and delighted in how much easier it was to work now that I'd found this balance. When I let it loose, fire blistered through the ranks of the enemy, who were spread out all over now. Trampled grass ignited quickly, but with a tweak of the spell, the heat was sucked out and fire doused. The fire lingered on them, but it wasn't hot enough to burn through their suits. I couldn't match Cyra's magic.

A gun blast shot at me. I covered myself in a quick protective layer, searching for Cyra. A pulse of my magic sang out, calling her.

She rose from within the battle, darting toward me.

*Fire,* I thought, and for once, the blast of magic matched. She could feel my meaning through the magic. She could feel the command.

She wasted no time in diving. Her beak opened, and

a large blast of fire covered a crowd of enemy fighters. It wouldn't get through their uniforms, but it would muddle their senses and burn any exposed skin. That would slow them down.

Hollace was next. Seeing me take the heat out of the ground fire, he let a large torrent of lightning loose. He missed as many as he hit, but it didn't matter. Those he hit went down for the count.

Shouts and screams rose. The enemy ran around in a frenzy, the middle of their forces now encapsulated by flame or being struck by lightning.

Through the cacophony I heard, "Yes!"

Edgar. He stood on the outskirts of the battlefield now with his fist held high in the air.

"You did fire, Miss Jessie!" he called. "I knew you could do it!"

Now I was leeching fire, but it was still a win.

I let my magic flood me, not hindering it. Not squishing it down or worrying what I'd do. I let that sweet darkness roll through me, and then I blasted it out. Time to reconnect with my team and get back to the plan.

Time to let my pretty beastie shine.

✧　✧　✧

THE SHIFT IN pressure was unmistakable. Niamh could

feel it coursing through her. Some came from the Ivy House bond, but more came directly from Jessie.

It pumped Niamh full of courage she didn't need, power she was happy to use, and a strange sense of community that had her checking on those around her to make sure everyone was on the same page and accounted for. It felt...

There were no words for how it felt. Niamh had been on many battlefields in her lifetime, and it had never felt this incredibly...natural. Like coming home. Like they couldn't possibly lose so long as they worked together.

The gargoyle had settled into her wings. About fecking time.

Jessie pumped her wings while throwing out a hand. A moment later, a zip from one of those magical guns slammed into some sort of shield covering Austin. It ricocheted off, headed back toward the one who'd fired it. Jessie turned again, flinging out her hand for Dave right before a blast reached him.

How in the hell did she know what attacks were coming when? It was like she was predicting their course and reacting before they could land. Ho-ly crap. The gargoyle was worth all the hype for that little trick alone.

Dave let out a ragged snarl before grabbing an enemy by the upper thighs. The man yelled in surprise as Dave picked him up and swung him around like a baseball bat. The enemy's body hit a bunch of others, knocking them down or back, disarming most. He let go of the body mid-swing, launching it, before descending on those he'd disarmed.

Without their weapons, they had absolutely no chance of survival.

Now that Jessie was safe, Sebastian resumed his quick-fire spell casting to the battlefield at large. He was obviously taking the attacking role, leaving defense to Jessie. And now that she'd sorted her gargoyle issue, she was handling it beautifully.

When her people went in for an attack, she draped a spell over the enemy, deadening their efforts to fight back. She blanketed a whole section of enemy troops at one point so that Austin Steele could barrel through and take people out with quick, vicious economy. All the while, she flew in among them, diving to help when needed and flying away again. She clawed through throats and ripped into bowels. Only Austin Steele could hold a flame to her newfound viciousness.

Well, Austin Steele and Niamh herself. And the basajaun, she supposed. Cyra shouldn't be left off the list. Edgar...

"Jessie," a voice boomed. Sebastian's voice amplified

by magic. "Time's up. We've got mages."

Jessie rose higher into the sky, a little lopsided.

Niamh shifted into her smaller form again. The pain from her back was mostly gone, and the surge of energy from Jessie greatly helped. She skittered up someone's back, saw Dave running in her direction, and decided to let him have this guy. Instead, she jumped from that guy's back onto another guy's face and wreaked havoc. *Jeepers, creepers,* she sang in her head, *you just lost your peepers...*

*Where are all the women in this outfit?* she wondered to herself as she scratched down another guy's stomach and then bit hard into his junk. This troop was solely made up of men. The mages, too. A bit sexist, that.

A body flew by her, one missing an arm. Another body followed.

Dave was having a grand ol' time.

He roared and high-kicked, catching one of the shorter troops in the side of the head. A resounding crack had the guy sliding bonelessly to the ground.

Cyra dove by and blasted someone to Niamh's left before continuing to barrel down the line, getting two more. They didn't die, though, just screamed and writhed and tried to get their weapons up to shoot.

Jessie was there in an instant, throwing a quick

shield over Dave before a blast struck him, and then dousing the fire Cyra had caused. She was gone again in no time, twisting to hurl a spell at the enemy mages.

Niamh hopped from one singed guy to another, taking them out quickly. They only needed a little help to go down.

Magic flew from the enemy mages. They aimed for the fliers at first, but their attack smacked into one of Jessie or Sebastian's defense spells. A ball of light shot back the way it had come.

Niamh jumped onto the ground and ran through the shuffling feet, swiping or biting if the opportunity presented itself. Those mages had to be taken down. The shifters could handle the rest of the ground crew, who were being thinned rapidly at this point, but magic was another story altogether.

She got to the edge of the milling crowd, only to find Dave again. That creature really made his way around. He picked someone up by their ankles and then slammed them onto their back as if the weight didn't bother him at all. She ran around and into the trees, climbing a tall one to better see her target.

What she saw widened her eyes.

Magic shot in both directions, but the enemy mages couldn't get through the defensive shield. As Jessie seemingly held it, surrounded now by her gargoyles,

Sebastian fired through it at the enemy mages. His spells came just as quickly as before, and even from a distance, they were incredibly powerful. They cracked against the enemies' defensive spells, scattering the mages.

The enemy had bottles of potions to help, though. They weren't doing this on their own.

Niamh climbed back down the tree. She ran through the grass and bushes, staying hidden. When she was nearly at the mages, Edgar suddenly popped into sight, shifting from his insect form back into a vampire.

"Oh, hello, Niamh," he said, running by.

"Have you seen this guy run, though?" Nessa laughed as she hurried after him holding just one of her knives.

Niamh kept with them, slinking behind trees and then sprinting toward the mages.

The one on the left saw them first; he swung his hands from the air toward Nessa's center mass, ready to shoot off a spell.

"No, no." Edgar puffed into insects, closed the gap faster than Nessa could run, and popped back into being right behind the mage. "Surprise!"

The mage howled in startled terror, jerking to the right. But Edgar was already biting down on his neck. The mage next to them gasped, and the spell he'd been casting went wide. Nessa was there in a moment, grabbing him and swinging him around to use as a shield. Another mage blasted him on instinct, or maybe out of fear. Niamh ignored that mage and went for the last, but a dome closed over him before she could get there. She slammed into the magical barrier and bounced off.

"Leave him," Nessa shouted as the last "free" mage ran. "We need someone to report their failure. We need to make Momar hesitate and want more info. Quick, get that mage—"

A spell hit the fleeing mage in the back. Another hit even as he was falling. Jessie and Sebastian had him.

Nessa dropped the dead weight she was holding and approached the dome. The other magic users switched back to helping with the ground crew.

"We're the sort of people you invite to dinner," she told the terrified mage in the dome. "Not the sort you sneak up on. Tell your boss that he'd best do this differently next time. Just because we're new on the scene doesn't mean we don't know how things work."

She lifted her hand high, and it had to be for Sebastian's sake. The dome winked out of existence.

"We're sparing your life," she said. "We'll expect to be compensated down the road. Go."

The mage took off running like his arse was on fire.

He didn't look back.

Niamh wasn't actually sure this was the best course of action. Momar should be able to come to those conclusions on his own. He certainly wouldn't want to get advice from a nothing mage who'd failed in his duty. She'd need to think about the possible repercussions of this decision.

For now, though, they had a battle to win.

Edgar smiled at Nessa. "Ready, shadow?"

Oh, great, Edgar had made a new friend. Now he'd never stop talking about it.

Only a slice of the enemy still stood, trying to hold their ground. Trying, and failing.

The magical blasts from the weapons hit impenetrable defenses thrown up by Jessie. Magical spells rained down on their group. The shifters didn't flag, just as ferocious now as when they'd started. The gargoyles dipped, ending those who'd survived the onslaught from Hollace and Cyra. The Ivy House crew and Austin's scant pack had been grossly outnumbered, but it hadn't mattered. Not after Jessie had gotten a hold of her magic and helped each faction shine individually so they could help the team as a whole.

The enemy now clearly realized they were fighting a battle they couldn't win. Momar's ground troops were used to being the strongest and best, to having a team of mages at their backs and effective magical weapons in their hands. They weren't used to what the Ivy House crew had going on, especially with Austin Steele and his shifter pack in the mix. They'd been gobsmacked. One of *them* should be the one to tell their friends. Their experience of the battle would carry the most weight.

Niamh made a snap decision.

She ran and jumped onto a guy, marking that enemy as hers. Broken Sue let her have him, and peeled off to club someone else with his big arms. Into the trees Niamh rode the man, avoiding his flailing attempts to sweep her off.

A basajaun stepped out of nowhere, blocking the enemy's way. The enemy ran into him at full speed, bounced off, staggered into a tree, and then fell. The basajaun snarled and reached down to finish the job.

"No!" Niamh said as soon as she'd shifted back. She worked to catch her breath. She'd had no idea the other basajaunak were hanging around. They hadn't joined the battle, but they'd apparently taken it upon themselves to pick off the runaways. Better yet, they'd seen Jessie and Austin Steele's crew at work. That was good news. "Not this one. Maybe beat him up a bit, that's fine, but let him go."

"You already let one go," Dave's mom said, stepping out from a tree down the way. "Why two?"

"I'm not sure letting that mage go was the right decision, honestly. I'll have a think on it. But this one is a highly trained and supposedly effective foot soldier. He's seen a lot of action, so he has. Unlike that mage, your man is at the top of his game. He's had a'lotta experience, and I'll bet he's not used to runnin'. He'll surely be punished for that. Regardless, his account will carry a lot more weight than the mage's. The story will grow, and the next time we have'ta deal with these lads, they'll be nervous. Jumpy. It'll make them easier to kill. It'll make the mages who depend on them as a shield slower to commit. *That* is what will stall the big boss in coming after us."

The basandere watched Niamh for a moment before nodding. The basajaun stepped out of the way.

"Besides," Niamh said before she turned back to the others, "they invaded your territory. You need someone to witness what happens to those who do. The magical world has clearly forgotten how basajaunak work. The enemy had zero regard for you. They didn't think you were a threat in your own lands."

Niamh wasn't giving the whole story, of course. The mages had certainly forgotten, but she didn't mention that the basajaunak were still very much regarded as a threat in much of the magical world, and their rules were known by all. Mages were proving to be a different breed. They either didn't know the rules or didn't care.

The basandere turned and melted back into the trees. Before she was completely out of sight, she said, "That had occurred to me, yes." And then she was gone.

They weren't ready to be part of Dave's new family, but they'd stuck around. They had even helped. They'd crossed the line between spectator and sport, just as Dave had last year. The younger generation would probably be jealous or sad they missed out and ask for *all* the details. They'd want to see for themselves.

Niamh smiled to herself.

They, as a collective group, were intrigued. That was always the first step. The curiosity, the interest. Then the gathering of more information. Maybe visiting. Maybe trying a flower or two.

It wouldn't be right away, and it wouldn't be all at once, but Niamh would place a very large wager that they'd win many of these basajaun to their side.

She'd better work on her alcohol tolerance…

# CHAPTER 30

I PUSHED HIGHER into the air to watch one of the wolves dash into the trees after a running soldier. Before the wolf reached him, a basandere stepped out from behind a trunk and grabbed the enemy. In a few very heinous movements, he fell to the ground in a somewhat grotesque shape.

Roars went up, followed by Edgar's shout. Looking back at the field, I saw why.

None of the enemy remained standing. Not one.

My magic still pumped through me, calling for more action. Wanting more blood. It raged and throbbed.

This was it. This was the part I was most scared of.

I found Austin on the other side of the battlefield, up on his hind legs and looking around. He spotted me coming and lowered to all fours, waiting.

I wanted to shift into my human form and drag him into the trees. I wanted to stay as I was and go find more enemies. I wanted to rip and tear and bathe the world in blood. Violent emotions pulled at me. Lustful emotions did, too, as I eyed that alpha gargoyle across the way. I'd never properly appreciated how handsome he was. How strong. Or the alpha gorilla, scarred and broken and safe, hot as hell.

Panic flared within me.

I landed, stumbled, and then hop-flew directly to Austin. He stepped forward to meet me, and I felt his calm assurance through the bonds. I felt him easing out of the darkness and now shifting into a man.

"Shh, shh," he said softly, standing in front of me now, his gaze rooted to mine. "Come back with me. Let it recede."

I breathed shallowly, too quickly.

"Shift now, Jess. Shift now and come back to me."

*"Do not listen to him,"* the voice whispered. *"Do not trust him. He wishes to claim your beast. He wishes to force your humanity away so that he can control you."*

I felt the pain in the words. The haunting loss. The loss of what, I couldn't be sure. Herself, maybe? The control she spoke of?

Just as I had when I sought the darkness, I ignored it. I did as he said and shifted into my human form. Spots danced in my vision, the effect of hyperventilating. My core throbbed with confusing tightness at the thought of the other alphas in my proximity.

But then my palms met warm skin covering hard, cut muscle. My gaze sank into the familiar cobalt blue. His power and his strength shocked into me.

*Mate.*

The lustful thoughts dried up immediately, vanished as though they'd never been. The primal part of me, the gargoyle, recognized her home. Nothing else would do. No other alpha could compare to this one.

The violence and the turmoil soothed me as his arms came around me. The surging darkness, the vicious joy of battle, eased into a calm vibration.

"It's okay, Jess, I'm here," he murmured, rocking me slightly. "I'm here. You're safe. Let it go."

I took a deep breath. Then another, coming back to neutral. My gargoyle was still there, now officially a part of me, but the darkness that Austin himself often kept at bay receded.

He didn't rush me to step away, even though I knew he was eager to check on his people. I clutched on to him for another moment, continuing to breathe, just to make sure all was well.

"Okay," I said, finally stepping back. "I'm okay."

He held my upper arms for a moment, looking down into my eyes, then nodded. "I'm proud of you. You did it."

I released a shaky breath. "I needed you, though. I

didn't do it on my own."

"It's better that you let me walk you into the darkness than to find it through rage like I did. Once you know your way, you'll be way better off than I am. I still find it through rage. As far as getting out..." He shrugged. "If you find a trick to that, let me know."

I gave him a little smile. "I'll ask Nessa. She seems to pop in and out regularly."

I could feel people through the bonds, but I wanted to assess their hurts and issues with my eyes as well. I needed to pick and choose whom to heal first. I didn't have the energy to help everyone.

We needed someone other than me who could handle this part of things. Someone whose job was *just* to heal, kept safe until needed, their energy never depleted through fighting. It would help me focus more during battles and rest after. A magical medic, basically.

The shock wave of magic blasted out across the battlefield, then beyond. I stopped with widening eyes before slapping my hand to my chest.

"Did you..." Austin turned to look down at me. "Did you just..."

"Sent a summons, yeah." I moved my hand to his shoulder. "For a healer. I was just thinking how it would be great to have another one besides me."

I started walking again, and Austin quickly caught

up.

"You shouldn't have to receive challenges or dominate or anything." I chewed my lip. "I hope. I'd just been wishfully thinking. I hadn't meant to send a summons."

"You don't have to accept whoever shows," he said, "but it's definitely not a bad idea. I wonder what type of magic it'll be. I don't think I know of a magical being specializing in healing."

I wondered myself.

Ulric had some nasty wounds, but he was still in flight. Hollace had taken a lot of hits, too. Those magical weapons didn't just puncture—they seemed to strip the magical wielder of their power. After I found balance in my magic, I'd tried to protect as many of my people as I could, but I hadn't been able to cover everyone, especially once the mages got free.

The rest were banged up, but nothing too serious. Niamh's back hurt, Dave had been hit by the blasts several times but didn't seem to notice the seeping wounds, and Mr. Tom was very annoyed about a torn wing.

The shifters hadn't fared so well, and a lot of that was my fault. I'd nearly been captured by the enemy, and they were the ones to rip me free. They'd paid the price.

"What's the damage?" I asked as I checked in with Austin again by the trees under which the wounded had taken shelter. Various connections fanned into my awareness. Most of the shifters had accepted my gargoyle's—my—invitation during the battle. The extra awareness had allowed me to know when they felt danger—exorbitant danger, since battle was always dangerous—and help as best I could. Those that didn't had been hit harder, as I'd needed to physically see their peril.

"No casualties," he said, and tilted his head. "Nearly."

I nodded as I knelt beside a wolf I didn't know well. He'd stayed in his furry form to help with healing, but he wasn't faring very well. He'd taken a lot of hits with the guns, including one to his eye, and had gaping wounds on multiple places on his body. If left to his own healing abilities, he'd surely die.

I set to healing him immediately, cutting out his pain so maybe he could get a little sleep and help himself heal. I still wasn't sure he'd make it, honestly. I wasn't sure this much damage could be fixed.

Isabelle's front right leg was broken in multiple places. The bone stuck out in two, and if it wasn't set to rights, it would heal incorrectly, and she'd never walk on it again.

"We need to see if the basajaunak can help with this," I murmured to Austin. "I can stop her from feeling the pain, but this shouldn't be healed yet, for obvious reasons. I can't *will* bone to straighten, at least not to that magnitude."

He nodded, glancing at one of his people to carry out the command.

Three more had broken extremities, but none so bad as Isabelle. Still, two would need help from the basajaunak if they could provide it. The guns had done the most damage, but thankfully, the enemy had underestimated shifters and wildly underestimated gargoyles. The wounds were intense and painful, but with the shifters' faster healing speeds, it took many hits to keep them down. Those bleeding the most heavily, like Kace and a couple others, could rely on stitches to sew them back up before blood loss became a serious problem.

I really hoped the basajaunak were set up for all that.

"Hey." Sebastian walked up after I'd checked in with the last shifter under the trees and moved away to find the lead basandere. He wore an incredulous expression.

"What's up?" I asked, looking him over. "Did you sustain any injuries?"

"What? Oh." He looked down at himself. "No, I was

too far away for that."

Broken Sue limped toward us. I could feel his pain through our connection, which was dimming but didn't seem like it would entirely disappear, now that I had a firmer handle on my primal side.

"Alpha, I was just making my way over to check on the wounded," he said when he reached us, standing tall even though I could feel what it cost him to do so.

"Jess just saw to them," said Sebastian. "She's healing the worst, and we have people checking in with the basajaunak about other issues. What's your status?"

"I'm fine," Broken Sue lied.

I didn't have the energy to help him, though. He'd have to tough it out.

"Half of you would be dead if it weren't for Jessie's ingenious spell work," Sebastian said, looking out over the meadow covered in the fallen enemy. "She shouldn't have been able to reflect blasts from those guns. That's the precise reason they use them—they strip away magic. If you'd just blanketed everyone in a defense spell, it wouldn't have been enough power. The way you applied shields individually, as needed, with your vat of power behind them, was"—he ran his fingers through his hair—"unbelievable. Incredible." He gestured around us. "A normal mage couldn't do this."

"You have enough power to do it," I told him. "It

wasn't at the top of my power scale."

"I might have enough power if I were *close* to the person, sure," he replied. "But a normal mage can't fly through the air and then use magic exactly where and when it's needed. I am… I'm…"

"Flabbergasted?" Nessa basically pranced by. "Verklempt? Shocked? Astounded?"

"Alpha Ironheart wasn't the only mage lighting it up," Broken Sue said, clapping Sebastian on the back. For once, Sebastian didn't flinch and move away. "If we'd had a weird mage like you fighting for my pack when those mages attacked, we wouldn't have gone down."

Sebastian shook his head. "I need to find a way to be closer. I need to start training to be part of the fighting. I feel like a coward way in the back. Even Nessa was in the action."

Broken Sue's demeanor changed, and his mood soured. "She shouldn't have been," he growled.

"What you need is someone watching your six," Austin said, studying him. "We should've had someone go around the battle and take the mages out from the back. It was an oversight not to."

"Hindsight is 20/20," Sebastian replied. "But I did have someone watching me. There were a few basajaunak keeping post. It, amazingly, made me a little less afraid of them."

"It's a nice feeling having the monsters on your side," Austin said, his joke hidden behind his stone façade.

"It's a nice feeling not being the biggest monster at the party," Sebastian returned quietly.

Broken Sue took a deep breath, and I could tell he barely stopped from wincing. "You've got a long way to go to be considered the biggest monster at these parties, weird mage. A long way."

"We shall see," Sebastian murmured.

A basajaun roared. I glanced that way in time to see an enemy bashed against a tree and thrown ten feet.

"Holy—! What the hell?" I exclaimed.

"It is done," he said.

I turned away quickly. "There's no way I can stop them killing the survivors as a punishment for trespassing, is there? Since this is their territory?"

"No," Austin replied, still looking that way. "To do so might cause offense."

"And then you'd be the one bashed against the tree," Sebastian said unhelpfully.

"Okay." I nodded. "That's probably my cue to get out of here. What are we going to do with the bodies?"

"Here we are, miss." Mr. Tom walked over to us with a handful of muumuus and Dave in tow. "And for you, Austin Steele. Broken Sue." He passed them out before moving on to the gargoyles, all sitting a ways away. Ulric had lain down and closed his eyes.

"The basajaunak will handle the enemy bodies," Dave said. "Maybe Cyra will give them a hand, though."

I grimaced again. I might have a better grip on my gargoyle now, but that didn't mean I found any of this tasteful.

"The basandere asks," Dave said, looking between Austin and me, "if you would like to return to the village to rest. We can carry the wounded on slings. They are being made now. *He* ran ahead to tell the healer we were coming. *She* can reset bones and stitch up flesh. She is more than capable."

I could feel the pride buzzing within him. We must've shown well to his people. He'd gotten what he wanted.

"That would be great, Dave, thank you," I said. "Thank her for me. And how about you? Make sure you get stitched up."

Dave looked down at the seeping red in his hair. "In time. But now I must carry out the punishment for trespassing before it is all done without me."

Someone screamed. The sound cut off quickly.

"It is done," one of the basajaunak in that direction said.

"God, this is grisly," I murmured. "Let's get out of here."

"Do you want a ride?" Austin asked, and I knew he was asking if I wanted to ride on his back.

"Yes, please. I'm exhausted and getting more tired by the moment."

"And she heals," Sebastian muttered, watching the basajaunak work. "She does spells that shouldn't exist, protects her people while flying, and she heals. Female gargoyles are now my favorite creature. And they're pretty—"

"Who's he talking to?" Niamh asked as she walked up, dressed in a muumuu. She hooked a thumb Sebastian's way.

"Oh, no one," he answered. "I'm just trying to process all of this. There's no way we should've wiped the floor with this crew. No way. It's inconceivable. I feel like I'm dreaming."

"Are ye *jokin*'? What with all your spell flinging?" She shook her head at him. "We're going ta need another talk here soon—"

"No, thank you—"

"You're better about stoopin' and scrapin' and embarassin' yerself around shifters, but you gotta stop underestimating yerself, too. Humble bragging is just plain annoyin'. Sure, those lot didn't have a hope against our mages. C'mon. Let's get back to the village. I'm hungry."

"I can probably walk," Sebastian said, once again stooping as he followed her. "I don't need to ride on your back."

"Ah, schtop. Ye might as well. It's faster. Let's see if I can shake ye off this time."

"Please, no…"

Another scream cut off quickly. I stopped myself from looking.

Austin looked at Broken Sue. "Wait with the wounded. Make sure they're all taken care of. Hear their stories if they want to give them."

He nodded. "Yes, alpha."

"Shall we?" Austin asked me, leading me away.

"Shouldn't we stay to make sure the wounded are looked after, being alphas?" I asked quietly.

"The gargoyles don't need you. They aren't that badly off. The shifters need some reprieve from authority, and Brochan is hurt. I've just given him a reason to sit and rest among the wounded." As he stepped away a bit to shift, he said, "I wonder if they can find more of that alcoholic fruit drink."

I frowned. "Why, do you want a celebratory drink?"

"No, I want to watch Niamh roll a basajaun through the fire. That sounded like some sort of spectacle."

Sadly, they couldn't find any more for Niamh to consume. She'd become a low-key celebrity, though. Apparently, the basajaunak prided themselves on their ability to handle that special brew, something their relatives to the north weren't as easily able to tolerate. She'd drunk them all under the table. A few wanted a rematch, including the basajaun with singed hair.

We stayed in the village for a little over a week. We hadn't needed so long to recover, but it was peaceful and beautiful. We went on hikes and listened to stories by the campfire. I watched Austin fish in the stream and sat with Edgar as he failed to find four-leaf clovers. Mr. Tom washed our clothes and complained about the dirty rocks on which he had to dry them.

"What is the point?" he'd mutter to himself. "You wash them in a fish-poop–infested stream and then attract just as much dirt when you lay them out on these filthy rocks. This is no way to live."

He wasn't as enamored by our surroundings as I was.

When it came to our turn to share stories with the basajaunak, Ulric told most of them, weaving tales with a storyteller's flair that had the younger ones riveted. At Niamh's request, he mostly offered Ivy House's antics in funny vignettes, like Edgar finding out Dave had eaten all his flowers. Edgar attempted to tell the story of the time I'd jabbed him in the eye, but he ended up sputtering himself into silence after tripping on all the words. Niamh then told them of our previous battles.

When it came time to leave, I was sad to go. I missed my bed and my privacy with Austin, but our woods just didn't have the same feel as these. They didn't feel lived in because the basajaun were at one with their home—protectors of their territory and everything in it.

I told the head basandere that, and thanked her for the welcome. She accepted my thanks but didn't comment further, not even when I offered to return the favor—and host them—whenever she wanted.

Before we left, the basandere I'd met by the stream sought me out in camp. She waited on the outskirts until invited in, and then asked if she could sit by the fire for a time.

"That means she wants an audience," Dave whispered with a knowing smirk before making himself scarce.

We had Cyra build it up a bit, and then I invited her to sit down.

"I have enjoyed knowing you," the basandere began, watching the flames. "I have enjoyed hearing your stories and interacting with your...crew."

"I've loved being here. Thank you for your hospitality."

"Yes." She braided a bit of the hair on her leg. It seemed like a nervous reflex, like fidgeting. "Buln'dan—ah, Dave mentioned that…" She let the words trail away and then shrugged a little. "I am young. Too young to set off on my own, my mother and father say. They say I will not be able to feed myself or keep myself out of danger. And while I am plenty old enough, it is true that I don't know anything about the outside world. But…"

She stared into the fire and took a deep breath. She was building herself up for something, and I held my breath for what I hoped it was.

"It felt as though you drew me that one day, by the stream," she said. "It felt as though you had called me. And Bul—Dave mentioned that you have a lovely and protected wood outside of your stick-builder home. He mentioned that you were sad that it was not lived in—that it didn't feel like a home. Not like here, I mean."

"True," I said, keeping my cool. "We have Edgar to take care of the grounds, but we don't have anyone to take care of the wood."

She nodded, a little more confident. "Yes, that is what he said. I am not sure if you know this, but among my family, I am known for my ability to blend nature. To enhance the environment. It is a gift. I think we can help each other."

"A trade?" I asked.

Her smile made me want to fist-pump the air. "A trade, yes. I will blend the nature in your wood with your stick-builder home—with your crew—in exchange for living within the Ivy protection. Until I can venture out to Dave's mountain, I mean. He has offered me to stay once I am ready."

"Ivy House protection—Never mind, you'll see." I put out my hand to shake, then realized Dave never did that and put it down again. "I accept. That sounds nice."

She wouldn't be going home with us, but would stay to say her goodbyes and gather her few things first. Dave had agreed to stay behind with her, to show her the way when she was ready and to take the blame if any of the family were angry at her decision.

We hadn't gotten an alliance, but this seemed like a step in the right direction.

The hike out was much faster because we took a different trail that wasn't nearly as arduous. It still took a half a day, though, and I was plenty tired by the time we made it back to the little town.

"This place still smells like incense, doesn't it?" I asked as we loaded up the cars.

"It does." Austin stood beside me. "It's nice."

"Well…yeah, but it's weird. Like…the whole place, inside and out, smells like incense. The same kind, too.

It's not like various people are burning different sticks of incense, it's like the whole place is perfumed by one massive stick. It's not right."

"I think you're letting it get to you too much."

"Very likely. But still…"

There were just as many snacks in the jet on the way home, and Mr. Tom asked me about them just as often after we landed. Niamh heckled him the whole time.

When we finally pulled up to the house, I couldn't wait to be in my little parlor with the door closed and a warm drink in my hand. Maybe curled up in Austin's lap, though I assumed he was eager to check in with his territory.

Our sedans were parked in front of the house, and I climbed out with a sigh.

"Hey, thanks for healing me, alpha," Kace said to me as I stood near the trunk. "I took a beating."

"I didn't help much, just made sure the stitching worked."

"You cut out the pain. That was worth its weight in gold. I hate pretending things don't hurt when they do." He laughed.

"Anytime. Every time, actually, as long as I'm able. You're a valuable member of the pack and the team."

He nodded and stepped back. "It's a helluva team. I can't wait until Alpha Steele makes his rounds and meets the other packs. It'll be a helluva thing. Too bad the basajaunak didn't want to join—"

He cut off. Something had clearly caught his eye. He turned toward Ivy House, and then I saw it, too. We all did, actually, because the sight came with shouting.

A short woman a couple of decades my senior and twice my girth shouted obscenities as she ran across the Ivy House lawn. I could just barely make her out in the moonlight. With one hand, she held what looked like a bat above her head. Her other hand gripped the hem of her flower-patterned dress so she could run faster. Short blonde curls bobbed on her head. In front of her ran a terrified gnome, holding up its pants.

"You're not going to get away," she hollered, gaining on him and then swinging down with the bat. It clunked on the gnome's head and knocked it to the side. She pivoted on a dime and dropped the hem of her dress. With both hands, she swung the weapon down, smacking the shrieking gnome. Three more times, and then she straightened up so she could kick it. "This is not your home! Get out of here!" she hollered at it.

It scrabbled up and limped off as fast as it could. Another peeked out of the bushes, and then the chase was on again.

"I see you!" She sprinted across the lawn in the other direction. The gnome jumped out of the bushes and ran away from her. She caught up to it, though, and kicked it when she was close enough, knocking it off its feet. Then she started battering down on it.

"Mom?" Ulric said.

The woman didn't seem to hear. She finished her burst of gnome beating before kicking this one as well. It limped off like the other. Only then did she straighten, brush a curl out of her eye, and spot Ulric.

"Well, hello!" She beamed, bright red lips pulling into a wide smile. She crossed the grass to us with the confidence of a linebacker, even though she was all of five feet tall. Her gaze swept over us before landing on me. "Oh, my gosh. Is this..." She looked back and forth between Ulric and me. "Well, don't stand there with your mouth hanging open. Introduce me, Ulric!"

"Oh. Uh...right." Ulric hastened my way, setting down his suitcase as he did so. "Mom, this is Jessie Ironheart, the alpha of this house and territory. And this is Austin Steele, the original alpha of the shifter territory and Jessie's enforcer of the house. Alphas, this is my mom, Patty. A little late, as usual."

"Hello!" Patty reached out for my hand and pumped it eagerly. "So amazing to meet you. A real female gargoyle, huh? I always dreamed that I'd suddenly find out *I* was a female gargoyle. I hoped and wished and—But no, just a gargoyle's daughter." She laughed and turned to Austin. "My goodness. When Ulric said the alpha shifter of these parts was powerful, he didn't do you justice. I can feel the alpha in you. Usually, I don't with shifters. You'll do splendidly as her mate. Yes, oh, yes, you'll be just fine."

"Mom, where have you been?" Ulric asked.

"Oh, here and there. I met this *wonderful* lady on the way, and we got to talking. Well, she'd heard of a female gargoyle, of course. Everyone has. But she didn't believe it. She just did not believe a female gargoyle was not born but made." She lowered her head and looked at us from under her lashes. "You know the mages have tried that in the past, right? *Mages.*" She shook her head and tsked. "Well, I told her all about the house and the original female—that's what I'm calling her, so it's easy to grasp—and repeated stories I'd heard from Ulric. She so kindly asked that I meet their cairn leader, and I said *of course!*" She put her hand to the side of her mouth. "He is *very* influential. I won't tell you who it was because I swore I wouldn't—they want to save face for not believing—but expect a nice connection request from them. Anyway, another large cairn was pretty close by, and I've met the cairn leader's mate before, so I figured I would stop in. We had a nice chat, and I found out they've already sent their connection request. I told them I'd put in the good word for them."

She gave me a look that said she was talking out of her butt on that one.

"And then I got the message from Ulric about the business you all had to attend to, so I figured I'd call on my good friend Vanessa. Her mate is a grizzled old fool, but he has excellent connections. A lot of status. That's the only reason she mated someone twenty years older and with the personality of a leather boot. Well…that and the money, but you didn't hear that from me. She was glad for all the gossip, so I piled her high with it. All good stuff, of course. It'll make us look good. Well, I finally got here, only to see the place over*run* with gnomes." She gave me a concerned look. "Do you have any idea of the infestation you have here?"

"I apologize." Edgar slunk closer. "That is my fault. I have asked repeatedly to be retired."

"Good *night*." Patty yanked her elbow away from Edgar. "Are you a vampire? I thought they killed vampires that got as old as you?"

"We're working on it, believe me," Niamh drawled.

"Well, anyway, I think I've got them on the run, don't you worry." Ulric's mom patted me, side-eyeing Edgar again. "Are you sure you want a vampire this old within your proximity? They can be quite dangerous. They get a little…" She made a circle with her finger around her temple. "Then they forget the difference between friend and foe and just bite anything they see."

"*Mom*," Ulric groaned.

"Well, be that as it may, let's head inside." She turned and looped her arm with mine. "You must be exhausted. I want to hear all about the journey. Basajaunak, huh? My goodness. I didn't think any of them were around anymore. I haven't seen one in…forever. A very long time. I can't wait to meet one. I hear they're very scary. From the rumors, I don't think I'd chase one off the property with a bat. No, no. I'd need something bigger for that job."

She laughed again, and I was too awestruck to say anything.

The door opened when we got there, and I saw that the little table by the door had been moved back somewhat and doilies covered almost every surface.

"Dear Lord, no," I heard Mr. Tom say as he came in behind us.

"Oh, this is nice," Edgar said a moment later.

"I hope you don't mind," Patty said as she led me into the large front sitting room. "Since you weren't here, I decided to make myself useful. There were connection requests all over, so the house showed me where to put them. I went ahead and got them organized. Then I had some spare time and saw a stack of these lovely attempts at doilies and wondered why they weren't being used. So I laid them out for you. I just love a home decorated with doilies. It reminds me of my nana."

"*Since when do you let in strangers?*" I asked Ivy House.

"*I... Well... She's not an easy woman to say no to, it turns out. After she organized the connection requests, I tried to scare her out, and she laughed at me. Then she started after the gnomes, and...*"

If a house could shrug, I knew Ivy House would.

"Mom, we just got home. Give her a minute," Ulric pleaded.

"Where are my manners. Of course!" Patty beamed at me. "Can I get you something to drink? Something to eat?"

"I beg your pardon, but that is not your job." Mr. Tom sniffed. "Miss, I will deliver something to your *private* parlor."

"That would be great, Mr. Tom, thanks." I took Austin's proffered hand, then gave Patty as warm of a smile as I could muster. "Thank you for coming. You'll be a great help, I'm sure. If you'll excuse me?"

She clasped her hands in front of her, holding her smile. "Isn't this perfect? She's pretty and full of grace, but our girl has grit. Yes, she'll do nicely. She's the perfect choice for a female gargoyle." She patted my arm. "You go. Go rest. I'll just catch up with Ulric and meet the rest of the staff. We'll start on those connection requests when you're ready. Tomorrow, maybe, or the day after. We have a lot of work to do, but you're in a unique position to make them wait. You can take as much time as you want. Make 'em sweat, girl." She winked at me.

Thoughts dizzy from the tornado that was Ulric's mom, I let Austin walk me to the parlor and lead me to the couch. Once we were both sitting, he let out a breath. I did the same.

"I don't envy you," he finally said, and I burst out laughing.

"It sounds like she's a helluva networker, though."

"Yeah, it does. Let me know when you start working with her. I want to be there with you."

"Why? In case she decides I need to be handled like the gnomes?"

He chuckled. "I can't *believe* she had those things on the run."

"I know, right? I'm both in awe and a little scared."

He cuddled me close, and his breath ruffled my hair. "I want to hear what she has to say about each cairn, and I want to ask some questions about how best to manage their leaders. I need to learn how gargoyles work if I'm going to help you handle them. I'm pretty sure that's what enforcers do."

"Given that their mates scare homicidal gnomes, I get the feeling they're pretty rough."

"So do I," he growled.

I rested my head on his shoulder. "How much time do you think we've granted ourselves from Momar?"

"*We*? Probably a while. I agree with Niamh that it was wise to let that ground trooper go. If mages think they won't have a reliable shield from shifters, they won't be so inclined to attack. I also agree with Sebastian that the mage he released will tell others about your might. They'll want to meet you like they would want to meet any high-powered mage. You'll probably go from physical battles to the cunning, in-the-shadows-type battling."

"At least Sebastian is fluent in that. I think we're good for a minute." I paused for a beat. "I'm sorry it didn't work out with the basajaunak."

He stroked the side of my face. "It hasn't *not* worked out. One is coming to stay, and we're welcome to visit any time we please. I think that's the best we can hope for right now."

"True. Hopefully, I can connect with a couple of big cairns," I said. "If we at least had that, we'd have something."

"After the battle in the meadow, I'd say we already

have something. More than something. If we add it to Kingsley's pack and Momar attacks sooner rather than later, hopefully, we'll be enough."

I didn't mention that we'd only battled decent mages, at best. It would be different when we had to defend Kingsley's territory. We'd likely be surrounded. Sebastian and I would have to spread out, and we wouldn't be nearly as effective.

We'd definitely need help. I felt it in my bones. I just hoped Patty could help organize it, and that I could lead whatever surly cairn leaders we brought in.

I hoped we had the time.

## THE END

# ABOUT THE AUTHOR

K.F. Breene is a Wall Street Journal, USA Today, Washington Post, Amazon Most Sold Charts and #1 Kindle Store bestselling author of paranormal romance, urban fantasy and fantasy novels. With millions of books sold, when she's not penning stories about magic and what goes bump in the night, she's sipping wine and planning shenanigans. She lives in Northern California with her husband, two children, and out of work treadmill.

Sign up for her newsletter to hear about the latest news and receive free bonus content.

www.kfbreene.com

Printed in Great Britain
by Amazon

15796849R00284